P9-DUB-689

WITHDRAWN
UTSA LIBRARIES

ACTS OF LOVE

ACTS

OF LOVE

AN AMERICAN NOVEL

CAROL BERGÉ

THE BOBBS-MERRILL COMPANY, INC.
Indianapolis • New York

LIBRARY
University of Texas
At San Antonio

ALSO BY CAROL BERGÉ:

Poetry
Vulnerable Island
Poems Made of Skin
Circles, as in the Eye
The Chambers
An American Romance
From A Soft Angle: Poems About Women

Stories
A Couple Called Moebius

The Bobbs-Merrill Company, Inc.
Indianapolis • New York

Copyright © 1973 by Carol Bergé
All rights reserved
ISBN 0–672–51780–9
Library of Congress catalogue card number 72–89688
Designed by A. Christopher Simon
Manufactured in the United States of America

LIBRARY
University of Texas
At San Antonio

THIS BOOK IS FOR

Anne Bentzen
Audrey Hamilton
Elizabeth Collins
Lois Jeffery
Jerry Wapner
Ron & Valma
Dwight & Rudy
The Two Andreas
Peter Bergé

: JOY & WISDOM!

My gratitude to the MacDowell Colony, where the second draft of this book was completed, in one-third the time it would have taken otherwise.

"In Peru I visited the ruins at Sacsayhuaman outside of Cusco. The way the stones go together got to me. It's not about huge stones. The experience of the object relates to particular intellectual inquiries: the decisions of mass and interstices, one never dominating the other. I had known about Machupichu, and always intuitively known that a relationship between Machupichu and the work wherein I was trying to define Set Membership existed. To specify a set, you must identify the objects in the set, that is, the members or elements of the set. The work called *Leveling* deals with how parts can be similar and yet maintain their differences; this is a consideration in Set Membership. For example, what constitutes sameness in the citrus family and yet what is the difference between an orange and a lemon? Seeing Sacsayhuaman was a reaffirmation; until that moment I'd been working in the dark. I was impressed by the way in which the work(s) function in the space they occupy—a beautiful, fertile valley. They turned the place into an object. Whichever ruin one looked at, one was in a circular situation: always in the center."

—*Dorothea Rockburne*

from an interview
in Artforum Magazine,
March 1972

"—Do not stop here to ask directions: I do not know where you are going, & barely know where we are right now. Besides, all directions are circular, and lead to the same center. Assume responsibility for your own travelling, as I do for mine, each and each along The Way."

—*hand-lettered sign near
the Woodstock road*

ACTS OF LOVE

CHAPTER

1

Not even a mile north of the hamlet of Wittgenburg, in the township of Trois (pronounced "Troys"), is the place where the mountain streams have cut through shale on their way to the lake that is the town's center, on the way from the Reservoir ten miles still further north. The lake, and this glade near it, are more to the people of Wittgenburg than the Hudson River was to their forefathers. In winter, the glade is alive with footprints of animals and birds; the dark water moves in a tracing of veins across the pale flesh of the snow and is never frozen over. And in summer, you can stand a moment on your own earth in sunlight, then run, perch your toes on shale smoothed by a century and a half of such feet, and do a fluttering belly-dive into the crisp, brilliant mountain-water, coming up sputtering and flushed, knowing just who you are.

Whichever, you are plunged into the center of life of Wittgenburg; always, Wittgenburg is summer and winter superimposed on each other until it is one circle, then a spiral of seasons which are the years. Edward Richthoven, born in Wittgenburg and living here now, loves winter best; it is his birth season, and the town looks best to him then: ageless, its identity not influenced by the gaudy dreams of summer people or other strangers.

He loves the town as he would love a friend. And one day each spring, the Friday of Memorial Day Weekend, Wittgenburg is like a friend whose face changes too radically, not slowly as with nature into age, but as with an old lady wearing too much makeup, or a young person who has dropped too much acid too fast. The town was built by Dutch and German, temperate and wintry people: thick food, warm clothing, no nonsense, nothing fine-boned here, even the luxuries are practical . . . these are oatmeal houses, heavy for the extreme seasons, made to last, favoring winter. The new summer cottages down by the lake are thin and odd, undernourished, made of unnatural products: they are breakfast-cereal-product houses.

"If you want to know who a man is, study the lay of the land he comes from," it is said; well then, Wittgenburg, a town of rich farmlands, at the edge of an alluvial plain of the Hudson, below Albany, near Leeds, south of Rensselaer (pronounced to rhyme with *penciller* by these people). Some Irish had settled in the 1900s, and now many Irish come, summers, for good air, cheap cottages (hopefully, by the lake), and the company of other City Irishmen to play whist with, to drink with, to lay, and to gossip with. Edward and his crowd shy away from the summer people, for the most part, but they are not separate from the town-born Irish. The rift is noticeable only on Sundays, when the town divides between the Irish Catholic church of Our Lady of Knock, which is down the street from the German Lutheran church, or the Dutch Reform, two blocks further down on Main Street. And everyone meets, like it or not, at school, and at Tom's Luncheonette, and evenings at the Sled Pub. And at the swimming-hole, and at that end of the lake furthest from the village, where rich waves of mallards and ducks rise for Edward and Marty and the others and for the strangers who come then from the cities in their new red jackets from Bean's, all kneeling together to shoot in the bright grey dawns and cold sunsets of Fall . . .

Edward's family, dark-haired and fair-skinned Lutherans originally from Hamburg, had lived in or near Wittgenburg for the past three generations or more; the Richthovens were tax-collectors who worked for the Friesian land-owners who came as merchant traders and stayed to push back the Indians and the woods. Edward, thirty-six now, is a worker, with a heritage of peasant workers and tradesman behind him, though his uncle, Fritz Rattermann, lives still on the money a Rattermann stole slowly and lovingly from a Van Bogart for whom he had collected, back then. (The middle generation was Big John Rattermann, a man still spoken of as one of the early successful stock-investors in the area, and who is said to have come out ahead on every deal, one way or another.)

But that was another branch of the family. Edward's father, a drinker and a hard worker, had gone from farming into smithing during the Depression, and Edward had followed him into it, learning the trade at his side. The younger man took naturally to it, loving the feel of metal and the satisfaction of solving challenges in a useful way, with his skill and his hands. It was a steady living, in this town. He was respected, he was even, people looked to him and counted on him.

He was beginning now to feel his own power: being Capricorn, he related well to things of the earth. And he is German, so he is doubly practical and earthbound. But also the idealist: the only area where he exceeded this weightedness was in his concern for music—it was his particular joy. A thick, solid man, he felt at his full height and as tall as any tree when singing with the Mid-Valley Choir or when he rose, surfeited, after a concert in distant Poughkeepsie or Kingston or nearby Albany, where he was usually the only man from Wittgenburg present. None of his friends cared for music beyond tavern singing or running the folk ballads handed down at firesides. He would meet with three or four others from nearby towns, and work at playing the old musics, Sunday afternoons in Fall and Winter. The Wittgenburg friends thought Edward odd and affected, certainly haughty, but he sought the music as they sought food or money. He would buy an old autoharp or lute, or sheet-music, before he'd buy a new car or an air-conditioner. They were not like that. He was different.

His involvement with music was, for now, a way of assuaging the horror of his marriage, which went slowly rotten as with certain diseases that take over healthy bodies. Kathy had left him almost a year ago, taking the boys with her. She had moved through the tiny town and his life, laden with her discontent and anger: she said she wanted all of them to move to the City, which she sought; Edward could not leave his land, this town; had been away from here, to that and other cities, to the war in Korea, and knew his own place as best. So she took the boys and left. After all the ugliness and bitterness. She was a waitress now, in a Greek restaurant in the West Forties. And so furious with Edward for not being what she needed him to be that she would not let him near his sons. After she found he would not give in and would not give her any money, she declared she would not ever give him the freedom of a divorce.

Now, some of the time, he didn't care. They were three and six now, the boys, and he hadn't seen them in more than nine months. It was Edward who used to insist that the boys come to the church on Sundays, to be near the music. Kathy fought him, on this as on everything, calling him a hypocrite, knowing he didn't give a damn for religion, for all his traditionalism. Unable to understand that music was his religion.

He did not consider any of them "his" any more. According to a call from his friend, Marty, who now lived in the City, she was with some other man these days; he didn't give a damn, except he did miss the boys . . . he could do nothing further for them; she would permit nothing. And these days, he was busy enough here, in the town, what with his smithing and his music . . . putting his life together, getting around, being active, working well again, and trying to move without pain again, but without a real sense of himself as yet, like a man who's been wounded and has not yet learned fully the use of the hurt limbs or muscles. As after a long illness.

He was not drawn to any of the five or six single women near his age who were living in Wittgenburg right now; at first, he tended to keep off to himself, warily, but then he found he could not stay alone: he was vitally alive in his own body, and in the habit of being with a woman, and not damaged irreparably by Kathy. So there were talks and nights with one or another of each of the single women. Some of the time he was depressed and lonely. But he felt free, too, for the first time in too many years. They'd married too young, just out of high school; he knew that now. In those months, no woman held him for more than a few hours, but he managed to learn a lot in that time about each.

Until Myra Shultis managed to attach herself to him: he thought of it, of her, that way, even now, and it had been a couple of months of sleeping with her; a baby she was, really, nineteen now, all of it some sort of nonsense, nothing he could think through sensibly; but it was Myra who kept it going so that he felt no anxiety, she kept it both light and intense, and he kept on with it, opening the door when she came, having nothing else except the pain, moving some of the time with her as if in a dream, involved but not knowing he was involved . . . whatever it was they had, he considered it a far cry from Kathy, or from anything he'd had with anyone he'd ever been with, few though there'd been . . . He was always surprised with Myra, so she was as far as he could get from the heavy predictability of his final year with Kathy.

So he was both ready and astonished to find himself wanting to be involved with someone else in the town: one night, when Myra said she'd be busy with friends her own age, an activity at the College, she said, Edward went into the Sled Pub alone and for the first time in years had a chance to sit down and talk with Ellie Elsen, a woman he'd always known in the soft crossings of their town lives: he knew her as a youngster; then as the wife of Tom Dykstra, who'd been killed in an accident earlier that year . . . she was lovelier than he remembered; the red-gold-auburn hair, the firm, freckled, heavy-boned Dutch body at full maturity now; she was a year or two ahead of Edward in school, a year or two older than he.

And that reticence of hers. She was standing outside the Sled Pub, seeming to hesitate. She wasn't at all beautiful, he saw now, just good to look at, soft-seeming; not at all like the tiny dark angularity of Myra, or the thick sullen flesh of fat Kathy. He took her elbow and teased her about her shyness about walking into the Pub alone. And they walked in, sat down in a booth.

So it was all "How are you, and what've you been doing?" and "How've *you* been," and the rest, the usual, and something more happening, with both of them glancing sideways, into the new consciousness of each other's senses. He was seated next to her in the booth. They drank beer. The difference in response between friends and potential sexual partners. He could feel the sweat wetting his shirt. If his hand brushed hers. If she turned her head, so—if they. When they. She would turn, and then she could smell his hair and his skin, and she was drawn to him. If he moved just a bit—she could see the dark, curled hair on his chest.

Talked, about the town, the social things, first, the who and when; and then discovered that just underneath the patter they were both still caught in thoughts of the death of lives near them both. Edward's brother, Arthur, had worked for Ellen's twin, Anne, on her farm, the Elsen family's place, until he had not long ago been killed in an auto accident. And of course Edward had known Tom Dykstra, who had been popular in the town: quiet, warm, strange Tom Dykstra, who'd walked out on his family's old money and gone to work on the railroad instead, for the love of it . . . and the train accident that took him and three other citizens of Wittgenburg, and fifteen others from nearby towns. So that this meeting, this talk between this man and this woman, had another layer to it; there was more than their attraction.

They left The Sled together, walking slowly and easily, toward his house, a good mile from the center of town. All of this seemed perfectly natural and reasonable. And then as reasonable, as expected, that their bodies would move so well together—but even so, a joy, a surprise. Ellen had thought she was with a good man, back then; her Tom had been good to her, very quiet with her, they were much alike, he pleased her often; but this, the new way, with Edward, seemed like the sea to her, turbulent and calm at once; he woke her to some blood-memory she could not at once identify. It had to do with her sea-faring ancestors, all the Dutch who had moved across oceans. And she herself was Pisces. So: this double memory of oceans and their motion. In her life thus far, she had not known such loving . . .

This she told quietly to Edward, as they lay resting. And he, never overtly the romantic, could only tell that Kathy had, over the years, turned him against her, had turned herself into a rhino of a woman; tough; not just put on weight after the first boy, but put on the muscles too, with her way of needing to try to run everything, that took all the joy out of his being the man around her . . . Now, he took pleasure in delighting in Ellen's passivity with his body, her sensual, slow way of warming to him, of coming to him, of being with him. He found he needed her, this pliant, warm woman, not the excitement of the edgy, angular little Myra he knew, and far enough from the tough, fat, bad-mouthed Kathy, herself not the woman he'd married back then.

✿   ✿   ✿

Edward, pleased, began to come by often of an evening to Ellen's house, and they would walk out, companionable on the streets of their familiar town; then they would come back and sit at the kitchen table in one house or the other, or sit before a fire, and talk comfortably about their work or the gossip of the town.

Ellen had to consider what she was feeling when she noticed that he had come by to her three nights in a row, toward the end of the third week they had been seeing each other. During the day, worrying in her Piscean way, she had just about decided she would tell him she had something else she wanted to do that night, or the next; or maybe she just wouldn't be there when he came by; maybe she wouldn't even leave him a note, so it wouldn't seem that she was taking it for granted he would be by . . . But all of that was against her nature. It might hurt his feelings. She knew the man was happy being with her; and if it suited them both, what harm could there be? Was it so bad, for him to know that she wanted him to be there? If she was there for him when he came by?

He came by as usual, and she was there, waiting; they would sit at the kitchen table, then move to build a fire in the front room (she still called it the *pronk-vroom,* as had her mother and grandmother before her), eating a bite of supper and smoking grass and relaxing into the evening; and always, at the end of the gentle time together, there was the rich security of bodies moving together beautifully (like Bach, he once thought; like the sea, she thought always).

On a Tuesday, he did not come by at his usual hour. An hour after 8, she began to wonder and then to worry, thinking herself a fool but remembering that awful night when Tom —ah, she had only been with this new man a few short weeks —had something terrible happened—But then, at 10, he came in, radiant and ruddy, affectionate and unconcerned, touching her waist and her hair, then grabbing a morsel of food from the plate. He had nothing to say about his "lateness" as she thought of it. So it existed between them only in her mind (where it lay like a block of dark wintry ice, solid and unsolved). He seemed to need for her to ignore it. She sensed him. He seemed into his own skin entirely and not inclined to talk; this was sometimes his mood, as a Capricorn. He looked once at her, in what seemed a cautioning, Please keep your counsel and don't ask me. She kept still about it.

They sat, talked, ate a bit, smoked, and went around the subject. He was watching her, for sure, in a sort of testing. Watching her face as she responded to him and as she moved around the little room. Finally, he moved toward the bedroom, motioning for her to follow him there. She stood still, tense beneath her grace. He felt the tension in her arm, under his leading hand. Her body would not lean to his, as it had so often. She was forcing him to speak. He would have to.

But he waited an instant too long. She turned away and started to move back. He grabbed her arm.

He said, as close to her as he could, gently,

"Sometimes I've got to be away from you a bit, Ellie," feeling her flinch back just that bit, "things I have to do, people I have to see; and I need a lot of the time these days just to be by myself. Really more than most people. Because of that marriage, I suppose. If you could just wait, do whatever you want to do with your time, I'd be back soon enough. Trust me. I'll get back to you." But she stiffened, her body close to him but her distance from him already established. What was the rest of it, she was thinking. She stayed silent.

And then, to him, "All right. Let me think." Walked into the kitchen, stood at the stove, bent to light her cigaret from the pilot light. Then stood naked in the cold room . . . Ah, that was it; it was *someone* else—yes. The old feeling of fear swept in. The terrible cold unsureness, part of her having been one of twins, of having been one of twin girls when it was boys who were wanted and needed in her family; part of something nameless that responded to anything that smelled of being turned down, or someone else being chosen over her . . . The Piscean, going cold in the blood . . .

Ah sure, if this, with Edward, was all that good, what a fool she'd been to think it could last. He was strong; he was in control, wasn't he. She *had* wanted to pull back, hadn't she, what a fool she'd been to be there when he wanted her, ah what a fool . . . she'd *wanted* to keep herself to herself, that good lean clear feeling of not depending on anyone, the feeling she'd built slowly in the time since Tom died—ah, she was so furious with herself in this moment! All the magic had gone out of her body. Hadn't she felt that the good things between them were worth more than any games of self-protection she would set up. And she had thought about *his* feelings! Ah, but now he was turning it all around. She was frightened. She felt alone. That damned sense of loss again, that feeling of coldness, of losing someone.

Meantime, he sat on the edge of the bed, where she had

left him, legs crossed at the ankles, feet stretched long at the edge of the braided rug, considering what to do. There had been no way to discuss any of this openly with her, before now. There might be no way now. He'd begun to feel himself entering a pattern—and any pattern, right now, was a trap, the stench of Kathy's pattern and trap; for him, time was precious—that was only a part of it. That was the part he could give a name to. There was more. He needed to feel alone, and free. Well, maybe she would understand some of it. He would try. He walked across the bare floor toward her.

The red glow of the cigaret in her hand and the softer glow of her ivory flesh as she leaned near the counter. "Look," he said to her, touching her forearm, "I'm not sure about all of it, but what I need is not to have to be afraid of what we are or what we're doing. Sometimes, in my dreams, I feel trapped, and I don't like the taste of it, ever. I don't even know who I am yet, but I'm trying to find out. And I'm not afraid of my own reality. I'm not afraid to take whatever time it takes to find out who I am and what I want—"

Her head was averted like an animal's, her back set now toward the metal of the stove, her belly half-turned toward him and the whole of her in torsion, the face held away, toward the wall at his right: away from the light coming from the hallway. He saw that she puffed the cigaret strongly, the smoke falling out into the dull air of the room in a screen. An arrangement of defense. She would not look at him. He had a sudden idea that if he reached to touch her again, this time his hand would pass right through her; her emanations were at once smoky and solid, like some minerals which are at the same time smoky and solid and liquid.

"Ellen," he began again, determined, but in his most gentle manner, "I need right now not to see one woman every day or night. I don't know what it's all about, but it's the way I have to be. Maybe I'll change, but I just have to follow my own sensing of myself—it's probably the devil itself for you to understand, but it's the—Look. There's a girl here in town I'd been spending some time with—before I met you. Before we began to spend so much time together."

10

He stopped, leaving a space for her reaction or comment. She said nothing. An evenly stanced fleshly statue. He wanted to assume a clear distance from her while letting her feel his support, his closeness; to leave room for what he was saying to her and for a reply. But it wasn't working out that way. She was already very close to him (the bodies' own nature had seen to that), and very far from him as well (the minds were taking care of it). He could smell her fear; she was confused, her body posture showed this, and waiting numbly for him to stop or to go on. Or this is what he thought he saw.

"I think you know her. Myra Shultis, it is; goes to the Community College; the little dark girl, I'm sure you've seen her around town—well, I've been spending time with her, a while now, a couple of months—and I think she counts on it—somehow—God, it's hard to explain, and I don't think I like having to—it's as different as anything can be from this—and as different as anything from what I went through with Kathy —I figure it's good if I can spend time with you, and with her, and no harm done—or anyone else I choose," he said, wistfully and defiantly. "You're both very fine people—and very different each from the other."

He was speaking quickly, with his head down, toward her belly, but blinded into his words. Not trying now to make her face his eyes or what he was saying to her. He felt defensive. An image of Myra set before him as he talked about her to Ellen, trying to explain how he felt, how he saw the way he had to live the life now, with the past being always part of the present, and a future very different from any of that. There was the image of Myra, set against the white soft screen of the other woman's belly, as if at a side show . . .

Ellen made a sound and moved her head, so he reached and tried to turn her toward him, to comfort her or to try to say with his body what he'd already said. She felt betrayed. He felt what he was saying was reasonable. To her, it was a violation of some principle of life, a heresy, it went against her grain. But why couldn't he have told her about Myra before now? And about how he felt about his own life? And then she remembered that he had indeed. He'd mentioned Myra in conversation more than once. It was really no surprise. Ellen had needed to overlook.

She knew her own value but she had so little self-confidence these days. She knew she was a handsome woman who didn't look the couple of years older than Edward—she knew about some of her wisdoms—many men in Wittgenburg had wanted her, proud Dutch lady that she was, in her rich flesh, with her slow, saucy wit and mild arrogance and vague charm. Tom Dykstra had been the only Wittgenburg man who'd been suitable for her. She felt always the line of tall, fair, well-fleshed aristocratic Dutchmen back of her, and had wanted to marry within that realm. But always that Piscean softness that made her shy from any competitive setups, all of her life. As now.

She felt deeply threatened. Yes, she knew the young Shultis girl; not so different, she thought, from the other young of the whole vulpine Shultis clan. She could visualize Myra's face, all sharp angles and foxy, the Scorpio baby, just leaving the teens but never having had the roundness of flesh some teenagers have . . . soft of mouth, all right, but crisp of cheekbone and of chin . . . Ellen could remember how the girl looked during a night at the Pub, the girl at the other end of the bar, the eyes too bright, the mouth gone sharp, the conversation overheard, Myra having had too much dexedrine and chattering beyond that and the shots of Scotch she was downing . . . the excesses, the extremes . . . Ah, the *idea* of Edward, with her, with that girl! of all people!

Well, but he and Ellen had had only this short time together, wasn't that right, what right did she have to demand or assume a bond between them? The man had to do what he wanted to do with the life! —And wasn't it true that Edward had met and known the younger woman first . . . Around and around, bounding off the inner segments of her skull, and with Edward standing there next to her, sometimes talking, sometimes just looking at her—did he really see her?

He was watching her. Myra had so marvelously distracted him from his memories of Kathy. Myra, so fast-moving, so bright and intense! and she seemed to feel that nothing in life was worth taking seriously. (She would sit with him, when

12

they were both stoned, and read to him, in a sarcastic mono-
tone, from the *Wittgenburg Weekly:* "The Mary Circle will
have a dessert luncheon Tuesday at 1 P.M. at the church, with
Mrs. Duane Sulzburger, Mrs. Alta Neiemyer and Miss Jean
Grundish as hostesses. Mrs. Montgomery Shultis will speak on
'Our Changing World: The Church,—Yesterday, Today and
Forever.' Mrs. Liona Shultis will lead the devotions.") She
would accept only her own realities. He remembered watching Myra once as she made love to herself before he went
into her, because she'd taken too many ups and couldn't come
easily with him; and his body responded now, not to the
woman he was near and with whose body his own moved so
beautifully and naturally, but to the thought of the nasty imp
who teased and distracted him, who was as German as he,
who gave in to all of his fantasies and would always have a
new one to urge him on. Her crazy-intense skull freed of the
old ethics and coming to him from bedding down with imagination and drugs and everyone in town, probably . . . He did
not feel possessive about Myra.

So to hell with her, for now. He would have to turn this
arousal toward Ellen. He was compassionate. But if she knew
he was thinking about Myra this minute. That was the
trouble—it was so good to be with Ellen. And Myra always
said, *"Now* is all that counts; forget the rest; if you think
about what was or what's coming, you just get all messed up."
She never took anything for granted. She moved like a hum-
mingbird . . . Edward thought he could stand damn near anything except being forced to choose between Myra and Ellen.
He was as afraid of losing each of them as he was afraid of
having to carry through and commit himself to either . . .

*   *   *

His eyes narrowed and focussed until all he saw was Ellen.
All he felt were his feelings of tenderness for her and hers of
fear of him.

"Come on, love, let's go to bed. I'm tired. But I want very
much to make love with you now. I think it'll do us so much
good now—"

She reached out and slapped him, quickly, with strength, her left hand coming awkwardly across his face, grazing his nose.

"What a hell of a nerve you have," she said, softly, straight into his eyes. "What's the good of it if it all disappears tomorrow? Do you think I want that kind of loving?"

"That's ridiculous! What makes you think this'll all be gone tomorrow? You *know* we've got something beautiful here. Take it easy! I said I'd come back to you, and I will! I just can't play out any whole numbers now. I need—"

"Oh, Christ, Edward! What you're trying to do is too hard. What you want me to do isn't me at all!"

"You can do or be anything you want, don't you know that? What the hell! This is 1973, not 1900!"

"Edward, you don't *understand*. I'm not one of these women who can sit patiently around while their man is out—"

"I'm not your man, or anyone else's, don't you see? And you're free, too; you don't have to *belong* to anyone. You shouldn't. Can't you just *be,* and enjoy being?"

"I can only be what I am. Everything you're saying goes against—I can't—if I'm going to have to do without, when you're off somewhere, what're you going to be doing without? —How about your doing without, right now. Doing without me. Go out and find—"

"No, Ellie. *No.* I don't want to. I don't want to do without you. Come on, Ellie, don't make me beg. You *mean* something to me. I want you . . . You want me, too, and you know it—"

He touched her hand, her arm, moved his hand slowly toward her armpit, toward the soft flesh of her breast. Moved slightly closer to her, slowly, letting himself surge till his body rose before his belly and touched her. His thigh against hers. He knew their bodies well. The bodies could be trusted.

The mistrust and anger still moved toward him from Ellen. But he sensed now that she would go with him. Not just that she was lonely. But that she did want him. Her thoughts now were not open to him, but he thought he knew the body-texture of this woman as well as he knew the soft tongues of animals or the leaves after rain. Thinking these warm, wet thoughts moved him against her again, leaving a tiny trail where his body first touched hers. He wanted so much to move inside her!

Finally, she would let him touch her, and then had to respond to him. She would have to let him move her out of her arrogant moodiness. There was that chance to take; the bodies were alive, were talking to each other through the space between them; they would have to walk toward life. They moved together then to the bed in the other room, holding each other fondly. She would have to decide to forget any *then* and *whenever*, and do her living now, in these moments. The small of his back was firm under her hand; his form was under and then over hers. He moved slowly and wisely into her and then they went into that familiarity of mutual motion they had attained in this amount of time together, a time not measured by calendars or clocks . . . the bodies were so glorious and rich! Edward noticed the small noises of pleasure she made near his ear: so much this Ellen, so much no one else on earth! And then the strong, low animal-howl that meant she was joining him in the great upsurge.

Afterward, they lay together entwined. Calmly. In their usual blaze of ordinary glory. He knew she would not then argue with him about his life. But when he told her he had decided to stay the night with her, to reassure her, she decided she wanted to stay alone. She was delighted to be that independent of him.

He rose, then, dressed, and left. He, too, was delighted to have this time to himself. He wanted, after those years, to have the early morning hours alone; he treasured the silence of the roads he walked on to get to his own house, and then the deep sleep, undisturbed by another creature near him, and then his early rising, alone, the time of day before the demands of his work and of his relationships to the other people of Wittgenburg.

CHAPTER

2

There were those men in the town who said, "The way my father did it . . ." to prevent change, and they were the same men who said "My wife says . . ." to prevent disagreements or further discussion or threat. Cornelisz, whose family was from Groningen those years ago, now an elder of the Dutch Reform Church in Wittgenburg, moving slowly around the streets in a maroon Cadillac, the new model every year, but who saw to it that the town passed an ordinance against television sets, against neon light-signs . . . The town was nicknamed "Repose" in the last fifty years, before it became a gathering-place summers for the Irish, and if a thing worked then, it would somehow work now, it would be followed until it fell of its own weight. Now it looked like so many other small upper New York State towns, except that the signs (painted) read "Reilly's Market," and "The Dubliner," "Erin Hotel" and "Mooney's—Tourists," and the words *Erin* and *Eire* appeared on streets with Dutch and German names affixed. The streets of the center of town held fifteen hundred more people in summer.

Myra and Mike were shacked up in a brown cabin that had been until recently used for summer rental. It was not insulated and was in a section near the lake that was pretty far from the center of town, and even from the little lakeside general store, so they were comfortably isolate. Besides, they couldn't get that much time out there lately: Myra was busy with school much of the time and was with Edward some of the time; Mike had a lot of school work, as it was near Christmas and therefore nearing finals, and besides, Mike was involved in the seasonal community activities of his family (with their political ideas and their real estate business, this was a big season). So it was a weekend now and then at the cabin, and an occasional quick snappy midweek breather.

They were both fed up with the things they had to do, so the cabin was filled with the kind of life they liked to do: two beautiful waterpipes, one of painted glass and one all brass; a woven reed box lined with brown wood and filled with a clean three ounces of grass; an ornate silver coke-spoon next to a silver snuffbox full of coke; glassine envelopes and small brown envelopes, full and empty ones; chocolate- and banana-flavored cigaret papers; candles; boxes of small matches and stove-lighting matches and fireplace matches; bead-incense in a bright pottery jar; magazines, records, a pile of cut-out photographs and a half-done collage, and piles of kindling and firewood for the franklin stove. A tin box full of stale hash brownies, gone slightly moldy. A portable hi-fi stereo.

Myra could make Mike do anything. He was so thick-fleshed, boyish, looked younger than twenty, though the resentful sulky line of his mouth and the weight of his flesh sometimes made him look as he would thirty years from now. He jumped for Myra; he was so drawn to her tense, slight, dark looks, her sharp face-bones and quick way of moving that made all space her own, so different from his own undefined way of shrugging off his areas. She would laugh at him, at the curly reddish-blond hair that grew across his back and

17

shoulder-blades (though you couldn't feel the blades, they were so covered by a thick layer of home-made-Jewish-cooking fat-pad). But her Mike knew where to buy or find anything Myra's little heart desired, and he fucked real good.

Mike's father (a worn-out lawyer), and his mother, Sally, ran the real-estate office that filled the town with visitors each summer and relocated the residents on their occasional moves into an upward or downward stratum. He knew all about advertising the cabins, the lake, the town, the hotels nearby. He got his big commissions. Sally (born Sarah), was ambitious for her men and even for her daughter. Her children were finally safely at college, Mike supposedly studying for law, and Heather at a teachers' college, a community college, a two-year college, nearby. It was through the daughter Heather that Mike the Jew had met his true-love, Myra. Heather had brought Myra home (both of the girls stoned out of their gourds) and Mike had adored her from the start. First sight.

What with no television and half the town preserved as historical sites, it was a hard town for young folk to grow up in. So many stone houses, set along the poplar-lined roads that ran radially out of the town away from the recently installed Village Green, looking like the roads and houses of old Europe, some Dutch with the peculiar step-roofs and *stoeps* and some German with the dark crossbeams of wood and that cottagy look—ah but these were land-lovers, land-valuers, who feared water in bulk; *so* a river wasn't the Zuider Zee, but it took more than two generations for the stubborn Dutch to use lakes and waterfalls without throwing polders across them . . . The Dutch and German, so slow to change. The youngsters, greedy for amusement and for progress. Kick-the-can and joke phone calls not enough by now. So Mike managed to smuggle a TV into their cabin, along with the other amenities and niceties.

Sally Mandelbaum had gotten the TV for the kids. Mike called her "Big Momma Magic" in reverence: her abilities. When Mike had gotten busted in Mexico last summer, it was Big Momma Magic who'd gotten him sprung in half the time it would've taken without her intercession: a few weeks. (She thought the experience would do her son good, and hadn't really tried as hard as she could've. Always believed she could've gotten him outta there in a day if she'd really tried.) Sally, despite her distrust of all Christians and her ambition for her children, loved Myra as much as she did her own kids: all that spirit!—maybe some of it would rub off on Heather. Such a quiet child, that one.

It was near Christmas. For Mike's family, it was always a season of compromise and of profit. First and most important, it was one of the seasons when the town would fill with skiers and with holiday visitors, and with those whose summer cottages were winterized or had space heaters or both. The Auction Barn and the restaurants and bars would fill and empty, fill and empty; goods and buyers, estates to be sold, people from the City to sell them to, the registers ringing. Like bells of the season. Sally would supervise the annual Carolers' Rounds and the visit of Santa Claus to the Village Green, an artificial clearing created by the local businessmen when a few stores became vacant some ten years ago. Santa Claus would land in a helicopter, and would hustle for all the town charities and drives. And Heather would be home from school and would have to be taught one home skill each vacation; this year, it would be baking, her mother had said. Mike had already arranged for her to make brownies and had set aside some beautiful Moroccan hash for the occasion. Sally would look the other way. She was modern. (She pronounced this "modren.")

Myra ran into the cabin on the day before Christmas, high on acid but beginning to turn it into a down trip, and began slowly and systematically to throw out or rip up or otherwise dispense with things in the cabin that upset her sensibilities; after the unfinished collage and the bead-incense (she never liked that jasmine smell, Mike had picked it out and it was too sweet for her but he always insisted,) the main offender was the illicit TV, which had been left on by Mike last night, and was now showing a day-time couples show, the Honeymoon Quiz, in which the couples revealed their concepts of the personalities of their mates by second-guessing the spouses' answers to highly personal and either stupid or titil-latingly suggestive questions. First she jammed the set, and then she put a lamp through the front of the tube, base first, and then she built a fire in the franklin stove, and set the TV frame and bulk so that when one sat in the only chair, one saw the fire glowing through the ovoid frame of the erstwhile TV. That was much better, she said softly, and wept. Seeing the tears flame-colored on TV.

Mike did not at the moment suit her. She yearned for Edward. But it was not her night to see Edward. He was doing his funny number. Seeing that older chick, Ellen Dykstra. Son-of-a-bitch . . . There was a picture of Mike in her wallet, and one (candid) that she had stolen from Edward's house of Edward when he was a lot younger (she had written "Eddie in his last incarnation" on the back of it and planned that he would never know she had it, would never see it). She put both of the photos in front of her on the floor of the cabin, on the scruffy rug. The two faces of the men rolled and pitched and yawed; the thought occurred to throw up over both of them but she couldn't quite manage it. Ran instead out into the snow.

And ran smack into her dear friend Heather, Mike's beloved sister. "Crazy old Heather," she said, and hugged her and then slapped her shoulder gently as one would a horse. "Ah what a helluva face you have, Heather, old horse." It was true. Heather's normally long-nosed oval face was elongated and bubbled-down; it looked like silly-putty, nice familiar horsey silly-putty. "I tell you what," Myra said, leaning up close to Heather so the blonde girl could smell the other's sticky breath, "Let's do a real number; let's take our threads off and go into town and see what shakes."

"Forget it," said the pragmatic Miss Mandelbaum. "What the hell are you *on*, anyhow?"

"Oh, God, you are such an asshole," Myra told her, and began to weep again.

"Don't be so goddam funky spoiled rotten," Heather said, "you can't always do just exactly what you want to do *all* the time, you know . . ."

20

"And where is it so written? And besides, who the hell are you to talk about being spoiled," Myra whined, "you've got all the best clothes."

"Clothes aren't worth a shit, dummy," Heather responded wisely. "But I *do* have good clothes . . ."

They began to walk slowly toward the artificial town green. It was almost nightfall, and in the distance they could see the lit-up tree, with its plastic and glass ornaments; Myra was hallucinating marvelous images around that distant array of soft-edged colors. All sounds were muffled in the snow. Heather pulled out a stick and lit up. She did not offer any to Myra; enough was enough.

"Where's your old goddam fucking brother?" Myra asked.

"Out balling someone, probably," Heather said, affectionately, willing to contribute to her friend's paranoia so as to get it all over with at once, if possible.

"Hmmmm. Hey listen," Myra bubbled, "supposing we were to meet Mr. Walters. I mean, supposing he just happens to be wandering around center of town, like, say, he had to come in for groceries . . ."

"Are you thinking what I think you're thinking?"

"Oh, right *on,* Heather, old horse; you are one *clever* person and you do know me well! Yes, yes!"

"You want to put the make on Sam Walters? Our *teacher?* You're kidding."

"No. Not kidding. If I can make it with old Edward the Edwardian, no problem, I tell you, no problem at all!" and she danced a sweet monkey step in the snow. Hands flailing the air. Angled face lit from within and pale. The quality of moving awake in a dream.

"What *is* it with you?" Heather said, staring. "Eddie isn't enough, Mike isn't enough, now you're after Sam Walters too? 'A decent married man,'" she said, mocking her own mother's tones with a bitter recognition.

"Fuck 'em all," said Myra.

CHAPTER

3

When Ellen met Norman, three and a half weeks after Tom was killed, he invited her over to have a drink and to hear some records and to see his paintings. She went to his house; that is, after they had had enough conversation to establish rapport, he invited her, and she, knowing he was recently divorced, was enough attracted to the idea, the possibilities, to consider the move. Norman had told her about the divorce; she knew his ex-wife; she decided he was possible. For his part, he had decided she was attractive and sexy and was good for his ego, and he would make his move. Time was not important; timing was everything.

They pulled up to his house along a tree-lined driveway. The house was dark red with white shutters; not an old house; a new house, built to look old. One story imitation add-on. As they got out of the car, Norman was suffused with the delight and pride he always felt when coming back to this house. His wife had seen it first, true; but he had preempted it at the time of the divorce arguments, the property hassles; gave her this and that and that in order to keep the house. It had been her idea to move to the country-house every summer, but he now felt it had been his idea. He loved this house beyond all reason and symbolism. There was the house in Forest Hills, too; that was part of another life, he didn't give a shit about it; she could have it, even though it was worth more. He had to have and keep this one. He was telling Ellen all of this as they walked.

"The waterfall," he pointed out, as he opened the car door for her. Its sound a cold susurrus through the white night. Ellen slipped going across the path and he caught her elbow. She wondered if she would be interested in him. They were both Pisces, so it was barely possible. He said he smoked grass sometimes but never felt anything yet. He told her (she knew already) that he was a wholesale meat dealer in the City. He wanted to get out of wholesale-meat-dealing and devote himself to painting and be another kind of person. Wanted her to see his life, his house.

He opened the front door. Into a tiny kitchen. Plastic everywhere. Formica table and four chairs covered in print plastic with tubular metal legs. Plastic wood panelling. She began to turn off. He walked ahead of her into the "living-room," as he called it. Something (was it a hassock?) covered in fake fur. Some bad oils on the walls; lots of them, in fact. Some on each wall and several over the flagstone fireplace, which had a Naugahyde couch set before it. Next to the couch, a gold metal stanchion lamp set with cones of fake brass, each with a turn-knob, which Norman turned, so that the lighting illuminated one of his paintings. "I did that about six years ago; my work's different now." Image of adobe walls of some better-known painting of the southwest; it was an imitation. A copy.

"Mmmmm," she said. "Yes." Rather than saying anything aloud. Rather than retching. Would he have an imitation prick too, she wondered. "Jesus," she said, softly; contritely.

She followed him, as he then proudly, diffidently led her to the—bedroom! Figuring the timing was perfect. She seemed to love the house. And there it was: a Round Bed. One of those. And lo, it was furnished with perfectly circular sheets, and you-know-what blankets, and ditto bedspread. And the spread it was of fake lee-oh-pard, and then he spoke.

"It's eleven feet in diameter."

She saw the curtains closed against the moonlight. She turned and left the room, dominated as it was by the bed. Paused for a moment at the Naugahyde couch; picked up her coat, which was woven of real wool. Handed it, without grace, to him: "I'm sorry. I have to get home."

He drove her home.

* * *

When she met Ronald, they were at church, the Dutch Reform Church on Main Street. It was a good place to meet people, in this town. His was a new face, to her. For his part, he had come to the town in the process of making a film for educational TV on historical towns of the Hudson Valley. A historical film of interest to historians. He believed in history. Ronald wore a beautiful thick woollen English handmade sweater, dark green, and heavy leather riding-boots, conservative enough to wear to church if the tops were concealed beneath baggy tweed trousers, as they were; and a suede jacket. A comely getup.

As she watched him, he was talking to the parishioners and the pastor, gleaning information about the town. She was trying to figure out a way to be introduced to the new man; just then, friends of hers began to talk with the group he was in, so she forthrightly walked over, knowing they would sense the necessary. They did. It turned out that he had rented a home from them, not far from where she lived, so that he might spend the necessary time in the area. He looked to be about her age. He seemed interesting and mannerly. For his part, he was interested in her at once—that red hair of hers! and the tall, well-fleshed Dutch body, the creamy Dutch skin! —She would have stories to tell, as well!

So all of them went out for after-church brunch to a Dorothy Murphy-type tearoom and dining-room on Route 74

24

nearby; many families took their Sunday repast there; lots of thick-sauced duck, seafood dinners (mostly fried), something as a special every week like ham and sweets or turkey, and the kiddies welcome for junior plates. It was the best place available for fifty miles. Ronald ordered his meat rare, while Ellen watched. Some chance, she thought, in this place! He was mannerly and out to impress her with his worldliness . . . she was attractive to him; somehow different from . . . not like . . .

Then it was late afternoon, and when the friends left for home, it was "Would you care to take a drive?" and conversation, and she was thinking, I hope he asks me to his place, I wonder if it would be marvelous to go to bed with this man, such soft fine olive skin; I'll bet he's Libra, the sensualist . . .

They pulled up to the house down a long tree-lined driveway. Dark brown woodwork setting off a white stucco front, the front of the roof with the characteristic step-shapes rising; the several chimneys; the four white stone steps . . . it was one of the early cottages. Stunning. She stared, though she had passed this place a hundred times before. Leaded glass in one bay window and in the oaken door.

He was proud of this house and of his luck in finding it; perhaps not luck, exactly; it had been his relationship with Sally, wife of Mandelbaum; what a flirtation that had been . . . she could have called someone else when this house had come up; she would call Ronald. She did.

It was a lovely old house and furnished accordingly. He and Ellen shared Cockburn's sherry at the fireside (he assumed she would recognize "Co'bns" as the finest when he offered it). The room was softly lit by the fire and one parchment shaded Doulton lamp. It was a gradual, civil time, shaded by centuries of culture; he talked of his English background, his royal ancestors, his bloodlines . . . this was delightful. You didn't get to meet this sort of man around Wittgenburg. She was hoping it was a reasonable preamble . . .

"Would you enjoy seeing the rest of my home?"

"Of course."

His still photography, matted and glassed, faces of famous people, magnificent detail shots; heaps of spirals of film-strip; a cutter, a splicer, an editor, two viewers, four cameras, all superimposed on a handsome darkwood study. And, upstairs then, a den, with his books, and

the bedroom, his, all brown cut-velvet and beige leather, a whiff of his good aftershave, he turns to her, she smiles, it's a natural, late dusk shines softly through a leaded window, he begins to embrace and to undress her, he carries her to the darkwood bed, he is very strong, he slips from his own raiments, they twine together, yes, his skin is magnificent, his back is so silky, he turns his body fully toward her,

and she cannot at first locate his cock. It is there. It is that the man is built very small; erect, (which he is, by now,) he is perhaps two inches by one-half inch. He does not touch her with it; rather, being very much the willing and eager lover, a man of much luxury, he leans down toward her breasts, and makes as if to put his mouth to her pussy, which is by now silky with the liquid of preambles . . . he turns her, raises her hips with his hand to the proper angle, "enters" her, and in a fast instant shudders slightly, and he is done. It is done. He moves away, smiling.

She is amazed. She rises, dresses with her back to him, turns, and leaves the lovely bedroom, dominated as it is by the fourposter darkwood bed. Pauses for a moment at the corner of the Duncan Phyfe couch; picks up her coat, hands it without grace to him: "I'm sorry. I have to get home."

He drives her home.

❀   ❀   ❀

When she met Edward, they were going into the town's favorite bar, the Sled Pub the familiar, the comfortable hangout. A good place to sit with people. Edward's was a familiar face. He had been part of her town, her world, in a peripheral way, for all the years she could remember.

They talked for a while; she had come in feeling quiet and thoughtful; he had four beers and was depressed. His brother,

Arthur, had been killed in an auto accident a few days ago; she knew of this because Arthur had been working on Ellen's sister's farm until then. Edward spoke about his ex-wife and their kids. (Ellen had been in Kathy's class through school). She talked a bit about how she felt a year ago when Tom was killed in the railroad accident. His story about the day of Arthur's death brought her back into her feelings about Tom's death. But they were both alive and in the present and both aware of each other as animals. They were both reaching for life amid the thoughts of deaths.

They left and walked slowly up to his house, down a long driveway which curved between trees up a hill. There was the quality about the night of moving awake as if in a dream. Edward was talking about ice-fishing earlier that week. Ellen was complaining mildly that the salt on the roads was ruining the fenders and muffler on her old car. They were comfortable together. Ellen was calm. She felt separate from him physically; they had barely touched. But they were aware of the bodies. They were alive in their skins.

The house was white clapboard, perfectly ordinary, set among several similar houses in a clump toward the top of the little rise. Its only obvious beauty was an oval glass pane in the front door. But he led her toward the back of the house, where a path was worn in the snow. Once they were inside, she saw that the front door was blocked from within, shut off with thick plastic. "It blew in from the north like God A'mighty's own fury early this winter," he explained, "so this was the cheapest way to cut the wind and save on heat. I did the windows that way too."

The kitchen was a mess, like one sort of bachelor diggings: dirty dishes in the sink, more of them on the ordinary wooden white-painted table; the garbage-container full, the instant coffee open, the milk container out . . . The newspaper open on the table . . . In the tiny living-room, a franklin stove gave off a glow from the bed of coals left of this morning's coals or logs. The room was furnished in a nondescript way, mostly, except for the evidences of music throughout. But this room did not seem like a part of Edward; she looked toward him, her question coming from her shoulders and her quizzical stance. He understood at once.

"Well, I haven't done much with it myself, as you can see," he told her, wryly, "Of course most of it is still left from when Kathy was here—" (Ellen felt a pang of anguish, was it jealousy this soon?) "—and one of my lady friends has put some energy into trying to set it straight lately—she's not so good at it—"

He meant Myra. Ellen did not really hear that part of it. Or perhaps she heard it and did not want to consider the information. It was to be this moment, and there were the two of them and the others were ghosts for now. Because each of them wanted to be here together.

"Ah, it *isn't* much of a house," he said, affectionately touching her arm.

"Oh, it's okay; it's good; the music is good, and you can see the place is where you get some work done," she said, totally absorbed in her response to this man. Really, she wanted to leave this place; it was messy and ordinary and filled with the clutter of lives other than his. But it was the radiance of the man, his sheet-music scattered, the old piano, the flannel shirt thrown down, the lute, the autoharp . . .

He did reach for her. He was direct and she responded to him at once; there were no words, but just the knowledge that they needed to hold each other and it was right. She went naturally with him. They were moving against the deaths each had suffered. Through rooms and

to the bed, the plain double bed in the warm bedroom with the faded flowered wallpaper, where they stripped, simply and silently, their backs to each other, and came to each other from opposite sides of the old bed. And as he lay facing her, as their mouths moved together and she felt his strong chest and prick nuzzling her, she turned her face into the hollow of the side of his neck and said to him, "Thank God for you, you are so real, you are so healthy and real."

He said nothing, but kissed her deeply and moved his fine healthy body into hers with tenderness and zest. It was for

28

both of them. Slow and tender and passionate to the point of no sense of space or place; no words, no thought, infinite and wide and deep passion; they came together, because each was with the other, even this first time, and laughed because it was so good, and then fell asleep entwined.

Afterward, they left his house in a feeling of ordinary glory, and Edward drove Ellen home. When they got there, he came in for a cup of coffee. And then each began the day's work separately.

CHAPTER

4

Ellen's twin, Anne/Frey, living on a farm four miles outside of the center of Wittgenburg. A fraternal twin: light brown straight hair, blue eyes, a firstborn girl, she favored their father; Ellen, their mother. The twins were more than half Dutch: their father was an Elsen, their mother had a Dutch father and a mother who came from French, Welsh, and English, with that one Indian grandmother of whom Americans are so proud. It is Anne/Frey who inherited that grandmother's wide, high cheekbones and her strong connection to earth, seen as mysticism by some, as madness by others. Her life seemed incomprehensible to those practical adults around her as she grew: she moved best with animals, had little use for most humans; she was most often "alone," she sought and loved animals and the earth as companions, she grew up asexual and proud.

She had been born half deaf. Learned speech by imitation, and used it only when necessary for self-protection. Her other means of communication she used for survival. When the parents died, they left the farm, which had been their family's for over a hundred years, ever since the Down Rent Wars. They trusted her: in Anne's hands, the farm would continue. Ellen had just married and left with Tom Dykstra to live in the town. Anne was part of earth wisdom by twenty-three: she had an aura of clarity, of directness bred of living more and more simply, she was out of touch with anything modern except as that thing pertained either to her Morgan horses or to her own increasingly subtle or sharp relationship to her sensings.

Anne's name became "Frey," though even Ellen cannot remember how or when it started. Anne feels it might have to do with the fact that her father's fathers' province had been Friesland (though this was only discussed once in her presence). She and Ellen call each other "Frey" and "Ellen" although that is not the given name, the correct birth-name, of either girl. Either twin.

FREY'S TEACHER IN THE FIRST GRADE AND SECOND: I started calling her Frey. She was little Freya to me. Those clear eyes and what they saw; that delicate distance between her and the other kids except her twin; no one thought it was to her advantage not to hear them all, but I did, I thought it was, I still do. We pass each other sometimes in town now; she loves me and knows me; we don't speak, but then we don't have to. *She* never had to, that child.

A NEIGHBOR, FORMER CLASSMATE, SAME AGE, MARRIED TO A GERMAN FARMER: I don't like Frey; never did. Something always been queer about her, not just the way she's living there on that farm and all, but something about her not speaking clear and a look about the eyes. You know, when John and me goes over there to pick up the kids if they gone over to visit her animals, she never look me in the eye and the kids behave sort of crazy for a while, a day or so. She's a cold sort of person. Something peculiar happening there, I don't trust it. And the way the kids is drawn to her animals, even the dogs, as if we don't have the same kinds of animals right here at home.

THE MAN AT THE AGWAY: What she is is, she's really an animal herself, not that there's a name for it yet, or maybe one them Morgans she raises. Lord knows she's no woman on this earth; beautiful lines to her, all right, but she don't *have* no sex, as I see it. But I'd sure like to get into her jeans and mosey around anyhow, maybe just to find out. Not that it'd ever happen; she just don't see me; or for that matter anyone else; it's like we wasn't here or something. Comes in, orders what she needs (takes good care of everything alive on her place, that's for sure,) regular as you please; when she's here it's strange but it's like there's nobody there, or there's space where she's really got her boots down firm on the floor (I can't imagine that gal mucking out a stable!) and after she's left, I always feel different than when the others come in and buy.

THE TWO HELPERS WHO COME TO WORK WITH FREY AT THE FARM:

1) Marty, christened Marthe, also of Dutch descent, a bright, wide, heavy-set student majoring in animal husbandry at the nearby Community College: "She's never touched me. Not even once. I wish she would. I watch the way she handles Marchwind or Wird or the foals and it just breaks me up. She's got the most beautiful hands I've ever seen."

2) Arthur, a brother of Edward Richthoven (killed in an auto accident at the end of a season working with Frey on the farm): "I wasn't there long enough. I was learning things I have no name for. It would never have been long enough. And I was thinking of her face when it happened."

ELLEN: She is my twin. She is both Anne and Frey. To her, I'm still Käti. I'm both Ellen and Käti. I feel I'm the only human she talks with. But even so not often. We have the same dream sometimes. She wears her fragility on the outside but not everyone sees it. She is the only one who sees mine. Knows.

ANNE/FREY HERSELF: People see what they need to see. Who teaches animals how to love?—and after that, each person who touches another person teaches another lesson.

HEATHER MANDELBAUM: I keep my horse at her barn. She takes less for it than the other barns around. But then Mom says she doesn't need the money. Mom says Frey's got a way with animals and she'd take better care of mine than the other people around, and besides, it's cheaper. She feeds 'em good, the grains along with the hay, keeps them groomed and it's only $12 a month. So when Myra and I want to ride or something, we just go right in; she doesn't go for any big conversations, and we like it better that way.

CHAPTER

5

From some place within his spirit, the phrase kept repeating in the man's head as he drove: "door and house; doors and houses, houses and doors . . ." How a man's ways in life are shown by, reflected in, the house he keeps, the car he drives, the woman . . . "doors and houses," he said aloud, tasting the words as if they were in a foreign language, until they lost their learned meaning. He could not think of an Indian word for "door"—ah, well, that was easy, they didn't have doors, did they, a flap or a tunnel but no doors, not till the missionaries came . . . yes, birth, slip through flesh flaps and out into the life, no doors there either . . . Change your wife, change your life—change your car because you've changed your ideas. But what if the door to your house remained forever the same . . . ?

The man drove from the Village Green at the center of town out along Van Kleek Road and down Boice Lane in the thawing snow. The roads looked both familiar and unfamiliar. He loved this season in Wittgenburg, not just because it was his season of birth and therefore of rebirth, but because of this quality of overlay: winter was the only season of the year when a town could look clear to him who had spent most of his seasons there. Assumed disguises; a magic beyond nature . . . The sun was in his eyes part of the time, softening. He drove with an automatically adjusting care: the road was partly mushy and sanded, partly slick icy patches where the sun had not come through woody sections that day. He was wearing a white shirt with dark tie and tweedy sport jacket and brown wide-wale corduroy pants. When he left town he had been wearing a turtle-neck sweater (navy issue), blue jeans, his old leather boots and a floppy, warm felt hat, and was driving a 1953 Dodge pickup truck that had once been bright red. As he turned to go back toward town, toward his own house, whichever way he turned his head the sun was in his eyes. He lowered the visor, getting ready for the down-streaming of the papers he kept stuck up under it: receipts for things ordered and not yet received, job orders; instead, a map of Europe, folded so that a worn edge showed, indicating a section of Austria, fell to his lap. There were the letters, not modern letters, anglicized, but in Germanic heavy script. Near the border of Germany. A town circled. A town he did not wholly recognize . . . When he started home, he went the wrong way on a one-way thoroughfare. But he knew this road, all right. His road. As he arrived at his driveway, he slid the Alfa-Romeo slickly around the familiar curve, past the three-rock marker, and set it down smoothly near the mailbox. He felt his hand locking the key in the ignition. It was not his usual gesture. He did it anyhow.

And stared. Instead of the old and faded white clapboard two-story house, there was another house set in its place, in this place. Set exactly, precisely, meticulously, with land-scaped plantings firmly around its concrete-block foundation, smallish shrubs and evergreens, barberry bushes and laurel and rhododendron, all of them tipped with snow on the north side of the house which faced him, all looking quite like a photo on a calendar. A one-story house, maybe four years old or so, painted barn-red in a certain manner, and immaculate;

tmas lights in the picture-window that overlooked the

_, well. In the door was the familiar oval-shaped amber glass window. Warm light behind it. He touched the keys in his pocket. Knowing that he never locked this house. Thinking that it was good he'd locked the car, though, never know who'd try to make off with a car that valuable in a town like this, full of car-crazy kids . . . hell, hadn't someone almost walked off with his Melton topcoat after church last week?—he moved toward his door; there was the sound of the water-fall back of him; delightful!

As he unlocked the door, he noticed he had not properly fastened the lower half with the vertical bolt—anyone could have come in, broken in—have to be more careful—these Dutch doors were not predictable, you have to think twice about them. . . . He carefully bolted the lower half to the upper, and walked into the hallway. Lit softly by a double-globe lamp of the Tiffany era, placed on a darkwood credenza, lovely against the creamy stucco wall.

In the livingroom, to his left, he saw all of his things, the harpsichord, the lute on a table near the sofa, the autoharp, the music-sheets scattered about from the last meeting for making madrigals and motets . . . But asleep on the couch was a large, beautiful Newfoundland, who did not run to greet or bark in alarm, but looked up, and, satisfied it was his master, wagged his tail briefly and went back to sleep. The man turned and walked to the kitchen. All of his things, but seemed somehow more neat than he had left them. On the table were things he could not recall having left thus: a half-eaten cas-serole of beef bourguignon, a wilting half-head of Boston lettuce, and a cheese-board on which was a crumbly triangle of Gorgonzola.

The man turned toward his workroom. Now it was filled with framed and matted photographs of his clients and his friends. The workroom was placed about the same distance from the Dutch door that had once housed his metals-work-room shed. The torches and workbench and scattered scrap-metal and jars of metal pieces and vises and sandpapers were

36

nowhere to be seen. But the smell was similar, a smell as if flame had been using the air. And the things in the room now —felt familiar. He lifted one of the cameras. His hands knew how to hold it. He focussed it on a jar of touch-up brushes . . .

He was suddenly very tired. His feelings were made of some substance resistant to whatever was going on in this house, yet he could not shut off. He would sleep. He went into the livingroom (he could not find his bedroom; in his own house, it had been on the second floor, and he saw no stairway here); he sat next to the Newfoundland, for warmth, and fell asleep thus.

When he awoke, he felt the Naugahyde cold next to his thigh; the dog was nowhere to be seen; the fire had gone out, the old blanket had fallen from him as it had when he was a child, afternoons; it was twilight, almost night, there was a sound of a cocktail party from the house right next door, and he had not been invited, Christmas and he was alone, alone again, alone still, as he had always and always been alone, an only child with five siblings, an identical twin with no other image in the world like his own, a skull, a bleached human skull in the desert of winter snows, an animal who had finally returned to a basic form,

he was more animal than human as he awoke. Somehow he had to get out of this room and go to a warm place with other humans in it. In the hallway he passed the mirror, the round bevelled mirror above the credenza, behind the Tiffany lamp. Yes, it was his own face. But smoother; rougher; as if it had a patina. As if he were older. Yes, that was it. Maybe ten years older. Fifteen.

He turned in the little hallway, feeling like beautiful metal. As if he had forgotten something he had to take with him. Yes. What was it. No. Nothing. Everything would be all right. There was the sound of the waterfall, thicker with the waters of the thaw, coming to him through the double glass of the picture-window. He could always count on that. He put on his grey Melton overcoat and walked to the front door. The streetlight shone through the leaded glass of the amber oval window, comfortingly.

He locked the Dutch door, first from inside by fastening carefully the latch connecting top to bottom half, then (in a rush of cold clear air) from outside, turning his key in the shiny brass lock in the top section. He walked down the road, the driveway, past the poplars and the elm, got to his car, found it unlocked, found his own keys to the truck, fitted one into the ignition, started it, turned it toward Wittgenburg and other lives, and began the long ride, the short ride. The ride to town. By the time he arrived in town, his town, he was again wearing jeans, a felt hat, a navy blue sweater, boots. The battered 1953 pickup truck was under his hands, under his rump, the back seat loaded with his own tools for his craft, next to him was his old carton of oil cans and rags and files. He was in his own Capricorn skin. His name was Edward Richthoven. Probably.

CHAPTER

6

Myra woke in the small hours. Edward slept heavily. Her feet were cold. Edward was dreaming of something she could feel but not describe. She was awake and restless. Her mother thought she was over at Heather's. She had brought some "angel dust" for them, they had mixed it into the pot, done the joints, balled, and fallen out. But he had been more active than she that day, and outdoors; he could sleep, and she was more sensitive to drugs than he. Well, so, she was up and he was asleep, damn. The house was cold. It must be ten below at least. She got up and threw on Edward's flannel shirt and went downstairs. To her, the house was just a shell. She hardly saw it. It was somehow not very different from Mike's cabin. But Edward was very different from Mike to her. He was sort of solid.

She and Eddie never argued. Whenever it looked like they might, he got so quiet that she dropped whatever it was, unless she thought that if she kept on with it in a certain way he might give in. So what if they didn't have the same basic tastes. He was that much older than she. She needed him.

* * *

He needed her: her dreadful sparkle and out-reaching and that quality of not caring. With her, he could be that wild part of himself that he had always been careful to deny. He was so deeply Capricorn. He could love rules, he could move with anything that looked systematic, he would even make his own versions of the rules. He was the mountain-mover and the mountain. He was the most aggressive of the Richthoven boys. Arthur and Levon would have nothing of their father's trade. Edward, the traditionalist, went along, and made his own version of it.

After these months with Myra, it was still her sharpness he reached toward. He felt that he never caught her, she was an insect that was never still, he understood nothing about her and how she moved, she could reach out to him and draw him to her even when he thought his heavy will was set against her. Her violence was magnetic. He admired her ability to hate; she could hate as easily as she could make love, but he did not think she could love. So he was safe. And he insisted on seeing her as an innocent, as a very old child who knew a lot but didn't know what she knew yet or what to do with it all. The whole child-woman was there before him, as Scorpio, but could never be seen entire. He would never know her. He would never know how long it could last; it was not designed to last. He was seventeen years older than she.

* * *

He was waking now from a dream of doors and houses. Myra was not in the bed and he was glad, for now. The house was cold, it was his familiar room, he wanted to be alone here, he had to locate his own soul before he could be with her in any way. She was so demanding. He could hear her downstairs, a tiny witch hurtling from room to room. It was distracting. He wanted to think about the dream. Then he heard her alight; the big chair shifted on a board as she leapt into it.

40

And then she was up again (all that angel-dust, he thought,) and he heard the crackle as she bunched paper to begin a fire in the franklin stove.

She could never begin the fire well, he thought, I must get up and help. It was her apparent inability to do such things well that drew him some of the time, but it was of his own devising. She was competent when she could do things without supervision. She hated supervision. But he needed to see her as a lost child, she had to be watched over and fed, she had to be cared for or she might die. After Arthur's death, after the departure of Kathy with the boys, Myra gave him someone to care for. She appeared to need him. Not to be dependent, God knows; but to need him.

He did not know anyone else her age. He was separate from her age; had had no reason to meet her or her friends. Or to consider how they lived or what they thought. Edward and Myra had met at The Sled, which was reasonable; Myra drank a lot, along with other extremes. A water-sign, who turned toward the liquids often. She came there often that summer, to meet men; sometimes she came there with Heather, sometimes alone; she was shy (Heather was) about going in there alone; of course Myra was not. It was May, not full Summer yet; Edward had been spending a lot of time alone, relocating his soul after Kathy's leaving . . . Myra spoke to him first; she made it all easy and easier . . .

He rose and reached for his shirt. Gone. She must have taken it. He went to the dresser and took out another dark flannel shirt and put it on, drew on his longjohns and a pair of heavy socks. As he rose from bending to pull his socks on, he caught the moon outside his window. It stopped him. It was a clear, brilliantly cold time; even at that hour a car was passing, and he heard the crunch of tires on crusty snow through the frosted window. These were the realities, he thought; he was in his own house, it was a good, solid little house, it was almost paid off, the view was familiar—he had his work, and he belonged to himself—

But then there was that dream. What was that about. Nothing was ever paid off. Nobody ever really owned anything. He owned nothing, he would never own anything. He thought he owned things, but it was all really renting, he thought. Because after his death, some other man would believe that he owned these selfsame things, this house, this land, maybe even this town, this country. And so it would go, a chain of humans on through time, thinking they could get some hold on things, on this earth, could actually "own" something. Pity they hadn't looked at this during the Down Rent Wars, he thought. For that matter, he thought, we never own anyone, any more than we own anything. This business about getting married and all. A farce. We just lease. And sometimes we just lend-lease. Nothing I've been counting on is for sure . . .

* * *

He felt a great surge of feeling for Myra, some alliance with her wildness; he wanted to see her. From below, he heard her starting the phonograph. Christ, he hoped she did not put on any of those loud bright rock things of hers. He could not sort out his own records from hers; she'd brought over some fifty-odd of hers and they had gotten mixed into his, in with the chamber music and liturgical music; the Pergolesi and the Vivaldi in with *Jesus Christ, Superstar* and Kris Kristofferson. Neither one of them speculating on what the mixture symbolized . . . (Ah, there it went again, he was thinking, and laughed: the 'his' and 'hers' of it, as if he owned that kind of music, as if she owned this. As if anyone could own music. What could be more unpossessible than music . . .)

* * *

She was looking for that record. The one that had been playing on the box at the Sled when she'd met Eddie. Earlier that day she'd popped an up and then another; it had been a very down day till then and she had to get things lively. Then, an hour before she finally went into The Sled (good name for that hill, Sled Hill, that bar, Sled Pub; she was giggling, when she was down, she slid down the Sled Hill to the bottom, and there was the good old Sled, ready to take her somewhere new, there and waiting for her, her own private Sled right there at the bottom of the hill!) she'd smoked a couple of joints, to take the edge off dropping down from the pills; so she was pretty stoned by the time she walked into the bar. Figuring, okay, that was a beginning, edge off it, but a nice little drink or two with maybe a new man or two and a good rap would make it, and if luck held, a good fuck to round out the night, and she'd be all set. Heather was off doing something, probably; maybe one of those damn family numbers she was always getting sucked into . . . which reminded her: that Mike could go fuck himself, he sure as hell wasn't giving her what she wanted these days, did he really think a good fuck was all there was to life, he was such a *baby,* and such a mamma's-boy, the both of them such big jerks, still on the tit; *both* of them could go to hell . . . Myra went into Sled wanting everything, content with nothing, expecting everything, a Scorpio kid, a tough German kid, she had been raised a Catholic and so now nothing could keep her down, nothing could hold her bound, nothing, not even a down like this one. Scorpio could turn any down around so the energy was useful.

The lights were pleasantly fuzzed-over for her and she saw a few of her friends. For God's sake, Heather *was* there, with her back to Myra; she never did turn to speak to Myra, so Myra knew Heather was into some new guy. She went to the bar and got a scotch-on-the-rocks, and sat alone with it, digging the music. It was Neil Diamond doing "He's My Brother," and it was thick, yeah, it was *true,* she began hurting just at the edges and went into a big heavy sliding back down, and then began to go up again with it. Fuck it all anyhow. But then on came, marvelously, something by Clearwater, that's better, up, up, and out into that big fat Aquarius medley, *Let the Sun Shine In,* then finally *Starshine* and she began to be filled up. She was thinking, I *got* to get that disc, I mean for *me,* not for Heather, *not* to share with Mike, *not* let Mike *buy* it for me, I mean *I* want to buy *that* for *me.* Hey hey, this is almost as good as a coke high, I'm getting there, wow, silky—this is what I needed—almost.

The man one barstool down was watching her and she felt it.

So she turned and gave him her full face, but not fast, slowly, so they could taste the first minute. She had flashed that he was goodlooking. She could feel the space, and she knew there was a thing going down from the way he had been watching. His vibes were good. She looked. His eyes were good. Blue-green, and the cat was very pretty, bit of grey at the edges of his hair, he was an older cat, good, let's see what he has to say for his self.

"Like that music?"

"Yes. I like it. I like most music. But I don't have to ask if *you* like it; you're sitting there just loving it; I'd guess it's very important to you! Right?"

"Yeah. Right on. It's heavy stuff—good for whatever's the matter."

"What . . ."

And more like that. She never could remember what she said next to him, or he to her; she was very stoned-out. He bought her the next scotch. Moved over to the barstool next to her. It was late Spring, almost Summer, and they were both just about ready for this. She arranged it so that her thigh touched his as he sat next to her. She was really grooving with his eyes. Who was he, she couldn't remember seeing him much around town. This would be a great groovy change from Mike. Damn Mike anyway, with his numbers about school and "busy tonight" and all. He wasn't this cute anyhow.

She left The Sled with the new man. He took her back to his pad. It was raunchy as hell and nothing hip about it, nothing happening. Not much in it she could dig. But he did smoke, and he had some good grass. They made a couple or three joints and curled up in the bedroom to do them. His name was Edward, which she promptly changed to "Eddie"; it was the first time anyone in all his life called him Eddie, he said. But was it okay, she wanted to know, knowing as she asked that it would be okay, that she could get away with probably any kind of shit she wanted to with this cat, he was looking at her like she was candy, said he was Capricorn and that meant she could match him game for game and outsmart him most times, he didn't know any of her numbers, and it

44

would be okay. She could teach him how she liked to do things. As long as she was cool around his Capricorn wish to run scenes . . .

* * *

"We ought to get some of these clothes off," he said, and she laughed up at him.

"Boy, I'm really *wasted*," she said. He was puzzled, and then he realized why.

"Jesus, is that what that means? Are we '*wasted*' when we get high? I mean, what the hell does 'high' mean, then, anyhow?"

She giggled. "Boy, are you ever *high*, Eddie baby, that's what that all means, you know?"

And he caught on, seeing how he was caught up in the semantics of it, seeing as if from a weird distance how high he was, to be playing around with the concepts that way— doing his Capricorn trip on it, even when high analysing what is happening in the being high. Wow, how *funny* . . .

She was walking around his room, dropping parts of her clothing as she went. She had a good body and she was doing her good little strut. She loved this. There was a radio near the bed and she reached over and put it on. He went into the bathroom and she could hear him pissing, and when he came back he stood with his back to her, taking off his clothes. The proper Capricorn, she thought; you could see his body wasn't used to being like this, just swinging out, he took off his clothes as if there wasn't a woman in the room, as if he was getting undressed to go to bed. Well, okay, he *was*, but not like he thought, hey, she purred . . . He walked to the bathroom this time to get a drink of water, and stood drinking it, his head tipped back, the light full on him. Jesus, a pretty cat, she thought again, black hair curled on his chest in a double butterfly pattern, turn of the torso, hard good body, and by Jesus if that wasn't a very fine and very pretty prick he had going there . . . Oh, couldn't I do some lovely things with *you*, Mister, she thought, looking him over.

He walked his erection across the room to where she sat,

crosslegged on the bed, with just a bit of her shirt dragged across her, so he'd have to guess about something, anyhow. Made sure he could see her good little sharp tits and shoulders, though.

"I want to make love to you," he said, and she laughed again, they both laughed, it was so superfluous.

"I'm not ready," she said, against his mouth.

He moved his mouth to the curve of her neck and she began to get ready. He turned her gently so that her right leg was turned out, knee bent, cunt toward him, left leg straight, and as she noticed what he was doing she began to get very hot for him (all the while somewhere thinking, none of this Cap missionary-style straight stuff for *this* Cap!)

"Not ready," she said, again, to him, but he had his mouth on her left tit, he was moving his warm firm prick against her belly gently, then down slowly along her cunt, she was getting wet, she wanted to wait a while longer, besides this was very good, and she wanted this part to last, and she was afraid. She thought he was going to be too big for her. He was trying her, and he was too big. She could not take him in. No way. But she was not afraid he would hurt her. Not this cat. She was really just not ready and he knew it. Okay. And Jesus what a luscious body, she had her hands all over him and he felt so good. His skin was much smoother than Mike's, for instance. And less hairy. And the hair was sort of straighter, it *felt* darker somehow. Mike, given to fat; and this man, without an ounce of fat on him; beautiful; and as she thought this, he smiled into her mouth and said, "Don't be alarmed, because it *isn't* the end, you better believe, but I'm going to have to come now. I'll be with you again and still, but I have to come now."

And he did, strongly and softly, having only been just a bit into her body, hardly into her at all (but it had been so long since he had had a woman), and he didn't move away from her. He still was with her and stayed with her, he had gotten somewhat soft, but not as soft as she thought he would be, Jesus, what a guy, he still had and kept the hard; but he

46

was smaller now, so he could move into her more easily, and he did.

He did; she watched it all as if from a great distance. All of him slid deep into her, good, it was good, it was marvelous; she cried out, "Jesus, that's *good*," and he was moving just right. Slow, and then moving them both so that she went into his rhythm, and then it was her rhythm too, theirs, no distinguishing the one body from the other . . . inside her, he was becoming big again, and she could take all of him well; the bodies were good. She said, "Good," and he said nothing, or she thought he said nothing, she was moving, he made a slight noise at her ear, said "Now" to her, he made her move faster when she didn't think she wanted to yet, and she came, in great waves, deep; her coming made him come too; they crested and sank and rose and sank. He fell asleep; she rose, and walked around restlessly, looking at his pad, his things, and then got dressed and went back to her parents' house.

* * *

The next day she began to move some of her things into his house; not in any noticeable or obtrusive way, she just left a jacket in one of his closets and a sweater on one of the chairs one time that she was there, and bought the record she had wanted and left it by his stereo . . . and she messed around with the kitchen a while, dropped some speed and washed some dishes, swept everything and made a pile of the laundry that was scattered all over the house. She could see that there had been a woman and some kids in this house, and that the woman and kids were not around any more, but she saw no reason to discuss any of this with Edward and he never brought any of it up. He never objected to her doing what she was doing with the house or his things, so she kept on.

They went down to the Superette the day after they met and they bought ten dollars' worth of groceries, especially four kinds of cookies (oatmeal; chocolate chip; coconut almond; and hermits), and four quarts of milk, and a bag of oranges (Edward was sure that pot leached some vitamin or other from the system, and he was making sure with the oranges and the milk). Apples and popcorn and a couple of chocolate bars and a can of Nestlé's powdered cocoa for making chocolate milk out of the milk. And they bought a bottle of good Scotch and a bottle of Bourbon and some N.Y. State white wine, to go with coke if they felt like coke. Now they were set.

CHAPTER

7

Now they were set. Into a certain pattern. Winter now; they had been spending time with each other since late last Spring; each got from the other something peculiar to their combination. Myra was balancing Edward's solidness against the giddiness and lightness of her school friends, including Mike and Heather, against Mike's tender, brave awkwardness. Eddie was always such a full man with her. But she would run from this too, run frantically, from Edward's great weight and back to the dilly-silly scenes with Mike and with Heather. But even though they were her best friends, she would never permit them to kid her about Edward. Anyone else, anything else, but not Edward. He reached some part of her soul that she would not permit others to mock.

She got the fire lit, listening to Edward padding about overhead. He would be glad she had gotten it done herself, and before he could help. She was a bit tired of his thinking she was some sort of incompetent baby. But then that was part of what he wanted her around for, wasn't it, and she knew better than to change it around too much . . . She took some more powder out of the packet of angel dust and mixed it in with some of the pot again and rolled a couple of joints. Had lit up when Edward walked in.

"You look wild in that shirt," he said.

She pirouetted and sank into the chair before the fire. "Glad you dig it."

Deep winter snow. Back of her, through the window, the big field stretched, glazy and waved under the moonlight. The rich curves of it, not angular like this child-woman, he thought, but richly curved, earth rich flesh like my other woman Ellen. Like Ellen . . .

He was too quiet now. There had been a thaw last week and beginning of this week, temp up to 40 almost, then a soft rain out of season one day, and then the freeze, and so a glaze across the field, smoothly icing over the snowmobile tracks, the animal tracks, the land heaved up with the thaw in a series of glistening low ridges in the soft high natural light . . . back at that edge, where the deer came in summer and where Edward would walk in winter to try to leave hay for them, it was dark and invulnerable, dark, dark and inviolate . . . Thus it was, he thought, with his soul. He was moving, moving, not questioning, trusting his nature, his own soul, moving in the life as he did in the dream, going toward that dark edge of the field.

Myra, her back toward him, was quiet, but not helpless. She was firm and very much a sensed if not known quantity. The tracks were covered; snow, soft at first and then dense with its own weight, and then the slip and glaze of the icy surface . . . so it was with Myra. Her arms bore the marks of experiments. Of her seasons. The acts were recorded. The seasons covered them but did not obliterate.

She was important to him. The sarcasm of one of his acquaintances, one night at the Sled: "Well, but here's Edward, isn't it, and is this lovely little girl your daughter—?" —and Myra's tiny, tight arm flinching under his hand, just that second, just enough, the moment before she smiled brightly up into the other man's eyes and said her wisecrack: "No, but he for sure *is* my sugar-daddy!" And the idea of sturdy, steady, solid Edward being anyone's sugar-daddy broke them all up, broke the inherent nastiness of the moment and all of them laughed . . .

But the remark didn't desert Edward. Returned at odd times, as in dreams: the dream of Myra as a baby, as *his* baby who had to be protected; good feelings; but then the dream-shift and he was fucking his baby, an infant named Myra with a little plastic body like some Didee-Doll, from which he woke frantic, horny and sweating, but stayed away from Myra for that whole week, unable to shake the idea . . . But she was part of his skin right now, and when he met her in the Superette, she saw to it that she left with him, and saw to it that they went back to his house and began the whole thing again. She made her flesh real to him, she made herself woman rather than child to him.

Now she turned from the fire, anxious for his attention. "Here's a really good joint," she said, "set you up just right," handing it to him. It was half-smoked. He took it, knowing that this would mean no work done most of tomorrow. They would make love again, she was already looking bright and greedy; that would bring the night to dawn or more; then, if he could sleep, it would be until after noon, and if not, they would spend the day mostly indoors, near the fire, she cutting pictures out for her scrapbook of ideas for jewelry. She had last summer worked with a man who made bronze jewelry for sale in the City and at the craft fairs of the area during tourist season, and she learned some of the craft from him; meanwhile, until she got back to it, she would add to her ideas, make drawings, put clippings into the scrapbook; and she loved to talk with Edward about this. It was a good bond between them, that they were both interested in working with metal, making something out of shaped metals . . .

While he would perhaps putter in his workroom, or sit watching her as she moved about the house. She was his wild bird. His dark small wild bird, all angular and tense, a little crow, a natural bony little bird, all the images came to him with the smoke they shared. Sometimes he had no desire to

51

move at all, just to sit and be, but this was always after they had made love. They would often make love after they had smoked, if they were in or near the house. In the crisp light of winter or the soft bright light of late or early Summer. Now, in deep winter, it seemed to him this way was best of all, the window open just so, the storm window open a tiny bit, so that a cold feather of Winter air moved at first across their bodies, was forgotten in their warm heated motions, and reminded them of the season as they lay resting and entwined together afterward.

* * *

Soon it would be half a year of this. Of them. Moving in their own pattern. But now there was Ellen, and he divided himself, willfully. As best he could. It was what he had to do. He could not do without either of the women; he was with whichever woman he was with; he did think of one woman while he was bedding down the other, and he didn't like that; he would try to gain a space of a day alone between seeing the one or the other, though he couldn't always make that happen. And he wanted his time to himself as well. He wanted to be on his own center.

It was now two months since he had met Ellen and she had become important to him in ways he was only beginning to name. Naming his ideas about Myra was much easier and safer: she was an unknown quantity, she was forever unattainable, she was a game, a choice, always irritating, sometimes exciting, always attractive to some negative side of his makeup, sometimes she made his teeth grit with impatience or annoyance, but always she had remedies for the pain, whether it was a folly of drugs, or a new way of making love, or a story he had not heard about the way the world was from the kids she talked to. She always kept the distance—she was German, too, but she was the dark, thin Catholic German, he was the stocky, firm, wide-built fair-skinned Lutheran German; his Capricorn nature was always vying with her Scorpio nature's power, and his Cap ethic was always alarmed by her Scorp amorality. He wanted to believe that she leaned on him, that he was feeding her.

But *Ellen*—ah, Ellen was Dutch to him, Ellen was the earth to him, Ellen was the earth's curves. Ellen was music, was the sea, she was calm and rounded, she was rich—and he was irritated because she had no angularities, and because her way of moving slowly, as a water sign, was different from his earth way of moving slowly; she was not ponderous or contemplative but was mystical and tied into earth's cycles in a way different from his . . . She fed him, she was giving him something he needed for his own hungers, it was a quiet deep rich substance he had no real name for just now. It *was* good.

CHAPTER
8

But along the roads of Trois, of Wittgenburg, the signs said
"POSTED, NO TRESPASSING," every eighth tree marked with such
a paper and all the roads lined with trees. A man put his sign
upon the land and upon the tree, saying it was *his* land, *his*
earth, *his* acre, his stone fence, his trees, his animals, *his own,*
saying this was his time on earth, he would possess some
things, he would design by his own work to keep something
for his own, to choose and to develop and to fabricate; he
would place his name upon certain acres, certain people; his
wife would take his name, his children would bear his sur-
name, they would be named for his ancestors, for his tribe;
there would be his own definition upon all of the nature which
he caused to thrive in his region of space . . . he would an-
nounce himself in this way and would fight for that which he
had labeled his own—by leaving his signs, his names, his
spoor, his residues, his heirs—that no other male might try
to claim that which was already fought for and won and thus
claimed. Or would run the risk of death by fighting.

A tree with a paper fastened to it, giving its message of the temporal, giving honor to the labor of the man who made the claim, the man who gave money to an office where he filled out a paper, many papers, confirming his right to this land, this tree, these people; who left his mark by using paper made of trees first; then metal into the paper and back with metal nails into wood of trees . . . metal of barbed wire onto fences made of the wood of trees . . . metal into a ring to go upon the finger of the woman to be called "wife" . . . the metal of bladed machines, simple hoes or clever combines, that taught earth to produce what man needed to feed himself and those lives he protected, those he chose to possess . . . to enable them and him to continue in an ownership pattern for their lifetimes . . . all this so alien to the Indians of this very land, who had lived here without thought of possessing; who thanked earth for giving of itself to them for their well-being and survival, who did not name their women or children after themselves but after the earthy creatures with whom their daily lives were intimate . . . who did not often kill idly . . .

The land that Edward saw from his window was not far from the scene of the Down Rent War, the challenge to possessiveness of the settlers of this land. Edward's grandfather had been one of the Germans who had challenged the local landowner's right to merely lease land rather than to leave it free for buying or selling. He had not liked the landowner's right to oust him and his family on whim, after all the work he'd put in, and after all his father's work before him, just because of some grabby gouverneur's whim and some paper called a patent which was really just a lease. Edward's father had told the stories to Edward. So Edward had a feeling for the land, though not much of it was now in his possession; he had sold off much of the farmland when he had married Kathy, who had not wanted to come there with him, and he was renting the old farmhouse, now, to some young lawyers from the City who had theories about agriculture and who were going to try organic farming there. Edward did not feel he was reverting to the spirit of rent-leasing. He felt he was still in touch with his land, that it would still be there for him when the time was right for him and when the people on it were through with using it for their needs. He did not play landlord with them; he did not need to. He remembered that he had not so long ago thought of living there, and of eventually turning that land over to his sons.

He and Ellen came differently to the question of ownership of land. Ellen's parents' farm, still owned and run by Frey, had been in the Elsen family since the original settling. Ellen's family had clung to that land, had succeeded in keeping the land. She saw this as reasonable and meet. She and Edward would talk about it. As Pisces, she believed in flow and continuity; she thought that "temporal" was really "circular," and all was permanent in the end; she thought water and earth were binding, a man's work earned him the right to keep land, forever if he could make it stick, a man's word was binding (as when a gouverneur gave his word that way); she went further: she believed that death could be surpassed, and that blood was equivalent to earth in its ability to bind (wasn't blood, after all, mostly water!). The losses she had suffered were through what was called *death,* and she didn't quite believe in the way that word was explained these days. Everything in her experience indicated that life itself could be relied upon, and she felt there was a strong possibility that the system of life was just.

In that fashion, she was relying upon Edward now. Although she knew about Myra and the time he spent with her, she trusted, from the nature of it, the warmth between her body and Edward's, the language of their flesh together, as it was part of earth. And the way they both responded to music: how well-made it was, how brave the combination of intellect and emotion.

One night, when Edward came by, she said, "You know, there was a time, not long ago, when your coming here and being with me was what I thought I wanted the most in the world . . ." He was looking at her. She felt the caught strangled pain in her throat. ". . . but I don't know any more. I don't *know* about that now . . . You keep talking about 'today' and 'now' and what I thought I knew best about was . . . just loving you . . ."

The words did not come out as she wished. She was moving restlessly around the room they were in, her own comfortable room, filled with her own artifacts. But she felt awkward.

For her the time was a jigsaw, moving, cutting out the periods when they were together and the times when they were not, shaping a series of morse-code chunks, dot-dashes, being-with and then not-being-with; as if she were being brain-washed by him into doing what was needed for him, without thinking of what she herself needed.

He was always contending it was what they both needed— he, talking from his discussions with Myra about independence, about how nobody was ever really *with* anybody, nobody ever could belong to anybody, the need to be free of the old-fashioned structures imposed by a messed-up society and its demands . . .

He could talk freely about Myra and her ideas to Ellen, he thought, because Ellen was his friend as well; there was an ease between them. But he did not talk with Myra about Ellen, or her views; for one thing, he was not all that sure he could reproduce them, because he felt he sensed her views, more than he heard or discussed them. He thought he knew her. He wanted her to be the woman he imagined she was . . .

Myra was not interested in talking about Ellen. She was not wide enough, really, and she was absorbed totally in herself and her world. Myra did not seem to be thinking very much about Ellen. But Edward would have to contrast the lives of each to the other . . . each woman's effect on him . . . it was draining. He would smoke more, drink more; when he was with Myra, he would dip into coke now, he would take some speed with her and stay up for two days and two nights, sometimes throwing the feelings into his work, sometimes just goofing off with Myra, often in the end feeling cleansed and free, but sometimes filled with distress and nightmares. It was Myra's highly touted form of running, and it was becoming his. Myra did not care, either way, really; she was only interested in his wanting her, in his seeking her out. She took pleasure in evading him some of the time, just to see him chase and find. Just to delight in his hunger and his appetite.

And Ellen: was always there when he came round; at one point this exasperated and disgusted him, that she be so available; most of the time, though, he was glad and very grateful, because of her softness and her affectionate nature. Her values were around the word "love," which was a word he would use in thinking of her, but which did not apply to Myra. Ellen as Pisces could be the complete romantic, to a fault, and sometimes, he thought, that's exactly what she was. Completely idealistic, completely romantic. Believed the world was round, was good, the sun would rise in the morning, Edward would some day give up Myra and would turn to her and ask her to marry him . . . As long as Edward understood her idealism, her romanticism, and seemed to respect, or at least let it be, they could blend. Had a chance to mesh and to move together. She would only strike out when this aspect of her nature was violated, when her romantic nature was forced into conflict with the hard edges of the practical or the pragmatic. Then Ellen would pull back, or come out fighting, offended, hurt, sometimes angry: not understanding it.

She told him: "The first man I was with after Tom was killed—I guess it must've been not long after the funeral, thank God, I don't remember exactly, but I hadn't gotten through the misery and the shock—this man, Daniel, he was so sweet, he was Tom's friend at college, and I'd met him just at the funeral—he was so *tender*. You know what I mean. Not just the gestures, but you could tell that he really felt compassion for me as a human being, not just for my being Tom's wife in that situation. We spent the afternoon, took a ride, had supper—you know. And all the time, oh, you know what I mean, a gesture, a touch, I don't know when it started to become something more—when I started to respond to him as woman to man. It just turned.

"So then it would only be a matter of time. I didn't really *think* we would make it, but I guess I *knew* we would . . . He told me a lot about himself while we were sitting around after dinner. He'd married when he was 17, because the girl was pregnant, so now, he was only 27, and had a kid that was almost 10 . . . who was with his ex-wife; the way your kids are with Kathy, I guess; they had split up, finally, about a year ago. You know, like this town, where he came from, somewhere around Buffalo, in that town he saw no way not to marry the girl, and he *liked* her well enough at the time—but not for long.

"Well, we talked and danced and we wound up together on the couch—the bodies were just drawn together. I guess we figured the bodies would make up for some of the pain we'd been through. He took off my shirt, and his own, and began with the rest of my things; I really wanted him by now . . . so then he leaned over me, and with his face real close to me he says, *'Hey, you wearing any protection?'*

"Christ, if that didn't turn me off. I turned to ice. Jesus *Christ*. I moved and turned away from him, trying to think of how to respond to the coldness of it, when . . . I heard him moving away from me, but I couldn't say anything. Next thing I knew, he was gone. Gone! right the hell out the door. And I've never seen him or heard from him since—and I don't *want* to, either. What a fool! What a poor graceless fool, all caught up thinking that *once* he's trapped that way, it will continue to happen with everyone!"

Edward stared at her. "You just let him leave?"

"What else could I do?—Actually, I guess I wanted him to leave," she said, from her Pisces passivity, from her terrible romanticism. "He'd broken the mood. Lovemaking *isn't* about asking such questions!"

Edward stopped: he had the urge to ask her, at this precise point, if she had or had not been using protection during his own time with her body. He was being practical and she could not brook that. He started, anyway: "But, Ellen, a man has to . . ."

"Not really," she said, "No, he *doesn't*," and turned away from Edward in this moment. The deep chasm between them. He flinched back. Still needing to know.

CHAPTER
9

In this Chapter, Mike and Myra get together and ball. Scene: the cabin in the woods, by the lake, after Myra has done what she has done to it. Has had to do. With or without acid.

MYRA: Jesus, man, you aren't getting any thinner, are you . . .

MIKE: Would you for Christ's sake just shut up and get your clothes off.

MYRA: Boy, is this place a dump. I wouldn't get fucked here if it were the last place on earth.

MIKE: For you it just might be . . .

MYRA: What'd you mean by that? (Mike slaps her face).

MYRA: Fuck *you,* you rotten sonofabitch, what'd you do that for?

MIKE: *Guess,* you fucking ingrate, you fucking tease. You don' always get what you want, baby, but you sure as hell gonna get what you ask for—*this* time, anyhow.

MYRA: And what, pray tell, does the Boy Genius of Wittgenburg think it is exactly that I need?

MIKE: Listen. Just for a change, shut the fuck up and listen. I know all there is to know about you and that Ed Rosterfrigger.

MYRA: That's not his name, wise-ass.

MIKE: Yes, that's his name. If I *say* that's his *name*, that's his goddam fucking *name*, bitch, you dig?

MYRA (wheedling): Listen, honey. Why don't we sit down and smoke something and cool it out a little bit . . .

MIKE: Jesus. You, putting out for a simpering old fart like Ed Friggerfinger. Je-*sus*.

MYRA: Heeeeyy, Mike—cut it out, willya?

MIKE: Not on your sweet ass, Lover. Not till I find out what you got planned in that freaky weird head of yours.

MYRA: Jesus, Mike, I came here with *you*, didn't I? And you know that I—

MIKE: I don't know diddly-shit. I know you're into a game, is what I know. I just don't know the name of the game. Tell me, pretty maiden, what is he, your father or something? That would—

MYRA: Boy, are you full of shit. He's a good lay, is all. Besides, I got a right to do whatever I want, with whoever I want to do it with and you know it. You don't own me, you know, Buster.

MIKE: You kidding? I wouldn't take you as a *gift*. What a big bargain package *you* are.

(It goes on like this a while. You know the sounds.)

The place is really a mess. It is a three-flight walkup on East Fourth Street. On each stairwell and each step-tread is a corner full of roach shit and like that. A hallway made for mugging. When Mike came home one night from gigging as a cab-driver (he does this in defiance of Sally and Herman who had him all set up for a really natty real estate thing with relatives but he quit because he wanted to Learn About Life On HIS OWN), he got ripped off for $49.52. However, he still lives here. He opens the door with a set of keys, one for the lower lock and one for the Fox Police Lock. Four guys share the pad. You enter the pad and see a cot, linens there but filthy and disrupt; next, a table, its top the only clean and cleared area: it's formica. The rug is invisible beneath the grime of a few years of city filth. The next room is the kitchen. Under the kitchen sink is a cat-box, loaded and running over with catshit strips: and the stench thereof is mighty. The sink, crusted with chemical residue and stain, is empty. Cleaned dishes stacked haphazardly on the old rubberized drainer. Stove, crusted with food overflow, gives off a whiff of gas. Heap of newspapers, another of old paper bags, shelf of dumped bags half-full of groceries, some open to the bugs, some shut. Two doors lead off the first room. Both are shut. One seems to be of metal; perhaps it was fashioned from two file-cabinet doors. Snores emit from behind that door. One of Mike's roommates. Another man asleep behind the other door. Mike's sack is the cot in the first room. He's the last to have come in to the deal.

Mike leads Myra out of the apartment front door, across the hall, to another locked door. This is the fourth roommate's room. It is he who rented the apartment and whose name is on the lease; it is he who takes in roommates, at $10 a week each. He's not in tonight. His setup is the only one with a private entrance. The Couple enter the Golden Chamber of All Desires, otherwise known as Bob's room. It is threadbare but very clean, in utter contrast to the other section of the apartment. Iron bedstead, painted black; improvised wooden shelves made from orange-crates; desk, which holds many paperbounds (Hesse, Watts, Laing, Castaneda, Burroughs, McKuen, Brautigan; books on cost accounting; books of actuarial tables). Myra is led toward the bed. Makes small grunting noises. Is obviously expected to speak.

MYRA: God, this place is a dump. I wouldn't get fucked here; it looks like the last place on earth.

MIKE: Bitch. For you, it might just be . . .

MYRA: What? (Mike slaps her face.) Hey, Miiiiike, cut it out, willya? O Jesus, why'd we have to go do acid . . .

The angular room waves all its corners into curves. Myra touches the heap of old sheets and blankets, she traces the many come-stains on the bottom sheet, Mike stands facing her, he grows tall and thin as well as he is able, he's the Master, it is after all his own design. There he goes, taller/ thinner, head touching the ceiling, ceiling a grey peeling cracking paint dust. But there Mike's bronze curly hair a halo against the naked aureole lightbulb halo halo. He moving begins to shed his clothing. Myra reaches up way up up and moving her hand across his shoulderblades lovingly an embrace geste. Her hand thus is India-rubber, her arm long six feet long six arm long. Tenderly she wipeth clumps of hair from shoulder shoulderblade and backskin of Mike Master. His shudderblades. Her face he sees as it sweet radiants, as he wishwashes, she his and The Princess for sure. Where acid blud runneth like en banks of all ribbers, or what do you thinkem on when it. JJ reacheth out tou tutch her six foot I mean arm in love. As hand leaves her it cumen away with Partch of skin & musiq back of it, as she hollows & soun as animalskide (th drum masq). As when Brandon iron skim hits the roof, or he wud be a new man. She smiles miles up to where he is her affection he seeks. Ah smiles Narcie such a hip hip. Look at the hip the eye of ankh tatu as Sanders say had but there is it, eye level perk-y and mayo never think to see another as gran, and lukin offaly find all danglin down-o fer man fer mon again to turn slig and an uncommon gal she wuz andtrim was he befor her with him dingle down o lims he'd dare long

MYRA: And what prey does der genies sur—? (Tears)

MIKE: Year suite asp . . . (Tears)

Of presence in circumstance. Honored guest here. He moves softly back from her as she sits on the bed, the better to see her magnificence. She seems rounded and full-fleshed, has grown fat and furry as were the queens of Solomon. Behind her glossy oil-rubbed shoulders gleamed the hanging gardens: cut-out prints of Van Gogh sunflowers, pin-up girls from East Village Others, notated calendars with photographs of sundials on them, other artifacts of a beloved and mourned civilization . . . they complement her rich dark beauty. He reaches a man's hand out to touch neck at nape. She reaches a woman's hand out to touch prick at base. He places white hand on dark mound cunt and when hand leaves it takes away dark hair on its palm as he is animal with hairy palm. Her dark hand on his white prick moves off it with patch of sear, as wen too hot iron &c &c. They will love to look tender upon each other. He rises to her und bent down, she lends up, as she marvs acrost the room his prig walks rising a loffaly thing to/toward her. Hence they lie down upon the grise velvet sheets, their bodies covering the centuries of stain dream ream reals across the grate graceless altar.

MIKE: Your lovely face it is made of mosaic, O Princess.

MYRA: Back of you the sky/ceiling extends blue as Dali, is also mosaic, as is the Master's skin.

MIKE: O love of this and all past lives, your mound is all the nurture and myriad warm colors of my world . . .

MYRA: Thy risen wand or rod is sceptre chambered like the hive of bees through which comes honey to me thus . . .

He touches her fur mound and it is the burial-mound of all his ancestors, it contains the death of all his old mothers, it contains his own death; his mouth opens and he howls out the silent scream of the most ancient fear. As he screams, she weeps, she has seen that his prick at her body is wet with the ocean of blood that filled her fathers' veins, it is the knife that killed them, it is made of her own death blood . . . They fly apart, to stare at each other from a distance that is not quite safe.

64

MIKE: Weird little . . . Don't want to . . . Don't know about . . .
MYRA: Rotten son . . . You're not . . . Cut it . . . You don't . . .

They stare through each others' heads, the room grows filled with the two body fleshes, each a mosaic in the basilica of years lived on earth and elsewhere. A universal old insect called now a roach is moving busily across the landscape, its sound crackly and enormous, its feet orchestrated by Morton Feldman. Music of the downstairs Porto Ricans' radio is clear as background, "Guantanamero" for example, memory of saffron rice and squid in ink & garlic and the sound of voices thousands of years old. Myra looks the long distance downward toward her toes. Toe-nails, lookin like they is mother-of-pearl. And the toenails of him near hers, corrugated as bread-knives. Mike looks across the long way to Myra's "face" which as he watches turns pale and ashen and then turns to ashes. A mask of ashes. From within the mask, she watches herself go out, a long corridor through and down and then out. She begins a laugh and spits ashes. "Gee honey I must look sorta like Anna in *Lost Horizon*," she whispers dry as ash to him. "Ah but I loved you for your tiny tit youth and beauty," he croaks back. His face has fallen away to its exquisite thick-and-fine bones. Each then looks down. Her cunt is covered with fine furry ashes. Bone shining through in spots like stars. His prick is gone altogether, fatpad melted, leaving the ivory pelvis, winging like buttresses. "It's been nice," he tries to say, before the fadeout. "Yeah," she sighs, "groovy, baby." "See you next time around," he says, reaching for her hand, but he meets only ashes.

CHAPTER
10

The walls of Ellen's house had long ago been painted white. Now, softened by the years, they were a dark buff shade, and in places where the water seeped through (since there was no one to do repairs, and Ellen did not notice or care really), there were traceries of darker ivory and ochre across ceilings, map-shapes and webbings over most of the walls of all the rooms. The walls were like her skin; it still retained the soft whiteness of youth, because these days, these years, she never spent time in the hot sun, she had long ago given up gardening, she spent most of her summers indoors in the cool shade . . . her skin was softly lined, like the walls.

And on the walls were words. Almost every day, or sometimes at night, Ellen would write messages to her dead husband Tom. Through years through space. Sometimes a quotation from a book she was reading. Sometimes news of a friend they had known together, that many years ago, or a relative of his or of hers. Sometimes a description of a new person she had just met, or an old friend she had met after Tom died:

someone she would like him to know about, through her eyes.

Most usually she would write on the wall-surface with a felt-tipped marking-pen that used brown ink; its tone on the buff walls pleased her and lent another dimension, she felt, an artistic touch, to her messages to Tom. But she also kept and used eleven other kinds of writing implements: a fountain pen with a three-pronged music nib, which she had gotten long ago from some man she had known who was devoted to playing and writing music; a thin-pointed Funk and Wagnalls desk-set pen, given to her father by a friend; a quill pen made from the feather of a local goose, fashioned by Ellen's sister Frey; a plain writing-nib set into a wooden holder which was painted in a swirly multicolored effect like that found in end-plates or on bookcovers made by floating liquid oil paint on the surface of water and picking up the paint colors on paper, after the swirl was turned in the pigments . . . with which pen was used permanent black Quink; a bamboo pen with aquamarine Schaeffer's ink; a sumi brush with ink she made herself from a block of Japanese ink-concentrate, using rain-water which she collected from the spout outside her door; an old Esterbrook fountain-pen filled with bright green Carter's ink; a Crayola crayon, usually purple, though sometimes she selected a mauve or violet one; a blue-ink Bic ball-point pen, the sort that used to sell for 29¢; a #2 graphite-filled yellow pencil with advertising for a local lumber company printed in black block letters on its side; and an Eagle "Charco" super-refined charcoal pencil, with those words printed in white along its dull black-finished length. Her mood would indicate which instrument she would use; and the weather would have an influence; and the time of day or night; and the time of year (the season: in Spring, for instance, she would use deep tones, preferring to keep the logical bright green inks for deep Winter, when they would refresh her as would a walk into Spring, a sudden change, a *grande geste* of the unfamiliar).

By now, the front room of the house, and the kitchen, and two of the upstairs rooms (technically, at first, bedrooms, but now, and for the past twenty years, not classified, not having any particular furnishings indicating a specific purpose for which humans were using them) and the hallway walls along the stairwell, were covered with segments of word paintings for Tom from Ellen. Almost a diary, covering the past ten or twelve years of her real and inner lives.

She had begun this form of, this system of communicating with him at four in the morning in the Spring of her fifty-fifth year. She had awakened from a dream of Tom, and, not finding him with her but feeling his presence as acutely as if he were indeed in the room with her, it occurred to her to reach out to him in this mode. She took up a brown-ink marking pen that was resting in the center of her kitchen table in a ceramic jar that Frey had made and given to her many years earlier. As she stood, in a flannel nightgown of a faded yellow, in the soft yellow light of the kitchen (she didn't remember walking to the kitchen from the room next to it, where she now slept most of the time), she lost all sense of place. It was all yellow yellow yellow, a soft great light, she was almost unconscious, she willed herself out of consciousness. She gave herself over to the feeling of Tom's presence. He was in the room. With her.

She said nothing, did not move, did not need to or want to. But then, with eyes open but not seeing, did move: toward the bare wall before her. Or almost bare. On the wall, near the stove, was a framed print of trees and land not far from this house. She moved with the pen, and began. She wrote "Tom" and then a colon. Then a dash. And then "I can see, I can feel you, you are here, in this room, it is as if you never left. Now I understand. Please, then, have this, read this, know this. And give me some sign of you. I know it is you, my love." And she signed her name. Not in full; just the "E" of it, the way she had signed the notes she had left for him during the time they had been married. Little household notes, that take the partner for granted, not notes of importance, the casual communication of people who assume they will see each other soon, who assume that each will go on forever, that the other person will always be there . . . that kind of "E."

At sixty-seven, Ellen was in fine health. Silver scattered

nobly through her still-partly-auburn-red hair; she had a sturdy, strong, soft body, the flesh indicating her two-hour-long daily walks through the neighboring countryside around Wittgenburg, which walks were a matter of survival of the soul to her and therefore occurred no matter what the weather; in fact, there was a certain delight and pride in continuing to walk out in every element, every extreme. The natural earth was a companion, and she was confident as well that Tom was walking with her. In fact, she was sure that Tom was with her. They seldom talked. She knew that he, too, took delight in her. In the way she was living the life out. She kept herself up for him as much as for herself.

Her bones were not as brittle as they might have been had she been a less active woman or a city woman. The skin of face and hands was firm and fair, barely marked by shadowy dark spots of aging, but covered with a fine web of lines that told of the emotions she had lived through, was living through now. The three vertical lines across the exquisite domed sweep of her forehead were the most deeply etched, moreso than the parentheses at the sides of her mouth: to tell, three times and strongly, of her nature of worrying, about any animal, any living being in pain or in trouble. Her glance was direct (except when she glazed off to allow her perceptions to enter into that which was not visible); her eyes, deep-set now, were acute and brilliant in their focus and their response. She saw all of the things which she wrote about to Tom.

All the satire was gone from her soul. She was serene and she was almost always in a high place. The tiny container of cocaine powder next to her couch (she no longer slept on a bed, but on an old couch, covered with soft dark-red velour, the one that had been in her living-room for years) was part of the days that were good, the clear days as she called them, and days when she wanted to crest the clarity, when she woke ready for the life but sunk beneath sadness or that automatic lack of her own majesty, the mantle slipped sideways and so everything ready to go awry. On such a day it would be a bit of coke, first thing, and cold water to wash in, second, and hot twig-tea to drink no matter what the weather, and then the day would unfurl, would wave out as she desired.

Often, during the day or night she was living through, she would receive what she requested, what she longed for: some sign that Tom was there or near. A brown feather exactly the color of his eyes, floating toward her from the tree she was walking below. Or she would round a curve in a usually familiar path through the woods near the house, and suddenly go blank, suddenly see it all afresh, as if it were all new, a feeling of being lost in the woods as she had never been even as a child, not panicked but utterly strange in the surroundings, and before her seeing on the path the branches shaped like T and D—directly across an otherwise clear part of the path. And then not there when she returned along the same path.

For the way she lived, simply and in her usual ordinary way, there was always enough money, and she trusted there would be: Tom had had a hand in that, and he was part of now as well. Even as his insurance money had enabled her to work on in designing and making fabrics after he died, the way he looked at things told her what to do these days. Some of the bigger milk-producing farms were going public, selling their goods to the City, receiving the huge tank-trucks which carted the stuff away as if it were white oil. She bought some stock in this process. She felt that Tom told her when to make an investment and when not to. It was his concern with nature, and hers, that suggested what to do next. If a project was concerned with the same kinds of growth that nature itself encouraged, she was safe to go with it. Frey moved in this direction, of course, and she leaned, as always, with Frey's ideas and enterprise. Frey knew well about Ellen's deep, steady relationship with Tom these days. She was glad for its substance, as it enriched her twin's life.

For Ellen there were particular memories. There was no memory of her parents or of her schoolmates, no memory of Edward Richthoven or of the Wittgenburg friends of earlier eras. There were the few friends of this era, and some of them had lasted over twenty years, but that was because they, too, were walking on the path that went through the woods to the north of the town, and had kept strength, kept the mantle. None of them was lonely. There was room for everything to happen that was possible, there was no difference between tangible and intangible, and so it was all in motion, all in flow.

11

Edward and Ellen were at his place. Talking about their childhoods. Which were as disparate, in many ways, as if they had been from different areas of Europe, rather than from different areas of the same community. The language of their elders was different, the folkways handed down, the names, the folkways' value; the families of their earliest friends and intimates were from the same ethnic group as their respective parents. This was the first generation in which the Dutch and the German of the region were beginning to blend, the old rancors, jealousies, pecking-orders and enmities beginning to blend into a bland mix called "American." The Dutch had kept the lines proudly taut till now; the German folk, sterner and more militant, observed their own boundaries. It comforted a man to have an enemy up close, someone he could recognize by face and name, someone he could order his children not to mix with or to marry.

But it was changing now. The tough elders of the tribes

were dying off. The younger people were more interested in escapes than in warring, and the land was losing many of them to the cities; those who remained were living less involved with the land and its old rules.

It was late at night, an early Spring night, they had been to the movie and found the town filled with visitors: the Irish who owned summer-houses were beginning to come up on weekends. Edward's telling Ellen his boyhood stories was reassuring. Everyone was upset when the summer people started to arrive, except those merchants and builders and tradesmen who stood directly to profit from the influx: the town lost its quiet and sanctity and seemed to change the quality of its values and basic structures.

Tonight, this Wittgenburg couple were sitting in Edward's house, by the dark-cool fireplace, drinking white wine; Ellen, in a white shirt and pale green pants, as pale as she had been in Winter, while Edward, having been working outside on a construction job, was already tanned against the yellow of his tee-shirt and the faded khaki jeans.

"The wind blew me to bits!" she said, and reached into her purse for her comb.

He said, without considering it, "Comb your hair after dark, comb sorrow into your heart . . ."

"What?" she said, stopping at once and looking over at him. "Where'd you dig that one up from? *That* sure dates back a ways!"

"Oh, it must've been one of my mother's, I'd guess. She used to say that to my sisters. Especially Gretch—so proud always of her long hair, always combing it, and around the kitchen, which my mother really got angry about. So she'd tease her. Not much. Enough to make her stop—" They both were pensive. Ellen felt depressed by the words of the old saw, their reality for her. He was remembering those scenes. "Come on, now," he told her, putting the comb gently through her hair. "You're past sorrow for now. That was a good movie, wasn't it? And it's finally Spring—"

But she could not be pulled back to today. She was back

into that other Spring night, when she had indeed been combing her hair and someone had called with the news that Tom was gone. And she did not want to tell this to Edward.

He wanted to bring her out of it. "Okay, try this one! How about: 'Never set a hen on Sunday, or the eggs'll hatch out all cocks.' I must've heard that one at least once every season till I was twenty, did you?"

She brightened. "I never did. I'd love to check that with Frey, though; she'd know if it was any good, wouldn't she!" She smiled, and he thought she was out of it. But: "I remember," she said, "Mother said that if you slept with your feet toward the door, it was an invitation to death—you know, they built the trundle-bed recesses so that your head was always supposed to be pointed toward the door when you were sleeping—"

"Bad luck, all right," Edward said. "In our house, the beds were always set with the head of the bed toward the doorway." Then he figured he'd get the others out of the way, all the others he could think of, and to hell with 'em, and she would be able to feel better. "There was the one about if a bird flew into your house, it meant death; and the one about an owl hooting outside your house—and all those weird ones you never even notice—you're so used to them—ladders, and spilling salt, dogs howling just at midnight—hey, that one really used to get to me, now that I remember; we had this beautiful red Setter, she liked nothing better than to howl, didn't mean anything when, in fact she used to make things up at night just to let loose, wait till all of us were asleep, and believe me, that lady really had an imagination!"

She looked up at him with a sad look. "Are you making fun of me? Are you saying I'm like her?"

"Oh, Jesus! No, honey!" He could swear she almost had tears going. He had all he could do not to laugh. "Silly! Of course, yes, how could I have missed it, here you are, the reincarnation of our nice old red Setter." He reached over and patted her auburn head. "Come on over, Lass, come and sit by your Edward," and patted the couch.

She slid from under his hand. "Ever hear this one? 'It's bad luck to ask a red-headed woman to a wedding.'"

"Depends on whose," he said, averting.

"Never ask for whom the bell tolls," she said. They were almost comfortable together. Serious, beneath the banter. Ellen would shift it over, now. "What was your mother like?"—although that wasn't so much of a shift as imagined; she was going on instinct now.

"She was—you know, I don't think she was anything unusual—probably different from yours, though. Worked harder. Kept things going—You know something? I wonder if I knew her—I mean, for people who saw each other every day of their lives for all those years, do I know today who she was or how she was as a *person?* We all just took her for granted . . ."

"My mother let us in sometimes, but she—you know, things I can remember about her now, funny things, the way her hair smelled when she tucked me in at night, how she looked, she was always busy with her house—the *pronk-vroom* had to be just so proper, the only time she got angry was when we went in there—never know when someone *important* would come by and that's where they'd have to be entertained—not that she used the place, I can remember maybe three times or four—she was always fussing to have that room just so and ready in case. I guess that was more the custom when my grandfather and great-grandfather had the house; or back in Holland, and she just kept it going . . . Her name was Annetje, did you know? (that's Frey's real name)—and she used to wear this certain perfume—I think it was made from carnations—"

"Perfume! Jesus, my Mom, she wore what looked like the same two dresses all year; two for winter, two for summer; one on her back and one in the wash. I think she made her clothes; I know for sure she made my sisters', all of 'em; that was what she did evenings. Sewing and darning. Didn't your mother have a darning-egg? That round wood thing you put into the sock or sleeve to sew on?"

"She had one. But she didn't *have* to sew, she *liked* to. She sewed mostly embroidery; embroidered all the linens on all our beds, and the collars and shirt-fronts—in fact, that was what began her doing seamstress work after Pa died. She wanted to be busy and it comforted her and she knew how to do that . . . Who lived longer, your mother or your father?"

"They died within a month of each other. We were all grown, mostly, except for Dorris, but Gretch could take care of her, so it wasn't so bad."

"Did you miss them? Did they love each other? Is that why they died so close together?" She wanted to know this: it would tell her more about this man. Ideas of loving.

"I wonder," he said, moving his head slowly. "Not the way we think of it. The way I heard it, she got married to get out of her grandparents' house; she never had parents for long, they died in an accident—funny, her grandparents survived all sorts of things and then her own parents were in a boat accident, the boat was crossing the Hudson and they both went down on it. At that time there was all this talk about witches. Nobody lived who was on that boat. So she was raised by her grandparents and it wasn't good."

Ellen was rapt. "What did they look like? Your parents."

"You never saw them around town? You must've. She was as tall as you, and fair; as tall as Pa. Fair, like Levon and Dorris. Pa was dark like me, and tall, too. She had me when she was in her late thirties, so she was never young to me . . . and Dad was older than she was. She looked like she worked hard. There was never enough money. She always smelled of the soap she made, out of ash-lye from the wood-stove, and lard saved from the cooking. You know, the Depression really got them. She was always taking care. Pa got into the metal-working, switched over from farming just about the time I was born, I think; they kept some animals, the chickens, a cow, and we grew vegetables—got so they were stopping up the wind with newspapers stuffed into the holes in the walls—she helped Pa a lot. She worked as hard as anyone around and looked it, too—looked sixty when she wasn't barely forty."

He looked across at the woman facing him: her white skin, smooth domed forehead, dark and bright red hair, soft freckles faint across her creamy flesh, healthy in the pastel palette of her summery outfit. So far and so different from the woman he was describing. But this was a worker, too—he'd noticed this about her, and it mattered to him, the long hours she put in on weaving and clothes-making, things she did to keep herself alive . . .

"Dorris must look like your Ma used to?"

"Right. But her eyes, they're Pa's. Levon looked the most like Ma, because he was firstborn; two peas in a pod. Those really light blue eyes, strange, the color of the sky over the lake in November; a lot of grey into it. The color that electricity would have if it had a color. And you know, when she was always talking about vibrations and auras and stuff, he was the one listened most to her. She sent away for all those little books from Vedanta and the Ba'hai and Rosicrucians, used to sit around after supper and while we did homework near the fire or at the kitchen table, sometimes after the darning she would be reading aloud from them. I grew up with those stories. It was years before I could understand there was any difference; I thought things that were real were things I could touch, but I thought some of what she told us about was real, and I still do. Like my music; some of it I can't touch, but it's real to me. I *feel* it. I can feel it. Like about my being Capricorn. When I got told about it from her, I read up on it, and it made good sense, fit in with the kind of person I knew I was all along, down to every detail . . .

"Ma used to say she saw things none of us saw, but if we just tried, or what she called *let them come in,* she was sure we could see too, because we were her children. Pa thought this was crazy-talk and said so all the time, so we never knew what to believe. As we got older, it was Gretch (who's the only girl who's got those eyes) who could perceive some of the things Ma saw or knew. Ma said it was because Gretch was *open to it,* so there was enough room for ideas or things, was why. She's a lot like Frey, though, you know that. Keeps off to herself . . ."

He stopped and looked across at Ellen. "I guess they did care, under all the teasing. I mean, they *cared for* each other;

and for us. The way you care for an animal you're in charge of, but something else, too. Pa was lousy about showing his feelings, unless it was tough feelings. One of those men who thought it was sissy to show feelings; probably he was raised that way. But lots of times his feelings had to come out and they did. If anyone was hurt, I mean really, (not the stuff Ma did, all the little things, she made a fuss about any old scratch toward the end of a day if she felt it would get her some attention from him,)—well, he was really very kind."

"That's so German, to keep the feelings down. What a damn shame—but you *did* know they cared about you, and you could *feel* they cared about each other, right?"

"About us, yeah. But not about herself. Thing is, she was very plain—her features were okay for a man, but not on a woman—that's why Levon's so handsome—she was too big and raw-boned to be good-looking except as a healthy animal. She's supposed to look just like her father, and the old photos show she was just like him, that sort of craggy rugged bony face—"

"What do you mean, she's 'supposed to' look just like him?"

"Genetics. Look. She was the first child and a girl, so she looked like her father. If she'd been a boy instead, she'd have looked like the mother."

"What on earth are you talking about?"

"It's easy. You probably come from a father whose features were rather fine, right? He was probably the first-born to them, and looked like his mother . . . so then, you get Frey's looks; she's got to look a whole lot like your Pa. And then you, a few minutes later, the second-born and fraternal and all, and you had to take after your Ma—right?"

"Exactly how it is. But I still don't see how—"

Edward held his arms out and crossed them, right over left; then dropped them down and crossed them again, this time left over right, and then again, right over left and lower. "This way: first child, if it's a boy, looks like the mother. First child, if it's a girl, looks like the father. Second child, reverse it, the way my arms go. So you get, in a natural order, an extension into the world of the looks and basic nature of each parent right away."

"But then, what about the third child? and what about if the first two kids are both the same sex, like Frey and me?"

"I just told you. First kid, girl, looks like Dad; second kid, girl too, looks like Mom. The third child, if it's the same sex as the first two, is a combination of the looks and traits of both the parents. Got it?"

"Yes, I think I see now. Hey, you know, it just works! I *do* look like Mamma, and Frey like Dad . . ."

"It's predictable. In fact, you can often tell when a couple has lost a child, because it's like there's a step missing in a row of stairs, the space where the face of that child would have been, so you can spot it, if you know the technique."

"So that's what you meant when you said your Ma looked like her Pa—what sign was she?"

"Never knew her birthdate; they didn't keep records real good back then, you know. Half the people around here don't know their birthdays exactly. Though most usually it was those who came from big families that got their papers mislaid. But she always said she thought she was born sometime around the end of July, so that makes her a Cancer, cusp of Leo, and it figures."

"From your description of her, though, she's got a lot of Pisces going—maybe a Pisces moon or rising." She smiled at what she heard herself saying.

"Aha! You know your own number that well when you hear it, do you!"

"Oh, sure; it's the worrying, and the mysticism, and the hypochondria. I'm only lucky I've got some Libra to give me a little energy to move around, else I'd be pulling a lot more poormouth than I do already!"

"We're both lucky. That we've got all the possibilities—all these tools to use, to help us get through . . ."

"*Lucky?* Us? Why? Does it say somewhere that our signs are compatible? Not likely, *dear* Cap—"

"Oh, it's luck, I think," he said, sensing the mood she was re-entering. "The signs are part of why I was drawn to you in the first place, and the shaking-down of it all's why I've continued to want to be with you, babe," he said, reaching for her hand.

But she would not lean with him. "You're *not* as good with Pisces as you are with Scorpio—the both of you power signs—you're one of the few who can take their crap, I'd guess!"

"Your sign is insecure but it isn't all *that* jealous, is it? Why bother now to bring Myra up?—when everything's smooth between us." He was gentle with her.

She felt as if he were being patronizing. "Because it *hurts,* goddam it, that's why, Edward. Because I've got lots of Libra and Libra *is* jealous as all hell. Because Libra and Pisces are vulnerable emotionally, you earthbound, heavy-trodding clod! Because Pisces is all about suffering aloud, and it *hurts,* goddam you!

"You just want some kind of reassurance, as if we lived anything like the monogamy our parents did! Hell, I can't give it to you. All I can tell you is that I *am* with you now, and a lot of the time, and I *do* care about you, and like being with you, as you damn well know; because if I didn't, I wouldn't be here with you now!"

"Oh, glory to the gods, *shouldn't* I be grateful for small blessings!"

"No. That jealousy thing is just a drag. What good's it to put a claim on anyone? We've got to be free, not feeling bound, or we can't really be together!"

"What I hear now is *Myra* talking, not you! I feel it. That little bitch hasn't been married, isn't barely off the tit, what does she know about being an adult, or loving, her big goddam nineteen years on earth?"

"I really think that's about enough, Ellie; move off and take a look; Myra may have talked with me about being free, but it only confirmed the direction I was going in anyhow; if I learn something from someone else, I'm not afraid to use it just because somebody else thought of it first. You ought to stop that hurting; it's coming from inside *you,* so only you can stop it. Stop looking for me to do your work for you! Remember that my Ma and maybe yours too, felt trapped in their lives; what *we're* trying to do is to feel good, not trapped —"

"Jesus, what a sanctimonious creep you are! You know damn well it's against nature to do what you're doing. Running two women. It's even against your own nature, your own sign. The most conventional-minded sign, proper-as-you-please. So what the hell!"

She had caught him. He felt it, inside his chest. Yet this was a good part of the reason he had to keep with Myra and the wildness of his life near Myra; how explain this to a woman like Ellen? She was too far, too shut.

"Listen. I know that and more. If you talk about animals and their nature, it depends on which one you're willing to study. There's an awful lot of animals don't behave possessively and a lot don't have just one mate at a time. Some keep a harem and some change off mates at intervals, and that holds true too if you study tribes other than this weird tight one we're both a part of right now. And I don't have any great testimonials to offer for monogamy; I wouldn't live those married years over again for anything."

"Oh, some people have an easy enough time rationalizing away everything they do, anything they want, there's a rule for it. But be sure, though, there's another rule—"

"Some people, dear lady, are like some animals; just being free to love whoever they wish is enough! I haven't noticed specific rules set up for us to follow like Moses' tablets, these days! There's quite an assortment, like you just said, and one to cancel out each one—"

She was furious by now. "Dissembler," she muttered.

"Really? The rule you seem to be talking from, the jealousy stuff, is really tied into a lot of beliefs hung over from the Bible, or maybe from the Puritans and—"

"Or else started in the caves or in the Garden of Eden," she said, bitterly. "Depending, of course, on which *theory* you favor."

"I don't mean to dishonor either one! I just think I have a right to find out my own answers; I've got to be free to find out which way *feels* right to *me* . . ."

And the devil take the hindmost, she thought. "And what about your own true nature? And your Capricorn self?" She was talking from an old magic, from her own womb. She had to turn away from him.

"Look, Ellen, you *don't* have to take it all as some kind of personal insult, don't you see?" He could see her suffering, but he felt he was right; he had to be right.

"Personal insult, is it! All I do know is, I don't have to take it, period." She glared over at him.

"That's up to you. I'd certainly regret it if you let all that old stuff get between us . . ."

"Oh, come *on.* I just wonder how *you'd* be feeling, how you'd act, if you knew I was making it with some other guy in town on alternate nights—"

"If you'd really like to find that out, why don't you—"

"You *know* I can't. I don't even want to. Not that I haven't thought about it. I just don't happen to *feel* like it—is that so bad or abnormal?"

"No, that's not a bad way to be—but you've got to understand that not everybody is where you're at. You have to leave enough room for me to be this way, at least till I find out for sure how I want to live."

"It's a dangerous business, Edward. I don't know how, but it is . . ."

"I hope you don't mean that as some kind of warning. You've known about me, how I am, from the beginning. After all, I was seeing Myra already when I met you, when I—"

"The time you've been with her doesn't make it right, or the time with me, or even the time we live in—it takes a while for me to put things together to say out when something makes me feel uncomfortable—how I feel about all of this, and I don't *like* it!"

"Take it easy, will you, and stop feeling so sorry for yourself! You haven't got it so tough. I'm someone you like and have a good time with and you don't meet so many of them, now do you. Don't *maul* the thing! Why not just leave it alone and see what develops?"

"One of the possibilities we have, as you put it, is the *right* to say out how we feel, and I feel goddam angry and fed up with—"

"Ellie, Ellie, don't do this! You don't *have* to—"

"Don't 'Ellie' me, you bastard!" she said, out of her frustration and fury, and she grabbed up her purse and slammed out the door and was gone. *Nice way to end the evening,* he thought, seeing no reason to chase after her, and no way to change how it was going. There was no choice.

CHAPTER

12

CHOPPED HISTORY: *A Pie. A Dinner.* The Gouverneur gave the man (Dutchman or Englishman) a lease on some land, and the man then leased it for three lives' lengths, which gave the man's son and grandson the option of leasing it or using it, and, finally, selling it off. This was not to the liking of some of the farmers. Mr. Lasher, for example, or Mr. Boice, or Mr. Shultz. But Mr. Rattermann like the arrangement just fine; he was the rent-collector for Capt. Van Bogart, for the DePuys and the Van Rijns, the Geertsemas and the Hasbroucks, and he was making out just fine.

Myra was the daughter of a Shultis family. Variations on the name abounded: Schultz, Schults, and Shutz, &c. Then there was her friend, a daughter of one of her mother's friends: Linda Schumacher, and her other friend, Bonnie Bamburger. Myra's mother liked it better when Myra stayed with her own kind. This is part of why Myra was fucking Mike Mandelbaum. "Well, he's German, isn't he?" And as for

Eddie Richthoven . . . *that* was too good to be true. German as you please.

Names. Everyone hereabouts was interested in names and put great stock in them. And everyone, at least at first, tried to keep the names from mixing. The town of C, not far from Wittgenburg, was Italian, and exclusive about it. The town of A, three miles from C, was Italian too, but P, just the other side of A, was pure German. So what: by now, everything was getting mixed up and mixed-in. The town of H was mostly German-Jewish. F, next door to H, was made up of Jews, but the Jews were subdivided into carefully segregated groups: Polish Jews, Hungarian Jews, German Jews, each with their own cluster of houses and of resort hotels. Then, in F, H, P, A, and C, there were the "red-necks," the farmers of French/Irish/English/Scottish original stock, the ones who came over as laborers, indentured prisoners, escapees, &c. So that by now you'd find a Shultis married to an Aaron Finch. Or a Shaffer married to a Van Gogh, with kids named Travis, Arlie, Levon or Lavon or Laverne, Linda-Bonnie-Susan, and Frieda. And Greta, and Dorotha, and Keith, and Sarah and Martha and John.

It says HAUSNER on the mailbox, and on the sign offering "All Kinds of Archery and Hunting Equipment," at the house of the man with the German name who has one Indian grandmother. In this landscape, with small white houses set, so, along the horizon of hills: breaking the horizon line so that it was a series of dark dashes and curves. Each house softened so that it was blurred by trees, blurred at its margins by the furry profiles of trees. House, long dash or curve of horizon, then house again, smaller dash, longer house. No color visible at this distance.

Theirs was the house just right of center through the windshield. The silo back of the car, visible through the rear-view mirror. "He carries it there; she places it where it will stay." Each of them wanted the house. They were both willing to fight for it—each other, if necessary. She swung her weight and her long legs, the thighs, walking down the road away

85

from it, looking backward at it through her skull: *the* house; *her* house.

She could always find a man; what she wanted was someone to love. She had found a man, and then found that he did not want to be loved. The only time he was affectionate with her was when he wanted something from her. It was all that planned. He thought of it as "priming the pump." She felt he was ugly and he was brutal, because she needed someone affectionate. But then, she was staying with him all this time. You can't have everything; her own mother had taught her that. So now there was a song which said it: "You don't always get what you think you want . . . sometimes you get what you need." It was another version of "I work best under pressure," in their minds.

*   *   *

He meant something to her. More than either of them could define. There was a lust between them, although they had never made love. Of those who come and those who go, there were those whose brief stay makes the act of passing through a memorable occasion. It was in this era that the drink erroneously translated as *Cold Duck* was "invented." It was not possible to move from gingham made of home-grown flax to store-bought satins made into tye-dies without some jarring noise.

1971, Shopping List for the Week Before Thanxgiving

eggs, 1 doz.	2 lg. bags popping corn
a doz oranges	2 Pepperidge Farm Stuffing Mix
1 qt reg milk	2 boxes Ocean Spray Cranberries
sweet potatoes	2 Freihofer Canadian Oat Bread
1 lb. butter	2 lbs. Blue Bonnet Margarine
1 lb wht flour	1 lg. box Campfire Marshmallows
2 lbs onions	1 bag Diamond Shelled Walnuts
2 lbs chestnuts	2 lbs. Rome Beauty Apples
8 artichokes	2 qts Lite & Lively Milk
4 lg. squash	1 1-lb. bottle Tupelo Honey
paper towels	1 Morton's Iodized Salt
paper napkins	

First she would take the sack of bread ends and leavings she had been collecting from the table and plates for the past few weeks, made of her own home-baked bread to begin with of course. then she would send Levon (he was not in school now) out to the hen-house to bring in whichever eggs (there should be at least seven ready today) . . . meantime Walt had brought in this morning's milk, there was enough cream to do into butter with, some left to make the bread and some for the table; she took enough off for the butter and set it into the churn, so it would be ready for Gretch to tend to when she got back from schooling. the comfortable familial churn with black marks charred at bottom where her grandma had poked in with a red-hot iron to keep the witch from Lake Ridge from keeping it from becoming butter. she was not sure it was all nonsense, no sense taking chances, we don't have a name for everything on earth, not by a long shot.

while Gretch and the boys was making the butter and then doing their chores she would begin to pick off the feathers of the turkey Walt killed. a nice fat bird this year and looked good. and scald it for pinfeathers (maybe Arthur would help with that part) and then she and the kids would mix up the stuffing if the sage was dry enough by now, she could send him down to where it was hanging drying, and he could get the onions from the storeroom down cellar, maybe begin the bread early tomorrow . . .

and tomorrow as some of the other families arrived she would get help peeling the sweets and turnips and cutting and then get out the big pot only for Thanksgiving and Christmas, good big pot they had given her and Walt when they was married, made by Walt's father's hand and his uncle and holding up just *fine* after fifteen years. what with the family getting big maybe she would leave that pot down and it could get some use the year round . . . then there would be putting the stuffing into the turkey, though maybe she could get to that before sleep tonight. she sure was feeling like she was further along than the sixth month, though that was what Dr. Schmidt guessed—her grandmother guessed middle of seventh last time she'd seen her; well, whichever it was, she was ready for some of that sleep *right now*.

but in the meantime there was all this to do and begin, she sent Edward down cellar to bring up the onions and turnips and acorn squash and some of the butternut too, maybe, and the chestnuts the Griers had sent over with their littlest boy last week, and some apples, the ones that had black marks or holes, they could be cut up for making sauce, easy enough . . . she and Gretch could probably get the apples done first thing tomorrow before everybody started to get here.

out the kitchen window through the ripply glass she could see at the edge of the far field the forms of three deer come to lick at the rocks down there. the red Setter lay quiet on the porch, also watching them. she would not go for them, Walt taught her to let them be, that was a good thing, the feeling of the man went over into the dog, good that Walt never hunted unless they needed the food . . . what with some of the folks around here shooting just for hides or God knows what-all reasons they dreamed up . . . some was for letting the deer be, a good thing, otherwise soon there'd be no deer at all left. well, what with the pigs, and the garden going good, the chickens and all, they really didn't need more than two deer a winter and they was easy to come by. at the beginning of the season. then the rest of the season could go by without the deer had to feel frightened to come out in the meadow. beautiful critters. maybe when she was born again she would come back that way. one of the books said it was possible. sometimes at night they would come in closer. once in a great while she would come into the kitchen around the hour of deepest nightfall and there would be one or two near the house against the snow, and the dog wouldn't bark and she felt she could go out and talk to them.

the money was a little easier this year but not much. they could do a decent Thanksgiving, though! that was all of it, wasn't it, feeling things were going good, all of them in pretty good shape and things going as the Good Lord wished. and giving thanks as well to all the Spirits there didn't seem to be room for in the Bible, as well. she had a feeling for the

Spirits of all the animals and trees, as well as for the people and the one called God, which she could tell plain as could be wasn't a single lonely God but had all that company. it was a wonder to her that Walt didn't feel them too, the way he knew about animals and the earth and all, all the other big Spirits around. well, but some of the kids was learning and seemed to see . . .

here came Levon in, dirty and cold and wanting some of the soup from the kettle. she ladled it out and some for herself too, with the baby inside it seemed she was always hungry, never seemed to let up, only a few minutes just after she ate. they ate in silence. then she asked him if he'd seen his father, would he be in soon. the boy said it wasn't likely, Grier wants his bits and bridle hardware end of this week. well, that wasn't too bad, he could've said *tonight,* and Grier pays right away, she thought. a tough year just passing. but Walt was talking about building a new house, so things wasn't going all that bad, or at least he must think things was going all right or he wouldn't be thinking about a bigger house for us all. ah but they sure could use some more room, this house getting smaller everyday, smaller every baby and harder to keep up . . .

❋ ❋ ❋

CONGRESSMAN O'NEILL: "We discovered that since the time of Christ, the male of our species has worn long hair and beards about 90% of the time. The Western world turned to short hair and clean-shaven faces only after the Prussian victory over France. All the great heroes of America have worn long hair. It's nothing for Americans to get alarmed about."
And,
from TIME Magazine also, this time an *Essay:* "To be sure, the children of blue-collar workers increasingly diverge from their parents over hair, dress and the use of pot, which is spreading in hardhat high schools. But politics is another matter: blue-collar children seem to be just as 'conservative' as their parents."
And,

from the *Letters to the Editor* section, another issue, in a letter titled "Recent History": "In my contact with marijuana users, I have yet to meet one who beat his wife or children while under the influence. (signed) Denny W. Walters, M.D."

❈ ❈ ❈

The woman was at the bottom of the hill, alone. By choice and by ultimate desire. It was Spring: the sound of dripping sweet water, run-off water, was the pervasive music, alongside the birds' song. Past the curve, and there it was: the new road. Moving along up the hill; a fresh mark against the aged land, this road just cut through the forest and scrub to what would be their, her, new house. They would move into it from the small old farmhouse they now lived in, that she had come to as a bride, that she had borne her six children in . . . Ahhhh. More room. More rooms. And it would have a bigger fireplace, and this time one in the kitchen, too.

All this grew even as she watched; the house rose before her against the background of patchy snow, against dark revealed earth and rock-juttings and outcroppings. An early thaw, thank the gods; good for beginning to build. The mud, rich, dark, turning umber in the spots where the iron of it surfaced and weathered—all sopping wet, all runny and thick and fertile under her leather boots, with rivulets of water making veins through the slope. She could not see the site for the house from this spot, from the bottom of the hill. But it was not all that far. When the house rose, the roof of it could be seen, just barely seen through the trees, from the road below.

Her house, their house. It would be the house she wanted for these years now. Since before the last two babies, the girl babies, came. It was the house that Walt wanted to build, with his sons helping. With his workshop and its sheds near it. A house big enough for everything!

As she moved a bit up the hill, up the new road, slipping and sliding in the thick runny mud, she was filled with a joy. She could smell the fresh-cut, wet lumber as she found the spot where her husband and sons had laid out the planks so the wagon could get on up the slope through the mud, and there was the big oak that Walt had used to fasten the "come-along" to ratchet the wagon out of the deep ruts last week . . . and here, finally: the site where the house would be. Was already begun! Stones and wood taking a form. Where they would all continue to grow, like the trees. Like the animals. Where the children would all grow up, where one son might stay and take over and the others would leave from. And where, she knew, she and her husband would die, in a natural order.

CHAPTER
13

Myra was never afraid: the Scorpio. Ellen was almost always
fearful: the Pisces. Edward, Capricorn, was conservative; the
kinds of fear he experienced were related to the breaking of
structures and patterns. Edward was concerned with the
search for order, for ritual, for the existence of a superior system and/or Being. He built a mountain, climbed it, surveyed
the world (part of which he had made), felt glory, then sank
into despair, having discovered disillusionment with a world
that was less than perfect; then, up from the trough, and began building the next mountain he would climb.

Myra could give out so much more dynamic (often nega-
tive-based) energy than any other sign around her, and so
was not concerned about being bettered. Everything was
yin-yang, life-death, black-white. She was able to make loss
and gain occur, and the world contained qualities of both,
seemingly at her own will for each. She was cyclical. She was
cynical and realistic.

Ellen, impassioned and fearful, was threatening to Edward.

She was the illogical extension of his own defined fears. Her fears were not definite: they were based on sensings, on feelings, they were wavery, seen through water. The only clear fear was that she knew she felt inferior to other, more energetic signs. But by now she had somewhat shaped the fear, getting it to work for her by providing for herself the kinds of life in which she would best survive: protected. She recognized her own fearful nature; even as her twin, Frey, had retreated from contact with most humans, Ellen had formed herself passively around the humans with whom she was in contact, depending upon them for the outgoing actions, and she moved with their motion, not in an independent fashion.

Now as to Mike: the Virgo, obsessed with details, concerned with unattainable perfection on an intellectual level, alive mostly in the skull, he was the perfect example of the self-defeating mechanism, built to work beautifully and to come apart in the act, like a Tinguely sculpture. He was not usually consciously fearful. (But watch that Cancer rising.)

Myra was good for Mike; she brought him out of himself, forced him up against her barriers, into views of the world other than his own; she was stimulating to him. His nervous lethargy became channeled around her desires. Myra was good, too, for Edward, not just the youth of her, but the aggressivity, the will, forward motion of the energy; even the negative energy was constructive for Edward these days. He was the Capricorn who would tend to become stuck in a rut; she was a creature of patterns but was aware of herself so keenly that she could will herself out of any attachment as she became apprised of it as a threat. She needed only to be free. She would remain free. She would be free in the midst of obsessive pattern.

Edward and Ellen were each dependent on other people to an extent. On what the other person thinks of oneself and one's actions; on the opposite person's initiation of ideas and action: Edward as leader, Ellen as natural follower. On the great roll and swell of the motion of groups and crowds and popular circles: Edward could, when or if he so chose, rule or dominate or dictate; Ellen could lean with any such leader, not just with flattery but by imitating the motion in process.

Edward and Myra would each as soon be alone, in an opinion, an activity; each was basically a loner, not dependent on anyone or on any group. Myra was a self-starter, defiant and at the same time powerful and conservative (in conflict): always testing from one extreme to the other, often settling for a pattern caught tautly between the extremes. Edward would try a new idea if he originated it; and if it were just that: an idea, rather than an involvement. He was intensely drawn to and set against involvement.

Edward, Ellen and Myra were available to astrology when each first heard about its possibilities. Mike was not and is not. (Edward is really ambivalent; he is open to it, having been exposed to it by his mother, but slow and ponderous in his dealings with the intangibles). For Mike, the pragmatist in minutiae, things *have* to be tangible, provable, realistic; he is a very nervous man, who loves to test and to argue. With Cancer rising, and Moon in Capricorn, he is stubborn, he is only mildly receptive to the mystical or abstract, unless he can view them in terms of idealistic and perhaps attainable concepts. He isn't sensual; he and Myra are well-matched in this respect; they are all about fucking and not at all about love-making. Of the people we are describing, Pisces is the only sign given to truly sensual behavior.

Myra is practical; she wants what is hers and knows what is hers, and is out to get it. Edward is practical, sometimes, mostly about possessions and occupations. The reality of his own world is a concern about possessions. He has a minimal potential to be sybaritic, but his fear of loss of control stops him; he admires adventurousness in himself (on rare occasions) and always in others. In this, he is much like Mike: both have admiration for Myra's recklessness. But Edward feels more comfortable with Ellen (her traditionalism, her easy, fluid motions through life) than with Myra. Myra enjoys both men, as we have seen, and knows exactly why. Mike enjoys Myra and knows why: her oppositeness to him, her freedom; her similarity to him (love of patterns). Ellen enjoys and loves Edward and is jealous of his relationship with

Myra, as we have already discovered. She knows who and what Myra is in the life, and by now does not like anything about her. (She is not a person of strong opinions and can be swayed, but she is capable of unreasonable prejudices and emotional overcharging.) Ellen does not know Mike to speak to, but she has seen him around town, and knows who he is.

Edward does not know anything about Mike except that Mike is a German Jew, which Edward feels very separate from; Edward is not anti-Semitic; he sees Mike as sort of odd-looking, fat and fair and awkward, young and pleasant, and an odd corespondent to his affair with Myra. Mike knows everything he can about Edward, all the details he can find out from anyone and everyone around town, and can see why Myra spends herself with Edward; finds it all reasonable (though of course it is threatening to him).

Myra does not give a shit who is with whom and why. She does not wish to consider, she does not stop to think; she is too busy moving. And Anne/Frey sees all of them, and knows about all of them, on some level, what each of them is doing and why. All of them/us.

* * *

Myra was asking Edward to feed her something. It was Easter vacation week for her, and she was staying most of the time at Ed's house, in defiance of her parents, who did not know where she was, but assumed (hoped) it was with Heather. Edward was not altogether happy about the arrangement, but she was, as usual, persistent and insistent. How could she be expected to go "home," she asked him, if her parents were such down-head squares? This was humorous to him because he thought them to be not a lot different from him, not a lot older than he, and of another Germanic tribe; Catholic, it was true, and that a huge basic difference, all right, but not as far away from his own tribe as were the Mandelbaums, for instance. They wouldn't let her be out after half past twelve . . . that was a major difference. He didn't like to see her suffer. So he let her stay.

There was nothing in the house to eat; they had done in

the last can of lasagna and the last bottles of Coke at four in the morning, leaving nothing but milk for their coffee when they would awake, whenever that might be. Now it was almost one in the afternoon. They drove into town. The likely place to go, in fact the "only" place to go, at this time of day, was "Tommy's Luncheonette," hangout and local bistro: greasy spoon ordinaire: *TOMMY'S* was outlined outside in red neon, with the rest in blue, and Tommy of course presided, with his fat wife. He himself being thin, a testimonial to his cooking.

Edward and Myra had turned on before coming into town (there was *always* enough of that), and by the time they got ready to order they were really giddy. "God," said Myra, close to Edward's ear, "I'm really wrecked, I don't know what the fuck to order, gimme a hand, order the whole place for me, I'm starved, willya?"

"Jesus, I don't know what you want, what in hell do you want, can't you give me a clue, silly bitch?" They both were giggling and felt helpless. "Jesus, I really could eat everything in sight; even you, babe," she said, slyly, watching his expression, knowing this was treading on his Cap conservativism but might tempt him into a trial run. No takers; he never batted an eye. "Well then, I could eat three fried eggs, up, and some sausage and wheat toast and a large milk, and I gotta have some of that nice plastic lemon meringue pie they have . . . Look . . ."

"You really sure you can do all that, babe? Oh, I forgot, you're still a growing girl . . . Okay."

"Yes. Yeah. Lay it out in front of me, and just watch it disappear, Mister. Just *try* me! I'm on vacation, remember! I got lots to do and lotsa energy!"

They were happy. For this moment. He ordered for her, two eggs and sausages and toast, then seconded the order, for himself. She whined because he hadn't ordered three eggs for her, but she was too stoned to bear a grudge for long. The food arrived and they both tore into it. She ate so fast that he watched egg-drippings smear the side of her mouth and drip down onto her lap (his fastidious little raccoon, eating like *that!*) Ah, but they were feeling good about the world today.

And then Ellen walked in. Into Tommy's Place, where she rarely came. Edward spotted her. Myra, turned toward him on the counter-stool, faced away from the door. If Myra saw Ellen, there might be a scene; she was so uncool right now, he thought. Probably some sort of brash remark and Ellen would be hurt. Ellen saw him in the first instant, then saw that Myra was with him. She paled. He couldn't imagine how he'd avoided this moment before now, in this small town. He would have to count on Ellen: she was a Lady, she could be responsible, she could somehow do something with this impending disaster, he hoped. He watched out of the corner of his eye as Ellen turned quickly toward the cigaret-and-candy counter. Stood thus, with her back to Edward and Myra.

It was her lunch break; she had eaten at home and had run out of cigarets; this was not a place she usually came to, and she had not expected to see anyone she knew. Usually Edward had been so careful; she knew this. Ah, but this is why he hadn't been over to her house for longer than usual, for three days now—her gut was cold, she felt the pain. She ran into anger and jealousy and a fine thin edge of fury. She could do nothing with it all. Ah, she thought, it was Easter vacation for the kids, that was it.

The door opened again, and a crowd of out-of-towners came in, noisy, wearing their version of country clothing: gaudy slacks-suits on the women, with high-piled hairdo's and wigs; short nylon windbreakers or collarless corduroy jackets and tight-fitting ass-hugging bell-bottoms of sleazy fabric on the men, and all of them with bright kerchiefs and large gold-colored link jewelry. The men stood at the cigaret counter, effectively placed between Ellen and Edward/Myra, while some of the women stood behind the diners, waiting for empty seats and talking busily.

Two of the City women found seats next to Myra and Edward. Myra leaned over to Edward and made a series of sarcastic nasal noises, which Edward hoped the City women couldn't hear, much as they were exact tonalities of their talk. Everyone was looking at everyone else in some way: the townies viewing the tourists, the tourists studying the natives.

Except that Ellen and Myra were separated by the new crowd, fortunately; Ellen was placing herself so as to avoid any confrontation.

Then, in the sudden lull that falls occasionally (as if planned) in noisy crowds, the guttural dark male voice came through: "*Kaput!*" and a chuckle, and then, again, more darkly, "*Kaput!*" it crowed. The strangers turned and stared in unison. The people of Wittgenburg did not turn. They were used to him, the town "madman," an old Shultis, looking perfectly ordinary and harmless now that he had finished delivering his message of doom and death. It was an everyday occurrence in the town: this Shultis helped out at the Luncheonette, picking up ashtrays and emptying them, sweeping, laying out newspapers when they came in, sometimes getting behind the counter and helping to clear away used plates, sometimes washing them. And always, as a necessary concomitant to his presence, a punctuation to his activities, a comment on the times we live in, the cry of "*Kaput!*" came, every ten or fifteen minutes, no matter where he was. A lot of the town kids called him that for a name. Some teased and some helped him.

Neither Edward nor Ellen turned to see Old Kaput. Myra turned, but it was to watch the reaction of the tourists to the old man, to old crazy Kaput. It was an unpredictable situation: the townsfolk felt somehow protective toward the old man in the face of the strangers' possible mockery. But there were so many people in the place, for a blessed change, that Myra did not see Ellen. She turned back to her almost-emptied plate and to Edward. She was very single-minded and ritually into her food.

Lucky, he thought, just plain lucky, this time. He'd been arranging his whereabouts with care; and the two women were that different in their activities and their tastes that there was little coincidence possible. Not likely. Yet it was a *small* town, and it was pushing his luck to suppose it to go on as it had for these many months. Once, Ellen had told him she'd run into Myra at some meeting or other, before Myra realized he'd been seeing Ellen (she had been mostly at school, he was seeing Myra only twice a week or so, and that left plenty of time to get acquainted with Ellen), but Myra hadn't known who Ellen was. At that time, Ellen had, as now, chosen not to identify herself to the other woman—the younger woman—how you say. Perhaps discretion, perhaps a lack of desire for competitive combat, known in some circles as cowardice, in others as pacifism; perhaps a desire to preserve the secret nature of her relationship to Edward, then so new; afterward, she thought of all the reasons she had not talked to the girl, and settled on all or none of them.

Since then, Edward had counted on his luck and on Ellen's will not to confront Myra. And sure enough, it was working out that way again. The crowd of *auslanders* was leaving, he saw, and Ellen simply left with them. The local people remained. Kaput began to clear away their eggy dishes, the whole counterful. Tommy's fat wife Mary fixed a new Silex of coffee. Edward could hear the cars revving up to leave. There they went, their bodies hurtling from place to place, whoooosh, their lives not touching his, their lives hardly touching each other. Where would they wind up resting themselves this night, he wondered, how did they get to be like that, so different from us, from me, what do they see when they see Trois, do they have someone like Kaput where they live . . .

Tommy's fat Mary leaned over toward him. Did he want to put something down on a number today. No, he told her, no, as usual. She was talking then about her son Tommy, Jr., who was training to become a mortician. Good, solid money in it, support a family nice on it, folks give you a bit of respect too . . . Tommy himself, she told Edward, had wanted to be a mortician, but then this place had come open, a good chance and not all that training needed and her pregnant at the time, so he took it, and doing okay too of course; but now he would see to it his son had the chance; but his son didn't want the luncheonette, he'd wanted to be a vet at first, but mortician was close enough, and Lord knows the town and whole area needed one . . . (None of us wears what we choose; we wear what is chosen for us . . . one way or another . . .)

The radio above the counter was talking, too. "W-A-B-Y Albany, folks," the announcer intoned, and then, "Modern

Adults Turn On, With W-A-B-Y!" he said, And "*Yeah,* baby! Do it! Tell 'em how it's done!" chortled Myra, full of food and good will, happy and grooving along. She smiled up into Edward's face.

He reached over and tenderly wiped the eggcrust from the corner of her mouth. He remembered a story she had told him, about her notorious childhood, she was such an angry girl, always looking for more than the life held, it was all so dull to her, none of what was going on around her made any sense to her, she hoped and kept looking for something magic, some Terrible Excitement that would make all the dullness worthwhile, would cancel it out. So that when she was not yet twelve, she got hold of her brothers' motorcycle, and one Sunday, instead of going to church with all of them, she pleaded illness so she could stay at home; and then she started the machine, quite capably, and rode madly down the main street and past the church—three times, during the service, until one of her brothers picked up the tone of that motor, caught on, hollered across to their father, whereupon not just her family but the whole bloody congregation leapt out to watch Myra the Terror do her bit. Nobody could stop her. (Of course not! Edward thought, fondly; not *this* girl!) And after that it was always "We'd best keep an eye on that child," they couldn't punish her, she moved too fast for them!

The door to Tommy's place opened again. Two construction-workers in green shirt and slacks came in; sat a few stools down from Edward and Myra, and ordered coffee and hamburgers, french fries and pie. ("Hey hey! that one's got a Utica smile!" said Myra to Edward. "He *what?*" grinned Edward, staring past her, not really understanding at once, but feeling her silly insight). Edward then had to order wedges of the plastic lemon-meringue pie for themselves; then he cancelled his, just one for Myra, coffee for both.

And became aware that the construction workers were jiving with fat Mary. She, gap-toothed, thick-accented, was used to seeing the working-men in her place. But these: they were teasing her, they were offering her a cigaret, telling her, "Go ahead, try one, it's good for you, won't harm you a bit, honey!"

The implication was that it was a joint, when it was really just a Benson and Hedges 100 . . . Edward nudged Myra to look, to watch the persiflage.

Mary was aghast. "No, no, thanks, boys, I . . . shoo! what you boys think I am, anyhow, bringing that stuff 'round!"

"No, no, really, ma'am, not only won't hurt you none but *good* fer ya, heals yr cuts and bruises, little while you'll be feelin' *soooo* fine . . . *we* smoke 'em all the time! Better for ya than all that nicotine rots your bones, and ain't hurt yr lungs none."

"Oh, you just get that dang dope out of here, don't bring it near *me*," she said, not knowing whether to believe them or not, not daring to look too closely. Skewered on fear, averting, pulling away from the proffered cigaret they were holding out. (And from a B&H box, yet! Myra and Edward couldn't contain themselves; what a riff!)

Mary ambled off, mumbling to the world at large about what this world was coming to, people walking around in plain daylight with dangerous stuff like that. Myra, stoned and feeling blessed with it, leaned over to the two men and said, "Yeah, you guys know where it's really at, don't you! You do dig the grass, in more ways than one, huh!"

" '*Course!* we-all got into it a long time back; probably knew about it before you, little Sis! Do some damn fine work on it too. Can't put weight on like with beer! Can't beat that! And just put a stick in yr shirt pocket . . ." He reached in, pulled one out, and offered it to Myra. "It's *good* shit; take it, folks!"

"Thanks, boys, *if* you're not fuzz!" Myra said, taking the joint and handing it to Edward. "Whereabouts you guys working?"

"Up to the dam, back of the Reservoir, know where I mean?"

"Oh sure, we passed there out riding a few days ago!"

"Well, folks," the taller, chunkier one said, "We gotta be getting back now. Nice meeting you. Stay happy," and he winked.

"Jesus, would you believe this?" Myra said, to Edward. "Right on, guys, right *with* it!" And as they went out the door, the tall one turned and called back, "Have a ball!" Oh, *yes,* Myra thought, that's what it's all about, isn't it; and Edward was trying it on, looking after them and then looking at Myra; is that what it's all about, having a ball . . . and then they both looked at fat Mary, back of the counter, hunched into her forty years of cooking, of being *serious* about life, into her fears of legal/illegal, of right/wrong, into her memories of Prohibition, into her rosary, into her next twenty years of life . . . "have a ball." Have a *ball!* Because, when all is done, thought Edward, the bell does toll . . . and for all I know, there's only this once to do anything I want to do, to swing out, *take* the big chances, keep with my conscience, at the moment be *in* the moment, and not lose one precious second of it . . . Have fun!

CHAPTER

14

In this chapter, Myra and Heather discuss sex. They are sitting in Tommy's Place, a/k/a The Busy Bee Luncheonette in some towns. They face each other across a booth. The booth is, variously, a table of red formica edged with stainless steel-type border and booth-seats of blue shiny plastic (marbleized); or a dark wooden table with initials carved in it toward the end where the sugar and salt rest, and paneled wooden booths with plain hard wood seats. It is about four in the afternoon in early Spring, this year.

MYRA: What was he *like?*

HEATHER: You'd never *believe* it. I mean, you'll never believe what I'm about to lay on you! We never made it at all. Steve and I never even *made* it.

M: You're *kidding.*

H: No; we just lay there like that, very stoned out and all, rapping a lot, for what turned out to be all night, and finally both of us just fell asleep! Just fell the hell *out*. End. Finis.

M: Jesus, what's his *story*, for God's sake? Did he turn you off, or what?

H: Oh, he ran me some idealistic shit about he wants to be sure before he gives his precious body to somebody; I mean he wants to be sure it's love! Would you *believe*? *Love*, you dig! He won't just screw, he won't ball, he's actually like lying next to a marvelous body like mine, a chick he's actually managed to get into the same sack with him, in a room *alone*, and what does he put out but this rap about *love*. Oh God. Was he ever *holy* . . .

M: What was he built like? I was thinking, I mean, like, maybe he's got an inferiority complex or shy or something.

H: How the hell am I supposed to know? Didn't I just tell you we didn't even ball?

M: Well, I just figured maybe you felt it leaning up against your leg, or necking or something. That's not *such* an unreasonable possibility, remember. Hey, you remember that joke—?

H: You mean the Mae West one, she says to the guy, Are you just very glad to see me, or is that a gun in your pocket—Oh Jesus. No. Not at any time was there B.C.

M: It knocks me out every time I hear you use that expression.

H: Well, if I *don't* use it, it'll hurt; it'll just seethe around in there, I'd rather use it, if it's appropriate at any rate, as in this case . . .

(They both fall silent, thinking about last summer. When Heather was in some posh mental hospital for two months. Myra visited her there and Heather told her that no one was allowed to touch anyone else: "No B.C." was the expression, no body-contact, not between staff and patients, not between the patients themselves. When what the patients needed was often nothing more, most of them, than an exchange of affection, of warmth, of some sort of demonstration that someone cared—some of that stuff they'd never gotten enough of—the real stuff, not the cop-out, Heather told Myra, not the stuff Sally handed out like food but it was really fake, like white plastic bread. Heather's father had gotten her mother to consent to committing Heather when he'd found what Heather called her "medicine bag" or else her "ditty-kit," that grand assortment of ups, downs, and assorted goodies she used to survive without B.C. at home in her world, including works for doing speed. Myra had hastily ditched her stuff, for the moment, and sure enough the Mandelbaums had called the Shultises and they had ransacked her room, to no avail. Myra had known she could survive trying to scuffle up more stuff for her supplies, more easily than going a week in a place like that, whether Heather was there or not. With the young drug-users, like Heather, the first move was to deny them any kind of medication whatsoever; other types of patient could receive tranks, ups, sleeping pills and mood-elevators, in any combination, seemingly both random and illogical. The second deprivation was to deny them, and the others, all affection: NO B.C., *no* touch-groups, *no* movement-therapy; nothing to replace the removal of drugs or supplant the reason for their original use . . .)

M: God, I hate thinking back to you in that place. *God.* Remember Dr. Denton, Old Tight-ass? God.

H: *You* hate it. Think how *I* feel. Well, nobody can say I didn't *learn* something from being there . . .

M: Yeah. How to avoid getting there again. How to be more goddam *careful* where you keep your *stuff*, you boob . . .

H: Okay, okay. Change the subject, willya?

M: With great pleasure. Would you like to know what Orval was like?

H: Would I ever. But then I don't know if I could stand it, the shape I'm in. I'm still so horny I could die . . . What a rotten trick. Stupid nut. He knew I was hot for him, of course. You should have heard the line of bullshit that went down . . . Okay, about Orval, I tell you what. If it was marvelous, then don't tell me. If it was lousy, or weird, you can tell me.

M: Weird. Yes. The exact word. Weee-ird.

H: How? How? He comes on like all the other dudes. What kind of interesting perversion hath he?

M: Unfortunately, none. First of all, he's *not* like any other dude we ever knew or made it with. I guarantee you. He has what may well be the most beautiful big well-done dong you could imagine.

H: Jesus, I *told* you not to give me any good news!

M: No good news. None. All that good dong, and he doesn't know the first thing to do with it. I mean, felt his way around with it like it was in a ground-fog, or something. Maybe it was his first time—

H: So what do you mean, "weird"?

M: Well. Let's see. Talking to him, like we did when we first met him at school and all, you'd think he was very together and in fact one good swinger, right? But then when it comes to the nitty-grit and you hit the sack together, *forget* it. He's very straight. Or not even straight; just sort of lost. And with all that special deluxe equipment. What a bring-down. And those weird *shoes* of his he always wears. They reeeeely shook me up. You know, they look funnier empty, if you can believe it, than full, you dig?

H: (after they both stop laughing) So, what happened? Friends?

M: Worse. It was worse than you can imagine. He came and I didn't and he didn't know the difference. All on his own trip. "I hope you had a good time with me," he says, right after he shrivels to what would be a normal man's erection size, and pulls out. And I'm lying there not believing any of it, stoned to the gills and ready for heaven. Just beginning to move with it. Hung the hell *up*. It's a good thing I was stoned, or I'd have punched him in the goddam mouth. I don't know.

H: How can a man reach the age of twenty and not know *any-thing*, like that?

M: Well, one theory is—he wasn't exactly the class valedictorian, you may remember . . .

H: Being smart about sex isn't about his being stupid or smart in school, for God's sake!

M: Well, part of it is. I mean, isn't it pretty reasonable to think about how the other person feels, not after but during? It strikes me it's pretty easy *if* one doesn't happen to be either totally ignorant or totally self-centered—at least get out of his own thing long enough to know how to get her to come or at least be *aware* if she did or not . . . Jesus . . .

H: It's not all that simple to most guys. Don't forget, they were just like us, they began to fuck like it was a terrible guilty secret, big hurry up thing, and nobody usually takes the trouble to say Go Slow or turn them on to how to turn a woman on . . .

M: Well shit, what's the matter with learning by doing? You've got more compassion than I do, especially right now. The night I just spent! What the hell makes them think we're there just for them to get off on?

H: I don't know, I have this feeling that a guy is just as worried how you feel as how he feels. I bet Orval felt like a complete idiot. You probably didn't make any secret of how you felt. And then think how he felt. They're supposed to be all worried about "performance" and whether we talk about them like this after.

M: Worried . . . I don't think so. I don't know. Maybe it's about instinct. Maybe a person either does or doesn't learn about bodies and how to fuck and another person just doesn't get into balling at all.

H: Personally I think it has to do with what sign a person is. What sign is Orval? He's Capricorn, isn't he? But that's the same as Edward, isn't it?—and *he's* not like that. Or is he? Tell the truth. You never talk about Eddie in bed.

M: I don't really want to. Well. Anyhow. He isn't like *that*. If he were, the first time would've been the last time, as they say. For sure, Capricorn *isn't* all about fucking . . . Maybe Eddie was like that a long time ago. Besides, they didn't smoke pot then, or at least he didn't. One thing, Eddie isn't any great

experimenter. You know Caps: conventional as hell. Everything just plain Missionary Style. Good thing he's been around,
and he turns on, so it's not all as straight as it could be—
besides, it gives me lotsa room to teach him all these interesting things—

H: *Now* you're talking, Scorpio! The fuckiest sign.

M: Yeah. Yeah YEAH yeah.

H: So that's how come you've got Eddie to ball with, and my
brother to ball with, and you *still* make all the scenes you
want to . . .

M: Correction; *not* all the scenes I want, not by a long shot—
meaning, Orval, so that's a pun, baby. If only he'd been good,
then it would've been the scene I wanted to make!

H: That's what I don't understand about you. Why ball with
Orval, when you've got it going with Ed, and you've got it
made with Mike, and you know already where it's at with
them?

M: That's it exactly. I know already where they're at. Jesus,
Heather-old-horse, there are so many kinds of men, why not
find out all there is to know, why hang in with one or two,
who knows what's right around the next corner of the bed?

H: I don't know, I just think it would be good to get with one
dude and if it's good, stay with him. Maybe not exclusively, I
mean I'm not against making it if the other person's busy or
something—

M: Well, my way, you get to find out how many kinds of good
there are! Why settle, as they say.

H: All I know is, you didn't get it off with Orval, and I never
got it together at all with Steve, so we're both sitting here
with some kind of weird equivalent of blue balls . . .

M: I know, I know. It's enough to drive me back into playing
with myself. Wanna make it, Heather?

H: What the hell for, Sister, when you've got Eddie and Mike
and half the human race on tap . . .

M: Don't be bitchy. It was pretty good when we made it.

H: But I don't know what you say about me after.

M: Don't be ridiculous.

H: I'm not. Besides, I'm off women for now. And all you have to do is pick up the phone for Eddie—

M: *Not* bloody well true! That's what *you* think. He's with that old lady Ellen half the time now. The half the time that *I* want him, as a matter of fact . . .

H: Now who's being bitchy? Damn dog-in-the-manger! *You* can be with Mike half the time, but if Eddie wants to go to *her*—if *you* can make it with anyone who walks on by, how come you get miffed if Edward has someone else?

M: He isn't like me. He just makes it with her.

H: *And* you. It *bothers* you . . . him with her.

M: Damn fucking-A *right* it does!

H: That's what I mean! You don't want him to play by your own rules. You Scorpios! Got to own everything you touch but ain't nobody can own *you!*

M: Something like that.

H: Afraid he'll quit you for her?

M: Not likely. Not a chance. Other way 'round, maybe, which would be just as bad.

H: How come?

M: Scorp's good for Cap; Pisces is too weak. But he doesn't *know* that I don't want him full-time, and if he tried to set it up that way I'd disappear. You know that. You know that's not what I'm about.

H: So how come you don't tell him, straight out?

M: Because I like watching the mystery unravel! Who knows how it'll go, really! I *think* I know . . .

H: Pretty tricky, all them theories . . .

M: You'll see. He'll lose patience with her. Pisces people are such a drag. So sloppy about everything. Caps are all about efficiency, remember.

H: So you got it set up so that—so it won't last all that long with him anyway; why not let him go now?

M: What? to *her*? Not a chance. I dig him, and *that's* the point: as long as I continue to dig him, I want him around and I want him to dig me! As long as I want him around. And not a minute longer.

H: Pretty uneven . . .

M: Shape up. What's "even"? It's even because it works! When it doesn't work any more, it'll get uneven and split. All by itself!

❀ ❀ ❀

Another dialogue. Also at the Luncheonette (which is the local Bus Stop, sells tickets and all). It's full of kitsch souvenirs of the Irish in the area and of the local Hudson Valley and Catskill Mt. attractions. From the darkwood booth drifts the smell of pot. A waterfall is visible through the coarse old screen door. It makes the outdoors look like a tapestry. The sun through the screen falls on the cheeks of the two girls. Afternoon gold.

M: I was here to meet Mike when he got back, and this really *fantastic* weird thing happened to me, did I tell you? Last week.

H: Well, are you going to tell me, or just keep giving me tantalizing fucking-well clues? It's a man?

M: I was standing outside a while and then I thought I'd get some coffee. And look at the people waiting for the bus. This time of year, you know, all the types, City people . . . I was feeling *very* good. I felt good behind what I was wearing—

H: What'd you have on?

M: That long yellow velvet skirt, you know, and the big hat Mike gave me, and the embroidered shirt, and boots, the brown ones. No makeup. Just the eyes.

H: Okay. Groovy.

M: So there was this guy, older man, older than Eddie, I mean very grey at the edges of his hair, that really sexy way, you know, very attractive; maybe not to you but he was to me. Sort of tweedy and quiet. I was just wondering what he was built like under all those threads and noticing he wasn't wearing a ring, when he gives me this *look*, you know, this little kind of considering frown, really a *deep* look—

H: Okay. Okay. Was he from around here? Anyone we know, had you seen him around?

M: Never saw him before. Virgin territory. Must've been visiting somebody, or up on business. Probably waiting to catch the bus Mike was coming from Albany on, it went on down to the City.

H: Right.

M: So he gets on line with me, I mean just in back of me, when I go for coffee, and I can feel him looking at me, you know? Well, so then he sits at one of the booths, I'm at the counter talking sort of to Mary and Tommy and all—he was in that booth there—and I was sitting up there, see? And giving me those looks, you know, sort of sexy, sneaky but direct, from under those eyebrows, and I have it all figured out, he's thinking how I'm so great-looking and he'd love to ball me but he's got this dull-headed tweedy wife, which is why he doesn't wear a ring, he doesn't like her, and how's he going to find a way to talk to me and connect . . . He's got this briefcase and I figure he's one of these professor types or maybe a business man up from the City, bigshot, type that really goes for fantasy trips with young chicks but you know, really sort of shy and all . . . he could—

H: Jesus, Myra, I can't *stand* it; what happened?

M: So, no action and no action and no action, just all these looks, you know, and then I figure, enough is enough, I drank the coffee so slow that's it's ice-cold and I look at the clock and Mike's bus is almost due, if anything's going to happen it's going to be me who makes it happen, you know, so I get up to leave to go outside and I figure to pass him up real close so he can make his move, the poor sweet shy type, and Jesus, he looks up at me, stands up, leans into my face and says right out, clear as a bell, "You goddam fucking *nut*. You freak. *Disgusting*."

H: Oh God. Oh my God. You're kidding. You're kidding.

M: That's it. What he was thinking.

(They look away from each other, down at the table. Thinking. Feeling. To be taken in a way other than one intends. Not to be able to guess. One supposes. One is wrong. The sun, through the screen, has moved slightly, and falls on their hands. Myra's hands are twisting a paper napkin and shredding it. To consider the unexpected. Heather's hands are folded with the fingers interlocked tightly, rigidly. She unfolds them and reaches out and touches one of Myra's hands, quickly, softly.)

H: It reminds me of something, babe. The time when you meet some new guy and you jump right out of your skin. You know, that instant dynamite thing, when you guess right, like when you met Edward at the Sled, like when I met Al; you just know that you and that dude are gonna be making it before the night is out and it's gonna be good and there's all this electricity—

M: Yeah. It's like being on acid. I did get that feeling when I met Eddie. But not with Mike.

H: How come?

M: *You* know. Mike's someone I'm *used* to, not exactly take for granted, but I've always known Mike from around town and school and all, so he was no surprise.

H: Oh, I dig. It's very different from seeing a new guy and you wonder how he'll smell up close and you wonder how he's built and this other stuff there isn't any name for, pulls you toward each other, all the chemistry going, you know you're beginning something great—

M: And then maybe it turns into a Steve. Or an Orvie!

112

H: Listen, downhead. It could be an Eddie or an Al!

(Heather lights a Marlboro and takes a puff, then hands it to Myra. They smoke in a companionable silence awhile, and then get up to leave.)

CHAPTER
15

Directly opposite Frey's bedroom window was one wall of the barn. Beyond the barn was the stable. At rare free moments, Frey would sit at a chair in front of that window and look out, for a long while—perhaps as long as half an hour, an hour, more. It would be Summer in a month. The air today was softening. The grass was not up yet. She could feel it, under the earth, waiting to happen.

Since she did not hear what usual people hear, she would stare there to see more than there was. Upon that dark wooden wall, at this distance a solid medium brown, she would sit and focus quietly, centering, thinking, and in a while images would appear on the surface before her, as though it were a screen. In addition to the imagined ones, there were the recalled ones, and in addition to these, comprising the ideas thought of as *reality,* she could see sites (sights) and objects not considered in available common dimensions; for example, she could see the stable that was set beyond the barn in her direct line of vision.

When Ellen and Edward drove up, they saw Marty pitching hay out to Marchwind and Wird and the yearlings and the other mares. Marty told them that Frey was somewhere around, maybe up in her room. But as Marty finished telling them, and as they started toward the house, Frey appeared at the door.

Ellen had brought Edward over to the farm a few times lately. It was at first difficult for him, since he connected the place with Arthur even more than with Frey and Marty. Each time, they had stayed perhaps an hour, Edward not speaking much, the conversation going softly between Ellen and Marty, and, in her own way, Frey. Ellen carried the least of it, between her and her twin, although hers was the verbal representation. Edward was fascinated. Frey had much of his mother's aura. And Frey was interested in Edward. She knew his sensual involvement with earth and with music. Music was her familiar. She could reach through to it because of its vibrancy whose vastness was made of minutiae; she could hear it. Once, she told Ellen that Ellen's weavings were the same to Frey as music: music looked or sounded like weaving. And Edward was familiar with this view. He could see music.

In the past months, Frey had learned Edward. His soul was available to her. The first time they had come over, they had walked in on a house filled with Mozart. Edward looked in surprise at Ellen. "She hears it; don't doubt it!" she told him. Now, at the hour before twilight, the house was again filled with music: Bach, the Toccata and Fugue that had been in this same house when the Elsen twins were girls. Bach, with all the resonances: as Edward sat, in the kitchen, he felt the roar and thickness of it through the floor, through the chair, through his bones; it was not that loud, it was that *alive*. He knew it would extend through the heavy old beams of the old farmhouse, and that Frey could "hear" it in any part of the house.

Frey signaled hello to both of them and came forward to kiss Ellen's cheek. Then, unexpectedly, she touched Edward's cheek as well, and kissed him on the mouth. He accepted it and gave it back. She motioned them to sit and sat down with

115

them. At one point lowered the music and made cups of herb tea. If Edward was to be included, the conversation would have to move into more of an audible level than she and Ellen used. And Frey wanted to include Edward.

So it was "What have you been doing," and talk of the changing season, the weather that mattered so much to all of them, especially as Frey was so woven into the needs and patterns of the farm: for Frey, it was the time when the foals dropped. Frey had said she wanted to have them choose one of the foals to share with her and with each other. There were three new foals.

After a bit, while it was still light, they walked out to the north paddock, where the foals would be with the mares till the air turned cool for full nightfall. The mares snuffled and swished around the small forms. The earth-smell and animal-smell were heavy on the air; it was the hour when the dew formed and earth's moisture rose up; in the pasture beyond, the ground-mist was beginning to swirl and would soon fill the hollows, so that the roads would be as clouded as the mountaintops nearby.

One of the mares moved toward them and her foal followed shakily, but moving fast. The foal was very new, dark and still furry, all bony and angular. Frey talked to the mare and Ellen reached to caress the rich little form of the youngster. Edward went to him and felt of his body, his lines. The young animal was perfect; breathtaking.

"God, he's *perfect*—what a little beauty! —what do you think?" to Ellen; he could not take his hand from the animal's flank.

And Ellen, to Frey, "How lovely. How absolutely lovely! What lines! *God,* what lines to him . . . he's so *strong.* What do *you* see?"

"Good," said Frey. "He's got Sirrah Sean as grandfather and Marchwind's blood too—and you can *see* Wird's his sire, can't you! Edward knows: he's a little beauty, best of this lot by far. And he came to *us,* didn't he! Want to share him?"

"That's that!" said Edward, and then, to Ellen, "If it's good with you, babe!"

116

"Yes! Oh, yes," Ellen said, moving through the fence and gathering the silky bony body and putting her head on his neck and nose. She was too quickly filled with feeling, fulness of the season's opening out and promise, worry about this tiny animal who was almost too perfect, the immensity of Frey's deciding to share the colt with her and with Edward (as if she and he were a unit and to be treated as such!). She leaned her head on the baby-fur and wept, and laughed. It had always been Frey who wanted to be with the horses; Ellen had kept away from them, for the most part, not considering why; it was always Frey's special domain and she had not gone out into it, she had deferred. Shared so much else, but never this . . .

Edward and Frey let her be. Edward only sensed a part of it but leaned out to feel the rest and then to let it be. This was special, between the sisters, between the twins. That Frey had chosen to include him was important to him. He did not back away from it. It felt good, and somehow reasonable, and he trusted it. It all had to do with his feeling for Ellen, and his feeling for Frey, both through Ellen and through his association of his mother with Frey: all of it related to earth, and to music, and to flesh . . . It was all right. He could accept it.

It was full night. They turned to go to the house. Ellen and Edward built a fire and Frey went into the kitchen. Marty came in and went to the kitchen. Then she came out with plates of soupy stew and black bread and a pitcher of milk and another of juice. A vegetable stew. "What's *in* this," Edward had to know, with his nose over a plate. Marty told him: four kinds of beans, three leafy vegetables from their garden, parsnips and carrots, potatoes, turnips, miso for flavor, garlic, lemon, sugar, salt . . . She and Frey were not meat-eaters. They grew most of these vegetables, put them up in jars, kept a root-cellar where the root-cellar had flourished for over a hundred years in this house. A cellar-full of all the garden's largesse from each summer, just as had their mothers before them.

Before the dinner, Frey passed around the companionable

thin cigarets, to mark the end of the work day and the beginning of relaxing as earned. And now, at the end of dinner, another smoke, and the music on again. Softer, this time, too, and the sounds of the animals outside could come in to them occasionally, the dogs barking, nightbird sounds, all of it part of the Chopin and the Pergolesi . . . all of it a nocturne . . . it was near midnight. Frey suggested that Edward and Ellen stay the night. To continue the sharing. They had never stayed here; it was many years since Ellen had slept beneath this roof . . . It would have been nothing to them to turn and go back to the town to their own houses. Staying would be by way of an additional joy, lagniappe to the visit.

Yes, they would. So Frey went into the kitchen and came back with the tiny pottery jar she had made to hold the cocaine powder, and the little spoon, and the four shared and laughed. A little glass of Barton & Guestier Sauterne with it. The time and the room flexed into a clear rubbery substance that was part of the music. Ellen reached out and touched Edward's hand and Frey's. Marty put her hands on the hands of Ellen and Edward. Frey put hands out to Marty and Ellen. A circle of hands and hands, flesh, and then the responses began. Warmness: Frey with her hands on and the magic that was in them, hand on Ellen's breast, hand on Edward's groin. Marty loving Frey's buttock, Edward's thigh. Ellen, beginning to lose her shyness, kissing Marty's mouth, feeling Frey's thigh near her own, moving against it. Marty, leaning to the nape of Ellen's neck. Feeling Frey's mouth at her groin. Edward with a hand on the breast of either twin. The round dance began, around it went, a Matisse dance, then a Breughel revel, but softer—rich, moving slowly and then with the music going through it, the three of them their animal selves, the sounds they were making blending in, their motion bringing them from separate places to one place before the fire, atop the old soft rug . . .

They were in motion, it was one body, making love, one body with many beautiful parts. Everyone became one and had the loving to do and to receive. All the beautiful rich flesh was one animal. The clothing began to fall to one side. Husks of the grain falling away in a wind made of music back of their flesh. Flesh shining out like grain in the firelight. Ellen and Frey together, wound together as they had last been in one womb long ago. Marty and Edward, shaped into a curl of ivory skin and dark fur near the fire. And an opening out, Edward with Frey, his hands grateful along her long shanks, her legs wound around him as if he were the tree and she his vine and foliage; Ellen with Marty, their heads at each others' knees, their bodies curved together like commas, their sounds the sounds of the fields . . . And, finally, Ellen and Edward together, Frey together with Marty, all of it unfamiliar because Ellen and Frey were making love too, Marty and Edward were together too, meshed. They were laughing, and then they were free to begin to come, which was no serious business but a freeing, Edward roared as he came, watching the stars spin upside-down through the near window, he did not know whose mouth, whose hands were touching him, loving him, he did not know which woman he had entered, whose life he was moving inside now—one animal, the room filled, one woman screamed, one sighed, one said, sharply, "Oh!" which blended, joyous

and then the beautiful, sudden silence, roaring at one end and softened at the other, as the animal lay still and separated into its various parts; as they lay, curled like cubs, loosening from each other, resting, marvelling, Marty humming softly, Frey sprawled against an armchair, Ellen with her auburn hair spread toward the fire, her face glistening wet . . . The devotions, as they were part of it; a liturgy to all of life, *their* lives, their bodies . . . Frey rose and went to the kitchen, came back with a great pitcher of icy apple juice and some Japanese crockery cups, and a basket of oat cookies.

Ellen was silent, now beginning to think about what had happened, what she had felt. Frey knew. "*Good*," she told her sister. "It's all so good, that's the same energy that grows things from earth," then Ellen said to Edward, "This must be the only energy that never dissipates; imagine! that every time a human—or an animal—a human animal, or the kind we were just then, whatever that's called—moves like we did, and comes, from loving, it adds a spurt of that cosmic energy to the envelope of energy—to the vibrations—"

"Yes, that's it," said Marty, "that's just what it's like! You know, we get a constant feel of it out here; we can feel it from the horses; when they're making it, you can feel it clear across the fields . . . sometimes we go over to them and join in; it's all the same beautiful stuff—us or them, us and them, just like now . . ."

"Marvelous," said Edward, softly, looking at the women, and then back up to the window nearest him, and out across the night sky. "Simply marvelous!" He was considering that this was the first time he'd ever felt that music and flesh were the same. So *this* was what Frey knew. Was part of. Could share.

Arrowheads, and magazines. Edward came out to Frey's farm to look for arrowheads; he brought with him ten or fifteen magazines, ones he'd read or gathered from friends, to leave with her. Sometimes Ellen came with him, to see the colt, to feed him, to walk him; often, when they arrived, Frey and Marty would be out somewhere, either shopping or on another part of the farm that needed tending, and they would have the farm to themselves, and would play the pretend-game: what if the farm were theirs, how would it feel?

There were burial-mounds out back of the farm, maybe a quarter of a mile back, toward the edge of the forest and before the hills formed into mountains. This had been an Indian campsite. Edward loved to walk here, rummaging, looking for the peculiar shape that was or might be a burial-mound, not a drumlin or other natural hillock but the man-made magic rising which contained souls and their material goods. Those who lived then . . .

❖ ❖ ❖

Courtship patterns procedures processes. When he, then she. If she, then he will. If he does, she might, and then they. At the end of which, they both. The use of cowry is. The plumage of. When the ears are. Is worth at least five cows. The exchange of. In some instances, blankets are. It has been noted that when the female. The hammock is swung three times over the. At the age of. When the male of the. At the time of the first. As the elders move toward. The neck and the lips are. The ears.

Among them, the tribal mode indicates that. This figure proves that the male goes to. The more brightly-colored of the. When the female begins the. At the beginning of. Or in the coastal villages the. After which, both sexes. By examining the artifacts, we deduce that. The jewelry worn by the. The male paints his face with. The female moves the beads from. The metal rings on the necks of the. The earrings worn by both. The oldest aunt weaves the cloth for.

In Spring the elders of the tribe would. If the male so indicated, then. When he made that gesture, then she. And the father of the maiden would. Before either of them could, it. When the kin of each. Within the same moiety. Through the blood of the Clan animal, they. Occasionally, the youth would. Before puberty, it was customary to. In this connection, the female is permitted to.

The names of both are changed if. The names remain the same in the case of. The name of the male changes to. The name of the married female becomes. The girl takes the name of the. The form of winding the braid is. The male lifts the flap to. The males smoke it only when. The male is allowed into. The female's relatives make a. The elders on the future husband's side move.

Ritual ceremonial form observance. On the Northeast coast, the. Among the Sioux, the. If one youth speaks for. If the girl rejects the choice of. When each has made it known that. If by the gesture of. If by the following morning, it. Although nothing has yet been said, they. If in the evening a red-painted hide is. After he has sung, if the gathered mar-

122

riageable females. When the young women finish the dance, all the. When the older married females form a.

In the Spring of each year, we. At the time of the first thaw, they. A week later, when. The first full moon after. Two weeks before. The females form a circle to. The males who are chosen. Each female who is approached may then. All males of post-pubic age will. When the females are told to.

In case of competition for. In a situation where two males are. On the rare instance of two females who. If there is competition in a tribe which. In order to protect the family of the. For there to be a fair decision reached, a. Someone related to the woman is. An elder from the man's clan is. When the music of. If it should occur that. The tradition of the tribe dictates that. The women are each represented by. Each of the women who competes is caused to. One of the two men must. The father of such a violator does a. Each of the women tries to. A pact is made between the. The law as written says that. The wishes of the Clan are invalid when. The convention of the tribe is rarely. It is said that seldom. It has never been found in the Northeast tribes that when. The folktales say that. It must never.

* * *

Pictures in the magazines. The Agronomist. Livestock Quarterly. The Riding Ring. Strout's. Agricultural Greeben. Farming Faiben. The Farmer's Fordesaddn. Saddle & Fraibisher. Teaching Your Horse How to Nurd. How To Figure the Cost of Grundish on a Farm. The Surndisch Almanac. Edward brought some of these with him each time he went by Frey's place. This time, she met him with a story about the alarmclocks all going off at the wrong time, no matter what time they'd been set for they all went off at 11 at night. Demons & spirits. The horses all acted spooked. Frey had tried everything, except, as Edward pointed out, music. He brought over a dulcimer and a clavichord and left them there, in the stables. When he returned, they were nowhere to be found. When they were found, they were torn apart and the torn pieces were covered with a dust as of many years.

The pine seedlings over to the east field were going wild. Some dying, some growing in too fast, long and spindly and high, some stunted. As if in a dream; that quality of moving awake as in a dream. Flies appearing mid-Winter on the inside of windowpanes. Ice-fishing and drawing up a hooked dead cat, perfectly preserved. Eyes open to the world. Half the Dutch door blown off by the wind on a windless day. A Cadillac, maroon, passing on the main road with no one in the driver's seat.

Door locking by itself. Kitchen sink flooding when the water's turned off, in a season of drought. Horde of rutting deer trampling a mare and foal. An article on an event that had not yet occurred, in a magazine Frey had never seen before. The name of it blurred by rain but seemed to be "Sacrament". Edward swearing he had never brought it by nor seen it.

There were twenty-seven old chairs in the front room of the Elsen farm. Frey loved and collected chairs. They had an appeal beyond the beauty of their wood, for her, as they had had for her mother. Wicker, oak, bentwood, cherrywood, cane-seat ladderback, Morris, Duncan Phyfe, and more. Some of them were in logical or reasonable places for human use: at table, at the ends of the couch, or in a conversational grouping. Others were just there. Set. "Set down a spell." Set. Down. A. Spell.

Kill the first snake you see in Spring and you will kill an enemy. Make a wish on a white horse. The more chairs you have, the more chances. Everything happens in threes. Old Becky was the last of the witches hereabouts; people said she took so long dyin' 'cause she couldn't find anyone to take over her power. If you want to hurt a witch, you gotta talk so she can't hear you, drives 'em crazy, and try it on Sunday.

❧   ❧   ❧

One of the grandmothers of Ellen and Frey, the 'blood Indian, was responsible for the girls' sensitivity to weather, their feeling for animals, their love for earth and the natural rituals. That woman had handed this to them. The teaching was that when you kill someone else you kill a part of yourself. That when you deprive the earth, you deprive your own body. That when you lend yourself to the processes of earth, you benefit from all the earth's own process. A sharing-process; the gods who live within and on earth. Frey had kept with this, worked with this, was involved in it all, more than was Ellen. Her choices had been made for her. Ellen could work a garden, see what was not visible some of the time, could tend to a colt; she considered many things her children.

❊   ❊   ❊

Love. Death. Magic. Masks. (Masks: ceremonies, thrones, positions, rites, deception, symbol of the thing signified, scepters,) Myra, when she was stoned, had a different expression, Nōh plays, white powder, red paint, black paint, wooden masks, ivory bones in ears, "You look as if your face is enameled," "I can see how your death-mask will look," Ellen when she came had a different expression; *déjà vu;* The Way; *I Ching;* container for the thing contained,

the Mask of Lu, time's masks, if you look under the mask you will turn to stone, the mask is stone, stoned, Edward when he was stoned could better find arrowheads made of stone; all the masks occupied by other masks; Mexican tin masks; "his face was a mask of fear" and thus recognizable (didn't you get an image when you read that? that taut features?); the masks of Beckett made of ashcans . . . the way the leather is shaped to duplicate the features in her sculpture; the way the weather lays on the land makes people feel good or bad, it is a mask, the land serene under it; the people become frightened with weather's mask; a huge wind blows, the volcano spews,

the alarm clocks dropped their faces toward the ground, their innards were vines, the sun spun on its axis, nothing seemed to be predictable, people voted for what kind of day it would be and it was so decided and then it turned out to be a different kind of day from that which had been voted, nothing could be done about it,

when the enamel peeled away another kind of enamel

125

was revealed. The soul was not immediately visible. The self was layering deep. Was concealed even from itself beneath layers of motive. All the herbs wiped across all the masks. All the elements forming the flesh beneath.

And the sounds coming from beneath the masks. Whine, as of myriad insects. Glory howl as of the finding of answers in one instant. The mendicant's supplicating chant: for wisdom. For the doors through the mask. Shape of the teeth behind the mask. An old heritage disguised behind a changed nose. The constitutional inadequate, beefed up with stilbestrol for the market. Goose fattened for pâté. Innocence of the farm-girl trained as a nightclub singer. Dancing with a man whose hardon strains through the mask of his clothing. The Pinocchio voices of certain rock musicians, the tenor of their conversations. Contrast of tapestry as mask of a wall cracked to admit winds of Winter; of books as conversational mask at a soiree . . .

Masks of *agape:* "What do you really want. Of me. For yourself. With your life. Our wishes for your survival. Best wishes on your trip past Molokai." Cards made of cardboard, masks made of *papier mâché.* The mask of Edward as he faces Myra; the Janus side which faces Ellen. The One in the Mirror. To need to find the self by looking at the Loved One(s) for reflection. Myra, as she looks at Mike; as she faces Edward. Ellen, her face seeming to be turned toward Edward but veering toward Tom. Toward Anne/Frey. Away from herself. All the trick mirrors. Masks.

17

Mike the Virgo is now fifty years old. Lots of grey in his curly red hair. He passed his fiftieth birthday alone on September 4th, watching a football game in his bedroom, stoned and relatively content. Within his structures: safe. The apartment is in Manhattan, not far from where he works. He is now the vice-president of a small advertising and public relations firm. He has been married four times (the first was Myra). Besides the wives, he could have married four other women. His friends say of Mike that he has a compulsion to legalize his affairs, that he should have been a lawyer, that he is an obsessive-compulsive; he does not have many friends but they know him well. It is true: he need not have married the ones he married. He never did get the hang of living with a woman without marrying her. Since his rising sign is Cancer, he is all about security. He has always been nervous. Soft covered by hard. Fussy to a fault, more each year. Soft, ordered by intricate rules.

Most of the people he knows now are near his age. He lives

in a high-rise which has a doorman and an intercom. It is on the 17th floor of a beige-colored new highrise which is in the East 70s. There is a long walk down a hall which turns twice before one reaches his apartment; one can view the visitor through a double device called the Door-o-scope (Pat. 2,026,-108). There are three locks on the door. Each of the 13 windows in the six-room apartment is secured with a bar extending in the side molding along the right edge, to double-protect, as well as with the usual turn-lock. Thus, no window can be opened from the outside. His apartment is on the top floor, and thus might be accessible from the roof. It has never been robbed, but it might be. But it could not be. The windows are never fully opened. There are air-conditioners, complete with filters, in all of the windows except in the bathroom, which contains an exhaust-input fan locked into the top of the window-frame.

On the twenty-by-ten-foot terrace outside the livingroom, there is nothing. To the north, east and west one can see other buildings, some higher, some very low (brownstones, probably, and mansions). And sky. Views of other lives being lived on other terraces: none close. The livingroom is 43 feet long. At one end is a bleached cherrywood dining set, a table with six chairs. Four are set at the table as appropriate; two are set to one side at either end, at a distance, against a wall. On the table are two pewter candlesticks, and a zebrawood salad-bowl and its fork-and-spoon. On the lightwood buffet are a copper chafing-dish and a tall bronze salt-and-pepper set. All of these oddments were wedding presents. Mike does not now recall from which wedding. Which wife's friends or relatives gave what, or when.

There are no fresh fruits or vegetables in the refrigerator. In the 43-foot livingroom there is one four-foot-tall potted plant with strong glossy leaves. It is a plant native to deserts. It appears to be thriving. It has an Indian name. Most of the time it is the only live thing in the apartment. In the livingroom next to the plant is a chess-table, made of inlaid wood of different colors. The chess-pieces are unmoved from day to year but there is no dust on the table. Two marble-andalabaster pieces, a cigaret box and an ashtray, are placed on the chess-table beside the chess-set. A modern painting, a black-and-white abstract, hangs over the chess area. It was done by one of his wives. It is bad.

On one of the two large coffee-tables is a stack of books, each about a foot long, 10 inches wide and four inches deep: "Bauhaus," and "DaVinci," and "Rembrandt," and "Botticelli," stacked neatly. In front of the books are five antique opium pipes, the nucleus of his collection. In the livingroom are twenty-five various works of art: modern paintings (done by an ex-wife and friends and others), prints and watercolors, seven metal sculptures (some smooth, some angular, some knotty, some large, some minute), jars and pots and small pre-Columbian figures, an old jewel-box of metal and leather, and of course the collection of pipes.

The livingroom, in neutral colors, gives back the bright characterless light of the sky (which from here never seems to change color or value). The rug and walls are sand-colored, the chairs are a slightly darker version of the same color, the marbleized linoleum tiles (one foot by one foot) covering the floor of the entry area and dining area are also of varying shades of buff and sand. One couch is dark blue. One is a medium blue.

In the bedroom are two silent valets, on each side of the room, opposite each other; an oversize double bed (because he hates to be touched when he is asleep or trying to sleep), a Magnavox television set, a custom-made Electra-quad Stereo 260, a Sony Radio Alarm (digital), a wine-cooler, a compact refrigerator, a teakwood record-cabinet, a Florentine leather cigaret box containing from five to thirty rolled joints, an engraved box made of copper and lined with bright blue ceramic, containing inch-square chunks of Moroccan hashish, a hand-blown translucent antique apothecary bottle with a figurine stopper, containing 2 oz. of powdered cocaine (a tiny spoon is attached to the neck of the figure of the bottle-stopper by a filigree silver wire), two early American chairs of cherrywood with rush seats, an oversize (floorsize) thin rug from India which is used as a bedspread, a modern teakwood double dresser, and, most of the time from 6 P.M. till 8:30 the following morning, Mike Mandelbaum, sprawled on "his" (the left, if you're in the bed; the right, if you're looking at it from the entrance of the room) side of the bed. Facing the lit television, next to the table filled with all the accoutrements for getting high and staying that way, plus three Coca-Cola bottles at all times (the one he has just emptied, the one he is presently drinking from, and the one he has removed from the small fridge and which he will drink next).

The windows in the bedroom are shut. The blinds are always tilted toward the room, downward, at a precise angle, which was determined years ago. His cleaning-lady knows this angle by feel now and returns the blinds to exactly that angle after she dusts or washes them. The thermostat is set in each room at 80° and is never varied, no matter the occasion, and the air-conditioners set at *Fresh Air,* just so, from mid-September through mid-May of every year. In mid-May, the thermostats are turned to Off, and are not changed, and the air-conditioners are adjusted to *Cool Normal,* no matter what the occasion, and they do not vary from one day or week to the next, from mid-May to mid-September.

Mike takes eight Elavil tablets each day: two on awakening, two before his lunch drinks, two at what might be other peoples' dinner hour, and two at 11:30 P.M. At the time he takes the last two, he also takes one chloral hydrate capsule. When he wakens, before his first Viceroy he smokes part of one joint of pot. Then the Elavils, washed down with Coke. Then he turns on the stereo radio to hear the news. Puts the water on for instant Taster's Choice coffee, gets out the pint container of heavy cream, sets up the cup, the spoonful of instant coffee and two spoonsful of white sugar; then goes to the bathroom he considers his (the one located off the bedroom,) and brushes his teeth (sixty strokes) with Crest (regular flavor), sprays on Arrid Extra-Dry (unscented), pats on his own mix of cologne/aftershave after he has shaved his face and neck with an electric shaver, slips into his jockey shorts (adjusting comfortingly into their firm control), dons his tie-dyed nylon undershirt (sleeveless in Spring, short-sleeved in Winter); then into a dark suit (of conservative cut, except that the jacket has a double-vent back,) the pants held up by wide suspenders, dark to match the suit; adds dark calf-high socks and black oxfords. He is almost ready to leave for his day at the office.

He is mildly hungry, but there is not much time for eating. He grabs a couple of cinnamon cookies from a box on the shelf in the kitchen; munches on them with his coffee. He likes everything sweet flavored with cinnamon: in his cupboard are cinnamon cookies, cinnamon-crispy cold cereals, cinnamoned hot cereals; there is cinnamon applesauce in the refrigerator, near the cinnamon-topped dish of Horn & Hardart rice pudding. There is a container of cinnamon-and-sugar mixture on the spice shelf near the stove, and a jar containing sticks of cinnamon for mulling cider or wine; near the cereals is a large container of cinnamon in a shaker for use on baked apples and the like, or on bread pudding, which his wife of that year would be asked to prepare for him. It was wise of her to like cinnamon, its smell and taste.

One wife had had a cat, and so in the kitchen are still all the accoutrements of keeping a cat: the plastic pan and the scoop for removing debris from it are tucked immaculately under the counterspace; the boxes of Little Friskies, Purina Cat Chow, and Purina Dairy Dinner are stacked below rows of jars of strained or chopped baby-food meats (veal, beef, pork, chicken, lamb) that his wife's Siamese cat was trained to eat. With which his wife's cat-baby was indulged. Babied. Fed.

Sometimes Mike oversleeps: goes to sleep at eight in the evening, while watching the basketball game, wakes at 2 ayem when the late movie is on, smokes a joint, drops his Elavils and chloral hydrate, goes back to sleep during the movie, sleeps through the radio-alarm, and finally wakes, groggy, at eleven or noon. Sleeping is not always a good thing. There are the nightmares. This morning, however, he is almost "on time," and feels good about that. He takes a Revereware pot from the rack containing the set of 5 pots and covers, which hangs next to the 7 pc. copper-utensil rack, which hangs next

131

to the 5 pc. copper saucier set; reaches for an aqua-colored paper towel from the copper-colored holder which has three compartments, one for aluminum foil, one for waxed paper, and, in the lowest section, the paper towel Mike needs for mopping up the residues of water and the grain or two of instant coffee he let fall while fixing his beverage. He is already quite high from the joint he smoked on arising. Or he would not have spilled a speck or drop.

Mike prepares the cleaning equipment for the advent of Myrtle. Three mornings a week, for the past three and a half years, Myrtle, a black woman of perhaps thirty-eight, arrives to clean the place and put things to rights. She began to work at Mike's apartment when Mike was in the last throes of the marriage of that era. His "wife" found Myrtle through a neighbor in the building; Myrtle was familiar with the layout and the lifestyle, the neighborhood, the building, the floorplan of the elevators, the underground facilities needed to keep the place looking shipshape; she apparently could be trusted with the keys, as other people in the building for whom she worked trusted her with theirs; she had formed friendships of a sort with the other maids working in the building, she did not seem to gossip; once she began, she did not touch any of the dope that was always sitting around in the open in Mike's apartment; she showed up reasonably predictably forty-nine out of fifty times; she was as methodical and fussy and precise and careful as could be desired (Myrtle was born on August 23, but there was no way for Mike to know this; and thus knew or felt how Mike liked the apartment to look). She did not steal, and it was not just because she did not recognize the intangible value of things like pre-Columbian dollies; it was because she was a church-goer and believed in salvation, and had a great fear in her soul. She was, in short, a natural, a pearl of great price, and so she was paid $3.25 an hour.

When the Wife of the Year left, Myrtle continued on. She likes patterns and she needs security in her jobs. She continues. She is an integral small part of the functioning of Mike's life. He counts on her but he does not know that he counts on her. He hates to do with care of his apartment. He leaves the house knowing it will be tidied to his taste when he comes back. Myrtle arrives in his absence, usually; takes her black cloth coat off, puts it and her purse on one of the dining-room chairs, cleans the whole place in the ways he wishes, leaves everything at 80°, knows where to place his possessions if they are scattered about after his last high; at about 1 P.M., after she has finished with the laundry (his towels, sheets, little else), she takes the money he has left for her on the dining-table, puts it in her black vinyl folded purse with the golden clasp, puts on her black coat, unlocks the door from the inside, goes out, locks the three locks, and leaves.

At the time of this telling, Myrtle arrives early, as she once in a while does, earlier by a few minutes than her usual, in fact just ten minutes before Mike is set to leave for his office, because he, for his part, is by now a bit off schedule. He is surprised to see her, because he did not think he is so late in getting going; and even so, he assumed somehow she would not be due for a while yet and he would have the place to himself a while longer.

Coming in, she starts a bit when she sees him standing there, herself surprised and off-schedule, and says, "Hello, Mr. Mike," a sort of shy smile, the smile of people who know each other constantly and have no real relationship; the smile of the averters. Not quite diffidence. Then she frowns, stares at him, and says, in a flat toneless voice quite different from her usual, "I heard that you telling folks about me, you talkin' about me at your office, tellin' them folks I'm a prostitute, why you do that?" Then she looks away from his face, which is blank. She moves away a bit. He turns and stares after her, watching as her intense, angry look smooths out as she withdraws the vacuum cleaner and begins to connect it. And when he calls her name, at a loss, she turns, all smiles and herself again, entirely. He shrugs, not knowing what to make of it all, and, not wanting to make anything of the episode, leaves. Her alone in the apartment. "So long, Myrtle."

When he gets back to the apartment at 6:00, he unlocks the locks and finds the apartment smoothly in order. Goes directly to the bedroom to turn on the TV; raises the volume so that he can hear it while he gets a bottle of Coke or two out and sets them up, goes to the other fridge in the kitchen and takes a bottle of cinnamonized applesauce and a spoon and some cookies to bring to the bedroom. Back in the bedroom, he stops to do a spoon of cocaine. Takes a quick sideways look at the oil-painting of Myra which is the only picture hanging in the bedroom besides the inanimates (watercolors done by some wife or other at some other time) and decides that he will masturbate later.

On his second visit to the kitchen, this time to refill the bedroom matchbox, he notices a paper on the counter, propped against the clean coffee-pot. It is a scribbled note: "I know you're telling yr frends at the ofis Im a hoar and you shudden do that you know." No signature. He looks at it, already into his nice high and very puzzled. Thinking that she doesn't know how he feels and he thought she knew by now. How he has fought his mother's long sad speeches about their inferiority, their unreliability, their "shiftlessness," their body odors, their dishonesty, and always the "Watch out! watch out!" of the Jew who must find someone lower in the present hierarchy than herself . . .

Mike is now thinking of black Nefertete, and of his mother's face, and of Myrtle's. Mike thought he never had listened to Sally, but he must've listened, he thinks now. He must've picked up a lot of Sally's bad-mouthing the blacks, because otherwise, what was this all about, why would Myrtle think he is not a friend of hers? Ahhh, he hums to himself, who is Myrtle what is she, she must be picking up some bad vibes he is giving off, and she's the only woman anywhere near him these days, not counting that hag secretary of his and who the hell wants to count her anyhow, anyhow. By now he is quite richly high and the TV is announcing the score . . . he goes inside, deciding to ignore the note.

The next week goes by without incident, without reference.

A mercy of no reference. And then, the following week, at about 7 P.M., his doorbell rings. Mike, stoned out and feeling just fine, peers through the Door-o-scope to see the face of one of his neighbors.

"I'm sorry to bother you, Mr. Mandelbaum, it's about your maid, Myrtle."

He lets her in. "It's okay; what's up?"

He doesn't want to hear. He wants everything to go along smoothly. If one crack appears, it all might crumble. And the neighbor, a rich young housewife, another Jew married to a Jew stockbroker, tells him of Myrtle's incident in the laundry-room that day. In which Myrtle accused this neighbor's maid, called "Sangie," of spying on her, of having taken photographs of Myrtle while Myrtle was using the laundry-room lav. Mike listens. What can he say. But Sangie was very scared, she rushed upstairs and she was crying after that, wasn't Mr. Mandelbaum going to do something about this? Mike says thank you. Okay. Then he takes an extra chloral hydrate. That night he will dream a little dream about Myrtle. He is beginning to resent all this. It will be quite a week.

The following week, Myrtle again appears a bit earlier than usual. Mike is clenched. Getting ready somehow to leave for the office. He doesn't want to see her, in the worst way, and has been trying to get out earlier than usual. Because it might happen again. So it does. He is putting on his jacket when she turns to him.

"You got it all planned," she says to his profile, having it all planned. "You rotten bastid, all them pictures of my vagina, ain' that a *rotten* thing you doin', why you showin' my vagina to all yr fren's and tellin' 'em I'm some prossy and not good 'nough for you or them no*how*, goddamn your filthy e-vil soul,"

and he standing there thinking that this *was* a form of woman, wasn't it, she *did* have a vagina somewhere hidden in there, this was Woman, this thing mouthing these words at him with this look of hatred and violence, a woman, a female of the human species, somehow with something, lots of things, in common with his own mother Sally-Sarah, with his own sister Heather, with his ex-wives Myra and her and her and her,

he stared, immobilized, hypnotized, while she continued to froth at him (it came out like foam, he was thinking, and he was by now stoned out on his morning joint, what was it she was saying now,) "You *got* to *stop* that, motherfucker, I got to make you stop it," was he, he wondered, had he ever thought of fucking his mother, what a funny idea, he was going to laugh at the idea of anyone wanting to fuck Sally, so he said to Myrtle,

"Hey, that's not just ridiculous but it's really pretty funny," grinning at her, "Just stop mumbling and foaming," he said to Myrtle, and meantime she drew a pair of scissors from her apron pocket and moved slowly toward him. He did not move away, just smiled and noticed, amused.

Mike's mother Sally always welcomes him back to Wittgenburg; all his ex-wives are one woman to her, she does not call any of them by name, by now. "They taught me how to talk fresh and act fast, where I was raised," she tells him and them. Her double chin, her energy (Gemini, like Heather), her wide chest, rosy across the clavicle as with many women of Russia; her thick soft upper arms. She and her son are both glandular overweights; her husband is thin and so is Heather (Heather having outgrown her teen-age chubbiness). Mike's mother, now seventy-one, wears a bright-red wig some of the time; her own hair is very thin at the crown. She attends Edw. Albee matinees down in the City; she loved "Tiny Alice" and thought she understood it perfectly, had little patience with those who didn't. She has no one to talk to, on an intimate level. Her husband left her seven years ago. She took an apartment in Riverdale. It is tiny and she sometimes sleeps over there. She keeps the house in Wittgenburg. She has developed a passion for Albee, Ionesco, and Gênet. Tries to see her own life as they might see it. Thinks she could have led a different life, what with her energy and abilities. When she went on a cruise to the Caribbean after Herman left her, she found herself with little in common with her shipmates. She

136

was the only woman aboard who could play bridge like a man, play shuffleboard as well as Mah Jongg, and would really rather discuss business and the modern theatre than discuss illnesses or grandchildren.

She thinks Mike is a schlemiel. He is *so* limited. She admires *The Fountainhead* and thinks she could have written it just a shade better. She has a feeling that her power in Trois is still that if she went to Wittgenburg to the Village Green and hollered out "You gotta squat and shit," everybody in Wittgenburg would do it. On the Village *Green,* even. It had been that way for so many years . . .

She changed the house around a lot after Herman left. After the kids left. She bought a lot of records and Mike helped her pick out a good hi-fi set. It cost a lot of money and she sort of resented spending the money but now she loves having the music around at her whim and command. She has bought Verdi, Puccini and Wagner, for starters, and is considering moving further into Beethoven than the symphonies, and has her eye on Schubert and Wieniawski. ("and don't forget Dvorak and Chopin, fa hevvins' sake!") She doesn't know anything about the technical or historical aspects of music, but she sure as hell knows what she wants to sit around listening to while the washing machine is going or the coffee is perking. Knows where she is and sometimes where she is going too.

Where she was, where she has been: to shape Heather and Mike into her images of them, to keep a clean house, to avoid fucking her husband Herman, to feel the fear of the retributive God, to feel the feel of Power, the power of Power, to back her husband to his hilt in controlling a town through him, to get jobs for her brothers and if possible for her son so that she could further confirm her control over the town; to try to form her son toward his father's image (and even more toward her own father's image), ah his innocence of motive, as she watched him accumulate, ah his lust for money, his inability to love . . . to have failed and to know it, to see her loved son leave her in disgust, first with one woman and then another and another and another, none of them in the slightest bit like her; to see him armed now only with a need for pattern, for money, for anything to supplant or circumscribe that which she had given, that which she had taught . . . anything, so long as it was different from that idea of a man offered to him by his own father and by her . . .

Her daughter is, at forty-eight, living on some kind of large commune in New Mexico; they had never communicated; there was nothing now between them, all the "old hates and hurts" had been screened out or screamed out, long years ago. A static peace. A time of silent arbitration, between the mother and the daughter. Each keeping the distance secure. Though the daughter is herself a mother now: Heather has five children, by three fathers, all of whom she remembers well. Mrs. Mandelbaum sends her $150.00 a month regularly as her token gesture toward basic survival. Mike sends his sister another two hundred. Thus they rid themselves of guilt. Thus they feel superior. In return, Heather sends her mother and her brother a letter or a card once in a while, and books and magazines about ecology, containing articles about Heather's kind of life experience. Receipt is never acknowledged. These articles are threatening to Mike and to Sally. The magazines and books lie on shelves in the City, unread. Soot gathers on them and is wiped off by someone.

As Myrtle stands before Mike, facing him, he is feeling simply royal: a state approaching a high, almost orgasmic. Myrtle is his mother. She is his mother and/but with a black skin. She is also hallucinated as Myra; after all, Myra would be even older than Myrtle is! So he starts to reach for her. She is all the earth to him; all his fantasies of Woman.

"Will you marry me?" he asks, as if by rote. That would do it, he thinks, make up for all the injustices, all the times he was nasty to her when he was a kid, all the times he sat in her class and looked up her dress or down her dress and lusted, all the times he watched her on the screen at the Orpheum and played with himself, all the times he fucked her and she didn't come but he did . . . Back of them both, the Electra-Quad Stereo is doing that old number, Gordon Lightfoot's "If

You Could Read My Mind," soft sweet jazz, white music in the clear white morning light,

"Darling," Mike begins, as the scissors reach their even destiny, as her lips curl, and then, "Well, how *about* that, bitch," he smiles up at her, blood at his mouth, hitting a great high, the greatest.

"So long, white boy," Myrtle said, and went into the kitchen; washed up the last few cups and dishes, dried her hands, put on her black cloth coat, let herself out the door (taking the money he had left for her on the dining room table), and carefully locked the three locks on the front door of the apartment.

Mike took Myra into the Sled. Always a scene happening here, friends and noise and ha-de-ha. Anyone under age had a bit of apprehension but usually the bartender looked the other way if it was someone he knew, or whose parents he knew. A townie, or long-time summer people.

Mike, Myra, and Fred-who-tended-bar had been in the highschool at the same time. Fred had gotten out the year Myra got in and the year before Mike got out. Myra had never spent any time with Fred; he was of the wrong class in several ways. All of the three were born in Trois.

Mike orders double scotches and Fred serves.

"Didja hear yet?" Mike asks, meaning the Draft.

"Just a question of time now," Fred says, expressionless.

"Shit," says Mike, "You're not going to just *go?*"

"Sure! You think I'm some kind of goddam cop-out? Why the hell not! I *live* in this country, don't I? So why the hell shouldn't I fight if they need me?"

Mike and Myra exchange a glance. They are all in favor of

sliding out from under what's expected of one, especially if it involves a risk of getting killed. "The schmuck doesn't know why they're fighting, probably," Mike says, low, to Myra.

"You *gotta* be kidding," Mike says to Fred, "you want to go and get your ass shot off you?"

"Well, what the hell else you want me to do? Chances are I can get to go to their school thing, get some kind of training; *this* way, I'd never get *near* any more school . . . Pop wants me to work here with him, he's goin' to turn over the place to me, and he won't even talk about it unless I go do my service . . . Besides," he says, wiping off a beer mug, "I'd sort of like to travel, you know, see the world, before I settle down here . . ."

"Good Christ," Mike says softly, thinking about what he's just heard. His father Herman Mandelbaum has taken him into the City to the Draft Counselling people and a good lawyer to learn the best ways of evading the Draft. Sally arranged it. Sally will not stand for the idea of having raised a boy to be cannon fodder. "I dinna raise my boy to be a sol-jer," she hums. She and Herman also have future plans for Mike; they want him to come into their real estate business here in the Trois area when he is a year or so older and has learned something in the City. They have already begun taking him with them when they show houses. He finds it dull as ditchwater and says so. They ignore it. Sally's favorite remedy for unpleasant things or thoughts is "Ignore it."

"I want to get the hell out of this ratty town," Mike tells Fred, leaning forward in a man-to-man.

"What for?" Fred says, filling a glass with suds. "All towns're the same! What d'you think you'll find anywhere else? Better twat? Better booze? Hell you say! Wittgenburg's as good a burg as any, and besides, the old folks have it set up to lay loot on us if we play it right . . ."

"Oh, that's really *disgusting*, Fred," Myra comes in.

"Ah, what the hell, a message of wisdom from the local speed freak," responds Fred-not-Friendly.

Mike doesn't like this from Fred but he laughs anyhow. The men aren't about to include Myra in all of this.

"Oh, come *on*, Fred, you really want to sit on your ass the rest of your life in this miserable dull place, taking orders from your parents like you were a little *kid* or something?"

"What's the difference? So *what* if I do what they think is good, if I get what *I* want out of it! I got eyes to marry Frieda, I do my two years, I come back, I saved some money, I got some kinda skill I can use if I want to, Pop takes me in here, I marry her, I got it made!"

"*If*, that is, you got your ass in one piece after The Nam and you can still fuck Frieda like you been . . ."

"I'm not worried. Never happen. I won't be one of those!"

A small silence within the intense noise of the bar. Myra turns to Mike, knowing he'll listen; he respects her. Her toughness. "Anybody with half a brain wants to get the hell outta this dumb town," she says to Mike. "You know that. What a dumb schmuck, that Fred."

"There's sure as hell lotsa dumb schmucks," Mike agrees.

"What about you, what're you going to do?" she asks, looking out for herself at all times; at least for now, she is with Mike and his interests are her interests.

"New York," Mike says, "that is, if I get off the Nam hook okay. The folks are getting me introductions to some of the real-estate-niks they know in the City, and I'll try it there."

"Boy, does that sound good to me!" Myra says, her hunger glowing and the whiskey glowing on her face. Her face is that of a young wolf, intense, hard under soft, her voice is sharp with hunger for getting out.

Mike sees his chance for making his bid. It's right on the subject. "Listen, I got an idea. Why don't you come with me to the City, when I go. We could get married."

"*What? What?* You're *kidding.*"

"No, why?"

"I'd *go* with you, maybe, or maybe even *live* with you or something—*maybe*, I said—but you gotta be *crazy* to mention *that* word to me!"

"But I just figured I couldn't ask you to live there with me without . . . you being Catholic and all . . . you know."

"Jesus, baby, how wrong can you *get! They're* Catholic,

which doesn't mean *I* am! What is this, guilt by association, or what?"

"Well, I thought—to make a pun, habits are habits, you know—you might just have a bit of that stuff left—"

"Shut the fuck up, you big boob," Myra says, fondly pounding his arm. "You're really crazy, aren't you. I wouldn't let myself get ripped off by letting somebody, even somebody I *like* real well, change my own name to theirs—and I'm sure as shit not going to give up a whole big chance to be whatever I want to be, by getting married, not to you or anyone; just because *some* people think it's the only way to do life—I mean, can you just *see* me washing dishes, or waiting till you or somebody comes back from some office or other?"

"Oh, come on, Myra, it doesn't look all *that* bad, I mean, we could run the show to suit ourselves, the way we do at the cabin and all, nobody says we have to do it like anybody else, right?"

"Don't be a simp, Mike, married people aren't *happy*. They just think it's the only thing to do. I happen to think *not* getting married is the big groove! I happen to think experimenting is the thing to do. And I don't *have* to do anything just because all the other folks are doing it. That's for *them* . . . Hey, you wanna know what's for me?" and she reaches over and firmly places her hand on his groin. "Wanna split?"

"Not yet, babe," he says, slowly, with her and not with her. He agrees and he disagrees. "Let's hang in a while . . . Besides, you haven't convinced me it wouldn't be a good idea," he says, weakly, not looking at her. "We could get a pad and it would be fun . . ."

"Not for *me*," she says. "What the hell you expect me to do all the time, while you get out there and meet all those people and stuff? You think I'm supposed to sit in some apartment and justhangaround?"

"You say it like it's some *disease*—how would it be any different if we just lived together, which you say you have no objections to? What would you do all day *then*?"

"That's *different!* Don't you see? Then I could just run around! Nobody *expecting* me to be some place at some time, just like at school or in *their* house. Jesus, does that sound like bad news to me! I mean," seeing his look, "I could see doing the *pad* thing, maybe, but none of this getting married thing! Please, Mike." She doesn't respect Mike, she doesn't admire Mike, for asking her. So she says, to the down look on his face, to his sad averted profile, "I tell you what." He brightens, turns to her, and she forges the lie: "I'll really *think* about it. I'll really *try.*"

"Yeah? You mean it's not so absolute as you just said?"

"Yeah. Really. I'll think about it." She thinks, if he gets a nice setup in the City, I can pad there and do whatever I damn please. Just like here but better. So *what* if I have to marry him or something! Fuck it. That doesn't matter. People get unmarried. Nothing is forever. And her Scorpio heart sings out a mosquito-whine glee.

Mike's mood lifts. He orders them another drink, says "Back in a minute" to Myra, and goes to the head. Myra sinks into the drink in front of her and decides that if Mike really gets it going, gets to the City and gets into a lot of bread and things, it might be very juicy indeed to go there and hang in with him and see what shakes—*Jesus,* all those shops and all those flicks and all the new people to meet, guys, clothes . . . But that wouldn't happen for a while, and I'll have to wait till he gets something together meantime . . . The shape of time; it changes, it depends on other people, it feels different when you have to wait for somebody else to do something . . . I don't like that feeling, she thinks, of depending on someone else to get their shit together, before I can do a thing around them.

And then: round face of the Irishman summer visitor at the bar on the other side of her: "Can I buy you a drink?" meaning, she flashes instantly, he thinks I'm here alone, he didn't see Mike leave; meaning, "Can I buy you? Will you gimme a cheap piece of you?" and she snarls at him, "*Not* very likely, old buddy; you *gotta* be kidding," and turns her back on him, toward the john, from whence Mike is emerging. Suddenly seeing Mike as he might look to this Irishman, who has also turned; Myra tries to see how Mike looks to just any stranger

144

around, for instance this man, and Mike is a very presentable-looking cat indeed. So she decides to provoke Mike, by telling him what's just gone down, just to see how he responds. He is so sexy when he is jealous.

But Mike, in a serious mood, barely takes notice and does not even turn toward the other man. He says, "We are not amused," and shrugs. He knows well that Myra would not be into that type dude. Who has nothing whatsoever to attract her, much less hold her. She'd be bored in a minute. He feels confident of his scene with Myra, despite the number she's running alongside with Edward and the other guys around town he knows she's made it with. She seems always to come back to him, he won't look too closely for the reason, the fact itself contents him. He reaches over, touches her breast, so the man on the other side can see.

They have another drink. The moon-faced Irishman starts working on Marcy Hoenig, who is sitting on the other side of him. Mike nudges Myra and turns her on to this bit of business, and they have a little laugh. Marcy is likely to leave with the man. And she'll give him one fat fucking run for his money, they laugh. They crumple at the images . . . Myra's sleeve slides up, revealing the delicate tracks along her arm; she is not yet tan, and the tracks are like the footprints of birds in fresh snow; Mike, tender, upset each time he sees them, pulls the sleeve down again. He wants her very much now. He feels he will get her eventually. He knows that Virgo can do a lot for Scorpio; he's counting on it.

He thinks how much he wants her. He gets a hardon. He sees to it that she knows. He is thinking how he himself isn't all that interested in experimental sex, just wants to get the hell out of this damn town for Christ's sake and take Myra with him; and then he turns to see Fred, dear old Fred, doing his thing behind the bar.

"Remember," he says to Myra, "the night old Fred was drunk as a skunk and fastened the deer-antlers onto his head and went roaring down Main Street on his bike?"—and they both laugh, it was indeed quite a sight, even afterward when old Freddie went right through a plate glass window in the front of Snyder's Butcher Shop. Some Fred! Always good for laughs; or *used* to be . . .

"Maybe that's why he's not afraid about the war," Myra says. "He's been running frantic around Trois all his life, and doesn't know it, maybe he thinks he's got no other way to get out and see something else besides this fucking town . . ."

"Yeah. And he doesn't make anything but booze, and where the hell's *that* at! Jesus, imagine what his life'll be like, in this rotten stupid town, Frieda *Schuler*, for God's sake, and a bunch of kids and working this bar and saying yes yes to Pop and then when Pop dies, wow, *woweee*, he gets the *whole bar!*"

"Big fucking deal," she laughs with him. "But don't think Frieda's got it so good either. She's got—would you dig—not just Freddie, but his whole *family* on her neck—in addition to her own . . . and stuck *here* for the rest of her life!"

They smiled fondly to each other, marvelling that they would get to leave this place, the gods favored them, they had energy and will, they would get to have a piece of New York City. They would make it. And leave it to simps like Fred and Frieda to stay put, and home fires and all that shit. They were greedy and they were smart; they would get out. "Hey, listen," he said, smugly, "I read where Gênet when he was in Chicago a while back, at the riots you know, the Convention, he said, 'I took Nembutal to forget I was in America!' Wasn't that right *on!*"

"Oh, *go,* baby; did he? That sharp old fucker! *Jesus,* but I want to get to France! And Tangier, and Morocco . . ."

"Then you *will,* baby," he said to her, his hand on her thigh, "for sure, you will!"

And I bet you'll pay for the trip, she thought, and I bet I won't be staying long with *you,* either! She ran the tip of her tongue over her teeth, her molars. By God, they were going fast! Only a matter of time now before she'd have to do something about them. God, but that speed eats them up. Booze is a whole other thing, tough on the gut all right, but I mean at least you can't actually feel it doing its big heavy down magic, like this bit with the teeth going right in front of your eyes . . . But then, she could always have them capped, she thought. I bet in the City they have real good dentists who can do all sorts of things like that and not ask any questions either, and when Mike's working he'll have the bread, and I could always deal too, and so the teeth'll get fixed. But it's all right for now, the front ones still look just fine and that's what counts, isn't it. And so I don't have to worry about a damn thing. It'll all work out.

CHAPTER
19

Masks removed finally for the agape: "Who are you? What do you really want?" Clothing as mask of bodies; lipstick as primitive lure; tight pants over the asses of both sexes; hair lotion and perfume and three-button jackets and Dynel wigs; vasectomies; bodies whose ovaries produce at the command of a pill whose ingredients are culled from the ovaries of another animal—a woman bears nine infants at once, all of whom die, and she was on The Pill; another woman bears nine infants singly because a human man in Rome says he represents God and that she should not use The Pill to prevent conceiving . . .

The words "constitutional inadequate" appearing in Wittgenburg. The ghats in India . . . A woman in Appalachia on a tenant farm losing her teeth when she is twenty-three; five babies; eats starch direct from the Argo box . . . The newspapers that line her kitchen wall say that that other president would fix it all, his old lady came down here to fix up things but all she did was plant all them goddam fuckin flowers . . . say, lady, how'm I gonna feed those *kids?*

Ellen was pregnant. She knew it from the third day after she conceived. She was totally familiar with her body. Her breasts swelled and were tender. When she took off her bra at the end of the day, the breasts swung forward and there was real pain, especially near the glands up under the arm. Not like any other body response, and she recognized it, although she had never experienced it before. She was startled; she *knew*.

She waited until she was a week late for her period; by then, she was almost two weeks certain. It was the tiny but strong and different womb-sensations around the time that her period would have been due, and the absence of the usual pre-menstrual cramps: no temperament shifts, and no small and then wide cramps. The slight nausea and the feeling of intense hunger between meals. She knew and knew, twenty times a day.

"Love is so dangerous," she thought. She saw Edward, said nothing to him, looked at his vaccination mark, tried to visualize what he had looked like as a baby. He had pictures of his own boys as babies; the oldest looked just like Kathy (thereby confirming the Edwardian theory of genetics), or what Kathy had once looked like; the big bones were there and the coloring and shape of face, but not the overlay of misery-fat Kathy had added. His younger boy looked more like Edward. But then, Ellen was thinking, what if I had a boy—he would look more like me than like Edward, and no one would know he was the father except me. And, *if* he wanted to know, Edward . . .

Maybe she would not tell Edward; she thought he would panic: he was now, over a year after Kathy had left, still in the pain of that mess with her. And, of course, he was seeing Myra. A lot. Ellen sat at the kitchen window every morning, looking out at the field in a manner that was parallel to the way her twin looked at and into and past the brown wall of the barn from that other window. And no answers came . . .

149

She wanted a baby. This baby. Edward's. But really hers—
she couldn't count on anyone else, she would have to assume
that Edward, if he knew, might move away from the closeness
with her . . . she could not think much or deeply about this:
touched it, veered away, came back to it. Could she decide
to have the baby and to raise it alone. When she couldn't even
take full-time care of the colt! But what else was there to do.
Not have it? Not possible!

She went over to Frey one day. Just to be around her and
to try to let the feelings sift out toward some answer. Frey
gave Ellen no answers. Said things that Ellen already knew;
that she knew Ellen already knew; things designed to keep
Ellen open to the possibilities: "Whenever a woman conceives,
there's a reason; no woman ever conceived 'by accident' . . ."
and then, "Humans are so different from animals, even though
they're animals; they're instinctive, but they don't have the
sense to organize it for themselves and realize they're a lot
more than that—they convince themselves that things happen
to them by chance, when they could finally realize that they
do things like conceiving for a reason, something more than
propagating the species, a damn important reason or two . . ."

As they walked around the farm, talking, Frey doing some
chores, Ellen helping or just being there, Ellen was thinking,
"flashing," as Edward called it, the small insights coming with
Frey's comments. Turning things over. True: she must recognize that she was glad to conceive because it would give her
a bond to Edward—in the timeless way of woman to man.
And it would be a way to force him to recognize her love for
him and the direction of it, and her own feeling of wishing to
feel bound to him. In this she felt blameless: it seemed a
classic gesture. But would he recoil. Having had two children
by Kathy. With his particular history, he would probably ultimately recoil and run, in despair at the entrapment. So she
would be faced with having the child alone, and keeping it
alone, and raising it alone.

The strong possibility of an abortion. The death idea again.
And Frey, saying, "When you kill another living thing, you are
killing a part of yourself—but then there's that other side of

it, a death gives more available energy to what is already alive on earth," and, later, "An early thaw sometimes means a longer season of growth, but then, a late thaw sometimes means a more intense shorter season . . ." and all of this Ellen took in and took away with her.

The ideas and feelings sifted slowly as she moved through her days. She would not tell Edward. She would assume total responsibility for what would be occurring within her own body. She would realize and face the reality—that Edward would not say, "Hey, that's *great*," or, "Let's keep the baby and raise it together," he would never say what she thought she wanted to hear from him. If Edward was who she loved right now, the idea of the baby would estrange him from her. And if she told him and he said *No*, she would feel bitterness; now, she did not feel bitter toward him or toward herself.

She worked in her garden. Noticing the pine seedlings that grew randomly near the tidy cultivated rows of her plantings. Each of them a strong little tree, a tiny well-formed tree. And when she drove past the Reservoir, there were the intentional plantings of pine trees, in which the rows were only clearly noticeable from certain angles, like parts in hair. An intentional forest, to enrich the land: thinned out scientifically: a planned forest, dense, the needles as heavy at their base as if they were not told where to fall.

She thought too about a photograph she had, of a sculpture made of four paintings and two plaques and a box: the sections were called, and the piece was titled, "A Birth/A Bird/A Man/A God/A Love/A Death" and it was torn out of a newspaper's art section and taped to her wall in the kitchen near her stove. Where she could glance at it, get into it, and ponder on it . . . And thought about what Edward had told her about his brother Levon: who had married and had two sons, but found out (or knew?) that neither of the boys was his; one of them was the child of his closest friend, Duane Rattermann, and the other, he never did find out about. He had already formed his emotional attachment to the boys by the time he found out, and the marriage was going to continue. The delicate thralls, the binds, tapes, webs between people. Levon Richthoven wanted his wife anyhow; the wife wanted the marriage, the boys, and, somehow, in her own peculiar way, Levon . . . Edward thought the whole thing was a mess and said so, from his righteous Capricorn conventionality, and said he was beyond trying to figure out anyone else's motivations, let alone his own—nothing seemed reasonable or predictable. For their part, Levon and his wife had made their peace. They said nobody could write the rules for *them!* Ellen liked them for that.

Finally, in one instant of desire, she decided to have an abortion. And the minute she decided, she acted on the decision. Then there was time to react to having made the decision. She thought about what Myra might say if she knew Ellen was pregnant by Edward. Myra!—would surely never allow herself to get pregnant—and Ellen laughed at herself, realizing the edge to that: her thinking of it that way confirmed what Frey had said, about every woman knowing damn well what she was doing when she got pregnant; Ellen had indeed "allowed" herself to get pregnant.

Ah, but she missed the baby already, having made that crisp decision. There was a hunger in her arms to hold a baby. And it was the destruction of a life—a life that was part Ellen and part Edward and totally itself. This idea brutalized her and she could not dismiss it. She had not been raised Catholic and it was not a question of ethic. But she was Pisces. She had to decide she could not afford such maunderings. It was just not *practical* to have this child at this time. Maybe there would be another child, another time; maybe not. Aaah, what if there were no other time, no other baby for her . . . to hold, to raise, to love . . . She had to hold back those feelings, those thoughts which threatened to change her from determination to emotionality.

The field she worked in was a reminder that there was this season, and the one before, and the one ahead—and the years. Perhaps there would be another chance for her to have a child. Earth takes care of its own. She felt she should go ahead now. Before she changed her mind. She called to make an appointment with a doctor in the City. Even from within the clarity of the decision, she felt the deep twinge of misery and resentment at having to go through with this. She arranged to take three days away from her work and went into the City to the metropolitan hospital. Superficially, the abortion went without complications; she was, as the doctor confirmed, wondrously healthy, and could expect a fast and uneventful recovery, and would find no problems were she to conceive again at a future time . . .

It was on the trip back from the City that the depression of the event hit her. She sat on the train and wept. She missed the child that had left her body, she felt bereft as after a death of someone one had known. She ached for it, she wanted to hold it, she knew she was not being reasonable; but then, was life reasonable? Wasn't it just as reasonable, as healthy, as life-confirming to *want* that baby, to want to raise that child; to want to confirm her place on earth as a woman by having that baby? She wept . . .

She wept. Mourned. And when she was done, she had mourned in a way that resembled her keening at Tom's sudden death. Part of the mourning was done now. There was no way to cope with either death. She would mourn now, as she had done then, and she would have to manage to be enough of a person to continue to move along within her own life despite the deaths. There would be no living separate from death. It was all of the same fabric. No way to separate the one from the other; it was not two substances, two states called "life" and "death"—it was *lifedeath*, it was a Winter that was also a Summer, a seed that was a tree that was finally back into earth again and a tree. She would live with this new pain as she had with the old. And time would change its texture as it had in the past. It was a reasonable pain; it came in waves, she thought she might learn to deal with it.

She felt a hundred, a thousand years old. She felt as old as every mother who had ever lost a child. As she had felt something in common with every woman who had ever lost her man, whether in accident or war or illness, when Tom had been killed. Strange—the abortion had brought her back into her close feelings for Tom; it had not brought her closer to

Edward. She would have to consider what she was playing out with Edward, from this new point-of-view. That she had not trusted him enough to tell him about all of her feelings around the abortion, this matter that was so important to her —she would have to learn, slowly perhaps, the difference between what she felt now for Edward and what she had felt for Tom in those years. Since Tom died she had not been able to consider her feelings for him; mostly, she had just lived them, let them be, not touching, not exploring or analysing or evaluating. But now: he was here again. What if it had been his baby.

Names. She thought: she could have had a daughter called Ellen. She and Tom had once talked about that. But now, with its "E" beginning like hers but also like Edward's, it would seem to be Edward's child as well. She dreamt about it one night. The baby was a girl and she called it 'Ellen Richthoven.' It had a good ring to it. Woke in a sweat with the baby gone and not ever to happen. And one day she considered, what if it had been a boy: would it be Edward, or Ned—Ted, or—she had heard that Tod and Tad were also nicknames for Edward.

It became important to her that she had never discussed with Edward her own real name. Tom had known, of course; she and he had grown up near each other, and there was the signing of the marriage license, if he had not known before then. She had been christened "Katryn," had been called Kathy or Käti; her mother had called her Käti and this had gone on strongly for the long time of the early school years. But some time during junior high school she had rejected these names. The kids in school had been calling her "Kitty" and she did not like that; she wanted to be a new person, separate from Anne her twin, herself separate by now from the others and called Frey by everyone; she, too, wanted to choose. In the first year of junior high school she saw to it that she became "Ellie," from her last name, Elsen. It felt more comfortable, more like her own self. Everyone new since then assumed her real name was Ellen. She became Ellen. By now, she *was* Ellen. And when she met Edward, he'd known her mostly as Ellie or Ellen—he had only the vaguest recollection of her as a kid, as Käti—she would never tell him she was or had been another Kathy. The last thing he would respond well to, in his life as it stood, was another Kathy. Especially another one pregnant. No question but what Kathy Richthoven had gotten those boys as a weapon . . . Well, but with the abortion, Ellen was changing all of that. She could tell Edward her real name. If she wanted to.

From this train ride on, she would see Edward in a different light. They might come through it and some of their feelings for each other might survive. But right now she felt there was a distance between them that she had no name for—not yet. The feelings were rolling and subtle, water-sign feelings—they would become recognizable later, and nameable later than that. He was so much an earth sign; she felt too soft, too malleable beside him. She felt he was forcing her to his own needs and tastes. To his own order of how the life should go. They might both be creative, yet it was Edward who had the potential of energy-into-life, he was the builder, it was Ellen who was impractical, and Edward was not patient with her. Would he be angry with her about the baby. About the abortion. Well, she had gone about it herself, independently, she had not consulted him, had not looked for his strength to help her, to shape her decision—there was a certain amount of pride in that, however dubious, a kind of bitter pride.

She tried to shut out the mourning, but it kept returning in dreams. She saw Edward on the streets of Wittgenburg, but only by accident. She kept away from places he frequented. Shopped at the little general store out by the lake, rather than at the Superette, so as to avoid seeing him. He would know that she was avoiding him and he would seek her out; this much she knew; somewhere in her being, she was counting on this.

But for her part, it was useful to her that the schools had begun summer vacation now and that meant Myra would be around constantly, so Edward would be with Myra, probably, and this would give Ellen time to heal. Besides, she wanted (so she told herself) not to see Edward. And some of that was true. She took long, gentle, quiet walks, mostly at twilight when the town was eating dinner, or early in the morning, before the summer people were about, while the farmers and milkmen and other tradesmen, the locals, familiar and comforting, were beginning the day. She would wake from a dream of a dark-haired daughter named Kit, or of a round-faced auburn-haired son named Tad, and her face would be wet, her eyes puffed with the grief that came out unbidden. And it would take hours of slow misery to rearrange her feelings, to adjust from the soft to the hard mask of reality.

When she did see Edward, she could not talk to him. Put on the crisp mask and shut him out. Allowed him no way to reach through to her. Knew somehow that he was innocent of inflicting this particular pain, and yet doubted him. Oh, he was entitled to living his life as he chose, so that he would not now want another child; he needed that other way to live, to be free; needed it badly. She was aware. So be it. She would not see him, then; she would shut off. She felt quite the wounded animal. Perhaps there would be scars. Sometimes, her fantasy was that she had gone ahead and had the baby; Edward had noticed the change in her body, he was pleased, he was delighted; or, in another version, she had gone away for a while, come back, blossomingly pregnant, and he had known it was his baby and was glad; she had been *determined* enough to have—ah. Ah. Aaaaaah. None of it. She would share none of it with Edward. Her womb was empty. She was bleeding with the wound of her emptied womb. She felt very sorry for herself. She knew she did not have the courage to go ahead and have the baby and raise it alone. She did not even have the courage to talk with him about it. She could not take the risk of sharing.

CHAPTER

20

Ah well. Well then. Well now, what have we here. A *novel.*
Isn't that *cute.* In *this* day and age? Some folks say *any* story
is a novel, these days, if it's sort of long, and has to do with
the same people all the way through. It doesn't even *have* to
be long. Even the word "long" is open to interpretation. And
some of the time, if you've noticed, it doesn't actually have to
be a *story,* or have a *plot,* or what might be called a beginning, end, middle, &c. But. If we've gotten this far and you're
still with me, if there is more to say about the people alive
in these pages (and believe me, they are as alive to me as
they are to you, I am the catalyst through which their lives
move outward to you, I listen to what they say, I watch how
they move, I tell it to you, that is what I do) then this might
be a novel.

"Novel," new, the news, *nouveau, les nouveaux,* everything's
been said but say the story, human nature's always been the
same but this might be interesting, have you heard the one
about . . . Can you top this: old stuff but from a new angle,

let's share the ideas, have a slice of some lives and try 'em on, see if any of it fits. Sit around the cracker barrel, you and me, I *like* you, *thanks* for coming, welcome aboard,

a novel, yes, *a novel is a story in which the same characters exist, and move, in the same or similar or parallel direction, throughout.* So here we have some people who have been with us from the beginning. You may by now even recognize their faces or their walks or mannerisms: Edward, and, on either side of him, Ellen, and Myra. I guess we've got to call them the Chief Characters in this Novel. Then we have Mike, almost a Chief Character but not quite; sort of a limb, or limbo character, whatever that is; and Frey/Anne, and Heather, and Marty #1 (you have met another Marty earlier, and you will see him again quite soon). All the others, Sally & Herman, Myra's parents whom you haven't yet met, Kaput Shultis, &c., are really there to be around the above important lives. The ideas of their lives. Is what this novel is about.

Sometimes a novel is short so we could end this now. Should we? We could stop the story now. We think we know enough about Ellen and Edward and Myra and the others to guess, and about Mike and about Heather, and Frey. How they would go. But we'd be guessing, and while that's fine and fun, I think you want to *know* more. If you've read this far, you're interested in these people, for your own reasons. Or in the ideas these people represent (sneaky but true). This is a novel of ideas. I bet *you* knew that. It is also a story which is like taking an acid trip. But you will want to guess whether or not this writer has ever dropped acid. Some people who know me know the answer. Others look at me and speculate. Even if I stated one or the other here, you would still not know. This is a work of *fiction*. I may represent myself to you any way I choose. In any guise.

But then, this is also a story about a lot of people living in a small town, and at various times in life this writer *has* lived in small towns; it is a story about a lot of people fucking, and this writer has indeed fucked a lot. (Do you believe me?) The more the better, as you well know, though quantity can never assay quality. This is a novel about some real people, with whom you may identify if you so wish, thereby feeling more comfortable or less comfortable with your own life. A story to keep you company on your trip. As it has kept me company on mine. These people have been my companions for almost two years! Who are these people? Myra is the Geraldine (not Geraldine Chaplin); Edward is Raskolnikov; Ellen is Isabella Gardner Tate. Myra is a wolf and Edward is a bear and Ellen is a sunfish.

This is Page 232 of the fourth draft of a long story about three humans we have called Ellen and Myra and Edward, for no particular reason. Nonsense. For *many* particular reasons, most of which you may decipher, if you so choose. On that subject, it should be said that Myra Shultis was christened Elmira; Ellen, as we discovered recently, was born Katryn Elsen; Edward, now called Ed and Eddie but never Ted or Tod or Tad, *seems* to have been born Edward; Mike can have been either Michael or Myron, which leads to some fairly dull comment and speculation; and we all know altogether too much, for sure, about the transition of Annetje (Anne) to Frey . . . and what can you do to or with a name like "Heather," much less *Mandelbaum?* Nothing.

Born, they grow and learn and sweat and fume and develop with a blossoming crash and burst forth alive and adult on these pages; you have to believe them, their lives intact, their faces real to you on your inner secret retina; Myra sits at the bar where you drink, no matter where you live; Ellen is designing clothing and/or making weavings, and she is your friend or someone you buy things from; Mike plans the advertising you read in TIME Magazine's pages each week; Heather is the reason you buy detergent marked "biodegradable" even though you may have only some idea what that word means. Myra is the girl your firstborn son first fucked, back of the barn or on a car back-seat in a drive-in or whatever; Frey is the Magic Lady of which every town has at least one, and who used to be burned for witches. ("Render unto Caesar that witch . . .")

But *you* knew that. You, who have ducked the stones. Who have read, or lived, Shirley Jackson's "The Lottery." "I look at each person and I realize that they had to go through so many things to come up the way they are," is one way. And: "All these people you can love, if you understand where they're coming in from . . ."

Now that all the musicks have become unlyrical and unfamiliar; "cain't whistle it so whut *good* is it; now thet them sumple thaings jus' ain't like they was . . ." Edward: is the hero, or an anti-hero, because he does some things with his life and does not do others and is struggling with The Questions, the definitions: is Edward *you,* or the guy in the next apartment, the next room, the next bed, is he the teacher in the next department, you know the one, the one who seems on the brink of discovery and may or may not that day take the Big Chance, make the big jump up and out?

And why should we not discuss this? Why shouldn't you and I talk? You must be my friend: if you are an agent, or work for a publishing house, or have bought this book in a shop somewhere, you have by now somehow cared enough for me and for these people and for your own life trip to come along this far; so you are my *friend;* doesn't this mean, Friend, that I can come out in the middle of a "novel," so to speak, to speak so, to talk with you? I want to be able to talk with you. You can write to me c/o the publishers, and we can get together and talk, damn near any time you say. I hope you believe me. And if we become friends, could I/you pick up the phone and speak, now, at midnight, on June the 17th in some year in some state in the U.S. of A.? To cut across the ineffable loneliness? I would say to you, as Muriel Rukeyser said in a poem she read recently: "I speak to you; you speak to me; is that fragile?" (Punctuation mine: I've never seen the poem on the page.) I would ask you, What are you getting here; are you getting it on with this story? What do you think this book is about, why do you think I am writing it, are you absorbed in the lives being described herein, do you identify with any or all of them, is it audacious by your lights for me to have picked up the telephone and called you, at this hour, or to have accepted your call, to talk about some people in a book (as yet untitled) that you are reading even as I am writing it? Why not? Who is it that makes up the rules, if any?

Yes. I *want* to tell *you* more about Ellen and Myra and Edward, and the others, because they are alive and will provide the necessary rest of the story. There is more to be told, yes. I can feel it: their lives. Can you? I trust you. I will let it flow on. I will let them do it. I will be flexible enough to allow alternative endings, because each person, you, dear heart, each alive soul should be able to choose the way he wants a story to go. For instance, I may decide, not so arbitrarily, to record one of the other endings possible for Mike's life; a calmer one, or a more average one. Or a more convoluted dramatic one, something more public. If you are living a life similar to that of Mike, it will comfort you to know that you have choices and that it can go any one of several ways. You need not look suspiciously at your housemaid.

It is that America is developing a history. A herstory. Not everyone has to live on Klutz Road in a town called Ineptfield somewhere near Iowa or South Dakota. Ourstory. I mean it. You don't have to be a Sadhu to know what I mean. You don't have to be Jewish to be Jewish . . . All the people in the "civilized" countries going crazy with loneliness, variously called alienation, isolation, cancer, the horrors, or Please Touch. Here we are: not ghostly for the old values, not a nostalgia (*this* is when to be alive, for us), but needful of any of the softer feelings, which words like *rip-off* cannot cover. The guardian vestals and nereids appear seldom and in guises, and are often involved in glossolalia . . .

* * *

When Myra was in high school, somebody called her (you?) Mimi, for short, and then someone else called her L. Myra, and then there was the wise guy who, when they got to Lewis Carroll, called her Mimsy, and it was all over school, the sneaky way kids have: she was Mimsy Borogrove and she hated it. She was too much of a person for such an indignity.

When Ellen (at that time, still Kathy, mostly,) was in high school, she developed a series of blinding headaches from feeling awry in the world (four hours of homework a night, it did not suit her temperament, she saw no reason for it); and her husband, Tom Dykstra, had *his* headaches developed to the point where they were cluster migraines; it is suspected this may have been one of the causes of the accident, if not the sole cause.

When Ellen and Tom were married, at the Dutch Reform Church, her eyebrows were not plucked nor shaved, nor was her head shaven, nor were her teeth blackened. The bride wore pale yellow, a just-below-the-knee dress, and walked through the trees as if they were people. The groom seemed at some points to have no face. The skin of his cock was so soft, so delicate, as to seem transparent. Shirley Jackson attended the wedding; came over from Connecticut: a friend of the occasion. Jakov Lind was there, wearing a suit of horsehide he had made himself while in the home of other friends in the Black Forest. Bob Creeley sent regrets. Thea Claire Bowering was Flower Girl. It was lovely.

The sorority that in different years rejected both Myra and Ellen from its membership, in the high school years, was called Mu Kappa Delta. Not many girls got into it, so it was called, by the many rejects, "May Cong Delta." Most of the girls who were taken into that sorority stayed in Wittgenburg for a long while after they finished high school (I should say, stayed *on* in Wittgenburg). They came from families who were churchgoing, ongoing, whose fathers belonged to the Grange and whose mothers had married without higher education, for the most part; those girls went usually to a state-funded "community college" for a year or the full period of two years, to study home ec, or phys ed, or nursing: in other words, the alternatives to getting married at once. Or what to do when the marriage is well on and the kids are well off, on their own: always nice to have something to bank on. Just waiting to get married to somebody local. In this part of the country, a man finds himself a wife before he's 25, if possible. A girl "settles down."

Anyone's father is called "Guv" by the guy who delivers the bottled gas. He rents a house on Pine Grove Street (every town has one); he works as a plumber or a carpenter or he works at the mill or the plant, he gets a salary, "ekes out a decent living," this is American life, none of that coal-miner stuff, none of that Appalachia stuff, the Agway is there and can be counted upon, the Sears catalog arrives, the Grand Union uniforms are waiting. The young man is married to Armentha Sulzburg, or to Janice Mergendahler, who goes often to have coffee with her best friend, Rosemary McClary Vander Molen (you can see how that marriage came about: Rosemary was a summer person, and met Ari Vander Molen, and it took, and there she was, and she fit herself in). Rosemary, Janice, Marie and Linda-Susan are in charge of making the posters for the Sodality Rummage and their daughters are virgins. Marie is married to Harley Reynolds who runs the Mobil station; Linda-Susan was named for the daughter of Shirley Temple, and she runs the local beauty parlor. Myra's mother, Liona, is a friend of these women . . .

Myra's tiny, fine-boned face shining and running . . . Let's talk about Myra for a while.

CHAPTER
21

The intensity of the hatred, the tight violence of the fear many people had around Myra. Myra: as she danced: what she believed in, what she stood for, how she lived her life. Simply when they *saw* her: as with the man in his fifties at Tom's Luncheonette, the bus waiting-room (that story she told with such depressed horror to Heather). It had to do with her vibrations, of course; with how she felt toward the way ordinary people were living their lives around her and with her intelligence and the ways in which she was using it. Her forms were threatening to the status quo.

Myra's parents are themselves the kind of people who fear and hate people different from themselves. They are carefully, rigidly Catholic. They are on a forced march down a boundaried, fearful road, the way marked out for them by dos and don'ts and how-tos—it is comforting to some folks to have the questions thus covered with answers. To prefer what was and is to what could be. Myra's parents are not all that unintelligent (an obviously bright girl like Myra doesn't spring unheralded from dullards); it is just that Liona and Joe Shultis are not given to taking risks. They avoid. Confrontation. Threat. Variation on the themes. ("At his weekly audience, Pope Paul described his church as 'tenaciously conservative. It is necessary to say this even if this word is not liked. But precisely because it is conservative, the church is always young. If it had changed all the time, it would have grown old.' "—is the way TIME Magazine gave it, and the way they would give it, too.)

Their house is light green clapboard and has a fieldstone fireplace. Myra calls it "ticky-tacky" but of course it is somewhat higher-class than that image; it is a substantial eight-room ranch house, twelve years old, in a nice neighborhood where each of the houses has at least half an acre, often up to an acre, of land. Many of the men, good honorable men like Joseph Shultis, Joseph Nicholas Thomas Shultis, work as executives for the ITT branch eleven miles from Trois. Living a decent life. Started out in modest circumstances, worked hard, used the energy in pro-social ways, provided more for themselves than their parents had had, more for their children than they themselves had had as children.

They took care of their own. In fact, they nurtured, they espoused, they protected, they advocated, they cherished, they looked out for—in a word, then, they were and are the gentle murderers, the defilers, the rapists, the commanding soldiers, the assassins of imagination, the defiers of progress, of vivacity, of the different among them and us in the world. Of Myra and the Myras, the ones who are different or who want more or want to *do* more or do it differently. Old Kaput the Madman is a first cousin of good, honest, bright Joe Shultis, and Joe would kill anyone who touched or mocked Old Kaput. Joe's mom is Irish Catholic and his wife is German Catholic, though Joe's father is Protestant: hence, Joe is a Catholic, a *good* Catholic.

Myra's mother, Liona, is Chairman of the Meeting. In a bright yellow rayon knee-length tunic dress with plastic buttons set decoratively down the side of the tunic; in her greying soft-cut short-nape-exposing hair, in her squinty twitchy fifty-year-old eyes (blue?) she is speaking well and clearly about the need to protect the town's waterway from the threat of the new proposed plant's possible sullying. It is she who recommends to Joe that he buy land instead of banking his money or investing in stocks. It is she who is glad that the Irish use the town in Summer, not in deference to her Irish mother-in-law, though that is probably part of it, but for the same reasons that Sally and Herman Mandelbaum are glad. It is good for the town.

"It is difficult," she says to the assembled Meeting, "for someone downstream to have an influence on those who live upstream. Our little river—" She is a Leo, with that powerful turn of head, those hands. Her husband is Cancer. It is not the most perfect match. She can coordinate; she is busy being a concerned adult. A good woman in the community of Wittgenburg and in her family. She has not given Joe a good piece . of ass in fifteen years, almost. She has no sexuality at all; the energy goes elsewhere. She stutters occasionally. "From the s-s-s-standpoint of possible legislature," she is saying now.

Joe is seated in the second row of the audience. Resentful. Wearing his gold wedding-ring. He looks like his mother, and she had looked like her father, so he looks very masculine, for a Cancer man. Handsome and with crisp classical features. Without all the flesh of age, and stripping away the creases, you have Myra's vulpine beauty. Thus it goes. His flesh is leaning down toward earth. After this meeting, he knows that their phone will ring and ring, perhaps twenty or thirty phone calls to discuss, corroborate, confirm and compress the action instituted here and now at this Meeting. "Regional concerns . . . motivations . . ." he hears his wife saying. Then he begins to think about his daughter Myra . . .

Joe, who when his daughter Elmira was entering puberty used to continue to just happen into the room where she was dressing in the morning or undressing at night or bathing, as if she were still a child, such innocence of his, who would pinch her nipples under the playful pretext of seeing if they were "growing along all right," who would fantasize and sit with his hand or a book covering the hardon in his lap until the day would arrive when he thought she would be curious enough to want to play with him, if he could convince her to. At first at least through the covering cloth; that was an okay beginning. He told her it was a good secret but not of the kind that was to be told at Confession; he told her it was indeed like a "little priest," though; it *was* his little priest, in fact, and to be treated with respect; told her she couldn't see The Little Priest, any more than she would see the Big Priest in church at Confession, but she could tell if "he" was listening and responding to her presence because "he" would lean toward her hand and try to touch it as she touched "him" or spoke with "him."

He told his daughter Myra that some time she could see his "Little Priest" and that it looked something like the hooded statue of Our Lady of Lourdes at the Shrine, a picture of whom hung in the hallway of their home, lit by late afternoon and dappling sunlight. And "yes," he replied, when Elmira asked her father was the little priest a magic person or did he worship with it or did it have a good power (remember, she is a mystical Scorpio). And "yes," he said, half a slow long year later, it is a marvelous magical being to have and all men have one like it, and women have a sort of small tiny being something like it, if she wanted to see her very own he would be glad to show her, and hers would respond to him almost the same as his Little Priest did to her. And explained to her that the way a girl person could share and partake of the Little Priest further would be to love it with the mouth, not exactly eating as with the Wafer, but just sort of tasting gently, and if she were lucky she would notice a sort of sweet wine would appear in a little while.

And told her that if she were as good a little girl as she seemed to be, reverent and all, and still respecting the Secret and all, in a while he might show her an even greater way that women and girls had of sharing their marvelous little gods with others. One night he did show her; very carefully, very affectionately, while his wife Liona was away at some Meeting, they both arranged it so that the Priest moved softly and sweetly after his gentle fingers toward that place Joe called his daughter's Chalice, which he wanted to drink from, and which was, he explained, a place that held a girl's most revered and special way of sharing. Joe told his daughter that the Chalice place was a secret wonderful place that "he" liked to visit, if the girl were really understanding of the visit and would never need to discuss it or refer to it (this part itself was *really* just like a kind of Confession, he told her, this letting the Priest come by and all; so of course she didn't need to discuss it at regular Confession, at the "Big" Priest's church).

By now they established that this took place, their worshipping, their fondling, in a hushed and private and ritual Church ceremony of their very own, just the two of them, in a corner of her room, set up to provide the needed privacy and quiet for the sanctity of worship. Joe had by now taken to calling his daughter's pretty, darkening cunt "The Little Chalice," or "The Little Church," which she enjoyed. She was, after all, a ritualist, as are all addicts. He patiently showed her the tiny body-bound tight lively almost-replica of his little Priest-god, just above her shrine-place, her sacred Chalice; and he touched it and showed her how to touch it until it swelled and rose mildly, in its horizontal way so like the growing of his own form as he watched. And told her, when she made her noises of delight as they both touched her body, that that was exactly how he felt when they both were touching his body, his Priest!

Near her thirteenth birthday, he promised his daughter a lovely surprise. They waited longingly until they were alone and quiet, after exchanging looks across the dinner table, and then, in her room, in their special corner, he showed her that it was not only his gentle hand that could slip toward and into her Shrine; the Little Priest would be welcome there too, he explained; that is, if she would be very loving to "him" and would understand that the priest was moving there with complete reverence for her Shrine and Chalice, they both would find a new wonderful way to worship. So be it. He fucked 'Myra completely. She loved it. She was full Scorpio, and ready. She came when he did.

What a fine addition to their ritual. Nobody knew about it but they both knew more and more about it. Joe was so pleased to be getting it regular again, and without having to go outside his own house. Liona had once been okay, but she'd shut him out years ago. He saw no reason for her having turned him aside, and this was a really good secret he had on her. Let her go do all her Meetings and all that goddam stuff. He was perfectly happy now with them. He had his own. He and 'Myra. Myra was getting to be pretty good, anyhow, better than Liona had been, when you get down to it . . .

Liona never did find out. But Myra did. When she was almost fifteen, she let something slip when she was talking to her girlfriend (Myra somehow assumed that all of this was some kind of wonderful ritual that all girls shared with their fathers; although she was secretive by nature, she began to take for granted some of the ritual's by-laws, as time passed and her father neglected to re-emphasize). The friend, astonished, amused, asked for more details, and since the two girls were both high on pot and comfortably loose-tongued and easy-going, Myra and she went over to the Ladies' Room, dropped her pants, and showed the friend the area referred to as The Chalice or The Shrine, explaining in great and affectionate detail who the Little Priest was and how he behaved.

The friend's reaction and response to all of this was such that Myra began to have mixed reactions to the thought of the secret ritual, which had by now become a habit with her and which she so loved and enjoyed. Her friend pointed out that Myra might bear in mind that there were plenty of cute boys around who would enjoy sharing such forms of worship with her. The friend laughed fondly, smitten with her own memories of fields and backs of cars and garages and porches and couches. She suggested that now Myra might want to experiment a bit with some people her own age . . . Maybe learn something new . . . at the very least, vary the menu a bit!

This was a very attractive idea to Myra, so she followed through on it. She was not against giving her Dad a piece now and then, at least for the year, but in a while she did find the boys her own age attractive, even though they were not as practiced or as used to pleasing her. It never occurred to her that her father was sadder and sadder, that he rued her turning aside, her turning to him less and less. He was always tender to her. And they always went to dinner together, and Church together, they and Mother. It seemed reasonable to her to turn to boys her own age.

She never used her power over her father. But when it seemed to flow through to her that she did indeed have this power, she began to understand something unspoken. When she was about sixteen, she began really to know what had been going down for the past years. That it was not only *not* customary, not only not a privilege, not a religious ritual, but was actually looked upon as a tribal taboo. That something was rather out of gear with Joe Shultis. Toward her. With her . . . Was she all right?

She went to the Priest, the real one, as she began to think of him. He, not so surprisingly, didn't believe any of it; he could hardly afford to, really, since Joe Shultis, one of the more prosperous members of the extensive half-Catholic branch of the Shultis tribe, married to a Catholic and raising his kids Catholic, contributed more than his tithe to the Church; and wasn't that where his money came from, after all!—so the Priest yessed Myra, and made no further reference to the whole story. Gave her to understand that she was, and her father was, blameless and unsullied. Not a word from him after that.

She went then to the Doctor, and what he did was to give her a diaphragm and a speech about conception. She did not tell him who had deflowered her, and he did not, of course, ask. It was a small town. She was getting on to the game; she was getting smart. She was a very cool lady and she loved herself well, she believed in herself. She enjoyed the subtle discomfort of the Doctor. She was feeling happy and relieved. Also, she was getting laid, as much and as often as she wished, if not as well; and that, for a Scorpio, is, as you know, penultimate.

The nuns at the lower-school across the valley thought they

170

were teaching Myra how to be virtuous, truthful, honorable and good. They in fact taught her how to lie and deceive, how to seek pleasure in ways other than those usually acceptable, how to seek the extremes in human experience, how to evade questioning, how to avoid mediocrity by acting in opposition to whatever examples they set; in short, to what extremes she would have to go in order to acknowledge and achieve the true nature of Scorpio. Myra's mother was responsible for Myra being at the school. Liona would not have married Joe Shultis if he had not been half-Catholic and if he in addition had not proven his devotion by promising that the kids would be raised Catholic. They were married in the Church. The local church of the town in which they had both been raised: The Church of Our Lady of Knock, which in the past fifty years incorporated both the small German Catholic population and the large Irish Catholic resident and visiting congregations. Myra's mother, Liona: a virtuous Catholic woman who would not use the Pill or other methods, who would practice abstinence because it suited her concept of self- and other-discipline; and it was all right that way because she had not been all that pleased with what she knew of sex with her husband (no other men before him, at least not many, she never discussed this with anyone in her life, Joe thought she was a virgin . . .) Liona drank a lot. Began with a drop mid-morning. You know.

Myra was drinking a lot by the time she was not quite six-teen. Wine bottles in paper bags down the fast highways and dirt roads and in the drive-in. Beer and highballs whenever she could. Then some buddy brought in some speed in pills. She loved it. So much possibility of reaching out further toward the extremes. Black, white, hot, cold, she could stay up four days in a row with this great stuff Speed, she could travel fast without ever moving from the spot where she rapped with her friends . . . not so great after a while for balling, but sometimes even then it was good, Great Stuff! And of course the pot, lots of it, every day, at school, and anywhere, it was everywhere. *That* was the stuff for balling, for sure! Nothing better except maybe coke. The speed took an edge off her sex drive, even *hers,* and she realized it acutely, and she was hooked on it, all right; but she was tough and stubborn, she wanted the one more than the other, so she could begin to kick speed, or at least control her use of it, and she did. She got it under her control. Figured there was nothing on earth could run *her*—she would run it all, from her own chair.

Began to hang in with pot, and sex as an up, a bit of angeldust mixed in sometimes, far *out,* and of course lovely coke when she didn't have to pay for it. She got the idea and began to steal from Joe Shultis' pockets. Figured it was reasonable: he owed her a lot. Even at ten bucks a lay, she had plenty coming to her! She had no guilt and this way he wouldn't have to, either. She used the bills and change to buy her coke and pot, so she could treat sometimes and keep a good stash. She kept it right with her school supplies in her room. She had no doubt at all that they would never mess around with what she had in her room; Liona was basically pure stupid chickenshit and ignorant, the way Myra figured her, and as for Joe, he was of course unable to do a thing if he should find out. She had him by the shorts.

Mike was the first of the younger men that Myra made it with who provided enough of a challenge for her. He was as much of a down-head as she was an up-head. He was a Jew, and she found that exotic and attractive. And he was a natural victim, in some way that she could smell. Only part of it was that he was Virgo and he was a Jew. The rest was all about karma. And Jesus but he loved to ball! And he was into drugs and into experimenting. And he always had money and ideas of how to spend it. And his family's house was so different from hers. It smelled different. The people in it smelled different. They had more flesh, for one thing. Mike's mother really got into Myra as a personality, Myra intrigued her. She told Myra, in confidence of course, that her own daughter Heather bored the hell out of her and so basically did Mike her son. So Myra moved with ease right into the bosom of that family. The father, Herman, kept his distance. He knew what she was and his wisdom bade him keep his mouth shut.

Myra saw that he was dead between the legs. Except for Herman, it was a comfortable warm arrangement.

Myra at this point was not into conning any of the Mandelbaums (except for the little con of not messing around with Herman, who, she knew, knew). She was busy learning something. The emotions they showed to each other, and the ones they reserved, were very different from those on tap at the Shultis menage. Myra's people were so cold, so orderly, they sliced the roast-beef paper-thin, they never touched when greeting, they were all about mailing greeting-cards on every occasion. Myra could contrast her own avidity and spirit against the fleshiness of the Mandelbaums and the thin-bloodedness of her own kin. In some way, she felt better in the jungle of the Mandelbaum flesh. She hung out with them, came there after school, enjoyed rapping with Mrs. Mandelbaum and Heather. She knew that her little pointy face was almost too different from their round, freckly fairness. When she was balling with Mike, she could always visualize how she looked with him, as if she were viewing the whole thing from the sidelines. It turned her on. Their difference, each from each.

She was an addict by the time she met Edward. Not addicted to any particular thing, but to many things. A Catholic, looking for other patterns to fit into. An ex-Catholic finding rituals. An addict, looking for a habit. An accident, looking for where to happen. Into, and out of, hard drugs, into and partly out of speed, messing around a lot with acid and digging it, all the time pot, pot, pot; and then she met Edward—who was himself an edge, a move somehow into danger, and she leapt for it, for him. She had no name for it, it felt right, she had no realization of why she went for him, or stayed around for more. She knew only that Mike wasn't enough, that she wanted to have both him and Mike, and, smart together chick that she was, she would and could have both. She was nineteen, she had her shit together, she knew where it was at, she was as hip as anyone, so she could. Can do. Did.

CHAPTER
22

(Parts of the dialogues herein have been translated, where necessary, directly from the Hintereub dialect into the Eloquatian.)

Edward got a call from old school buddy Marty, who wanted to come up to Trois with his wife for the weekend. So what if it was the beginning of the summer crowds and the bus trip took a half hour longer than off-season; he wanted to talk to Edward, and he needed to get the hell out of the City. Edward told Marty the house was empty, at least for a few days (both Ellen and Myra were busy with other things; neither of them had been in touch with him that week thus far, so he could assume he could keep the house free). He told Marty they could come on up. Friday would be good.

At the last minute, Edward felt he didn't want them to stay at the house with him. A sense of malaise, a wish for his own privacy, a sense of encroachment—so much of his time alone

174

seemed to have been preempted by Myra's presence, lately
. . . He walked over to the Clover Motel to see if Brian could
give him a room for Marty and Marie. As he walked, he
realized that he was valuing these few days without either
Myra or Ellen around. He valued their absence, his total own
presence. A great feeling, this, being alone, being off to himself, in his own home and out, beholden to no one for attention or affection, for his time or his thoughts or emotions. Now
if he could get Marty and Marie a room, then he could get
together with them and they could talk and he would not
have to have them in the house with him, everyone tripping
all over each other. Good idea.

But Brian at the Motel had no rooms. No possibility of one,
either. Edward walked over to the Erin, definitely a second
choice (Marty would hate it, it was all plastic, real cheap shit,
but what the hell) and there were no rooms available there
either. Nor at the Hotel, or the Inn. By now, Edward was dis-
passionately observing his own panic. "I guess I'm the Inn for
tonight," he smiled, feeling fierce and desperate. They were
due to arrive in ten minutes. The afternoon had gone and it
was almost 6 o'clock. The town full of cars of people up from
The City, all the Long Island and Brooklyn license plates; the
Superette still open and would be for three more hours, on
their account. An atmosphere of impending barbecues. He was
depressed. He was getting a headache. What the hell. What
was he getting so het up about, he knew Marty for years,
what's the big deal . . .

The bus from the City arrived. Marty got off, alone, carrying
a canvas bag. Edward caught himself resenting that Marty
had not driven up. What kind of a guy is it that reaches 38
years of age and doesn't drive his own car if he wants to get
someplace. The guy *used* to drive his ass off, how come—A
man who has his ass in gear, Edward thought, should have his
own goddam *car* . . . So Marty was alone. No wife. What the
hell. Edward reached out for Marty and shook hands, grabbed
the other man's shoulder with a solid thwack, bid him welcome. How the hell *are* ya, man, how ya been . . . Where's
the wife? Marty, shorter by half a foot than Edward, stocky,

175

wide of forehead, tanned, looked as if he'd been on vacation already. Jesus, you look *great*. You been taking care of yourself! What you been doing? Sun-lamp at the Club, Marty told him, smiling up at him. But Jesus, I needed to get the hell out! My old lady is driving me crazy. I left her back there. She wanted to come, but . . .

Let's have a beer, Edward said quickly, thinking, this'll get us a little space before he feels like we should get into any kind of deep talk . . . I'm not ready. Not with Marty. Not with anybody. But maybe especially not with Marty; *not now*.

The bar was fuller than in the Spring season: mostly men, tonight, and lined up two or three deep at the bar, so that there was almost no aisle space for the two men to get through. Marty wanted to sit at a booth. Edward said no. They would have to talk then. He wanted none of it. At least not just yet. He wanted to lick his wounds, and he didn't even know the name of the wounds yet, just knew the feel of the pain and the smell of his own blood. Maybe part of it was about Ellen, he was thinking. Beer, he said to Fred; two, make it; one for my friend here, you remember Marty, he hollered over the noise and motion.

Ellen; yes; what was it; she was really pissed off at him lately; she was avoiding him, that was it, ever since the abortion. Things had been strange between them since then. He missed her. As simple as that. Even when she was talking to him, on the street, things were different. As if she weren't really talking *to* him, *with* him, but alongside him. Nothing like it used to be. Different now, for the last weeks. Since then. Just since *then* . . . Marty was here. He needed something. They finished a second beer, and a third, without saying much. There was no way to fend it off any longer. Let's get going, Marty, Edward said. Let's head out.

They walked the long walk back to Edward's place, through the clear, bright night. Marty saying how good it was to be back in this air again, the town looked good, what a relief to breathe real air again, Jesus he'd been missing this sort of sky, he thought Edward hadn't changed much—a mildly nervous patter with an edge of agitation just under the surface pleasure. They picked up two six-packs at the Superette. *Good* to be here, Marty said, Jesus I hate the City sometimes! How come not *all* the time, Edward asked, I hate it all the time! So do I, really, pretty much, said Marty, but I get some goodies too, and I can never get things to the point where we can get out, much as I want to, you know? I know, said Edward, not knowing. Not believing it. Not wanting what was going to follow. The Story, whatever it was, whatever Marty had brought up here to his home town, to lay on his oldest friend. But what about me, Edward was thinking, what in hell am I going to say to you. And how much do you want to hear of what I say. I know you. I know what you're made of. You're Cancer, you won't want to hear what I have to say, what I'm thinking. No matter what it is. It's going to have to be all your trip, hours of it . . .

As soon as they were back in Edward's kitchen, Marty asked him for a joint. Just to get out loose, he said. They smoked. Edward figuring it would help. Marty focussed on the kitchen (painted that bright blue by Myra last Easter when she was on vacation and constantly up on speed and stoned and busy). Marty said he liked the color, liked the changes in the place. Last time he'd been here was when Edward was still with Kathy, just before the second boy was born, Marty had fallen by for an hour, just passing through, hadn't wanted really to get into anything, just to say hello. And his wife wasn't with him then, either.

Then, Edward was thinking, *then,* when he was with Marie and I was still with Kathy. But Marie is never around; why? Kathy gone; he would have to tell Marty about Ellen, about Myra; was Marty still with Marie, or what? What was he saying. Edward tuned in.

"I don't know what in hell she wants. I don't even know who she is any more, if I ever did. She's shut me out. Somehow. Whatever I do—isn't exactly wrong, it's just never exactly *right.* You know? I can do the same things I've been doing for six years and now it's suddenly not right any more!" He shrugged and moved impatiently, making rings on the table with his beer-mug. Edward stared at him. So. Marie was wising up to Marty. Or was she. What was he saying now, ". . . ignores me completely. As if I weren't even in the room. I say something and it's as if no one spoke at all, what the hell. Or she looks right through me. But can you imagine what it's *like* when that happens in bed." He stopped, wanting what he said to have shock value, wanting a response from Edward.

Edward was not shocked. Just listening. He had part of the number already. Marty-the-User. Marty, the guy who'd blame anybody but himself for what was happening. A refusal, but very subtle. Marty, who wanted everything to go for him always, whose big thing had always. been comfort, then pride and security (Edward thought then about Myra, the Great Risk-Taker, what a laugh, she'd run *him* over the coals, wouldn't she, wonder if even *she* could reach him where he was, all shelled in and cozy). Edward remembered the one time he'd visited them in the City. The image of their life that he'd gotten then, how firm it was, how clever, how slick. How dead. Well then. What could it be now. Probably just like what had gone down between himself and Kathy—only their own version.

Static. Marty always wanted things to stay the same. Wanted things to go along as usual, he'd gotten used to the pattern he'd set up, the pattern of Marty-and-Marie-and-the-kids; he'd set it up for his own comfort, got it all snug, gotten set in it, his shell, his Cancer Creature Comfort shell—and Marie, let's see, she was Spring, wasn't she, Gemini, yes, busy and active and flippy, she'd probably gotten fed the hell up. But what could she do. What would Marty let her do. Not likely he would let her go or even talk about it. He wasn't about to talk to *her* about it . . .

Marty looked good. Here he was, talking as if he were suffering his ass off, that slight whine to his voice, and he looked better now than four years ago, better than when he said he was getting everything out of life that he wanted! Then, he had been so smug. Gave out the word that anybody who stayed in Wittgenburg was really *crazy*, they had *the* life in The Big City, just that shade of superiority Edward had always felt put off by in the old days when they were in school together. Marty's girls were always the prettiest, the best lays, the richest, &c. As if they had to be. Marty needed them to be. So Edward let them be. It didn't threaten him, Marty's need to have the best or be the best. That understanding had been part of the base of their friendship. So many people wouldn't put up with that kind of shit from Marty. Edward had always liked him anyway, for his warmth, affectionate energy, his constancy as a friend. So Edward had wound up Marty's only close friend in town. Neither of them was easy. But by now Edward had changed. Fallen out of the pattern of having to understand what it was that Marty meant when Marty talked, under the bravado. He had to reach back twenty years to hear what Marty was saying. To feel what his friend was feeling, under that. A long uneasy trip . . .

"Jesus, man, you want to hear what I think? It sounds like more of your old bullshit!" He turned to Marty.

"What the fuck do you mean?" Marty snapped.

"Life is marvelous, you got it all by the ass, nobody has a better life, like you always have to have it—and on the other hand, something right dead center, something very important, is all wrong, and you won't face it!—because if you did, it would give the lie to the rest of your Big Story!"

"What the hell—?" Marty stopped and turned to him, for a second. His fist clenched and unclenched on the table.

"You look good. Better than you did last time I saw you; better than probably in your whole life. So how bad can you be hurting?"

"Jesus, Ed, you don't *know*—"

"If I don't, it's because you aren't saying it. You aren't saying it to *me*, straight, so you damn well for sure aren't saying it out to *yourself*—or to Marie. Maybe *especially* to Marie . . ."

Marty's fist was by now clenched and staying that way. "So *what* if I look great? It's part of my *job* to look like I'm in good shape! Besides, I *do* feel great—I mean, in one way, I— You think because I look good and feel okay, this thing with Marie isn't doing me in?"

"*Nothing's* doing you in, old buddy. Nothing ever has, and

chances are, nothing ever will—because you're still taking *damn* good care of Marty—through anything, keeping the shell tight, just like you did when we were kids. It's not only not getting to you, it's sliding right the hell off your shell. Only reason I ever saw you caring about anybody else was because it might make *you* uncomfortable if *they* were uncomfortable." Edward said it all flatly, quietly, firmly. Hoping. To be heard. Marty sat still, expressionless.

"I mean, look, Marty, who *are* you, man? I mean, is your life really who you are? or even were?"

"Now what the hell's *that* supposed to mean?"

"It looks to *me* like whatever it is you've got with Marie has been good for you . . . you like some parts of it . . ."

"Jesus, of *course* I do! She's my *wife*—"

"Yeah, yeah, that's a big part of it. *Your* wife. Everything is always 'your' this and 'your' that, Jesus, I can't believe how totally self-centered—"

Marty was there this time. "The shit you say. That broad's had everything from me. Everything in the *world.* There hasn't been a thing she's wanted—nothing—she hasn't gotten —Jesus, she's got me *crazy,* I tell you. If I *didn't* take care of *myself*—you just don't know. She doesn't cook, she doesn't supervise the maid, she's got this bug she wants to get out and '*do* things,' whatever the hell *that* means, to hell with me or the kids, who *knows* what she's into, half the time I come home from work and she's not there, no one knows where she is, the kids're parked with some neighbor in the building, no food, the fridge empty, Jesus, what the hell! *I* should be the one who's drinking, and it's her, there's always a half-empty glass of straight Scotch around . . . But Jesus, she's not even really into *drinking!* It's something else. The goddam fucking bitch!—and it's not *that,* either, if that's what you think—she's not into fucking someone else, not even that! I *know* Marie, goddam it, I'd smell it on her, I'd be able to tell, in *fact,* that crazy broad, would you believe, she's a better lay than ever! We've had a better sex life the last few months than all the years since we got together, even better than at the beginning

180

—that's *all!* Oh Jesus—I think I'm going out of my mind. It just—I don't get it. I just—don't—get it."

Marty stopped, run down and out of breath. Edward moved from his angle of listening, shrugged a shoulder and then got up and walked around the kitchen. Pretense of opening a cabinet and getting out a box of pretzels. (A box of pretense, he was thinking, or, how can one guy while seeming so sincere be conning himself so heavy!) What was he really going through, so hard to hear Marty through all the words . . . So whoever told Marty it was supposed to be easy, Edward thought, and chuckled.

"What the fuck are you laughing at, man," Marty said, low and dark, turning toward the sound, furious.

"Listen," Edward said, feeling soft and benevolent, "Whoever told you anything makes sense? The only 'sense' is your goddam sense of perspective, and maybe even a sense of humor, which I'm a bit short on myself, right now, tell you the truth . . . Whoever told you things stay still, even if you want them to? Listen. Are you the same guy you were six years ago?"

"*Yeah,* I am! You're goddam fucking-A *right,* I am!"

"Well then, you might just be the exception that proves the rule. But I doubt it. Though I can see where you'd try like all hell to maintain the status quo. Ah well—maybe you are. Maybe you just goddam well *are.* All you fucking Cancers— go try to explain to a Cancer that something in a house can change besides adding to the furniture—that sometimes *people* change—Jesus, I ought to know how hard that is to realize —I'm an earth sign—Listen. Do you *really* think that you're the same as when you married Marie?—that *she's* the same as six years ago? Nobody any different?"

"Now wait a minute. I didn't say that. I have a better job now. I make six times as much money! We have the apartment. The kids."

"You're too goddam *much.* You self-centered blind bastard. You motherfucking self-centered blind bastard," Edward said, angrily, furiously, fondly, not to Marty's face, off into the room, toward a cabinet door. Thinking, maybe I mean myself as well . . . just maybe.

"How? *How?* I want to know what I could have given her, given any of them, that this whole world has to offer, the whole goddam *world,* that I haven't given them. I break my balls at the office, kiss ass and push people around and play the goddam game to the hilt and get paid goddam well for it, make it work for me, and now you're sitting here, in this god-forsaken small town in the hills, goddam hicksville is what it is, telling me that she—that I—she doesn't even *talk* to me— she—"

"She, she, she," Edward said, blandly. "She, indeed. I get the feeling that all you'd ever talk to her about, if you *did* talk together, is you, you, and *you.* I get the idea that there hasn't been *anyone* talking to *anyone* in that sane-looking insane asylum of an apartment of yours for years; am I right?"

He was looking at Marty's and Marie's apartment, posh, big, flashy, view of the East River, fake brownstone beams, lots of modern art, doorman; Marty was in industrial public relations, home town boy broke through and made good, came in solid, Marty the nephew of Wittgenburg's all-powerful Sally and Herman Mandelbaum, high school buddy of Ed Richthoven; fellow road-runner, beer-guzzler; but Marty had always been different from Edward; was it that thing about being a Jew, neither of them had known there *was* any difference till they hit high school and there were the two fraternities, one for Jews, one for Protestants only, and of course the Newman Club for the Catholic kids, all this division, so early, in a tiny town like Wittgenburg . . . So that when the Difference hit, it hit Marty hard, so hard that he wound up changing his name, wound up marrying as blonde and tall and Christian-looking a chick as he could find on the New York scene (took him a few years to find someone he would feel he looked "right" with, someone who would help him to "pass," which he needed to do, someone who *wouldn't pick up on his game*).

"—anyhow," Edward was continuing, "I thought you said when you phoned that you and Marie were supposed to be coming up here *together*. That indicates *some* degree of communication—"

"*Can* the sarcasm. I thought it would be a good idea. She did, too, at least at first. You know how little time she's ever spent up here . . ."

"I'd be surprised if she was *ever* allowed to come here. The scene of the crime. But then, you'd just love showing off your Christian captive, wouldn't you—"

"What the fuck do you mean by that?"

"Just this: why would you want her to *really* see where and what you come from? In the face of all the stuff you've sold her. The whole bill of goods. Everything's been some goddam *image* of who you are, not who you *are*—do you see what I mean? —and made it all very clear, too clear in fact, you want her only because she happens to fit into that new goddam image of who you are *now*, and who you *want* to be—it's all got absolutely nothing to do with who *she* is. Who she might really *be*, herself. Who *is* she? Do you know?"

Edward was getting tight and frustrated, even through the easing effect of the pot and the beer; how do you tell somebody who's never dropped acid about that insight that lays off all the masks, all the rôles, what do you do when you suddenly see that the other guy is into playing rôles, has his old lady into rôle-playing too, and then has the nerve to wonder why she's turning off him, looking for something real to do with her life,

and then it hit Edward, Ellen's never dropped acid but I have, thanks to my little gaudy Myra-bitch; how can I have the goddam fucking *nerve* to sit here preaching to Marty; even if I'm right about him, what about what I'm doing, myself? In my own life? Putting Ellen in some kind of box, not caring about how she feels except as it affects me; avoiding thinking about what *she* went through—what she's saying to me by moving aside, by avoiding me . . . He wanted to concentrate on this. To center on it and work it through. He felt its importance.

But Marty was busy jumping with what Edward had just said. Fully Cancer, he was determined to keep it centered on himself, deep. Full speed ahead, Edward thought; okay, baby, let's do your trip, I've got plenty of time for mine. I move slower and I can wait. I'll damn well *have* to.

"Shit. *Shit,* man. I know who my wife is! You mean it? You think I don't know who my wife is? You think I don't give a damn for my *wife?*"

"You give plenty of a damn for your 'wife,' Marty," Edward said, in an exaggerated slowness, "just that you maybe never really stopped to notice who your 'wife' happens to *be.*"

They both stopped. Sound of a beer-can being opened. Sweat-beads on Marty's forehead, though the summer night is cool.

"Well, what the fuck," Martin said, slowly.

"Yeah," Edward said, into the silence. "Yeah."

But Marty wasn't about to follow the insight and hang in with it. He would try to mess it over: "What do *you* think she wants?" he asked, petulantly.

"I sure wish you'd do your own work, for a change! Try this for starters: from what I've seen of Marie, at least up till very recently she must've been nice and orderly and wanted just whatever *you* wanted her to want, not an inch or an idea more than that . . . Just for a *change,* you might try asking *her* what she wants! Only I keep getting the feeling that the way you asked her, it would be more of your telling her what it was *you* wanted her to want! If you see what I mean. And I bet you do. And her just trying to hold off till she understood what you wanted her to say. You know, you're a pretty manipulative bastard, when you want to be . . ."

"You mean when I *have* to be." Caught. And then chuckling, embarrassed, seeing being caught, the whole thing opened. "Jesus. I see what you mean. Holy shit. Holy . . . sweet . . ."

"Do me a favor, will you. Don't say 'Jesus' again, okay?"

Marty stopped. Shut. Open and shut. Edward got up from the table again. It was past ten now. He felt drained. He wanted to get away, get back in tune with his quiet self. He had to. He hoped that Marty would stay put and put some of this together for his own use. A chance to be taken. Could one expect it from a guy this age, was there room. A guy this age who couldn't get his ass together enough to drive a car up from the City. As he went toward the door, Edward remembered when they both used to go like blazes around the Reservoir (how it had taken years for both of them to learn there was another way to say it than ending in *-vore*), how the guy *used* to drive, goddam it, what happened to all that push—

But then, who the hell am I to talk, he thought. Marty had got his ass out of Wittgenburg. Marty was married to the same broad he started the trip with, and he did seem to continue to dig her, if for the wrong reasons. Okay, so he'd married later than most of the guys in the class . . . Maybe they would split. So what, it was the fashion nowadays. So what. Marty would have a bad time if they did. He never could make adjustments. Their way of running to some kind of concealment, the Cancer trip of protection and evasion—funny how the original Jew-boy had turned it into having money and buying art and Passing, and that whole game. Somehow it fit into his Cancer number. Jesus, but he took everything so goddam tight and grabby—scared? Maybe Marty could catch on that he didn't have to take everything in as if he had to own the whole world. Even though it was his sign to try to . . . Ah, Edward thought, here I am doing *my* sign, taking Marty too seriously. Losing perspective.

Edward leaned his head back around into the kitchen. "I'm going to split for a while. I feel like a walk. Back in a while." Good. Marty didn't move, just nodded his head. He'd stay there, and maybe put something together . . . When Edward got outside, he breathed deeply. He walked along the path back into the woods, his feet placed so solidly on the earth that they seemed to indent it. He wanted to connect with his earth again. Wanted to feel like he was part of a mountain again. The feel of his own weight, not the feel of his friend's weight upon him.

His own pain was still very much there, he wanted to work on the problem about Ellen, her feelings, the abortion, all of it; he did not want to escape it. He would work through by himself, slowly, ponderously, in his own way. His mother had taught him the value of considering himself a symbol of all people of his sign, thereby using the power of it to the fullest. But in order to do that, he *had* to be alone. Now, walking the field back of his house, he felt, for the first time in almost a year, totally, blessedly cleanly, strongly alone. A man who belonged to no one; who, at this time, finally, somehow, belonged with no one. A good feeling. He felt clean and whole, he belonged only to himself.

CHAPTER

23

O yes o yes Ellen was weaving. O yes o yes the wool is made of blood. Shapes of large and small moons Streaks and each moon streak a stream of blood that was not a child never—O yes

NO.

Soft wool into flesh into glass breaking/ the sound of samisen thin as glass clavicle of tiny bone song breaking like glass wires The glass voice saying NO.

Light of the moon the blood moon Cold cold not-voice empty absent You are the cold side of the moon I am lost in snow The warm light of then The then light of the violin warm but always the *No*. The samisen sound of No.

So little blood such Great Silence and life gone into it A person a Being ah Jesus a baby even as Jesus even as you as I.

Was weaving. The reds were blood the yellows were soft as amber sun flesh. Could make an image a small body from the stuff Was all fabric the same Not on earth of the earth Was all fabric made of flesh of blood of bone

NO. Dissonance cacophony   The simple noises of the street The whirring mechanical world   Going along as usual out there   The Land of Metal. Ah she had let cold metal into her body instead of flesh to take flesh   and it had taken. What right to live now that she had taken life   She would die   She was dying   Telling in the weaving about it   She was alive in her body   She was

weaving. A fabric of flesh. Skull body bones who lives who dies. Who decides. The White Doctor immaculate in decisions. As if   as if   I and the White Doctor with the NO the NO the *No* in his hand   In a room full of blood air full of a cry of some human not to live. Ordinary operating room into tomb,

full of gentle waves of blood. No sound as soft bones scraped out from softer envelope. To have destroyed someone else's tiny bones O my God. "Thy perfect symmetry" and o God what music what colors to tell it the caco-phony. Violin based on death of cats and of colts like Wird and Marchwind. Some machine said it could hear the sound of live trees felled. An enormous music from her trunk—

Coming back from the hospital and after the blinded weeping of the long train she got into her car that time and the clock of her eyes off kilter, down the familiar roads and then the close road and then in God's own name a beagle pup had started across the road TOO CLOSE a baby blindly unaware of metal "place where no dog had ever been"   She jammed on the brakes and no thought

slam spurt smash and over

into the lane of oncoming   *Jesus. God.* hit this car and then that and glanced off all. Went blindly toward space a hundred feet   Turned back. The pup lay there on its side   Blood flowing from its mouth   Dead

The drivers of the glanced-off cars off to the side trying to understand   And Ellen crying Howling not being able to see but still with wisdom understanding

blood from the pup and from her own body flowing flowing   She went to a house nearby to ask for Help   First to Edward but no answer there (the same NO, was it) then to ask for Don Bowart to come in his patrol car   Had gone to school with her and Frey   He would know how to help   Came and did know. Arm around her even as he took down all the terrible information   And then she could tell him the rest only leaving out who was the father of the dead the missing baby for whom she was making red tears.

In her head and also out of the eye saw it   Saw the blood flow from the mouth of the pup as he went   Seemed to be flowing from the mouth of her own babe   seemed to be flowing from her own eyes/ from her own eye-shaped lips between her legs.

Don made her sit down "We can't keep on with this now can we, you have a lot to do, you're gonna be just fine, come on now Ellie," and his arm strong around her His hand patting her back to comfort

and where all this time was Edward   Where for God's own sake   Off with Myra probably and *NO*where. (The *NO* again.)

Done. The other drivers got back into their cars—one of them hardly scratched, made no fuss, the other a left fender gash just as her own car had   And they were gentle with her

The owners of the pup showed up   They were in their sixties and saw everything differently   Kept saying Look my dear it's all right it's only a dog   It's not as if it were a person   And Ellen wanting to tell them, No, it's more than a dog, it's a life, it's a loss, a loss, *I have lost*—

They kept saying "an accident" and so did Don

and finally she just got back into the car and drove slowly back home almost believing all of them

Had a cup of tea and then went over to the farm where she had been born where Frey lived now the other half of her duality Frey who would never have or lose a child Frey who was a child forever and an ancient forever   And the look of Frey's eyes comforted her finally   for the while

*   *   *

Now weaving and it was of this design and fabric. Now she wanted nothing so much as to take all this folding stuff and bloodied as it was throw it into Edward's face. Proof. She had wanted to give him in a package the soaked sanitary pads she had worn. Would he believe, would he suffer at all, would he feel . . .

She was fully conscious during the abortion despite a shot and two pills they gave her. When they told her to relax and just go along with the medication instead of tensing up, she had been unable to reply, but in answer had held out her hand toward the nurse, who was the only other woman in that ghastly room, and spread out the fingers tight and taut till they looked like a scream—a starfish-shaped scream, silent sound of a woman pinioned and impaled . . .

Weeks ago. Now her fingers were busy with the weaving. She got up and went out to the garden. That always helped; that ought to help. She cut three tea-roses and brought them into the kitchen and set them into a tiny clear green bottle. Smell of them came to her. She put up some water to boil, it would be good to eat something, she felt herself moving in the gestures that would give her back her own life.

And when the eggs were done, she put them under cool water so she could handle them to crack them. But then there was the feel of them. Feel of the egg still warm. Egg still warm from the hen's body, as she remembered from the farm when she was young, and something she had talked about with Frey and with Edward as one of the special warm feelings about life that were left over from their childhoods. Ah, egg still warm . . . and so again she wept, still the salt flow, and still the slight blood spotting from her body; wept for the lost child, for herself, for her ripped body and for the ripped dreams, for the ache she would always feel, dreams of that baby she would never hold, never be able to raise, love, teach, nurse, embrace, watch, to care for, to mother . . .

Right here, in this her kitchen, the smell of tea-roses, would they always bring back this moment, this time of agony, would she smell tea-roses in her dreams of that baby that never breathed, that never won the right to life,

all her wisdoms deserted her. All of the calmness, the thoughtfulness, the rationality that had kept her moving toward the abortion weeks ago—all the sanity, gone, gone, done,

because of the dreams. Because, in one way, each sleep was

good and took her further from that day; but then sometimes the dreams—because she had, at the last minute, told Edward, and he had said NO, or she thought she had told him and she thought she remembered his having said NO,

what part of it was dream and what part reality,

all she knew for sure now was that she dreamed and dreamed about it,

the dreams bred a bitterness and a misery and there was no stopping them, she had blocked out the accident with the dog almost completely except for the reminders in the dreams, where the baby had a pup's face or head once, and the pup had the eyes of a human infant and did not whimper but cried, infant-like . . .

❖ ❖ ❖

For a week or more, after the abortion, her life had gone on seemingly well, an almost normal procession of activities, excepting, of course, that she did not see Edward, except briefly. And that was without incident, without reference. And then the dream, and others, had taken over, and she refused to see him. He seemed no longer innocent of inflicting pain. He was no longer someone she could let into her life.

She became furious with him, blaming him. And this was the feeling that came out along with the sorrow. Once, she dreamed he killed a child with his own hands, with his own body. And one time she dreamed she watched him taking a knife to his penis, and she screamed, *Don't,* and she realized in that moment the extent of her love for him, as it had carried, below and beyond her fury and her need to blame him. But then she blocked the love out, too. Somehow, her own survival depended on her being able to be angry with Edward. At least for now.

There was a terrible melancholy in being alone. She could have gone to Edward at any time, she sensed this, she did not want to believe this, did not want to share her grief. Therefore, she was her own prisoner. She saw him, walking about Wittgenburg, and part of her soul reached to him, and she gave a cool hello and turned and walked on. Trying to avert;

trying not to notice his expression. She had no way to reach for him. She said to herself that there was no man on earth knew what it was to lose a baby this way. What sort of pain could he know, to equal this. She could not tell him any of this. The days passed and the time grew thick between them, palpable and more definite as each night fell. As she healed, the scar tissue formed. With each sleep, especially the dreamless ones, she rose into another way of life, a way that did not include Edward.

Marty asked Edward if he could stay on for a week or so. It was all right with Edward. Things had gotten better between the two men, and within each of them. A loosening. Good talking, and Edward had been able to take his time for himself, without which he would have had to deny Marty.

Marty had it in mind to stop by and say hello to his family, finally, including dear old Aunt Sally and Uncle Herman. "It's not that I owe them anything, all of them," he said to Edward over breakfast rolls and coffee at the house, one morning. "I know they all fucked me over, in their way. Sins of omission and commission. It's something else. It's—like—that I look at my folks and I realize that she had to pay some heavy dues to get to where she's at—they had their own shit to do; so what if it was different from mine, it was a tough trip, when I stop to consider it . . ."

"Yeah, I know," said Edward, thinking of his own father, how tight and tough he'd been, and of Marty's father and uncle, "the Great Nutsless Wonders," as Marty had called them the other night when he was drunk and bitter. What kind of men were they all, on earth!—and what kind of image of Man had they been able to give their sons . . . a bequeathing of violence or of weakness, of fear, of avarice instead of benevolence, the survival in a moving away from nature . . .

"Well, it's okay; what they couldn't do for us or give us, life's done and given," he said to Marty. "The Old Ones are dehorned, aren't they. I wonder if they *ever* saw us as we see them. Or even tried to." Thoughts of the old bull mooses. Flesh settling toward earth. What wisdom had been gained . . . Edward was reading a lot lately, suddenly. Last week, after he and Marty had gotten through the beginning breakthrough of Marty's upheaval about Marie, and where his head was at and could be at, Edward ran from all the talk, ran from Marty and everyone else, sought his Capricorn solitude as sustenance. Ran at first toward his music, always the prime source. And then slowly went back into a couple of books he'd begun months ago and had never found time or motivation to go back to. And when he had taken his time thus, he quieted down and could come back to being with Marty again.

The two men took a long walk through the woods. That favorite walk, along the narrow path through the woods that edged the fields back of the houses of the town. As they went, silently now and in tune with each other and with the day, heavy with Summer, each man softened out further, into the land in which each had been born. These were familiar woods. But neither of them felt it as totally familiar. Now, with the new insights, there was surprise in the familiar.

As they rounded a curve, Edward ahead of Marty, they saw, off to the left, the first full, clear view of the mountains that surrounded the town. Set crisply against the dark curve and crescents of the hills were three tall birches and, alongside them, a tiny, spring-fed, shallow pool, in which the birches and dark hills were reflected. Edward stopped, bent down, and gathered three triangular rocks from the scattering on the path. Then placed them, thus, set aside from the others, clear, stacked, so as to mark a spot, if one noticed that they were not a natural arrangement.

"What—?" Marty asked.

"It's for others to notice, when they come this way. I mean, it's to say that there's something unusual to see. To notice. Here."

"Why three; and why that way?"

"Because it's not natural. It's intentional and it looks it. It's not an arrangement that could just happen."

"Where'd you learn that?"

"Frey taught me. You know: Anne, Ellen's sister."

Marty didn't reply. They walked on. It had often been like this when they were boys in the town, and much younger men. Each knew something that the other needed, wanted. Marty had nuances, turns of mind that Edward could appreciate; he was softer and more rounded, he had subtleties. Edward had strong dynamic gestures and a weight of perspective that Marty valued. Each had sought the lessons and used them, one way or another, willingly or not, through the early years in Wittgenburg. None of it conscious or planned. Always a translation necessary before each could use the new knowledge in his own life. Their contrast was the fabric of their friendship.

Marty needed now to get back into nature. He would have valued the seashore more, as Cancer, but this was good, his place of origin, this was almost enough. He was telling Edward that for the most part he was fed up with what he'd seen of what Trois people had become. All of them so *alike*, no sense of adventure, no perspective to make them push themselves up against the risk coffins of the cities. And how they tried to keep their children within their mold! "Jesus, Mom looks *terrible*. All gone to fat and all! She got some interior decorator up from Albany and you wouldn't believe what that house looks like. Looks like the whole house's got a corset on. And Sally and Herman are disgusting. She won't leave off Mike or Heather. Finger in every pie; runs Herman's business, her brothers' too, can't let any of them wipe their ass themselves, you know?"

Edward passed him a lit joint. "Aren't all parents like that?" Edward was remembering his own heavy-handed father and hypochondriacal mother. "I always would rather talk to *your* father, I remember," he told Marty. "At *least* the man was warm, he had a joke to tell sometimes, he was out in the open where you could see him! He worked hard, you knew it, but he had time for a kid. I always felt he had time to talk to me! Where my own father didn't."

"That stuff looks better in retrospect, and besides, he never one time said anything intelligent to me. He probably saved it all for impressing my friends. Especially the 'goyim' friends. I think everybody else's parents look like the real article! Listen, now that I got kids I know what kind of job it is, and I'm lousy at it. I'm just as bad as my father was, only different. Oh, *sure*, I wish I could do better—if I knew what doing better was . . . there *is* no 'better', I think. Jesus, my big kid is still sucking his thumb, would you believe—you know what that's like? Sometimes I want to reach out and grab him and punch, and sometimes I know just exactly how he feels—what kind of world is it, can I brag on the world as a really great place, he should leave off the thumb and jump out into the chaos without his thumb in his mouth? Shit. *Let* him suck his thumb! I wish I could, too."

"For sure you couldn't do worse than what Myra's dear Catholic folks've done." Marty had met Myra the other night. Edward had seen her at the Pub and the three had had drinks and gone for a walk. Afterward, Marty had had strong opinions: envy, that Edward was with such a young vibrant physical chick; and apprehension, that that kind of trip might only end in disaster.

"Not *this* man," Edward had said. "I know what I'm doing. I know who she is, and what she's about—don't you give me *any* credit?—and anyhow, it's not *supposed* to last! We just have to learn from each other . . ." Marty had given him a sharp glance, and refrained. Their experience of women was different. Marty had been with several girls through high school, a couple during his army time; they all looked like Marie. He always claimed to know a variety of women. Edward came to women philosophically, an attitude Marty didn't understand. Marty came to them as if they were possessions.

Edward was saying now, "Listen, I've got an idea. You know Myra already. Now, Ellie's different—Ellie's nothing like what you imagine her to be. You only remember how she was in high school. And she's—well, different now. Why don't you come and meet her? We could walk past her house on the way back through the Van Bogart woods."

He wanted an excuse to go to Ellen. And he needed for Marty to see her now, as she was. Maybe it was to offset the idea of himself as the kind of man who ran with girls like Myra. He didn't want to be seen that way. Jesus, he thought to himself, am I ashamed to be identified with Myra?—and if I am, what the hell—why am I letting myself be identified with her, in this town? But I've *had* to see her, he answered himself. She draws me, she pulls me—she's so bloody *alive!* Crazy and sharp and bloody. Makes me more alive. Keeps me away from my own pain. It's what she does with the pain . . . Myra, saying once to him, "Stop *caring* so much, you silly serious dude, can't you see none of it makes sense except having fun?" And a flash view of her tiny white pointed breasts with the tannish nipples, the skinny-baby-body still seeming adolescent, thin ribs and belly, lean shanks and narrow agile hips . . .

And they walked then out of the woods to where he could see Ellen's house. The lights were on. The town was sullen in Summer heat of early evening. Smell of dinners just eaten, sound of peepers from the swampy pond just to the left of the road over near Zimmerman's place. Where he and Marty had caught frogs when they were kids. All the walking visitors out for their after-dinner strolls, everyone over fifty, all the Irish visitors and some of the townsfolk, the ones who hadn't the money or the wish to get away for the Summer, or those who were making money from the Summer.

"Good," Edward said, as they approached the house. "She's home. Sometimes she leaves the other lights on when she's out, but she never leaves the kitchen light on when she's not there. Funny habit . . ." He enjoyed revealing to Marty this intimacy he had with Ellen's life. But when they got to the house, he knocked at the front door and waited.

She came slowly, having seen who it was through the front windows on her way to the door. Saw his face, with its odd expression, and then saw Marty, just behind Edward.

"Hi, Ellie, thought you might be home, you remember Marty, don't you, Marty Lipschitz?" (Marty quailing at that old name he hated, even though he was in the town where he was so known; he was "Levitt" to the rest of the world, the world he had chosen.)

"Yes," she said, and then, "Yes, how are you, nice to see you . . . do you want to come in?"

"Love to. Love to." Edward was looking at her, at the familiar soft profile of her face and her rounded body. But her mood was raw. This was not what he had come here for. Maybe he had made a mistake, coming here. With Marty.

They followed her. She passed the parlor, led them to the kitchen. Good, Edward thought; she's letting us be kitchen company; yes, well, but she's *cold;* just look at that back . . .

"How've you been?" he asked her, as they pulled chairs up to the kitchen table, where her half-empty cup of tea rested. She gave him a sharp look. "Oh, just *ducky.* Just fine-o. And *you?*" There was no missing her tone.

Marty glanced from Edward to Ellen and back. Then he decided to concentrate on Ellen. Ah, yes, this was clearly something else, Marty was thinking. Quite a jump up from the skinny junkie-looking chippie the other night. *Quite* a different story. Will you look at that body! Jesus, how I love big chicks like this. None of this skinny intense model-looking stuff here; will you look at that chest! and those big wide hips—he felt a gentle hardon begin. Long time since he'd felt like this. Marie's type sure didn't bring him to this, did she! He felt like a teenager. How come this broad hadn't turned him on like this, all those years when he saw her in highschool . . .

He turned to Edward and smiled, guiltily. Forced himself to say, brightly and coolly, to Ellen and Edward together, as if in respect for their unity (he supposed there was a lot going here—even the evident hostility meant there was a lot behind it—) "God, it's been forever since I've wandered around Wittgenburg! Feels like a goddam *century.*"

"How long has it been? How does the old town look to you, Marty?" She was being social. Marty knew she felt his eyes on her body. You'd have to be deaf and blind not to. He didn't think Edward had noticed. His body was already having a discussion with Ellen's. And she was responding. Like fumes from a bowl of incense. But Edward seemed oblivious to what was going on. He was answering Ellen, as if he were speaking for Marty.

Marty watched the two of them. What the hell. This was supposed to be a scene that had been going on for months, according to what Edward had said; okay, but then what was all this semi-formality shit, why was this broad acting like this, and how come Edward had brought him over to meet her if he thought they might get this kind of reception?

Then Marty let go. He was stoned enough by now to stop worrying and lean with whatever it was that was happening. The conversation. He felt himself responding, joining in, just being with two people with whom he had grown up, done the Summer and Winter townie things, lived a lot of years with. All the memories. People. Edward and he even got to riffing about chicks they'd been interested in, balled, taken to dances. The fraternal feeling. The names flowed out and around their heads. Rattermann, and Sauer, and Van Bogart, and Van Wagner; Shultis and Shultz; Lasher, and Boice and the Sickler brothers and the Smith boys, the only twins in their crowd besides Ellen and Anne, (who'd never been much like twins anyhow; Duane and Travis Smith were identical, even traded dates on the sly—) the four Lindas, the three Bonnies and the two Sue Mays, three Waynes and three Johns and it came around to Arthur finally; Marty had to be told about the accident . . .

Ellen got up and set out coffee and a plate with brownies: "Hash in these over here, go with care," she said. "Those over here are regular; eat away. And here's some cheese."

A half-hour more passed. No one was touching any feelings. Only half of what was felt was being said. But then, with the hash and the pot, Marty's pain began to surface. Ellen began to feel angry and fell silent. What the hell, she was thinking.

What is all this jazz. How'm I supposed to keep this up. Edward felt just plain tired, or so he would have called it if forced to define, at this point; he just didn't want to go on with whatever was happening. He was tense and responding to Ellen's tension and rising fury, which moved in slow waves under the surface. She was wondering if he wouldn't ever ask her how she was feeling as if he *meant* it, as if he really wanted to know. Marty felt the heavy vibes in the room; he was feeling rotten and wanted to be able to swing out behind the loosening effect of the drugs, but these two wouldn't let him. *Damn* them.

Edward made the move, finally. "Let's move out. Let's go sit in the front room. I feel like making a fire. I need to watch a fire now."

Ellen was watching him. What was this move. That familiarity of his. How far did that get him, she thought. Not so far, buddy-boy. She was in great pain. They went into the other room. Edward, moving so familiarly around the room, getting the kindling, the newspaper from the pile behind the wood, knowing where everything lived. Marty noticed. How could he help it. Edward was acting as if he lived here.

The fire started, they settled around it, each separated from each. Until: "How's your little nun?" Ellen said, directly to Edward and cutting Marty out.

Ah, so that's where we stand, thought Edward, ah, but she's sore at me. "Quit fucking around," he said, "don't spoil a lovely evening. We don't need your cute mouth at this point; don't get dangerous."

"Dangerous!" she said, ominously. "As if I don't know about danger! It's *you* play a dangerous game, dearie."

"Don't be so lily-white-princess-pure," Edward said drily, not wishing to parry. "Leave it alone. Everything's okay; can't you let it be?"

"That's what you'd like, isn't it. 'Let things be.' Make believe nothing happened. *You* sure get off easy! I wish *I* could." Where was his sense of reality, she wondered. If a piece of him were torn out, how would he be acting now . . .

"Listen," Marty interrupted, "I wish the fuck you two would

get off it, or I can leave. This begins to sound like a very private conversation. Now either you stop or I leave. I tell you what," he said, getting up and moving restlessly around the room, "what we need right now is some music. And for all of us to be quiet and commune with our souls a bit . . . Here we are. How about this?" He held up a record. "I don't know this kind of music like you do, Ed. You pick." He didn't want to be caught in the middle of their games. He didn't have the name of it, but the smell of it was familiar. It had a dark, bloody smell. Just the faintest whiff like what had been going on with him and Marie . . .

Edward, grateful for Marty's move, chose Pergolesi, and the music filled the room. *His* records, here in Ellen's home; and his jacket hanging in the front closet, and his desert boots still under the bed in the room where she slept, where they had slept in deep harmony for so many nights . . .

There was no way for any of them to resist the music. It worked on them and for them. The soft richness of it, the crispness, the intelligence. Edward was walking on it, as if it were his natural element. And Ellen knew quite well she could breathe in it, it was the first clear breath she took this night, as if in a dream she were underwater and breathing nicely. Soft and strong and fine, bassoons, violins, the reminder of other centuries . . .

"What this country really lacks is a sense of history, like in this music," Marty began. "You just can't imagine any country that got its civilization together a thousand years ago having as low a . . ." But the others didn't respond. Ellen was languid, leaning back in her chair, legs loosely arranged, looking over at him through the smoke in the room, her heavy Pisces lids half-covering her glance. She was smiling. Marty caught her and turned it into an eye-contact number. Will you *dig* that woman, he thought, wouldn't I ever want to ball her, *is* she Ed's or what, well, whatever, isn't she something! Edward, turned from them, was facing the midsummer fire, crosslegged before it, back to Marty and profile to Ellen, and so couldn't see the look that passed between them.

In a space of time, Ellen moved into the kitchen and came

201

back with iced coffee, in tall mugs Frey had made and given her. The music continued. The talking could continue. Edward, as always, was able to strengthen and center through the music. And Ellen could respond to what he was saying about this land; nothing else could have reached through to her now.

"*My* town," Ellen was saying, "this is my own little piece of the earth; I don't know *why* it makes a difference, but knowing my father worked the land, knowing Frey's still with the land . . . I guess that's my own sense of history. I don't think this country's really all that different from Holland—or from Germany, where your folks came from; just newer; but it isn't the land itself that's newer—You know," she said, more to Edward this time, finally, "sometimes I feel like I'm part of a long film somebody's made about history; I mean, here I am, in the middle of it, living it, but at the same time—you know? —just a little flash, now and then, once in a while, especially over at Frey's; I can see myself doing the life;—me watching me, sort of . . . a quick *déjà vu*—I'm not *separate,* I'm the same women that lived here before—Jesus, it's hard to describe! . . . that business about the lives we live *instead* of living a life, some of the time . . . at times . . . I can see—you know what I mean?"

"Yes! Yes. I do," Edward said, catching that glimpse of her seeing her own life, glad for the sharing she was permitting.

That's why I love you, she thought, That look you've got right now, my Edward. And the strange way you understand me. The area we go to where there are no words. Edward— if only some traditions could be reversed—in the old days, a woman held a man's hand when he went through the ordeals, the initiations, the trials; she wore his favor, she watched— Edward, Edward, if you could have been there, if you could have held my hand, or seen me through—But we both made it a separated thing, didn't we.—No fault. No blame. I *have* to stop blaming! We are alive *now*—the only time I can change history is now; I can't change our memories or our history . . .

But she did not say any of this aloud. The room was quiet.

202

Neither of the men wanted to disturb her peace now, not after the way the evening had begun. Marty thought Ellen was very stoned, but then he was very stoned as he was thinking it, and he was thinking that he himself was very stoned. He saw his own mind like ripples that overlapped instead of going concentrically outward from a central idea. Several ideas that occurred at the same time, not building but all of the same material, all in motion at the same time. He felt marvelously light and very much in love with himself right now. Laughed at that idea. How could they call this condition "being wrecked" when it was all about building? he thought. I am my own god, he thought. In the old days, the people had beasts and plants for gods; well, I'm a fine beast for sure, so I'll be a god too! I'll be especially my *own* god! Okay, he said to himself, with a grin the others had to notice amid the silence, then if I'm a god, I can do whatever I try to do, even to think about myself as a god!—they say people can't conceive of what a god is like. But wasn't it people who made up that idea?—so then it has to be wrong. If I can think of myself as a god, then I can *be* a god, because I can conceive of myself! so that's *that!*—And he snuggled into his chair, arms around himself, delighted. He loved himself. He loved his mind. Hey hey, he thought, this is quite another kind of love!

Ellen focused on Marty's grin and felt herself grinning in response. She was so light. Both kinds. The light came to her aureole hair from the fire, and touched her fair skin, and the light came from her skull and aureoled outward in the form of hair and came from her body and radiated out from her skin. And her body felt light. She felt she was not touching the floor of the room. She felt she might move to any other plane she chose at this time. If she chose!—and she *would* choose. She rose, and, not saying anything to either of the men, not looking at either of them, moved out of the room and through the little hall and up the stairs. Edward heard her footsteps moving toward her own bedroom. And then no sound.

He and Marty sat companionably. "Well, I guess I'm all talked out," Marty said, not able really to share this part of the trip with Edward. "But boy, I feel *good* . . . God, is it *wild* being back here again! Fantastic!"

"Glad you're here. Glad you came," Edward told him, meaning it. "It feels important that you did." He was really thinking about Ellen, upstairs, where was she, yes, in her room, but was she sleeping? After the last hour, it would be a shame if she slept now. He wanted to see her. Be with her. Maybe she would accept him now.

"Think I'll check on Ellen," he said, and, without waiting for a reply from Marty, went upstairs, moving firmly and intensely, his feet striking the earth right through the wood he walked on. He was part of his own body and seeking to be part of Ellen's now. Again.

She was lying across her bed, apparently asleep. Her eyes were closed. She had taken her skirt off, and her shirt; she was wearing a pair of beige underpants that were so much the shade of her own skin that he only knew she had them on because he could not see the line where her buttocks separated. She looked so beautiful to him. Turned on her side, so, one arm flung up in repose, head resting on that arm—and all that mass of gold-red hair dark-shadowed and shining in the pale light coming from the hallway. He slid onto the bed and put his hand on her breast. She stirred slightly and moved away from his hand.

Her eyes were closed, and she was quite awake. Intense into her own mind. Oh no, she thought, not *this* time, old buddy!—I belong to *me*. I can do what I want with my life, it's *my* precious life, I don't belong to you, I don't even belong *with* you, and I don't have to be what you want me to be any more. What you need me to be. Enough of being Easy Ellen against you and your whorish little nun-games. You and your ideas of right and wrong and how life should be lived . . . I'm a person too! Too easy to fall into your way of looking at things. Too easy to remember what loving you is like. What making love is like with you . . . you and your sureness you've got me all tied up tight and waiting. You and your little dead baby, you had me there for a while didn't you, Edward my sweet! But look now: I belong to me! I don't belong to you, *or*

204

that baby, and I'm sick of the foul taste of what you think my life should be . . .

She had known he would come to the room, come to the bed, seeking her out. She felt his hand on her, familiar to her as it was; sure, so sure . . . and moved away from it. From him. He could arouse her so easily. He made his moves and it was like a conditioned response by now. She was so turned on by him. Their acts of love were such acts of life. She felt the warmth of her vulva in response to his hand's touch. But would not respond. She felt his weight on the bed. She would not move. *This* is being honest, she thought, this is not gaming. I wish I could say all this to him, but short of that I can at least *think* it out straight finally! I'm so sick of the game called "being honest with each other"—hypocrisy—when we change what we think, what we feel, who we *are*, too fast to report to the other person anyway!

He had stretched out near her; perhaps he was waiting. Quiet. Downstairs, Marty waited until the end of the record and then walked over and turned the machine off. "Damn fools," he mumbled, "irresponsible stoned-out bunch for sure, leaving everything like this," as he put the screen in front of the fire's glow. He knew he was fond of this feeling. Knew he was as much stoned-out as anybody else. He picked up the plates and cups scattered around the room and moved with them into the kitchen, taking care of house-business like any Cancer and enjoying noticing this about himself. He put the dishes in the sink (*damned* if he'd wash them at this hour!) and poured himself a glass of milk. Stood drinking it and looking about the kitchen at Ellen's style of doing a room. The artifacts. The pottery, the bright hangings she wove, the reeds in a jar, all of it soft and bright, She sure was interesting. This was a very different room from his and Marie's. Funny. He hadn't thought about Marie all day. All night. And now that he had, he could live without it. Without her. Imagine. After all this time. Habits. He could live without Marie. He *would* live without her . . . He made his decision. His decisions. Two of them. About two women. And started up the stairs. Why not. Why the hell not. He was a god. His own god.

From the hallway, he saw them. Ellen, sprawled across the bed on her belly, separate from Edward; Edward stretched on his side facing her, his face hidden; both of them motionless and seeming to be asleep. How come nothing was happening with these two. It didn't figure. None of this figured. What the hell, he thought. What the fuck; or, for that matter, what the non-fuck, as it looked to him from here!—and he indulged his godlike self a little, round chuckle at his own humorousness in the situation.

Ellen heard him and knew her opportunity. Without disturbing Edward, she raised her head, as if Marty's little laugh had roused her from her sleep. And looked at him, across Edward, as the friend stood in the doorway, silhouetted against the hallway light.

He moved from the doorway, following an instinct. He moved back, toward the other upstairs room, the other bedroom, the tiny room at the back of the house which he'd remembered seeing earlier that night when they'd shown him around the house. With just the clue of that woman's look to guide him. Walked in, took off his clothes, and simply stretched out on the bed, on top of the white candlewick spread.

In a moment, in the quiet darkness, Ellen came in. She stood a second against the light of the doorway and then she shut the door back of her. She came to him. "Marty," was all she said, to make it quite clear she knew who he was, knew what she was doing, what was going on; and that he might be sure, ultimately, that she was aware.

Sat next to him and put her hand on his chest, on the breastbone, where the dark thick hair curled richly. Then moved her hand to his belly and downward slowly. He reached out and drew her shoulder down toward him.

"You damn fool," she said softly, "you're smoking; put that cigaret out before you kill the both of us . . ."

"Oh, right," he said, and again that little chuckle. Very ungodlike of him, to try to take a woman while smoking . . . did the gods smoke cigarets? No way, he thought. But his face was quite serious in the light of the last drag he took before putting the cigaret out. "Droit du seigneur," he said to her. "What?" He went to her mouth so fast, so hard, that she received all the smoke of that last drag and her mouth filled with it. So she had to laugh too, confused, trying to concentrate, filled with the taste of the new man who was also an old friend, who was also such a friend to Edward—but then, didn't that make all of this even more attractive? And what did he mean, saying "droit du seigneur," wasn't that only on a first night? That's what he meant? This was supposed to be a beginning. Of something. With them. For them . . .

Then her mind spun out and left, Marty had his hand strong on her belly and on her groin, she was all dark groin-feelings, he pulled her on top of him, his tongue filled her mouth and he drew her tongue to him till she filled his, their motions rocking the bed till he was sure the whole house must be heaving and moving with their rhythms . . .

Jesus, but what a luscious body, this broad, she was taller than he by half a head or more and outweighed him, and he was her equal in every way here in bed, he felt his prick was big as a tree for her; was she ready, yes, ready, very ready and wet for him, luscious broad, rich-fleshed noble Dutch luscious bitch, okay, babe, *okay,* here we go, here we go, and he began to go in, he went in, slowly, right on in.

"Aaaaah," she moaned. "Yesssss . . ." Still confused, knowing some things and not others. "Yes," knowing for sure that she was aroused, wanted this, wanted Marty; this was the first time for her body since the abortion, weeks ago it was, so long ago it felt, she was so hungry, so damned *hungry* for this pleasure—no, Edward wouldn't get this pleasure! Marty— that's who this was, this new taste, this fine new body . . .

They rocked and swung out, enjoying, loose and hearty, two fine animals; he said to her, "Okay, kid, come now?" and his saying it made her closer, brought her close, brought her almost there, and then he made his move, the sudden rhythm she found at once and met, she couldn't stop, the world could have blown up at that moment and she would have been found pinioned on this man's body thus, in a rocking she could never separate herself from until it reached its destiny

—so then she would come, and the waves afterward, which brought him there just after her, on the edge of her coming.

"Good! *Good*," they said to each other, forgetting everything, forgetting the man asleep in the room down the hall; and then Ellen remembered, and the flash of guilt, and the amazement that she should feel guilty, *him* with his dear little Myra and all—to hell with them both—she felt marvelous, free; she felt saved from the weird kind of loneliness of the past few weeks . . . Now that the simpler motives won't do, she thought, now that all my music has to become unlyrical and unfamiliar . . . Nobody's baby has a pappa any more . . . I can learn the new rules to these new games, yes I can, I can stop being ghostly for those old values if they don't work . . . oh God, I am so *glad* this man wanted me, reached for me!

Marty was lighting a cigaret. "How you doin'? Want one?"

She laughed across at him. Whereupon he did it again, put his mouth on hers after he'd taken a puff, and hers filled again with the puff he'd drawn.

"I feel—I feel *weird*," she told him, "Still stoned! and something else. Something *light*."

"I feel *great*," Marty said, abstractedly. He was thinking about the last time he'd gotten laid unexpectedly. That dark-haired woman at the houseparty at Nyack, three weeks ago, wasn't it? Oh, no, it had to be more recent; his secretary, Peggy, that strange little scene, that quickie on the couch in his office. But could you really count that. That was just getting it off. That wasn't even *interesting*. That wasn't getting laid or making love. *This* was getting laid, and something more, all rightee! What a good trip—he could go it again right now! Wondered where she was at, could she maybe—?

But she seemed abstracted now. Looked to be nowhere near here.

"Second thoughts?" he asked, feeling friendly toward her, the sex impulse waning.

"I think I just started feeling guilty," she told him. "I was considering if we've done 'the right thing.'" She couldn't look at him.

"You're *kidding!* How could anything that feels so good, be

208

bad?—is your god the kind that stands around getting even, like ours? You got to *suffer* if something's *good?*"

"Oh, come on, you know what I mean. About Edward. It's a bind. I *wish* I could get out of that kind of thinking, but—"

"Time, I see, for the philosophy of my sainted father again!"

"Yeah, that's *just* what I need, a little fast Jewish philosophy!"

"Okay, fasten your seat-belt. Pappa always said, 'If you have to ask the Rabbi, *Is it Kosher?*, it isn't Kosher!' "

"Translation, please! I think I get it, sort of—"

"Meaning, if you have to ask the question, you already *know* the answer . . ."

"Oh, heavy, *very* heavy! But then, it's also very *funny*—"

"Us Hebes have this number where it all looks funny and it's really very *very* serious," he told her, making a very serious face for her, "*and* it's really very very funny . . . On the other hand, sometimes something that *sounds* very profound, like what I just said, means absolutely nothing serious at all—am I reaching you?"

"What?"

"You know," he said, laughing, "It's not just being stoned, I think something's getting in the way of your understanding of this wisdom!"

His body was set next to hers so that she could feel his new hardon. Oh, very funny, she thought. And then noticed for the first time that Marty was circumcised; this would be the first time she'd made it with a circumcised man; *was* there a difference . . . She giggled and told him what she was thinking.

"Well, how about it?" he asked, "is there any difference?"

"Who cares! So long as we're both healthy!" she said, in a silly imitation of an old dialect.

But she knew the answers to the questions. And that was one of the answers, really. Guilt had no part in any of this. This feeling of lightness, this feeling of gratitude at the bodies warm together. Sometimes, she thought, joy is merely the absence of pain, the lifting-off of loneliness! She was grateful.

She got up. He reached for her. "Where you going?"

"To the bathroom. And then I'm going—to sleep. I have to. Let me."

He said nothing; patted her hand. What a broad. He knew where she was going. After she came out of the bathroom, after the faint sounds of her urination and her washing, he heard her steps go toward the other bedroom.

She walked to where Edward was still lying asleep and lay down beside him. She fitted her form to his, lying against his back with her belly, so that they were a blended Z-shaped form across the white spread. Another good feeling. She said, her mouth against his black waved hair, "Edward, Edward, I really love you."

He made no move, no response. He was deeply asleep. She fell asleep thus. In the other bedroom, Marty, content and only very slightly puzzled, began to fall asleep. Guiltless, without answers, he felt the answers would come, slowly, of themselves. He didn't need to push for them. They were there.

25

Motion of the hands of the woman winding the clock in the kitchen, before dawn each morning. Edward's mother, in the kitchen of the farmhouse, new strong big farmhouse on the hilltop, finished just a couple of years ago. Putting a match to the fire her boy Arthur set last night before he went to bed. Pumping water into the big tin kettles Walt had repaired; putting them to boil on the black iron stove moved up from the old house. Planning the second kettleful for dipping the brooms, to keep them sweet and tough. Setting out bowls for the oatmeal, and cups for the milk and for the "beef tea". Motion of the woman around the kitchen. Shine of lamplight on the old dented brass clock her mother had left to her. Sound of the boys waking up in their room overhead. Firm, familiar sound of Walt's boots on the stairway.

A few miles away, across the valley, another woman's hands on an old clock: the mother of Käti and Annetje, in her kitchen, touches the shining brass of her old clock as if it were a friend. As it sits over the big kitchen fireplace faced with blue and white tiles brought by her husband's father those years ago from Friesland. The slight dawn light through the window over the sink, as she puts a match to the wood set by her husband in his late-night ritual before bedtime. Ah, I love this room, and now is the best, the woman thinks, this hour is mine here.

She looks again around the room, this woman who is Libran and loves beauty and the luxuries: enjoying again the fruit of the work of so many hands, the woods, dark and polished, light and polished, carved and straight and shaped for use . . . she reaches under the old clock for the key and turns first the left and then the right spring-winder, so that the comforting sound will continue in a soft susurrus under the stronger noises of the house that day. And will be clearly her own in this hour before the children awaken. This clock that had belonged to her mother and to her mother's mother. (How funny now to think that Henk's grandmother had never had a clock! told time by the sun and moon! was Indian!—Did she have other luxuries; what was her morning hour like!) This clock had been made in Groningen. Its sound was history, and civilised. This comforted the mother of the twins.

From the north windows over the sink and the laundry-sink, their fields stretched to the horizon and beyond. At her left, opposite the sinks, the windows gave on the road Henk's father's father had cleared, with its row of poplars. She could see the corner of the brown barn near the house; light shone from the barn windows, where Henk and the helpers were milking and tending.

Above her, the twins were still asleep in their closetbed, under the quilt she had made for them. This was a school day, so the mother would be able to count on having a few hours to continue embroidering the new sheets. While the water was heating, she got out the pile of linen from the oaken chest near the door to the *pronk,* and the basket of needles, embroidery threads, and oval wood frames to hold the cloth. She set her materials out on the long oak table in the kitchen, looked them over, planned the day's work, then gathered everything to one side, so that she could give breakfast on the end of the table in a little while.

It was a mild day; Henk would be outside most of the time. His dark eyes turned toward the sky, watching the season. He had wanted to be a sea-trader, as were his grandfathers, and on such a day he would be sure to mention the sea at least once. The last time, little Käti had listened to him, her auburn head next to his, had made him tell them all again the story of how he had gone down the Hudson once, long ago, and seen the sea, smelled the sea . . . Maybe they could all make that journey some time. He did want it so!

Meanwhile, his woman knew that when he thought he smelled the sea, it would be the river, only so many of miles from their farm . . . How he felt bound to this land, and how she loved it; they were both bound to it now, what with the portion the family kept to farm, and the supervising of the tenant farmers' duties and affairs, there was more than enough to do . . . A good life. But she would as soon have been in Holland. Born here, and born to wealth, she felt ambivalent; she would go if she had the chance . . .

She went to the water-pump, its copper covered with the pretty dark-red-and-yellow paint and shiny in the firelight, and drew water for the table, and for the dishes that would soon need to be washed. It would be a busy day. She heard the Holsteins moving out. The men's figures near the barn, sound of Henk's voice over all of them. At that moment he looked up and saw her, framed in the window, and lifted his hand to her.

Across the valley, Edward's mother got out the milk-pail. Levon would ride across to the Elsen farm and bring some back. Gretchen would go down cellar and bring up a horse-radish, grind it up, and set it aside for putting into the milk to keep it sweet. Then it would keep for the week. And there was the pot she had cooked the onions in, she had to get that smell out, later in the day when the ashes had accumulated she would take some out and boil them around in the pot, and that would take care of it all right. She must remember to get some buttermilk this time, too. For a pudding; and then for getting the stains out of the clothes when she washed things tomorrow. Things were in such a state. So much to do. Maybe Dorris would help . . . She looked out the kitchen window across the valley. It would be a mild day. Busy.

❋   ❋   ❋

When Edward was sixteen, and first getting laid, Joe Shultis gave Liona the baby that was born as Elmira. When the twins Katryn and Annetje were eighteen months old, Edward's mother conceived him. He was born at home, in the big double bed upstairs, as were all of his brothers and sisters. When it was Spring, all of the children of the town ran out after school, ran past the waiting adults, ran to the trees, to the stream; later, they walked in groups, sucking sour candies and gum, breaking twigs from the bayberry and sumac and lilac hedges; when Ellen was seven and Edward was five, they swam in the creek naked, as did all the children; and went properly dressed to their different churches with the adults; and rode their bicycles to the lake after school . . .

Mike Mandelbaum and Myra Shultis were born at different ends of the hospital in Rensselaer. They were in the same class in school all the way through: from kindergarten with Miss Sulzburger through primary grades with the Misses Van Wagener, Schultz, Fletcher, Wilhelm, and Vander Molen, through Schuyler High School, three towns away. The bus rides, the football games, the cribbing, the necking, the gossip, the cliques . . . They never touched each other. All those years.

❋   ❋   ❋

Along the wall there are cubbies, each with the name of one of them marked in black ink. Along the wall there are boxes where messages are left. *All the names are real. Nothing is changed to protect the innocent. All are innocent.*

Along the road there are mailboxes with the names of each of us. The names by which we were known as children. The other names are added under it. Nothing is ever crossed out.

All the names are needed. Are important. Along the road, shaded by elms and poplars and oaks, the boxes stand, in all seasons. In each box is left the name of "The True Love" (there may be several names). And of "The Teacher Who Has Had The Most Influence on One's Life In Retrospect." Of "The Field of Endeavour In Which One is Most Likely To Succeed." A record is kept of birthmarks and moles, of scars, of "lost" teeth (never lost, of course), and of incidents which demarcate the struggle and the valiance.

In the hallway of the house are a series of bellpulls. If you pull the first one, nothing predictable occurs. If you pull the second, everything that will occur is predictable and justifiable. If you pull the third, everything that occurs is logical and does great harm to all concerned. Two of the four bellpulls are made of coarse twisted rope of great strength. The other two are of velvet, with golden cording as trim. The first and second bellpulls are unmarked. The third bellpull is labelled "Dignity and a Certain Degree of Courage," and the fourth is marked, "To Summon Mr. Eldridge."

The bellpulls are changed around every fourth day. Sometimes even this varies.

✻　✻　✻

Last year, in an attempt to clarify their feelings, the youngsters of the town set fire to the high school. The previous season, which happened to be Autumn, they held a potentially huge anti-war rally, to which only twenty-four adults (out of a possible three thousand) came. There are no Negroes, Orientals, or "foreigners" at the high school. The night of the first moon-shot, only Sally Mandelbaum was impressed. Four summers ago, an outsider attempted to form an ecology group to study the problem of water pollution as it affected Trois and the surrounding river-townships. It almost didn't happen. It would have failed but for the dedicated and devout efforts of our famous and influential friend, the great and powerful Leo lady, Liona Shultis, for whom such causy activities had now become a way of life and an excellent substitute for good clean (dirty) sex. Organizer, ringleader, matriarch before her time, Carrie Nation of the Hudson Valley Association-of-Anything-You-Can-Name, spender of energy without liberation, Grande Dame, guardian of the morals of our children, protector of the sanctity of Happy Valley, and, in short, a miserable and reasonably annoying personality of Wittgenburg, she was feared by most and loved by no one. She had been scheduled to give a talk on abortion and birth-control (in a discreet way, with films sanctioned by the Archdiocese, of course,) at the highschool, the day the kids started the fire . . .

The layering of the town. Some still playing "we" and "they" —Irish, German, Dutch, and the overlaps—the people who set great store by, those who were sure that the town would fall apart if, those who believed that . . . All the gods must be appeased. And men play games of making up new gods who then must be appeased. Tree gods hearth gods metal gods earth gods visible invisible omnipresent gods built of *fearlove*. A word that contains "evolve" and "revolve" and "free" within it, but not visibly. The god-filled ones, the young, causing the atom-shift, the speeding-up of time—"Nothing happens fast in Life" being refuted, finally, with "Nothing's going to change unless *I* change it," which came from "I want it *different* from how I was taught it, I love *me* more than the gods, I *am* the gods, *I am God*" . . .

And in almost every house with a chimney, every house over fifty years old in the town of Wittgenburg, the "witch-catcher," of sturdy, blackened iron, prongs turned skyward in readiness for the feared, the Unexpected, the Unnameable . . . And the ritual chants believed—plant things that will grow aboveground on the wane of the moon; plant things that will grow belowground on the waxing of the moon . . . Summer and winter would come, don't worry, you can be sure of that if nothing else . . . The date of the first snowstorm is the number of snowstorms you can expect that winter . . .

EVERYTHING
HAPPENS
IN
THREES The weeping/the laughter/the birthdeath the mar-

216

riages the gossip the thrall the huge moon the music from the one window still alight in the darkened town at midnight The deviant the innocent the variable the nonconformist the renegade the maverick the hermit the

mailboxes along the road swung silently open in the darkness in the half-light all in a curved row shadows of the trees upon them Waiting

* * *

Young Anne/Frey, lying in the bed (yin) asleep? No. Young Käti/Ellen, lying next to her (yang) asleep? Yes. Frey is awake. Awoke as she woke every night of her life at some time. A time after midnight. Not always the same time. Sometimes it was at that minute when the moon slipped over a certain precipice. Or the hour before dawn. Occasionally it was in response to the call of an animal nearby.

But she would awaken, naturally, and sometimes would rise and walk about, unobserved by the rest of her "family." In a totally dark room she would walk with surety. In later years, she noticed that there seemed to be a faint light that preceded her, not definite, not from a determinate source. It never occurred to her that it might emanate from her own body. If it had occurred to her, she would not have thought it noteworthy. Her body was her clock, and was her seasons; it did not always correspond to what she saw around her as the experience of other people, so she early learned not to remark on the differences. But just to be them.

* * *

That which is said between lovers, without words. Son et lumière. The frogs shouting at night; the crickets, the peepers, the nightbirds, and then the voices of the silent lovers, talking to each other through the navels, shrieking silently, asking for a cure from each other: "Don't you understand me? Don't you hear me? I need to love you! Are you really there? Are you really you? Are you really the one?" And the lover's mute reply: "What? I can't hear you. Can you see me? See who I really am? I can see you. But I can't quite feel who you are.

217

I need for you to touch me. Then I will know you are really the one I want you to be."

So he reaches out and touches her. She loves him for this. He feels her love, and loves her for this. Each is the one the other wishes for. Then each of them moves away for a moment, in a natural way, something like the need to go to urinate, but this time it is simultaneous, and therefore subject to interpretation. To misinterpretation. "You're leaving." "No, *you're* leaving." "You started to leave *first*." "No, *really*." "Yes, you did!"

One of the lovers manages to overcome the need to be right, and reaches out to touch the other. At the same time, the tenderness of the gesture is cancelled by the words, said in a whining tone, "You don't ⎯⎯ enough!" The lover interprets this to mean that a kiss is called for. And so they kiss, openmouthed, openhearted, lustily, willfully, and from a distance, both watch the mouths become A Mouth, a cavern, a chasm, into which they are both liable to disappear, into which they *might lose their identity*, it is all one connected channel, through which flows the lifestream of both of the humans,

the force of the joining is enough to break small capillaries in the inside of the cheeks, the throat; *ah*, now the substances of anguish and of beauty can flow freely between them, since there is no longer audible speech as a divisor; it is all then one long soft tube, it is then, it has then become all *The Lover;* it is then connect all perfect at the groin and the circuit becomes complete; her blood and his can mix and do, even if not of compatible types, his and her fluid are *The Fluid,*

an energy is approached and built up; it has begun with the fluids of the Mouth-as-Unison, it extends to Groin; sometimes it moves and changes its charge in such a way that it becomes a Child and issues therefrom; but much of the time

it builds rises wells up, from the whispers of the loving tones to the whines and the whimpers, into the naggings, up and out into the shrieks, the screams howls shouting, the uncanny musicks of the confounded trapped Unities the souls connected at the body orifices and unable to separate,

and it is at this time that it becomes *Navel Talk,* which in no way resembles human communicative conversation; the positive "charge" becomes discharge and therefore visible as well as invisible; it can be the color of a mixture of menstrual blood and of sperm fluid; the sound of it is so high-pitched, so low-pitched, it cannot be heard by humans; it is awesome and it can be felt, as strong in a negative way as is the positive strength and power of the mutual orgasm—it is felt not just by The Lover as Single Animal Extant, but by all of the smaller sensitive beasts of earth nearby—and by certain few people, those whose bodies are all antennae just under the skin

CHAPTER

26

"It's just that my state of being these days is constant pain,"
she tells him, finally, when he convinces her to sit down for
coffee with him.

"Well, then, you must be doing *something* wrong," he tells
her, smilingly. Trying to keep it light.

"I'm not in the *mood* for any smartass stuff," she says to him.
"If you have something constructive—I mean, if you can *do*
any—"

"For people in a state of constant pain," he grins at her,
"*this* company always suggests a good night's sleep and—"

"Never mind," she interrupts. "You do have your insights,
every so often, babe. . . . But you've missed the Big One."

"The one about 'It's what you *do* with what you've got.' et
cetera . . ."

"Well *yes,* Edward, but what if what I've got is nameless,
what if what I've got is one big Question Mark, feels like one
long sad loss after another—too many deaths—in a word,

Pain, and *none* of your blessed home-remedies would . . ."

"Crap," Edward says, into her eyes, affectionately. "All you Pisces people do is feel sorry for yourselves, as if everything revolves around Your Pain—"

"Capricorn speaketh. The original Tough Guy. What a snot you are, from your peaky old holier-than-thou mountain. The nasty tough pseudo-idealist; turning everything around himself!"

"Must've been *something* about me you really liked!—Maybe it's exactly that I *do* act as if my world centers on me; but *I* don't get hysterical over it! Maybe You could *do* with a bit of that, dear Pisces lady, dear soft-and-sweet, dear gummy-sloppy-boundary-lacking Pisces lady—you could *do* with just a *bit* of my edges!—just enough to figure out your pain's a simple device that the body or spirit has, warning something's wrong . . . What I mean to say—*if*, on the off chance, you can hear me—is, Pain is designed to cause Action. You remember what *that* is, Ellie, don't you? Response. Like removing the hand from the hot stove. So you'll get up off your self-indulgence and *make* something better happen than what's been happening! But I'll bet Adam's off ox *that* never occurred to you! You just want to sit there forever telling me or whoever'll listen, how much Pain you've got."

She smiles, thinking smugly now about Marty. "Oh, *Christ,* all you Caps ever think about is action! You know, I think you guys *think* you move right, but to me you move weird. I guess if you happen to be an earth sign, all you think is how you're going to get moving again. Of all the static heaps to talk to me about 'action'—that really makes me laugh!"

"Well, I wish *something* would make you laugh! Maybe a sense of humour is the antidote to all this self-pity. You *could* consider the possibility, you know . . ."

"Oh, I move; I *move,* all right, I just don't move the way *you* want me to. I'm a *water* sign. I don't do that ponderous dance *you* do. You can't even begin to understand. But whatever it is about Pisces, you seem to have enjoyed it for lo, these many months now . . . Everything's changing, yes, moving to the next stage, the next permutation. But *you're* the one wants it all to stand still—because this whole mess suits you, you want it to stay the same always."

"If something feels good or right, I want it to go on, Ellie! Sure, I want to keep being with you—"

"All I know is, nothing seems to make sense to me now. Okay. Okay. So our signs aren't compatible. This we knew. So how come it winds up like this? How come we get *this* far and then wind up name-calling?—and then start tripping over if my way irritates you and yours irritates me?"

"*Need,* my dear woman. People see what they need to see in each other. And ignore what they need to ignore. Until they trip on whatever it is. Till it gets to be too much to ignore. Like now. Here I am, feeling hideously annoyed because there you sit, being hopelessly 'self-indulgent.' So here I am, philosophically denying you what you consider your goddam birthright: to be self-pitying all over the place—I can't *stand* your lack of continence, Ellie, you're just all sloppy when it comes to anything emotional . . ."

"Edward, for Christ's *sake!* All I said to you was, I'm in *pain!*"

"Sure. Sure. But what did you *want* when you were telling me that?"

"I wanted you to know I hurt! I wanted you to understand! or think about it! about me! God, but you're a pompous ass. You righteous, pompous, cold, self-justifying bastard!"

"Ah, you finally got it all out, you finally got it off! You finished? Got it all said? Then hold your tongue, bitch, or you'll find yourself losing everything you think you're trying to win with your games with me! You forget pretty quick what you're doing here. *You* came *here.* This is *my* house— not some rich posh place my daddy passed on to me—something *I* put together *myself!* You got yourself a real one, for a change, a man, instead of all those soft pricks you been messing around with since Tom died—and you haven't begun to value what we—"

"Oh. Oh. You are really too damn fucking much. I was just—"

"What you were 'just' doing—I'll tell you—is, you wanted dear old Doctor Edward to listen to your problems, all the juicy-watery-Pisces-worry-problems, and kiss the bubu and make it better. You wanted dear old sympathetic Dr. Jean Hersholt Richthoven to hold the kid's hand and ask little Pisces girl, 'Ahhhh, poor honey, *what* is it hurts, li'l lovey, is 'ums having some narsty ole pain, well, the world *is* really tomato jelly and I will fix it all with my, forgive the expression, instruments . . .'"

"Shut *up!* You really *specialize* in viciousness, don't you! That's your long suit."

"Well, what *did* you expect? Be honest, with me at least even if you can't be with yourself! You are so damn provocative! I am so damned *bored* with your whimperings. Sulkings. You *could* at least begin to learn something about why you do what you do! What a damn drag, to have to go through this! You mean you really don't *know* you said that for effect—so I'd do something you wanted me to do? You came here because you wanted something from me—something that wasn't happening! Am I right, or not?"

"Jesus, I came here because you *asked* me to! You always have got to be so awfully goddam fucking *right,* don't you! You have to be such a piledriver, such a goddam sledgehammer! You—you—you're in the right business, aren't you—with your pounding at metal till it takes the shape you want —you—bastard—I'm made—of *flesh*—"

"Quit it. You have no idea how messy you get. I don't buy all that crying; not now. I told you a long time ago that I didn't want to be part of anything thick or heavy. Not after what I went through with Kathy. And I still don't. Not with you—not with Myra—not with *anybody!* And it doesn't make you any better company when you go into this whining around me, be assured. I'm made of flesh too, kiddo, and you better know it. And *this* flesh makes up its *own* mind how it's going to feel, and won't be manipulated into sad stories somebody else made up. Not by your tears or anybody else's either, dammit."

"Well, but what am I supposed to *do* with when I—"

"Just *see* what you're doing. Everybody's got pain; it's what you do *after* that that I'm trying to make you see! Making speeches to someone else is trying to get *them* to change the way you feel, when you are supposed to be responsible for changing the way you feel *yourself*."

"Oh, you're so much *smarter* than all the rest of us, Edward, I can't see how you can lower yourself to spending time with the foolish stupid rest of us unenlightened souls who move in blind ignorant darkness around you—"

"Not smarter. Just fed up with people leaning all over each other and calling that 'being together.' Just not conceited enough to think that my own pain makes me stand alone from every other creature—my pain isn't different, it's the same as yours and everyone else's! Jesus, Ellen, don't you ever realize that nobody's isolate? And when you start mewling this way, it's a gimmick to—"

"You *don't* understand, do you. You get so bloody removed —You get so hung up in your damned broadscope view, you don't leave room for any real feelings. You're always off somewhere making up a universal theory to cover what you're feeling—putting it all into some box with a label—What's wrong with feeling everything there is to feel, the moment you're living it? So, if I'm in pain and I tell you, does it have to be some sort of device to suck you in, or something? Can't it be like a weather report? If I feel *good,* I say so. If I feel lousy, I want to be able to *say* so, without your being afraid my pain would suck you in! *Is* that what you're afraid of?"

"Well, maybe that's a part of it . . . maybe. I'll have to look at that."

"You *could* be wrong, you know. But of course, *you're* never wrong, though."

"I could be wrong. If I am, I could admit it. I try—I just try to keep my sense of perspective—there are so many kinds of people, you, Frey, Marty, Myra, my brothers, the people I work for, Freddy, they all *look* so different, they all have 'different' kinds of pain, who can say who's got more than the next fellow?"

"Why measure? Why do you have to tell me *you* have pain,

when I tell you I do? Can't I just *tell* you, and then let it *lie* there, and you don't lecture me, or do *any*thing, not drag it out like this?"

"I *wasn't* comparing. Like I said: the human condition. There's things we all have in common."

"But the texture's got to be different. Or else we'd all look alike, we'd all be the same age, we'd all have the same experiences, we'd all be the same sex . . . It's not just quantitative. If I feel—what I feel as a woman has *got* to be different from what you feel, as a man—"

"Why different? How different?"

"Don't be a fool. You know what I mean. I'm talking to you from *this* body! It's an 'inward' body. My sex goes inward. I revolve around my womb. That's my center! I don't just feel with my body; I *think* with my body. I think *from* my body. I'm never independent of it; how could I be? Just as I don't live *on* earth—I am part of earth; I *am* earth—how can I separate myself by saying I live on earth?"

"That sounds too simple. As if men don't think or feel the same way, or use the same methods, as women—"

"*Exactly. You* have to think 'outward' because that's the basic shape of your body, because your sex goes outward from your body; you're the seed-planter, you're the hunter, you're the theorist; you never have anything growing in your inside, but you have work on earth that goes outward in its own forms—"

"Well, I see what you mean. The bodies shaped for the functions—for the work we do. For the human race thing. But if I'm the 'hunter' and you're the 'baby-tender'—"

"Ah—Edward—ah—aaaaah—"

"What is it?"

"Edward—I—I—wanted—I wanted—I wanted that baby—I wanted—to—"

"Ellen—Ellie, come over here, don't sit all the way over there and cry like that—I can't stand it—! you think I don't feel anything about all that—? Listen. Listen, honey, come over here to me—"

"Don't—don't touch me—I—don't want you—ever—"

"Don't *be* like that. Ellie—don't. Listen. Honey. Listen to me. I didn't even *know* until you'd already made up your own mind and done it. Don't you remember? *You didn't even tell me. You didn't even let me help decide* . . . Ellie, listen! *Let me*—let me hold you—let's help each other—"

"Don't—don't—Let me alone—"

"I don't *want* to let you alone! You've been alone about this too much already. That's what it's all about, isn't it, all this talk about pain! Isn't it. Honey. Listen. We can talk about it. We can. Sit with me. Let me sit with you. Look. Listen. I didn't even know until after you'd made up your mind what you'd do, don't you realize? By the time you finally told me, you'd already made up your mind. What difference would it have made if I'd said different? We *both* knew this isn't the right time! Not right now. Not for what we're doing with our lives . . . We both knew that. You'd never have gone ahead— would you?"

"Let me go. Get away from me. You *knew. You knew, and you didn't stop me, and you could have*. You could have. You didn't want it to happen, I could be here now with a baby inside, I—"

"Wait just a minute. *We* is what you haven't said yet, Ellie! —all the I, I, I—Okay, I won't touch you, and I *will* listen to you, but you have to listen to me too. If you want to get this thing out in the open, stop pushing at me, I won't try to hold you in any way—I'll sit over here. Now, quiet down, can you? And we can talk—"

"Oh, sure. Nice. And logical and orderly and rational. 'Be nice'—goddam it, just like my mother—God, I'm so *sick* of being *nice*—of not saying what I feel—of feeling lousy and not saying or doing anything—anything about it—I AM SO SICK OF BEING NICE! I *hurt!*"

"Ellen—stop screaming—you'll blow the roof right off the bloody house—you want everybody for miles around to know our troubles?"

"Why the hell *not!* It's 'part of the human condition,' isn't it? Is it any different from what *they* feel in *their* house? Just why exactly the hell *shouldn't* everybody know what's gone down? Oh, you big, sad, rotten fool—my pain is like every-body's, you just—said—so—yourself!"

"Okay. So we're back to that. Okay. Something is happening in every house on this road and on all the roads—somebody's hurting . . . But all I keep trying to tell you is, it's what some-one *does* with that pain—it's how you get it behind you—somehow, make it *work* for you—I really *do* have faith in you—Ellie, if you let the pain take you over, you *lose*—if you get through it, put it off at the slightest distance, you've got it licked—then you have a *chance* at least to change something! Otherwise, it's just going to sit there and fester—and keep on hurting—"

"I'm *talking* to you. I *am* doing something. I didn't start out to talk about *this!* I started out just to talk to you about every-thing—"

"That's the only reason you started talking about your pain and all that. You wanted this whole scene . . . Don't pretend! *I'm* not afraid for us to talk. It's you who's been afraid. It's *you* who didn't tell me, until after you'd made up your own mind which way it would go!"

"Don't put it all on me. You knew. And you could have stopped me, even after I made the decision, and you didn't. You *didn't.*"

"Look, don't you understand? I wanted to see you. I tried and tried to, before and since because I knew things are wrong between us—I know, and I knew. All about it. I didn't need that rotten clever little scene with Marty and you, to convince me, either—"

"Ah. So you knew that, too!"

"Don't bother with that shit. Of course I knew. Did you really think I was asleep? I wasn't asleep, any more than you were when I came in and lay down next to you, bitch!"

"Big deal. So you knew. Well then—I hope you know too it was *good.* It was *great,* for a change, to mess up your games of showing me off to somebody and then going off and balling Myra! If *you* don't want to play it straight, how come you want *me* to with you! You must be crazy! Wouldn't you imagine a time would come when I was damned tired of—"

"Yeah. You're damned tired. Sure. Too tired to bed down with me, that night or since. But not too tired to take a roll in the hay with Old Buddy Marty, were you, bitch—"

"Aha. Hit a goddam *nerve*, did we. *That's* the '*we*' that I'd like to talk about, mister! That one right there. You and your goddam fucking double standard. Your double standard for fucking. Perfectly okay, is it, for you to go to Myra, whenever and however, isn't it! But *I* make one goddam *move*—out of your orbit, your goddam charmed circle of possessions, just *once,* and with goddam good cause I would say—and just *listen* to you! Just *listen* to the righteous man. I just wish you could hear that righteous smug possessive whine you get—bastard—"

"Is that why you did it? Is that why? Just to be provocative? Because you knew I would feel—"

"No. No. *No!* Is that why Myra goes to Mike, just to make you mad? Not likely! Why don't you work on that one? And *work* on why I made it with Marty that night! And not with you. If you care to. If you're all that interested. No? Let me tell you. I made it with Marty because I *wanted* to. Because I *needed* to. Because he wanted me, and I liked that, and because you were being a phony shit, coming in and acting as if I were some kind of possession or property of yours, all tied up, after what's gone down between us! Waltzing in with Old School Buddy Marty for a li'l ole social visit, 'want you to meet Ellie, you remember Marty, don't you.' But he fooled you, didn't he! We both did. We insisted on not remaining spellbound by the famous Edwardian charm."

"Boy, you're really incredible. This is really incredible—that you both should think I didn't know what was going down—"

"Just exactly what *did* you know, that night? Just exactly what were *you* doing, with the both of us? You can't tell me you really were here with *me* that night. You weren't being real—the whole time! The whole while we were sitting in the kitchen, and then later. Same as you evaded me when I was pregnant. You didn't confront me once! You never saw *me* at all. You just saw what you wanted to see! What you needed to see!"

"Don't get hysterical."

"I'm *not* hysterical! I just *see*. What's good for you *isn't* so good for me. You get into the bed, and you come, and you get out of the bed, and then you go about your business, and that's the end of the story as far as you're concerned! And *I'm* left with the rest of it—*I'm* the one has to go into the City, and face some *creepy* butcher who's got a streak of sadism *not* so well-concealed, and *I* have to go to everyone but you for some money and some good feelings! *I* have to be the one who goes and takes care of business—mine *and* yours—easy for you; *not* so very damn easy for me, I can tell you—!"

"Ellie, that's ridiculous! Making love with you had *nothing* to do with feeling responsible for your getting pregnant. You're supposed to be taking care that that doesn't happen! I thought you were watching out."

"Oh, you *did*. You did, did you. And what about you? What about *you* watching out? How come *I'm* the only one supposed to think about whether or not I get pregnant? Suppose there's an 'accident'?"

"Come *on*. There's no such thing. There's always some woman sort of 'forgets' to take precautions or something. You as much as admitted that, a long time ago. You wanted it! So *you* started it, without consulting me about what *I* wanted! And when it happened, (I should say, when it worked,) you still did the same thing: didn't consult me, till it was too late for me to really have a say in how things would go . . ."

"You certainly are sensible. And practical. The one thing you leave out is a little number called human emotions. Feelings. *You are the coldest person I ever met.*"

"Ellie, you *know* better than that! I *care* about you. I *care* that all this happened to you . . ."

"That's *it*. Happened to *me*. It didn't happen to *us*. Or to you. It happened to me. To *me*. *To my body.* My *feelings.*"

"It didn't *have* to go that way, I keep trying to tell you! I told you how I felt! I could have done a—"

"Shut up! Shut the bloody hell up, will you? What *you* are is, glad it's over! What *you* are is—what you *are* is somebody who doesn't have to get another life going inside his body and

229

then have to go get that little body *ripped* out of your body, *scraped* out; what you are is somebody who shows up afterward all ready to play kissy-face as if nothing unusual had happened at all—what you are is a *creep,* with explanations and excuses, well, I can *tell* you what it felt like to feel that damn curette—"

"Ellie, Ellie, listen—we come at this from such different places, even the way we think about the same thing is different, it's all like you said, but listen, it *doesn't* mean I don't *care*—it doesn't mean I don't feel for your pain—and it sure as hell doesn't mean I'm not *sorry*—God, don't you see that I *do* care, that I *am*—"

"You can't know. You can't *know.* You don't know. You never will. You won't ever know. What that's like . . . aaaaahhh, there's no way to ever make you know—"

"Tell me. *Tell me.* Don't shut off from me, the way you did! I care about you. That's why I came over last week. And twice before that. Listen, just because I don't have the same kind of body doesn't mean I can't understand. And it doesn't mean I don't hurt too. I do! I've *missed* you. I wanted to talk to you. To *listen. Really,* El."

"Ahhh. No. It's no use. There's just no way . . ."

"Yes, there is. We can talk about it. We can talk about anything. We can *do* something. We can communicate—"

"Oh, you don't *feel* close to me. It's all so *pat,* to you. I'm *tired* of feeling all these things, and then have you come along and explain away all my feelings and put them into boxes, all labelled. I'm sick of feeling whatever it is I feel, alone, while you're off with Myra or something! I'm tired of going through all of this alone! And then hearing you come along and make me out the fool!"

"But it really *is* a good idea to get out of your feelings, *sometimes*—don't you see? Then you can get some perspective on whatever it is—"

"You *see?* You see? You're doing it again! You just can't stop, can you? Can't you understand, there's no *way* for me to 'get outside' my feelings! They're part of my insides—part of my guts! I—Don't you goddam it understand? How can you separate how you *feel* from how you *think?*—Oh, you can get a distance on it, all right—I can't! I'm all contained, my womb is here, my brain is here, both *inside* me Listen. Let it go. This just won't work. Let's stop talking. Let's get out of the house. Let's—let's take a walk. Let's get out of here! I don't want to stay in here. Come on."

"You sure?—are you sure you aren't running away from talking to me? Or something?"

"Sure. I'm sure. Honestly. Let's take a walk. That's what I need now. Some air and a look at the town."

"Okay."

CHAPTER

27

Myra is now a Zebra. (Patterns.) Ellen is now a sorrel mare. Or, perhaps, a salmon, pink of flesh. ("What animal would you be . . . ?") Marty (the one who lives with Frey, I mean), turns out to be the long-lost twin of the other Marty (yes, Marty Levitt, I mean), taken by gypsies from the Lipschitz family while he/she lay stoned out in the cradle. Frey? Frey is now a grey cat. (All cats are, in the dark.) Or Frey a Grey Morgan. (Le Grey.) As for Edward—ahhhh—

At the County Fair, fifteen miles west of Trois/Wittgenburg, in a covered stall, shielded from the eyes of those who have not purchased tickets (and from the exigencies of the weather!) stands Giant Ed, a sport, a mutant, a treasure, a dark brown bull who stands 25 feet high, I mean 25 *hands* high; he is 18 feet (I *mean* feet; no mean feat) from soft black nose to firm black ass; magnificent, marvelous, a marvel, so perfectly like every other bull of his breed (Angus) except of course for his size; he fills the space so beautifully; he *is* the bull in W. C. Williams' "The Bull," his forefoot a foot around, ah, I'm sorry, but it *is;* the TeRritOrIeS of his heavy head, his GRAND broad back, his HUGE pizzle for which there will never be enough cow on earth—he *fills* the space which has been built especially for him, in the two *tethered stories* of his shelter he moves slowly and with ponderous grace, he is *himself,* he seems always full of wonder, his eye does not confront directly, he is apparently never bored, having trod his boundaries and learned his arena, there is the music in his head, he is aware of those who come to see him, to watch him . . . At night, he is kept with the other, lesser animals, and so seems less massive: the language is the same.

You may wonder how he came to be here. ("I know you are all wondering why I called you all to this place tonight.") Well, the couple who "own" him, folks called Tom and Mary, used to have a little Mom-&-Pop business in Trois, and then this opportunity came along, and. You see. Any of us would do the same. When asked, Tom says, "I don't like freaks. I'm normal and so's my wife." Her weight. His lantern jaw.

* * *

Frey/Anne has evolved to the point where she can be awake while seeming asleep. Awake to the naked eye but in some sort of clear sleep. Some kind of. The state of being of. As on the night the bear came and took Ellen's foal; she was awake, was Frey, while the bear was still half a mile away and lurching in. She did not, however, stop any of it from happening. There was no interfering with the natural order of things. The bear began it, and Frey's own dogs finished the job. (Ellen did not need to be told; Frey was teaching her, and by the time dawn came, Ellen knew too.) Fear itself was the killer. That, and nature's own lust for blood. Circular blood. Death as the perfect orgasm. Later, Ellen was one of those who can foretell the time of death's arrival. She knew the taste; it was familiar, at least in part. And the rest was so rich!

* * *

Some few miles out of town is a farm which breeds Dwarf black Brahma cattle; they dot the hillside, the side of the Catskill (KaatersKill) mountain, like some kind of punctuation mark as yet unnamed, or they are Chinese characters expressing their own exact form; above their grazing wheels a group of dark birds of the area, resembling circumflexes. The largest of the cattle is the size of a Shetland pony. It is not often that they will reproduce in captivity. The owner is not sure how he came to raising them; his wife has stopped vomiting at night since the cattle came here; he has made big money; she wears her old mink coat for another season; he is a man whose predecessors came from Germany, and ordinary Holsteins do not satisfy his hunger for the unusual. He may be the real father of Myra. His wife may be Elionora of Aquitaine reincarnated. She of the iron visage, dowager/doyenne; long torso, short fat legs, *glad* when the women started wearing pants into town instead of just on the farms.

* * *

Always wishing for different forms. Relationship of bones to the rock under the land where you were born. Row of mountains looking like the spine of the earth; yes, you *did* read that somewhere before. People, set up in their houses, minute and precarious, labelling everything theirs: 'their' land, 'their' possessions, 'their' relationships each to each—GETTING HOLD. And some of them letting go, letting out, letting down, letting loose, moving light as air in and out of the houses and leaning their spines against earth . . .

You, an animal, get to the place you've planned on getting to for so long—and the place is not there at all; or it has changed from what it was originally, so that it is recognizable only by glancing sideways, a peripheral-vision vision; or it is not as it was in your concept, but, right before you, it seems to be possible that it *will* be the place; it just isn't *there* yet, quite—a sort of déjà vu in reverse . . . Or—if you are still with me—you, as Animal, get to The Place, and it *is* the place, yes, it *is*—this is IT—and the place is not marvelous, not exciting, not amusing, not even very interesting—not even possible! But there you are, having invested all that time and money. So what can you do. You are no longer an animal.

234

You stay there anyway. You make up reasons to have to stay there. Turning your emotions and responses inside out. Go to sleep a cat in Holland and wake up a wolf in Germany— during the War. Hoping they will not notice that you are a Jew who has changed your name. That you have not left spoor on the trip. But.

* * *

The leaf and bark of the beech tree say it is a beech; thus, for a maple, or what-have-you; thus it is that Capricorn looks unlike Pisces and cannot be confused one with the other . . . Humans sometimes choose which rules they wish to follow. Which systems, which gods, which handles, of the few currently available . . . all of the systems being part of the earth at any given time. To the last syllable of. Some people try on one system at a time, in sequence; some try many at once; some choose one or two, decide they work or fit, and stay with it/them, in simplicity. Nothing has ever been clearly established as superior; some say the excitement is in the choice available . . .

Edward, human animal, male, Caucasian, 37 years old at the time of this writing, (if you count from time of birth rather than from time of conception as do the Chinese;) Edward, of Germanic heritage, of Lutheran persuasion; Edward, born in twp. of Trois, hamlet of Wittgenburg, N.Y., attended schools in or near there (here), learning the trade of his father and improving on it; his own variation on the old theme . . . Edward, Capricorn, lover of Winter, stern, strong, sure of himself, powerful, concerned with what happens in his world and the world outside as it affects mankind; Edward, whose religions at this moment are music and experience; whose greatest connections with life are through his feet as they touch earth, and through his head as he works out ideas; Edward, Capricorn, of earth and on earth, stronger than Taurus but as stubborn, much stronger than Pisces; stronger even, in deep ways, than energetic, high-pitched Scorpio; heavy-boned, wisdom-seeking, aspiring, idealistic Edward. American. Today.

* * *

Saying the towns the way your father said them. The way your mother taught you. Wah-tur-vuh-leet. Ah-say-bull, and Care-oh. Dell-high. Ligh-mah. Not thinking. Not connecting. Not considering. The source. The reasons. The mystery. When the child is very young, he marvels that there is another person with his own first name. That his mother's name is Linda, and there is someone right across the street *also* called Linda! And then the realizations. The sharing. Even unto names.

Smith and Fletcher. Johnson. Wilson. The principal's son becomes a mortician. The banker's son becomes a bartender. The real estate man's son becomes an advertising executive. The seamstress' daughter becomes a weaver/designer. *None of us wears the original clothing through choice.* Someone sometimes gets to choose later on. The raiment can become a symbol, a corner of the life. The junkie becomes an honorary nun. The twin becomes a mystic. The farmer becomes a collector of erotica. The son of the veterinarian becomes a botanist.

The mortician's son becomes a drop-out. The nun's illegitimate daughter becomes a designer/weaver. The bartender's son becomes a bartender! The son of the soldier goes to West Point, loves it, and becomes a Regular Army man. Devices for dealing with the fear. Answering the unanswerable. Systems for ordering the unorderly, or for avoiding seeing the inherent order . . . history, always/never repeating itself; stasis into dynamics; earth growing older.

In Wittgenburg, a woman of fifty collects bottles, old and new, soft greens and umbers and clear, displays them in her windows, so that the light of morning shines through. This is her delight. And Loretta Somebody, her neighbor, gets a license to become an agent and sell real estate, and takes a job working for Sarah Almond-Tree, A/K/A Sally Mandelbaum. And Loretta Otherbody is the town whore. The town Visiting Nurse. The Town Clerk. She runs the town's dry-goods shop . . .

✽   ✽   ✽

What do they *do* in Trois? Wittgenburg: the burg you pass through to get to somewhere else. "In Spring and Fall, they take in each others' washing!" What do they teach you in school in Trois? They teach you the way things have been done before now, hoping you will continue it. Unchangingly. In Summer, the summer-people and the tourists come to Trois and spend money, and the local girls lie down and spread their legs for the visitors, hoping for a change in their lives. Each July Fourth, at the Memorial Field of the town's school, the fireworks are splashed, the kiddies sing, the preacher says his message of war-and-peace memory. This year, the fireworks were quite psychedelic in aspect (Myra's influence on Mike; Mike's influence on his mother Sally; Sally's, on everyone in town who sets anything up ever.)

And what are the Wittgenburg children made of? Ellen is made of *rijstafel* and cheeses. Myra is made of cabbage and pork. Edward is made of turkey and turnips. Ellen is made of fish. Myra is made of scorpions. Edward is made of goat-flesh. All three are made of country milk made into icecream, so is Heather, so is Mike, Mike is made of Scotch, so is Myra, Edward is made of beer, so is Ellen, Ellen is made of pot, so is Mike, so is Edward, so is Myra . . .

Fried Spam, cold bean salad made with vinegar and 3 kinds of beans (kidney beans, peabeans & stringbeans), ham salad, baked beans, cracker-meringue pudding, hot German vinegar potato salad, pickled tomatoes, preserved beets, tomato jelly, persimmon jam, home-baked brown bread, white bread, rolls, what are little girls made of, oatmeal, mother's-milk, Pablum, Enfamil, Van Houten's cocoa, milkshakes, frappes, cabinets, submarines, hoagies, blimpies, heroes, franks, wieners, hot dogs, colas, what are little boys and girls made of, True Romance, True Confessions, Mad Magazine, Reader's Digest, Encyclopedia Britannica, Boys' Life, The Bible, A Clearly Illustrated Manual of Sex, How to Develop Your Frabbis, Mark Twain's Life On the Mississippi, Charles Dickens' Tale of Two Cities, The Girl (Boy) Scout Manual, How Far To Go and When to Say No, Herman Melville, Nathaniel Hawthorne, The Evening Courier, The Daily Citizen Sentinel, The Weekly Freeman, The Albany Post Herald,

what do little boys and girls look like, windbreakers, mittens, gloves, Chapsticks, condoms, pencil-cases, Tampax-cases, sawed-off jeans, hot pants, jockey shorts, pony-tails, dirty fingernails, clean socks, torn sneakers, miniskirts, book-straps, boots, padded brassieres, nursing-bras, Estee Lauder or Avon perfume, panti-hose, underarm spray, vaginal spray, Cupid's Quiver douche concentrate, nylon underpants, foam-rubber roller curlers, bobbie-pins, scarves, kerchiefs, fringed jackets,

The Rolling Stones, Glenn Miller, The Beach Boys, Tennessee Ernie, Kris Kristofferson, Bob Dylan, Simon & Garfunkel, Elvis Presley, The Mothers of Invention, Glen Campbell,

Mars Bars, Clark Bars, Good 'n' Plenty, Hershey bars, Charleston Chews, Bonomo Taffy, M&Ms, Raisinets, popcorn, Goobers, in the movie-house, the only one in town, once a week, on Fridays and Saturdays, in the afternoon till you're thirteen, then at night, then after the movie to the drive-in, and at the drive-in, into the back seat,

on the back porch, in moonlight, in shadow, legs, breasts, hands, pricks, cunts, backs, lips, arms, in magic, in reality, in lust, in love,

in the sunshine on the front lawn, the baby-carriage, the play-pen, the washing-machine, the Ford, the dishwasher, the Green Stamps, the eggbeater, the Mixmaster, the power saw, the power mower, the power snow-thrower, the Ski-doo, the milking-machine, the baby-bottle-sterilizer, the Rotisserie, the electric barbecue set, the electric can-opener, the patio, the playroom, the second car, the family room, the new wing, the new house,

the trading-stamps, the life-insurance premiums, the bank loan, the new flatware, the guarantees, the warranty, the lease, the amortization, the interest, the

meeting of, the rally for, the benefit for, the shower for, the welcome-home, the send-off, the

get-together, the ceremonial, the observance of, the separation to, the funeral for, the birth of,

✿ ✿ ✿

Ellen, at the station, to see Tom off, that day long ago, not so long ago, that day that was to be his last day, and her last glimpse of him—Ellen, waving goodbye to Tom. And thinking, then, knowing, later, "It stops, when it is supposed to stop; it stopped; there was apparently no reason; *there doesn't have to be any reason.* Not for any beginning, and not for an ending. And anyhow, these are only *names* we give to things. To our feelings about what happens."

At home, in the days that followed, she found his spare pair of eyeglasses and put them on. "Beasts and plants and ghosts," she said aloud, "all have gods." The eyeglasses slipped and slid on her nose-bridge until she felt as if they had become another lens of her own flesh, set before her own first original set; a great, curved lens as a gift from Tom, so that she might see it all as he had seen it, as he would see it . . . Looking at the rain, the lens would go translucent sometimes, a tiny sudden shift, the look of the world would change, she was underwater, she would then become The Fish, she was the salmon, she would be a huge pale Mesozoic version of a fish, she was two fish in one, she was freckled in her pale flesh, dappled, spotted, touched by light through water, she was part of his state of being of . . . And he could see what she was seeing. He could have that much of her world! Gone, or not gone, it was all the same. To her. During those first weeks afterward. There was no sharp line between her dreams and her waking hours: all were the same fabric. She kept the glasses on part of each day and each night. Though for her the line between day and night was slow and quixotic.

That had been one place she had gotten to for a brief while —not planned for, but wanted to be—the place with Tom. And now it was not a place. Or, rather, it was still a place, both of theirs, but it had changed from what it was originally. So that it was recognizable only by glancing sideways, the life now and as she had known it with Tom; it was a peripheral-vision vision, seen through his glasses, shifting from transparent to overlay to translucent and back and forth. She stayed put. There seemed no beginning or end; just a continuum, of a sort for which she had no name. She would not change her name from Tom's. She would not pretend that she had not been married to him. She would not pretend anything. She had her gods. She did not want her father's gods. She could share Frey's gods. She could stay in this town; she could remain a part of the town where she and Tom had been born.

❋   ❋   ❋

Births and deaths. Ceremonials. Observances and recognitions. Acknowledgments. Rituals. Gods. The spirit death. Departure of the body. Loss. The bridges of convenience between worlds. To know the hour of one's death. *To know the hour of one's birth!*

Animal and spirit. Frey, advertising in the local *Pennysaver:* "Marchwind, pride of Elm Farm on March Acres, will stand his first season in the Trois area to a limited number of select Morgan mares. Come by and visualize what champion blood will do for your foals. Fee: Private Treaty. For appointment, call—" And the foals are born; one belongs to Edward and Ellen; on the night they come to choose him, many people make love; on another night of making love, a baby is conceived between Edward and Ellen; on another night, the foal is stolen and destroyed by a bear; on another night, the baby is destroyed;

birth and death, melting into the earth, which is what Trois is made of—mid-winter into mud-water—the seasons in motion. And what is Wittgenburg made of? Earth, mixed with Campbell's soup, until it is palatable; a lake, mixed with Lipton's powdered chicken noodle soup, until it is Soup Yet. Flour from wheat grown on earth. Noodles made from flour. Water of the streams on earth. Milk from cows to woman who gives breast to new child. Some young Wittgenburg women are getting back to nursing the babies at the breast. It has taken fifty years for this cycle to complete. So then: what is Trois made of? : Time. The time of animals.

CHAPTER

28

Edward isn't getting any lately, for sure. The ladies of the town are used to seeing him with either Myra or Ellen; everything is gossip; being a loner lasts just so long; philosophy goes just so far, he is himself a bit spoiled by now, having had both of them to turn to, in turn. And there's precious little pot around town, too. It's the Season of Drought, in effect, Summer, when the fields of grass in Mexico are burnt to the ground by governments who get all they need to smoke elsewhere. At the borders. So that two out of four basics are in short supply in Edward's life.

He makes his move, like all Caps, by considering the possibilities first. It's evident, of course, that Ellen isn't going to be in the slightest bit receptive to him; she didn't even nod when she passed him on Gribble Street yesterday. So he will search for Myra. Most always she's accepted him. He finds Myra at the Sled, with some friends from school (including Heather). She is acting stuffy. After all, she's almost twenty now, and so sees herself.

Tells him she'd rather try to score for some dope tonight. Has heard that there's some great stuff around, only she's not sure who's got it, and if she hangs around, she's sure to run into somebody she can connect with. He says it's eleven o'clock already, he's got plenty of Scotch, why not try for the stuff tomorrow. She's wearing her denim skirt and her see-through shirt and she knows it. Sees to it he knows it too.

"Let's get it on tomorrow," she says to him, not letting her friends hear her. "That way it could be a birthday fuck . . ."

"You gotta be kidding," he says, "It's nobody's birthday then!"

She sees how horny he is and is figuring that by tomorrow she might be horny too. "Well, it'll be *my* birthday," she laughs up at him. "I picked a new one. I figure I might as well be Cancer for a while." Besides, then I'd be twenty already."

"Not a chance," he says, dourly. "That's really ridiculous. *You* couldn't even make *believe* you were a Cancer!" He is thinking of Cancer people he knows. Not a chance. He was not able to flatter or wheedle to get what he wanted. "You're silly," he goes on. "You can't do that . . ."

"Sure I can," she says, furious. Nobody can tell a Scorpio they can't do something. "I can do anything I want. *Anything*. If I want to do something, I can do it. You better believe it."

"Okay. Okay. I believe it. So if you can do anything you want, how come you don't want to fuck with me?"

"Because I don't want to. Not now. Because I want something else more. The stuff that's around is supposed to be mixed in with some great DMT. And that's what I need right now. Who cares about anything else."

"*I* do," Edward says. "*I* need *you*."

"Isn't that *romantic*," she says, not looking at him; having heard that particular sentence some years ago from her father, and not liked it then, and not done anything about it then.

"Oh, well," she says, thinking she probably wouldn't score anyway and it was always good to have Eddie in reserve, Mike was going into The City this week, and who knows . . .

242

"Let's go, Romeo." He looks at her, delighted. "What'll it be, your house or mine?" she says, impishly.

"What? Are your folks away?" That would make it even more interesting. They'd never made it in her house. Her parents' house.

"No, no, of course not—they're home, dummy! I was just kidding."

"Oh. Okay." He has no sense of humour. And what little he's ever had is obviated by his horniness.

They walk over to his house, without touching. Scorpio is not big for affectionate gestures, and neither is Capricorn. Time of the Big Summer Drought, all righty, she is thinking, all this grass around and no Grass. The two of them get to his house. It is dark; he walks around putting on lights. They have their pattern by now—a drink of Scotch or two, and a joint or three, and then they will ball. But this will be reality. They have some Scotch and some more Scotch. They get together awkwardly, their gestures bumping and clashing. Myra is very disinterested and unusually passive. They're completely out of synch.

He asks her to suck him, figuring it will get both of them started. She refuses, for the first time. Her head isn't here at all (sorry about that). "I'm not into that tonight, Daddy-O!" So he moves to go down on her. Maybe to get them both started. He doesn't really want to "make love," that isn't his orientation with her anyway, and he's all for himself tonight; and she knows it. But then, she's always been. No love between them. So she isn't with him. She isn't here. And it all feels very mechanical.

The ground outside is steaming, even at midnight. Their skins are wet and slippery—with sweat. Myra is as cold as Winter. They miss their smoke. They hear a soft wind beginning outside. They hear the creaking of the old house. They both get up and leave the bed, on opposite sides. Walk about the room. Both uptight and aflame as if in a bad shirt which is on fire and made of rough fabric to begin with.

"Jesus. What a trip," Myra says.

"Pain is one of the basic elements," Edward says.

"Jesus Christ," Myra says. "And we don't even *split*. We *stay* here!"

"Ah. Wise, *Dear* Little What's-'er-Name," Edward says, having reached that stage he calls "drunk as a skunk."

"Call me Elmira," she says, heading for the almost-empty bottle of Scotch. "L. Myra Shultis, In The Flesh," she says, prancing naked. He stares at her. Forgetting what it was he'd ever seen in this girl. And then remembering, as she dances.

They wind up near the bed and trying for it again. He can get it up this time and begins to go in. They go at it for a while, in a desultory, sweaty way, like barn animals. Suddenly he laughs. She snarls, "What's so funny?" "I just thought of a grownup joke. Not so sure you'd appreciate it."

"Tell," she says, quite seriously. "I'm almost twenty, remember."

"You won't be till November, weirdo!"

"Try me, creep!"

"That's just—what it's about," he says, laughing, not looking at her. Tells her the "So you can't think of anyone either?" joke. She doesn't respond. He still thinks it's very funny.

Considers that he now feels pretty all right; in fact pretty stoned, even if it isn't pot it's okay. Reaches over her for the Scotch. A drop left. It helps. Thinks again about the joke, thinks that Ellen would consider it in extreeeeemely bad taste, especially under the circumstances! Ah, that prissy aristocrat . . . wasn't she. Thinks, she almost always moved under *my* circumstances, didn't she. Notes his own use of past tense. Immediately loses his hard.

Myra seems to be upset. She was really just beginning to get interested, if not excited. "God*dam*, every time I get going, you change the position or the rhythm or something or you lose the hard, how do you expect me to get *off?*—you *ape*," she says, flatly, without a trace of affection. "You aren't all *that* much better than Mike tonight; at least he digs where I'm at, some of the time—"

Edward begins to get angry: not at her and not at himself, just generally. Gets his finger up into her and begins to get his hard back. Maybe the anger helps, he thinks, *something* better had! He feels lousy now. Their backs are cooled by the wind coming lightly through the window open near the bed.

He reaches out and pulls Myra toward him, in a rough way. Expecting a fight; wanting it. She, however, digs it. She's completely dry now.

"Wet me, wet me," she orders.

"Damned if I will!" he says, and tries to enter anyhow. Memories of Kathy ordering him to do this or that or everything for her in the bed. And out of it. Then flash to that scene where Marty Levitt made Ellen in the room down the hall from him. He hears every sound they are making. Watching those two, in his mind's eye. The fuck with Myra becomes frantic. It gets edges to it. ("onto it," Edward catches himself saying, and quickly changes it, after all, *he's* no redneck!)

Myra's frantic, too, in her own Scorp world, and halfway there. It's all the edges of cliffs, and the climbers' hands are bloody. Edward is really into watching his idea of Marty and Ellen fucking. What if it were the other Marty, Frey's Marty, doing the male Marty bit. What if it were Frey's Marty, doing Ellen. Flash to the scene at Frey's farm, that time, all the bodies making music to each other. Concept: what *if* Marty Levitt, Marty Lipschitz, had been there too, that time? How'd it have gone? New instrument in the orchestra—

Myra breaks in, at that moment, of course: "Jesus—too much speed today, Eddie—I can't get there—I won't be able to come! Why—"

He shuts the sound of her voice out. Pretends she really hasn't said anything. He's pursuing the fantasy that was keeping him going, a minute ago. What the *hell.* Nor are we out of it. The scenes in his head are beginning to get somewhere, maybe somewhere he needs them to go. Somewhere he needs to go. Feels that way—feels like—feels—right. Like the—Yes. Marty, there . . . Oh, *I* see. That's it. What if I were there, in the sack, with—Marty Levitt? *What?* Is *that* where this is all going? Fantasizes Marty's body erect and ready to go into Ellen. Puts his own body there instead of Ellen's. Himself taking it in the ass from Marty, his old buddy. One of his oldest chum-buddy pals. Pain but good feeling. Jesus, what a high idea! Himself sucking off Marty. Marty and himself in a sixty-nine. Wow! Risky, but it works. Maybe that's why it works! Boy, does it ever work! All the thoughts about having touched Marty (Marty the straight, the square, the predictable, the unquestioning,) over the long years as friends in the town. An arm casually thrown around a shoulder. But I'm not gay and neither is Marty. So *what*, do we have to be gay to make it with each other, suppose it's just affection, suppose it's just sex, suppose it's just a logical extension of the friendship—if we can love, why can't we make love? If we can fight, and talk, and walk, and be *friends*, how come we can't fuck? What would be wrong with it going along that road as well as on all the other ways of being close? We've fucked each others' minds, all right. So why not? Why the fuck not? But barely an *abrazo* now and then, on greeting or meeting. Now no way there could have been trips along any other street. Not in America. Had Marty ever thought—Edward wondered. Once, long ago, Edward had thought of them as brothers and at that time he couldn't figure out which one was Cain and which Abel. *Now* he would know which was which! :he, Edward, would be Abel. Would be able. And he would raise Cain. Raise him from the dead, from the square, from the American deadness, the antisexism . . .   Ho ho, what a bit of *business*, he laughed, beginning to move inside the body next to him at the moment. Hmmm, now, let's see—here I am, inside Marty, up his tight ass, this is Marty I'm going into. His broad, chunky back, the hairy chest, the short compact torso— hey, what kind of penis does he have? That kind. He must be circumcised, for one thing, and with that body-build, he must have a wide, short one, not like mine . . .

The images in his head melted together. He could see Marty making love with Ellen. With Frey, Ellen, the other Marty, with himself. The scene *needed* another man anyhow, didn't it? He remembered he thought so at the time. He saw himself making love with Marty on one side of him and Frey at the other. He saw Marty's mouth on Edward's cock. He could feel it all. There was Ellen, watching them and touching herself.

246

And there was her Marty—Jesus, what a group!—So now he could begin to think about coming. Actually, he could begin to stop thinking, because he could come—

At which point Myra moved and got off him. *Of course.* "*Myra!* What the *hell*—"

"You're *hurting* me, you creep," she said, in a dull, low voice, absent of anger.

"Since when don't you like it when I hurt you?"

"Since *now*. Since whatever is going down right now!"

"But *you* just did what you say you hate when *I* do it to *you*—"

"And what might *that* be?"

"You didn't see where *I* was at, at all! You quit just when it was great for me, just when I was getting there—just when it—"

"Oh, now, *did* I do that to *poor* sensitive old Eddie? Isn't that just too biddy-poo lousy old bad, too tough for words, Daddy-O—"

"You *bitch*. You goddam surly mouthy little bitch! Get over here!" He reached. But no. Loveless and hung up and hurting, she slapped at him. So he reached over and got her clothes and threw them at her, and kicked her out of his house. Without once looking at her fully.

She left, cursing him. Back in the coziness of her own room, she took out the last precious tiny roach of a joint and lit up; sipped from the bottle of Scotch she kept in her bureau drawer, and sat in front of the mirror, wanting not to think about any of what had just gone down. Her feelings were surfacing. Four ayem now and no chance in the world to score for more pot or DMT or *anything*. Might as well forget it. She was supposed to meet Heather at the waterfall near the end of the lake, tomorrow morning. Something would turn up . . . She fell across her own bed and began to finish what she and Edward had started. It would take a long time, what with the speed, but then she knew what she liked best to get herself there. She'd come, and then maybe some sleep, or a walk downstairs to get something to eat . . . and then some sleep. Not much, but some. She felt lousy.

A little comfort. A little warmth of some kind. A little excitement; a little relief. A big relief. The Lucky Big O. Always, for the Scorpio, the Lucky Big O. At the sure end, the rich round pot-O-gold at the end of the colorful trip; no matter who or how you get there; so what if the rainbow is the part about being with someone you dig; Myra wasn't about that part, maybe never would be, it was the Big O she was after, the brass ring of the Big O. No cons, no connects, no holds; she knew too much already about *that* kind. No gold ring of possession for this kid. She would possess only herself, she would never be possessed. And if someone around her wanted to be possessed, let him look out for his own ass. Not *her* problem. Never again! Dear Dad had turned her off *that* side-trip, for good. Thanks to his teachings, she was so good at getting the Big O's—for herself, from herself or from anyone. Damn near anyone.

Still in his own house, Edward walked around. Loveless and hung up and hurting, devoid of both questions and answers, he figured he might as well stay awake; it was well after 3 ayem, damn near four already . . . He had a drink of the Scotch he kept downstairs in case he ran out of Scotch, and then still another belt of it. Figured maybe he was turning into a rummy like Dear Old Dad, keeping a hidden bottle he didn't tell anybody about, and hitting it when nobody else was around, like now. He felt strange, cool, delighted to be alone, so that he could get back into his fantasies. As he sat sprawled near the cold fireplace, and as his thoughts ran and slipped and went back to the scenes he had been thinking about, earlier, he reached down and unzipped his fly. Slowly, almost tenderly, as if someone were being tender with him, he began: the loneliest art. Began, slowly, firmly, toward a little warmth, a little excitement, a little relief, as if it were—as if it were—who?

CHAPTER
29

CHOPPED HISTORY, *All those who are present today become the Past,* at this moment we are looking at the rocky gorge which feeds into the lake at the end of Trois, it is hot, *hot,* July again, Wittgenburg full of visiting Irish again, and all the locals are unified by their regional, cherished secrets: only they know about the rocky pool, which can be reached by hiking across the land of one of the oldest families; here, the various tribes of Trois are superficially one, sharing a barrier against the Barbarians, the Intruders, the Auslanders: the Irish of the Summer. Those who haven't the sense, or haven't had the luck, to live in this most blessed of towns on earth . . . those who must earn a living in cities, or who have, for whatever reason, chosen to; or whose parents were perhaps farmers but who left, and who now must pay the price of exclusion . . . A vanity, a possessiveness, an accent . . . On this, the several tribes of Trois blend. For the moment. *On the surface.* At the beginning.

High Summer, and half the town wants to be high, and the

other half is drinking sloe gin at noon out of thermos jugs and pretending to each other that it's iced tea . . . And also everyone is drinking beer. Everyone over the age of ten is drinking beer, whether or not he is smoking pot or drinking sloe gin . . .

* * *

Let's see now. In this Heather, Myra and Sex discuss chapter. No. I mean. In this sex, Myra and chapter discuss—Mike and Heather and—no. Mike and Myra, Heather and Al—who the fuck's Al? *A new character?* At this late date? You've *got* to be kidding! Ah well. Fuck it! Why *not?* It happens in the life, doesn't it? Does Al have to cease to exist just because I haven't mentioned him (except once, briefly, if you care to check back!) Is his life worthless, like the damn tree in the forest that nobody's heard falling? No. *So:* Mike, Myra, Heather, and a newie-but-goodie, Al, in *this* Chapter, among other things, discuss How The Other Half Lives. Let the rest be a surprise. As much to me as to you. But you are safe to assume that at some point, since we are nearing the end of this tale, that either Ellen, or Edward, or maybe both, will make an appearance. And that Frey won't.—Here they are, then, the Youth of America, in whose hands the future lies; midsummer, and they are at The Ole Swimmin' Hole. Doing their thing:

* * *

Chopped Strata. A History. A Spillway of Time, Recorded. And all our yesterdays . . . thereon: along the shale sides of the Gorge, names are chalked; the whiteness, softened by the years, is often a buff shade, and, in places where the water seeps through, there are punctuations of dark moss and lichen: names of people who have loved or who want in other ways to be remembered; hearts, or clubs, or the clever chiaroscuro of affection's connective tissues . . . And here, as along the roads of Trois, there are metal signs (rusted at the edges), saying: POSTED, NO TRESPASSING, on every eighth tree, in the old attempt to possess. But this is nature, from whom one may only borrow. Sign: PLANT ENTRANCE, not on some road, but on a granite rock, where a tree has split through and grown strongly toward life . . .

* * *

"Hey, listen," Myra says to Heather, as they walk down the steep path, "the peepers are going, and it's broad daylight! What the hell time is it?" "*Not* peepers," says Heather. "Them's '*gommels*', and you know it! Comin' for to carry us home." "I wish *I* could still believe in '*gommels*'," says Myra. "Well, you've got saints, that's just as good," Heather says. She unrolls a ragged towel and lays it across one of the flat rocks about thirty feet from the flowing water. "Sun's gonna be plenty hot in an hour," she says. "It's hot *now*, dummy," says Myra. "You got no nerve endings, or what?" "No; I'm just a wee bit stoned, I guess," Heather says, delightedly.

Heather kept at it last night, trying to score for some dope, and finally made it for a very light oh-zee. She came by Myra's house at a little after 8 ayem to give her the good news, or rather a taste of same, and Myra was quite awake, having briefly napped and woken up crying and not been able to sleep again; she was playing the radio softly and doing her breast-development exercises when Heather walked in. They rolled some joints and smoked two, at least. Myra has yet to tell Heather what went down between Edward and her in bed and all. That awful scene. She may or may not tell Heather. Sometimes Scorps keep things to themselves for quite a while. Secretive. A thing about privacy.

Now the girls stretch out in the sun and light another joint, passing it back and forth silently. No one else is there. A twig snaps in the silence, near their heads. "There go the '*gommels*', again," says Heather. "Right *on*," says Myra, "I saw one once, did you know that?" "*Sure,* you did," says Heather, half believing it. "Okay, so what'd it look like?" "Like your mother." "Oh, Jesus."

Half an hour passes. Then a sound of voices. Mike appears, with friend Al, who is also Heather's current interest. "Perfect!" says Heather, "We got a lot left, right?" "For sure." Mike curves around the big rock and spots the girls. "Ho *ho*," he grins, "Look who scored! Got some left?"—knowing the answer. "Only for close friends," Heather says to her brother, handing him a stick.

The boys settle in around the girls. "God, I thought there wouldn't *ever* be any more grass," says Al. "Who'd you connect with?" "Chuck had a pound to divide. And there were about a hundred vultures converging! You should have seen it," Heather told him. "He asked for fifty an ounce—" "You didn't pay *that*, did you? Where'd you get that kind of bread?" "Don't be silly. First of all, we knew he'd be shorting us all, so the first ones to get some got it for thirty-five . . . I guess the ones at the end of the line paid fifty or even more." "What the hell. He's *crazy*." "But he got the dope; right?" "No, dear. *We've* got the dope."

Another half hour passes. Myra goes down to the water, reports it's still damn cold. "Still got the night air into it," she says, mockingly. "Come on," she says, pulling at Mike. "Now what do I need to do *that* for?" he whines. "Keep your old damn ice-water! Here I am in this nice warm body—" "Yum," says Myra. "Let's go over behind those trees, what d'you say—" "Not on your *life*," Mike says, always the conservative, "not a chance. Not with all that cold, wet skin you got sticking all out of the jeans and your goose-pimply legs all dangling down-o!" She puts her hands on his crotch. "That'll do you no good, I tell you. But talk to me in half an hour, when you've warmed up a bit." "Screw you," says Myra. "Exactly my reference," says Mike. "You should be so lucky," says Myra, fondly, and lies in the sun next to him, her leg draped over his. He turns over on his belly, to conceal and control his mild hardon. But Myra knows.

✿　✿　✿

A lot of noise from the woods at the top of the path. "Oh, Jesus," says Heather, "Here come The Common People! I knew we couldn't get away with this glorious peace for long." "Well, it must be getting nigh on to ten o'clock in the morning," Myra says, wisely, pronouncing them "way-ell," and "tay-enn" and grimacing as if her teeth didn't fit. Along the path and through the trees come three women in their early thirties, and several youngish children. "If *they* come, I *leave*," says Mike. " 'Smatter, you intolerant or something?" says Al. "Don't worry," says Heather. "They won't come too close. They're afraid it's catching. And besides, it's too deep here for their kid-dees, you know that; *that's* their place, down there, where everything's all nice and *safe*." "Shit-ass types, never took a chance on anything in their whole lives," says Myra. "Watch. None of them even goes *near* the water. Watch closely, folks, at no time does the fat fanny of *any* lady leave the security of the sunny rock ledge."

"Clue me in," says Al, who's been away at agricultural college in Andes, N.Y. for the past year and a half, "who's the fat broad leading off? I recognize the others—" "That, my dear man, is the imported wife, the new second wife, would you believe, of our beloved Church leader, Neumyer, who seems to have lost no time in mourning the departure of the late equally fat Armentha Hawley Neumyer, who he probably killed in her sleep. You wanna be fixed up with her? Name's Linda. Just what this town needs. Another goddam fucking Linda," says Myra. "They don't have *enough* fat broads named Linda, so they have to *import* one." "Better they should import a new pastor, too, while they were at it," says Al, sweetly. "My folks made me go to his service last Sunday, and I can't *tell* you how impressed I was."

"Hey, dig it," says Heather. "*The Girls* . . ." All four turn and exaggeratedly peer at the arriving humanity. "All them *prints*," says Myra, "looks like they done gone and bought out all the Agway flour sacks there was!" With one hand, she pushes the stash under a corner of the towel, never taking her eyes off the newcomers. The arrivals veer away from the four youngsters. They settle in their habitual place. It is even and level and unlike the deep-channeled rocky ledge where the four students are located.

"Buncha creeps," says Mike. "How can they stand to go around looking like that, in broad daylight?" "Ah, it's not so bad, if you like plastic people," says Myra. The three older women have their hair rolled on large pink plastic foam-rubber curlers, not quite covered by gaudy kerchiefs. All of them are wearing Capri pants, one pair aqua, one light blue, one pair bright yellow. And the aforementioned print shirts. And Corfam sandals. The fat woman carries an infant in a device called an Infanseat, a device that prevents the baby's body from contacting that of the mother much if not all of the time. ("The twice-told tales of Infanseat" might be said at this time, but as none of our characters is quite literate enough yet to make that comment, I will once again step in, unable to resist.) The infant is howling. The women and the other children are talking above the sound. "Welcome—I say, *welll*-come to Wittgenburg's Ladies' Social Club, Sewing Circle, Straight-On-Fucking-Missionary-Style Organization, and Quilting Bee Branch of the Grange," says Mike. "They're disgusting," says his sister. "What the hell do they have to talk about so much?" says Myra. "What to cook for dinner for the old man; what else?" says Mike. "Fuck 'em all, I can't stand even to look at 'em," says Al. "I seen better tits on the cows I'm training on."

The women set up low plastic beach-chairs and plastic mats, turn on a portable radio, and get beers from a cooler. "Oh, *shit*," says Heather, "there goes tranquility. If it isn't enough to look at them, we have to listen to their bad taste in music, too!" The radio is tuned to some disk jockey in Albany. Rock music from the early sixties. "Buncha fucking *fossils*," says Mike. "We oughta bring along some Frank Zappa some day, and drown 'em out." "All right, folks, how you doin' and how's the folks, now for a stroll down Memory Lane, meet you at the Bowling Alley, glad you came?" says Myra.

Heather laughs. "Imagine it. If we were all done in as we are right this minute, and some smart archaeologist digs us up two thousand years from now. What would they find of us? We don't even have any interesting metal!" "Yes, we *do*," says Mike, producing his hash-pipe. "And aside from this, there'd be the fillings in our teeth, and the nubbies around the shoelace-holes in my sneakers," says Myra, "but really, the most *interesting* thing would be the imprints of the bodies on the slate . . . you know, like big brachiopods . . ." "Oh, *neat,*" says Mike to her, "Let's fuck! Can you think of a more interesting way to go out?" "Oh, so the bod is warm enough for your highness now?" He has his arm thrown over her back and is watching her face intently. "Yeah. Yeah, and *yeah.* And besides, imagine what fun it'd be for those people two thou years from now, to find us that way! Linked at crucial points." General laughter.

"I wonder if people will still be fucking then?" says Heather, seriously. "If they haven't found a better way in all this time, they probably won't by then," says Al. "I wonder if people will still *be,* period," says Myra.

❊ ❊ ❊

By now, there are perhaps thirty people gathered at the stream: divided into two clear groups, each is withdrawn from the other. Demarcations. Mike and Myra and their friends, their crowd; and the wives of the Gas Station, the Constabulary, and the Church, and their friends, downstream from them. In the latter group are perhaps eight or ten children under the age of ten. In the former, one nine-month-old infant.

MIKE: Know what they are? They're reality. Ree-*al*-i-teeee. *That's* what the hell *they* are. Adults. Grown-all-the fucking-way-up adults, would you believe. In the flesh. In their miserable, stupid, good-for-nothing shrunken-head flesh. *Look* at them, willya? Boy, are they weird . . .

HEATHER: Take it easy. The word "weird" begins with "*we*," dear sibling.

MIKE: Well then, *you* look at them and enjoy them, if that's your bag! It's not mine, for sure. All they think about is trivia. Stupid shit.

MYRA: Like what? What do you call *stupid,* smart-ass?

MIKE: Like what war to get us into next, and like what kind of plastic to wear today, and like money.

HEATHER: You think about money a lot, babe.

MYRA: Their kids are just more of the same mess. Look.

255

HEATHER: Not necessarily. Our parents look just like them. And we're so groovy. There's hope.

AL: Well, for sure they have to be on *some* kind of big ego trip, otherwise why would they have all those kids? Or maybe they don't know fucking makes babies. All that churchy hard-sell . . .

HEATHER: My mother told me she thought birth control was about going to take a piss after you have intercourse.

MYRA: So how come she only had two of you? (Laughter)

HEATHER: Do you suppose those people *think* about why they have babies? If they *do*—

AL: Ego. Ego. Wanting somebody around who's smaller than they are, that they can beat up on. Or wanting something around that looks like them or their old man. Yecccchhhh. Imagine wanting more people around who look like them! I'd sooner look at a bunch of Jersey heifers, any time. 'Least the color is good.

MYRA: Well, if there's gonna be a world a hundred or a thousand years from now—and I wouldn't put a bet on it—I can't see having it populated with creeps like that. *I* think it'd be better with just *us*. No more unenlightened slobs.

HEATHER: Not logical. They have more kids than we do. Lots more.

AL: We could change that—beginning right now.

MIKE: You're all *crazy*. We *need* them. We need people to pump gas and wipe off the bar and put the drinks out. Chop the trees to make the paper we wipe our ass with.

HEATHER: You don't have to be such a fucking elitist about it! Sure, we need them, but they need us too. Even tho they don't know it. It's a balance and it's good. You remember what you learned in Smitty's class, last year? *I* think it's going to be okay; that is, if we don't flip out and give up . . . I think the world's a good place; I mean, not *good*, exactly, not the way it is *now*, but it could get better. And then it would be great. Listen, if we can get days like this, that makes it all right!

MYRA: Oh God, are you ever an idiot.

AL: Heather, I don't *believe* this. Just *look* at them. Neumyer's wife. You just know how it is with them. He's her meal ticket and she's his real reliable twat. Not a brain in the bunch.

HEATHER: So what makes us any better? Is it better to be smarter? If I'm so smart, how come I hurt so much? Are we smarter just because we don't have to have it dark when we fuck, or always in one position all our lives? (Laughter)

MYRA: Listen, babe, we *are* better. Seriously. Better genes, or something. We *look* better and we're *much* more interesting. And—

MIKE: What makes you think so? The way they live is a vote of no-confidence, and so is the way we do the trip. Sucking up time without paying anything back in.

HEATHER: I'm not like that! I want to put back in. I *want* kids. Lots of them. So isn't that the same as *their* wanting them?

MYRA: I for sure don't want a lot of smarmy brats cluttering up my life. The noise is deafening.

MIKE: That's your usual selfish point of view. We gotta look at it scientifically. I have this theory that everyone with an IQ lower than 130 should be prevented from reproducing. That would begin to clean up some of the mess.

MYRA: Good, but it doesn't go far enough. Remember what I said the last time we dropped acid? That there should be a very carefully selected hundred people from the whole world, and they would be the only ones who could have kids. Really *selected*. Remember?

HEATHER: Remember! I wish I could forget!

MYRA: How come?

HEATHER: I told you. I *want* babies. And your idea would cut me out right away. I'm not brilliant, but I think I'm smart enough to raise kids better than those people over there—and for another thing, I'm going to be pretty careful about who studs them. Because if I weren't, then I'd be stupid just like they are. I'd just fuck and make babies on instinct or on instructions from the church or whatever. Dullsville.

AL: What about if you had a good offer from a really handsome, smart man like me?

HEATHER: I don't know. I haven't studied your family.

MYRA: You have to learn, sooner or later, Heather baby, to live dangerously . . .

HEATHER: Not about *that*, I won't! It could get me a kid I didn't dig, for example. Or, at the very least, a bad lay, is what . . .

MYRA: He's not.

HEATHER: Oh. You been there.

MYRA: Naturally! Scorp, remember?—No kidding. I'll give the testimonial. *"Try* it; you'll *like* it."

AL: Yeah! Yeah!

HEATHER: I'll think about it.

MYRA: That's the wrong approach.

HEATHER (gently): Your way isn't my way. Dig it.

MIKE: Seriously. The thing that gets to me is how they sell us all this crap about how we're supposed to do the life. *Their* way, of course. They want us to live like them. As if they were anything like us. The cretins. Not an insight in the whole lot. And when you think that that's something like 90% of the population—

HEATHER: They don't smoke grass, even! But—

MYRA: Darling, I think you're *very* wrecked.

AL: What *they* need is—I know. They need us to go over the ridge to the watershed, and just set in a half pound of nice sandy acid into the fabulous Trois water supply—

MYRA: Good, but no cee-gar. What we need is some kind of marvelous unsuspected way of getting the stuff to them, but *slow*. Like—like—how 'bout THC in their toothpaste? Not a lot, you dig. Just enough to turn them on a little bit every

258

morning and night. Boy, would they ever lay out! What would happen to all their automated heavy working trips!

HEATHER: But that would leave out the little kids, the ones who aren't old enough to brush their teeth yet.

MYRA: Forget it. Those people got their kids brushing their teeth when they're on the way out of the cunt, practically. Ritual, remember?

AL: Turning on a little kid two years old isn't such a big idea. They still have natural highs.

MYRA: Not with mothers and fathers like those.

MIKE: I think I was a full-fledged fuckup by the time I was two.

HEATHER: You were *not!* You were a very together kid.

MIKE: Seen through the eyes of love, if not hero-worship. Folks, I'd like you all to meet my kid sister, Heather.

HEATHER: Listen. There should be a way that THC or acid or whatever could get into their heads by osmosis. Like, they would have to put it near or on their heads.

MYRA: Too *much.* I have this image now of some sorta weird helmet, with input funnels.

AL: No. What I think would work is, some kind of salve. Works with animals; why not with them? Maybe in their vaseline—No, they don't fuck that much . . . Okay. I *got* it. How about this. The stuff they put on their hair before they stick on the curlers. And for the men, in the shaving cream. Or after-shave. They all still shave, right? So that way, it stays there a while, right up close to the brain.

MYRA: Great. Right *on.* And then we could distribute pamphlets as to how to *use* this new imagination they'd get. Jesus! —imagine one position, all your life!

AL: *What* life? You call that living?

MYRA: Do you suppose there's anything we could do to get the message to them that life's supposed to be fun?

MIKE: Sure. Starting now. Let's throw moons and see whether they'll laugh.

AL: Forget it, they'd just call the cops. Gimme a toke, Mike, you old bastard, what're you trying to do, keep the whole thing for yourself?—What you going to do in the Fall?

MIKE: Head for the City. Deal a little dope. Bring you some, if you play your cards right. Mamma has her usual idea of how she wants it to go, has this gig set up with some of her good old relatives—

MYRA: Fuck that! I'm going to see to it that all we do for at least six months is go to the movies. I want to see everything that plays on Forty-Second Street and then start uptown. All the sex flicks.

HEATHER: I don't know what you need *them* for. You live it better than they're filming it!

MYRA: Oh, I don't know, you can always learn something new! In the City they develop ideas faster.

AL: You know what? Those jerks over there never even *go* to the City. I heard Travis Bregman say he'd been there one time, says when he was a little kid they made the big trip and they all took in the Easter Show at Radio-City-Fucking-Well-Music-Hall! (Laughter)

HEATHER: You're not going to believe this, but when Mary Lou and her crowd are talking all the time about going to the City —she means *Albany!* (Groaning)

AL: I once took a bus up to Canada and you know what? All the cities we stopped at looked alike. Albany is just like Rochester and Schenectady and Utica—you couldn't tell 'em apart without the driver told. You could put any of those people down on any o'those streets like a bunch of cut-outs and they'd fit right in. Curlers and all.

HEATHER: Curlers *especially*. God, they're so *ugly*. I never saw anything so against nature. Will you dig the color that one's got her hair dyed. She could just about use the label from the bottle stuck on her forehead because you're never ever anywhere going to see that color enough to know what to call it!

Jesus, but I *wish* they were beautiful. Hey, just imagine if we were on some *island* really and if they were jet-set people . . .

AL: Why the hell's all that so important to you?

HEATHER: Because I'd just rather look at something *good* than something that looks like it's made out of somebody else's idea of a mass-produced person. Like the way *you* didn't like it that the cities all look alike and none of them look good. I'm just sick of looking at ugly simps, is all! They look just as bad as my relatives. I just wish I could see some grown-ups who looked good like we do.

MYRA: Well, some of them aren't all that bad. Edward does okay, and some of his friends. Anyhow, we don't look all that good to them, remember. That man at the bus-stop that time. And you must really be crazy if you think *we* look so good—"

MIKE: *You* look good to *me,* babe!

MYRA: Blind love again. I didn't sleep but one hour. I feel like shit.

HEATHER: Speaking of Edward's friends! Ain't that John's Other Wife, coming on down the ole garden path? Who's that she's with?

MYRA: Oh, Jesus. Whaddya know. Yeah. It's Ellie.

* * *

Just past noon now. High noon, and such it was; Heather, Myra, et Cie., having put away three more joints, were taking nothing for granted. Al had made a run back into town for munchies and more beer, in his 1955 pink-and-beige Chevvy. The older women fed their broods, and were getting ready to leave for town, for nap-time. They left behind a litter of beer-cans, used Kleenex and plastic-coated diapers. "Disgusting," someone younger said, loud and clear, but nobody moved to clean up the mess.

"Wonder what the new day brings," sang Mike, in a sweet, tenor voice. He and Myra were lying so that their sides were as one line. He felt protective toward her; no one could see if it was Edward with Ellen, approaching. He knew Myra was nervous. "Who the hell's that with Ellie Dykstra?" asked Al. "Don't know and don't care," said Heather, caught up pondering on the curve in Al's wet bathing-suit. "Looks familiar though . . ."

✻ ✻ ✻

The man walking with Ellen was Marty Levitt. He was pretty much absorbed in his return to a scene of his childhood, and caught up in his memories; he saw none of the youngsters stretched out on the rocks before him; he was acutely conscious of Ellen, as she walked next to him. But Ellen saw Myra at once. Despite her nearsightedness. By now, she had become used to that fine-thin, tight shock of spotting the younger woman somewhere and then making it her goal to avoid running into Myra. To avoid any sort of confrontation.

The pattern was set, by now. The fear invaded her body in a reflex. She shied slightly. Marty touched her arm. "You all right?" "Sure. Fine." "Okay." This was different. No Edward. And no possibility of avoiding Myra. She and Marty would have to pass the kids to get to the area beyond them, just before the Flats.

Ellen dropped back of Marty, and considered. Probing her feelings, she found she lacked some of the hard edge of panic she'd been used to. As they passed the group, she gave them all a vague, general smile and wave. The others returned it. When she and Marty got to a spot Marty liked, they sat, facing the water and with their backs to the group.

MARTY: So what was *that* all about?

ELLEN: What?

MARTY: Oh, come *on*. You know damn well what I mean. That little jump you gave. That no-so-little jump.

ELLEN: That's Myra, over there. You met her. You know that's Myra! Don't you!

MARTY: Okay; so what? So that's Myra. So what? Who are the others? I can't see from here.

ELLEN: The other girl is Heather. Mandelbaum. And you know

262

it. Your cousin Heather. All grown up. Your other cousin Mike is sitting with his back to us. What a shit you can be. You just *want* me to have to *say* all this. You even knew that's Myra. You *met* her. With him.

MARTY: Okay, okay, so what's the jump about?

ELLEN: It's an old reflex, is all. About that she also goes out with Edward. The whole mess. Months.

MARTY: What's that mean, "goes out with?"

ELLEN: You know. Dates.

MARTY: No, I *don't* know. You're really infuriating, the way you mess over the language. The way you say one thing and mean something else entirely.

ELLEN: What do you mean?

MARTY: You *know* fucking well what I mean! What a prissy broad you can be. You say "dates" and you say "goes out with" and what you really mean is, she's fucking with. They certainly weren't doing any of this Saturday-night-at-the-movies-with-popcorn thing . . . I mean, don't you have any integrity about the language, for Christ's sake, if not to the relationships you're talking about?—and I notice you used the present tense. You said "also goes out with Edward," I noticed.

ELLEN: It's just a manner of speaking, I guess. Don't get all fussy and fumy over it. You know I'm not seeing him any more!

MARTY: There you go again! What a damn drag. Why don't you call a thing what it is, instead?

ELLEN: I guess I don't *want* to say it that way . . .

MARTY: Why the hell not? It's in the past, anyway—or is it?

ELLEN: Yes. You know it is. But—it's not *enough* in the past, I guess, for me to understand all of it—all of what's gone down. Or for it not to hurt. Or for me to get over the reflex feelings involved—

MARTY: Jesus. If I can walk the hell out on Marie, after all those *years,* and no sweat—Jesus! Can't you stop paying dues behind that scene?

ELLEN: We live in the same town. You walked out on Marie and the kids and they're there and you're here. But Edward's *here,* and so's Myra . . .

MARTY: Forget it. For*get* it, I tell you!

ELLEN: I wish I could. I know you're right. It's just not that easy. I'm not like that. I'm—

MARTY: I know what you are, you're a beautiful and delicious and nice lady, and I'm beginning to love hanging out with you, and you better believe I don't intend to stand for your going all rubbery in the knees when Ed's name comes up or his other ex-girl's around, or *any* of that shit. Maybe *he* thrived on that brand of excitement, but *I* don't, and you know it. He's a good guy and he's my good friend, but you know damn well he's just a bit sadistic.

ELLEN: I never thought of him that way. At least not very often. (*Turns her head away.*)

MARTY: So how often is often enough for you? Anyhow, let's not get into that kind of a head. Not on a day like this. —You know what I'd like? I'd like to smoke some of that dope the kids have, over there.

ELLEN: Well, I don't have the nerve to walk over and ask. Why don't you? They're *your* relatives, et cetera—

MARTY: Hmmmm. Maybe it'd be better for you if you went over there . . .

ELLEN: Not on your life. I'm not ready. You go.

MARTY: Okay.

He walks over to the M-M-H-A group, who stiffen just perceptibly as he approaches. At a distance, one of the new group of older-women-with-kids, the townies, stares overtly at the upcoming interchange. Marty grins down at his cousins and greets them. With his back to the straight ladies, he asks Mike for a J. "Not this minute, but sure," Mike tells Marty. "Go back and sit down. I'll walk over to you in a minute. The locals are just longing for the opportunity to get us all busted, and you'd go along with us. That one—the one with the blue hair-ribbon that says "*Miss Bovinity, 1938,*" is affiliated with the Politzei. So cool it." "It's a pity we can't turn them on," says Marty. "Worse pity it isn't legal yet," replies Mike.

He walks back over the rocks to Ellen. She reaches over and touches his arm. "You feel different now. Different from two weeks ago." "Sure I do! I *am* different." "I mean, even your *skin* feels different!" "Of course. I can breathe through it now!" He flops down beside her and puts his hand on her back and moves it down. "You know what?" he says to her, "You have the greatest big beautiful rump in the whole world." "You should know," she says. "What's that supposed to mean?" "Well, you've just spent six years in the great big wide wonderful world of advertising in The City, so I suppose you've either seen or felt 'em all!" He preens, enjoying her view of him as a man of prowess. Knowing it is not true. She knows it is not true. "This is the way I like you to be," he says to her. "What do you mean? You mean kidding around with you about sex like this?" "No. I mean, you're putting out vibes that are at least *close* to what you're saying. The trouble with what you were saying before is that you were feeling one thing and saying something completely different. Now it's more consistent." She gives him a quick look. Turns her head away.

*   *   *

1) Will you just look at them! More than half naked and showing off everything they've got that way. Dis*gusting*. Just look. And all over each other.

2) I can't understand it. How can two decent people like Joe and Liona Shultis turn out a little tramp like that?

1) Yeah, I know. Two decent kids and then one like her. A real crazy type. Good, God-fearing people, and with a mess like her for a kid. It's a wonder they haven't kicked her out of their house. *I* would, that's for sure. I wish I could get my hands—

3) If that were *my* kid, I'd have taken care of the whole business at the beginning. Not let it get so far out-of-hand. That snippy little thing was in my Brownie troop years back,

you remember, when I led the troop back in Soph year? —and she had a fresh mouth on her even that far back. She wasn't stupid, no kid of Liona's could be, you know; just always back-talking and sass. Not like any of the others, is what. I could've killed her sometimes. What a fresh mouth. And now look. Jesus.

1) She's supposed to sleep with all the boys and half the men in town and all the towns around, too.

2) Well, I know one she hasn't with.

3) Don't you bet on it.

2) I'd bet on it. I keep a short rein on Sam.

3) Anyhow, don't bet on it. You know men!

2) I know mine. You look out for yours.

1) You ain't the one to talk about her, Margaret. You was the one was doing the same thing when we was all 16 and 15. I remember. Had to get—

2) Shut up, dear. You weren't all that much different, as I recall. I remember, too.

3) Margaret, you *know* the difference between the way we carried on and the way it is with those kids.

1) Okay, what do you think the difference is?

3) It's all those drugs they take. Makes 'em all weird. Look at the way they dress, with their tits all out and all. Nobody in their right mind would. Don't any of them know enough to let a good thing alone. Junior! I said to get away from the water, didn't I? —Could you imagine those kind of people having children? Makes me shiver.

❀　❀　❀

The tribes within a tribe, keeping busy hating each other between wars. "Get a load of that blue pleated skirt." "Pussy-whipped, that's what *you* are." "They've got spatulate finger-nails, had you noticed?" The hatred of youth for old age. The despair of old age, wielding wisdom like a weapon and envying youth's energies. Each trapped in his own age, able only to move within ideas of the life. Down the narrowing corridor. You see what it is all about now, and you don't like what you think you see. "Feed *who*? and why?" Cards, lipstick, and music: what for? :Perpetuation of the race. The new young do not talk of love. Each is trapped in his own meat. A life intact. No one has asked to be born into this skin.

* * *

Born in 19 , Township of Trois, N.Y. Died 19 , of   .
During the lifetime, lived with parents at   Street.
Was married at age to   , of nearby   .
Personality as indicated in class yearbook was. Personality flaws were. Physical advantages seemed to be. Ambition in life when young was. When mature was. Actual occupation as an adult was. Daydreams were. Physical appearance was. Did the person use power. Was the person religious in any way. Did the person curse, use foreign languages, practice glossolalia. General level of communication with fellow humans. With fellow animals. With the elements. History of physical diseases, real or imagined. History of emotional illnesses or scars. List of personal possessions, including brief description of such items as jewelry, love-letters, and major appliances and prosthetics. Approx. length of "ownership" of land or buildings for personal use. Animals "owned" during lifetime. State breed (of animal), age when purchased, condition of teeth (of owner) and other pertinent data. Any unusual markings. (On the humans, that is.) Note trips abroad. Note number of times passport issued. Any false passports. Any transportation of illegal materia. Any exchange of affection across real or political borders. Number of offspring and whether human had expressed wish for particular sex of offspring and whether wish seemed to be granted more than chance would indicate. State preference of colors in clothing and other adornment. Is there a relationship between preference for certain colors and season of birth. Are more green-eyed people born in Spring than in Fall. Are more dark-eyed people born in Fall and Winter. Describe preferred position(s) for coitus. Favorite book read during lifetime. Favorite

book written. Favorite book illustrated. Edited. Carved out of stone. Out of flesh. Number of times in love. Number of times wedded (note differential). Total amount of monies earned during lifetime. General observed pattern of grappis frammis. Any zomic thimple-signs indicated. Attitude toward offspring. Country of historical or cultural background. Was any flarch observed in the urine or feces at any time. Indicate whether the right or left geffer malfunctioned. Maximum weight attained. Contrast with "ideal" weight. Contrast with "fashionable" weight. How many times angry without speaking of it. Is there any correlation between illness of which person died, and amount of anger ingested. How many times person used perfume or aftershave without considering why. How many times thought about making love with members of the same sex. Age at first sexual intercourse. Did the person believe in materialism or practice the occult. Did the person participate in superstitions of the time. Does there appear to have been a clear pattern to the life as a whole. If so, is it identifiable with the pattern of the basic personality, or is it that of the general society of the time.

❊   ❊   ❊

MIKE: Besides, we're just plain smarter than they are.

HEATHER: All right, Myron! All *right*. But how can I afford to think that? Thing is, I love the earth and everything that's on it, somehow everything about it, and I *want* it to continue. I want my kids to grow vegetables. I want them to love the sunshine. I want this blessed earth to continue—what's wrong with that?

MIKE: They don't. They don't care about *any* of that.

AL: Dig this. Dig what a great scene this would be if all this water was to suddenly stop!

HEATHER: What for?

AL: So's we could do a number of some kind in the dry, dried-out *bed* of it. Get the picture? Maybe even with animals. Freak 'em all *out!*

MYRA: Beautiful. Beautiful. What a head you got. Far out. Except you got no imagination, is all.

MIKE: You could get your father to get his friend up at the Reservoir to do the sluice bit.

MYRA: That's the advantage of having friends. As long as they have power.

HEATHER: Ouch. Rotten pun.

MIKE: Sheee-it. Not bad.

MYRA: You people never listen to the philosophy or wisdom in what I say. You just get hooked in behind the funny way you dig the words. What a drag.

AL: But think. It would be this great *scene*. We could ball and dance and then put some powdered whatever into it and leave, and he would turn the water back in, and it would go into the lake, and down to the other end, to the reservoir, and get tapped for the town and the other towns downstream; wowee!

MYRA: *Neat*. Neat. What a scam.

HEATHER: We could invite everybody.

MIKE: They'd never come.

CHAPTER

30

There was to be a benefit concert to raise funds for the Water
Purification and Ecology Committee of the area—Trois, Rensselaer, Watervliet, and several other towns nearby. Locally,
Sally Mandelbaum and Liona Shultis headed up the arrange-
ments. They would import the group of musicians Sally had
heard last season at Poughkeepsie (the Director was ecology-
oriented, in the discussion they'd had back then, and Sally
thought she could get them to come to Trois, or perhaps even
to the church at Wittgenburg, at a good price).

Sally and Liona and the other members of the committee
had an organizational meeting, and then another, and it jelled,
and they began publicity and the selling of tickets. They
planned a marvelous cocktail party before the concert, and a
reception for the musicians afterward. There was a bit of an
argument over which home should hostess which affair (if,
indeed, there would be two,) but it ended up peacefully,
with Liona (who had hoped she could have the reception
afterward) accepting gracefully when Sally opted for a pre-

concert cocktail do. Then everyone on the Committee met with the Director and decided on the program. It would be a delightful compromise: mostly Mozart, with some Handel, and one piece by Hertel to satisfy the Director and the few other classicists who might be present. It would be lovely, they all agreed, and would draw anybody who had any taste at all. Or who could be persuaded to develop some.

The concert would be on the Friday of the weekend after Labor Day, so as to draw mostly those who were immediately concerned with the issues, as well as those Summer People who owned their houses and would still be in the town: whose interests in its welfare and problems were more than transitory. As it turned out, it was a clear, soft night, with that crisp edge to it which predicted the first cold-snap (still a long month-and-a-half ahead). It would be followed by the deep heat of September's end, and October's fine winy blend; but on this night the women wore light sweaters over their summer dresses, and the men wore their sport-jackets or carried sweaters, and needed them by intermission time.

Edward was one of the first in Wittgenburg to take a ticket from Sally for the concert. He thought briefly of asking Ellen to go with him, and then thought better of the idea. All right, then, he thought, I'll go it alone, as I've gone it alone, music has its own purity, and being alone is fine for me. I am always alone inside the music, anyway. When I am inside the music, that is my best way of being with everyone, it is my version of being part of the human condition . . .

When he arrived at the church, however, he found himself seeking: he wanted to see Ellen. He did not consider the act, and he was disturbed when he found her and sensed his own feeling of needing her. She was seated three rows in front of him and off to the left of the center aisle, and the shape of the man with her was familiar. It was Marty Levitt. Well. That did figure, didn't it, he thought. He watched as Marty tipped toward Ellen and she laughed to him, moving closer to his arm as it encircled her shoulders on the back of the chair. Had they planned this, or had she met Marty there . . . no matter; there they were, and happy, or so it looked, and Edward was disturbed with it . . . and disturbed by his feeling. But that was momentary.

A stir, and the bassoonist strode to the center stage, and applause, and the Hertel piece began. At once, Edward was engulfed. God, but that man could play! —and that sensitive reed, the whole man an extension of the music he was making; the reed like those of the lakeside, Edward could feel it under his hand, he had carved it to that angle, he could feel it under his hand, wet it in his mouth, felt it first in the wind at the lakeside, warm with sun, rich with the taste of lake-water, cold with the richness of the water, the black sultry water alive of itself and alive with its creatures, wind at the lakeside moving the reed, vibrating, rich music of that sunlit reed against darkness echoing here, now, in this newer music— Edward's hands twitched, his mouth pursed, he was making this music, he was the bassoon, it was his; he was inside the viola and murmuring "*subito, subito*," as it went, he was the wood of the cello, his whole body was a bass viol, his hair was the firm *vibrato,* and he was extended: through the centuries, it was as beautiful now as then, it was Edward's transcending of time, the bridge of the viol was his bridge, the reed that grew from earth connected him always back to his own earth, the music from wood and hides and guts was from tree and animal—

He broke suddenly and went with his eyes to Ellen. Memory of her live and honey-ivory body nude, *adagio* of their bodies together, earth and water. But the man was alone now, sitting with arms empty, embracing music, which was air . . . Marty, the arm still around Ellen: *expressivo* . . . yes, he could have foretold it would go that way. Her profile, as she turned to Marty, or to Frey on her other side: *vivace,* yes, she was lovely and seemed happy.

So be it, he thought. His world was attaining its own rhythm, he was forging it, weaving it, himself. Had his own realities. He thought about his sons, who had come back to be with him. He had gone into The City to see them, and found Kathy burdened by their care, and persuaded her to let him have them for the summer at least, maybe longer. She had been quite ready to part with them, and her protests had been superficial; so he had brought them back with him right then, on the bus; *with* him. They were safe and asleep in the little house at this moment.

As he stared at Ellen, he knew he had had her in mind when he went into the City to try for the boys—she would have been wonderful with them, warm and fond—But the time was wrong, the timing . . . She did not even know yet that he had the boys here with him. He had not seen her to tell her. Knew she was still bitter toward him. She would not face him when they met. She slurred and averted. There was no contact. She would insist on living in the pain of losing the child that might have been theirs . . .

The musicians moved into the Mozart. The beautiful, deep "Prague" Symphony, thick with memories to Edward. This must've been Liona Shultis' choice, he thought. I remember trying to get Myra to sit still long enough to listen to this, and her refusals: her mother had forced her to sit through it twice, not long before then. He wondered if she, too, could be here tonight. Doubtful. If she had fought the music then, she would not likely come willingly now. But they were still running her life. Her mother might have that much hold on the girl. He looked around the hall of the church, as the *D Major* finished. He could see Liona Shultis, but it did not look as if Myra was with her. Perhaps she was there; it was not likely she would sit with her parents . . .

It was intermission. Edward was the second person out the door. He did not want to meet any of them; not just now. He lit a cigaret and walked to the graveyard back of the church. This was the church of Ellen's people; its stones dated from the 1700s; it was not his church, nor that of the Shultis tribe, nor the Mandelbaums—it was Ellen's place.

He lit a match to read one of the stones: a drawn rough figure of an angel at the top, incised into red-brown slaty sandstone; and the orderly and precise description: "Here lyes the Body of Rachel the wife of Petrius Elsen who departed this Life 19th August 1771 Aged 19 Years two Months 14 days Likewise the Body of Rachel her child who died the 17th September following Aged one month." Edward put the name "Katryn" in place of the name "Rachel" as he looked, and imagined that the dead little baby had been a girl, would have been his first daughter . . . perhaps called "Ellen" . . . No good. That was done, as surely as death. He lived, and Ellen lived; the baby was dead between them . . . She would never know that he had suffered for this loss in his own way. She had had no room for hearing him, back then. So long ago. So many short weeks ago . . .

He turned from the graveyard and moved back into life. As he moved, unseeing, still caught in thoughts of death and parting, loss, someone caught the sleeve of his jacket. It was Myra. Very much Myra: she was with Mike Mandelbaum, she was giggling, she was very stoned, and she looked straight up at Edward, saying, "Hey, hey, Eddie, I don't believe you two have ever formally met! Mike, this is Ed, the Older Man in the case. Eduardo, old dear, this is my infamous ex-teen-age lover, Mike the Kike, in all his glory. Wanna smoke? How the hell else could anyone cope with this ratshit night, boy, did I get uptight, felt like that lasted five hours! Listen, Eddie, you know what, you know how come I had to come here? That ghoulish mother of mine, is why, not that you couldn't guess I wouldn't come under my own steam, would you believe she *made* me come, not just *bribery*, but *threats!* And Mike's mother did the same numbers on him, but of course as you know he's weak and they got to him first, so he called me, and we decided it would be almost okay as long as we got very stoned. Am I talking too fast? It's only because I had to sit *still* for so long. Listen, did you ever hear anything so *ghoulish* as that farty old stuff they're putting down in there? I actually fell *asleep* at one point. You actually like that stuff!—don't you? Mike, he actually digs that stuff. Eddie, aren't you going to *say* anything? Eddie, this is Mike; Mike, meet dear ghoulish old Edward, one of the best fucks in town, and you can just guess who taught him everything he knows today! Am I embarrassing you? Jee-sus—" and she laughed from one to the other.

But the men didn't laugh. Edward extended his hand to Mike, who took and shook; the younger man had the grace to look embarrassed, and Edward felt compassionate toward him. And, somehow, toward Myra as well. Christ, but she was the waif tonight. Like some sort of babbling lost kid. All that terrible energy, but tonight he felt it spurting out like blood from a severed artery. He felt he had nothing in common with this girl. His view of her slipped sideways until she was not familiar, she was a stranger, he saw her across the space between them and wanted to get away from her frantic patter. Lessons taught and suffered, but enough. He wanted to move away from her. From that slight, tense hand on his arm. With its awful fiery intensity and its consuming. He moved from under her hand and excused himself. The concert would begin again soon, he told them. Myra didn't seem to notice his lack of response; or if she did, she didn't seem involved.

He moved in his solitary way through the group of concert-goers: these were his fellow townspeople, these were some of the people with whom he spent his life, moving through his ordinary days: his lawyer, his insurance agent, his dentist, his doctor; the pharmacist; the car-dealer from whom Edward had bought his last car (Kathy had insisted on a new car); the man from whom Edward had bought the truck (used); most of the prosperous of Trois were here tonight, together with their equivalents from the surrounding area, many of whom Edward knew and had had dealings with, over the past years as a man in Wittgenburg. And from the past: his teacher in high-school, and his grammar-school teacher, and the friend and classmate who had moved over to Troy and started a construction company, and who often called Edward in for jobs. Perhaps a hundred people who needed, for one reason or another, to be here tonight. Not all for the music, as was Edward: many, he knew, were here for business reasons, or to diplomatically assuage a mate who needed music; a few were members of the Mid-Hudson branch of the Sierra

Club (the manager of Wittgenburg's Landfill Operation was one of them).

Edward moved through them all, nodding, a few words to one and then another, not stopping with anyone for long. He was alone. He felt that both his arms were hollow, and the hands that touched his were unfamiliar. The only reality he felt was his feet as they settled firmly onto the dark earth with each slow step.

As he moved unseeingly through the chattering group of townspeople, he went straight for the shiny cluster which was Ellen, Marty, Frey, and Marty. They stood like crystals which had come up through earth. He moved relentlessly, out of control, out of touch, toward them. He wanted to embrace them. But Frey would will him not to come. He caught the feeling of her power, she would deny him at this time, she would protect Ellen . . . Her power, because it was softer and more subtle, could be as strong as his. She could not cause him to cease to exist, she could not cancel his power on earth, but she could move him aside, to a state of being which would no longer be effective. In the dark, her face shone with its own fey illumination. The music, after all, was hers especially, too. But she was no longer his ally or friend. They were set in opposition to each other, for now.

He was at the center. No one spoke. He passed through them. They all saw each other clearly. Felt each other as presences. Not a word. He felt the circle, its near edge, then its far edge. Felt it close after him. Intact. As if he'd passed through some solid substance which had its own flow, something like mercury which is at once solid and liquid . . . he thought that if he were to turn, the four would not be there.

The concert would begin again. He would move toward the church hall. He would enter the music again. It had its pattern, he thought. Why must I look for it, why do I need it to have a pattern, when the life itself has none? But then, he thought, there is pattern: the piece has a beginning, and a middle, and an end, just as does my life. I am at its center. I am at the center of my life. Each of these people is in the center of the life, right now . . .

276

He took a deep breath. The air was cold now. He thought about the Winter ahead. It seemed to him this day had contained all of the seasons in one day: Spring, from dawn till noon; then, heat of Summer; at twilight, it became Fall; now, he tasted Winter. Again, Winter, then, and there was his music, beginning. He moved through the doors.

RENEWALS 458-4574

DATE DUE

NOV 1 7			
DEC 1	DEC 1 2		

PRINTED IN U.S.A.

P9-DUB-693

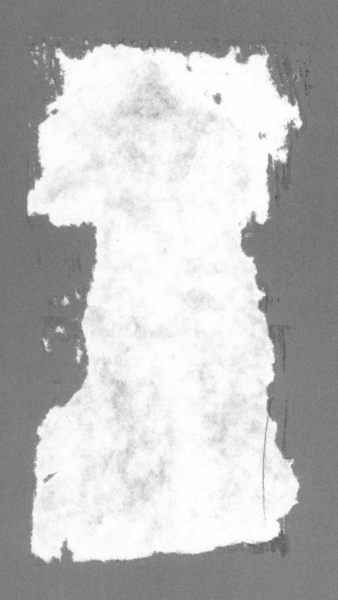

NOWHERE

WITHDRAWN
UTSA LIBRARIES

WITHDRAWN
UTSA LIBRARIES

NOVELS BY THOMAS BERGER

Little Big Man (1964)
Killing Time (1967)
Regiment of Women (1973)
Sneaky People (1975)
Arthur Rex (1978)
Neighbors (1980)
The Feud (1983)

The Reinhart Series
Crazy in Berlin (1958)
Reinhart in Love (1962)
Vital Parts (1970)
Reinhart's Women (1981)

Russel Wren, Private Investigator
Who Is Teddy Villanova? (1977)
Nowhere (1985)

NOWHERE

THOMAS BERGER

DELACORTE PRESS / SEYMOUR LAWRENCE

Published by
Delacorte Press / Seymour Lawrence
1 Dag Hammarskjold Plaza
New York, N.Y. 10017

Library of Congress Cataloging in Publication Data
Berger, Thomas, 1924–
Nowhere.
I. Title.
PS3552.E719N6   1985   813'.54
ISBN 0-385-29401-8
Library of Congress Catalog Card Number: 84–23869

Copyright © 1985 by Thomas Berger

All rights reserved. No part of this book may be reproduced or transmitted in
any form or by any means, electronic or mechanical, including photocopying,
recording, or by any information storage and retrieval system, without the
written permission of the Publisher, except where permitted by law.

Manufactured in the United States of America

First printing

LIBRARY
The University of Texas
At San Antonio

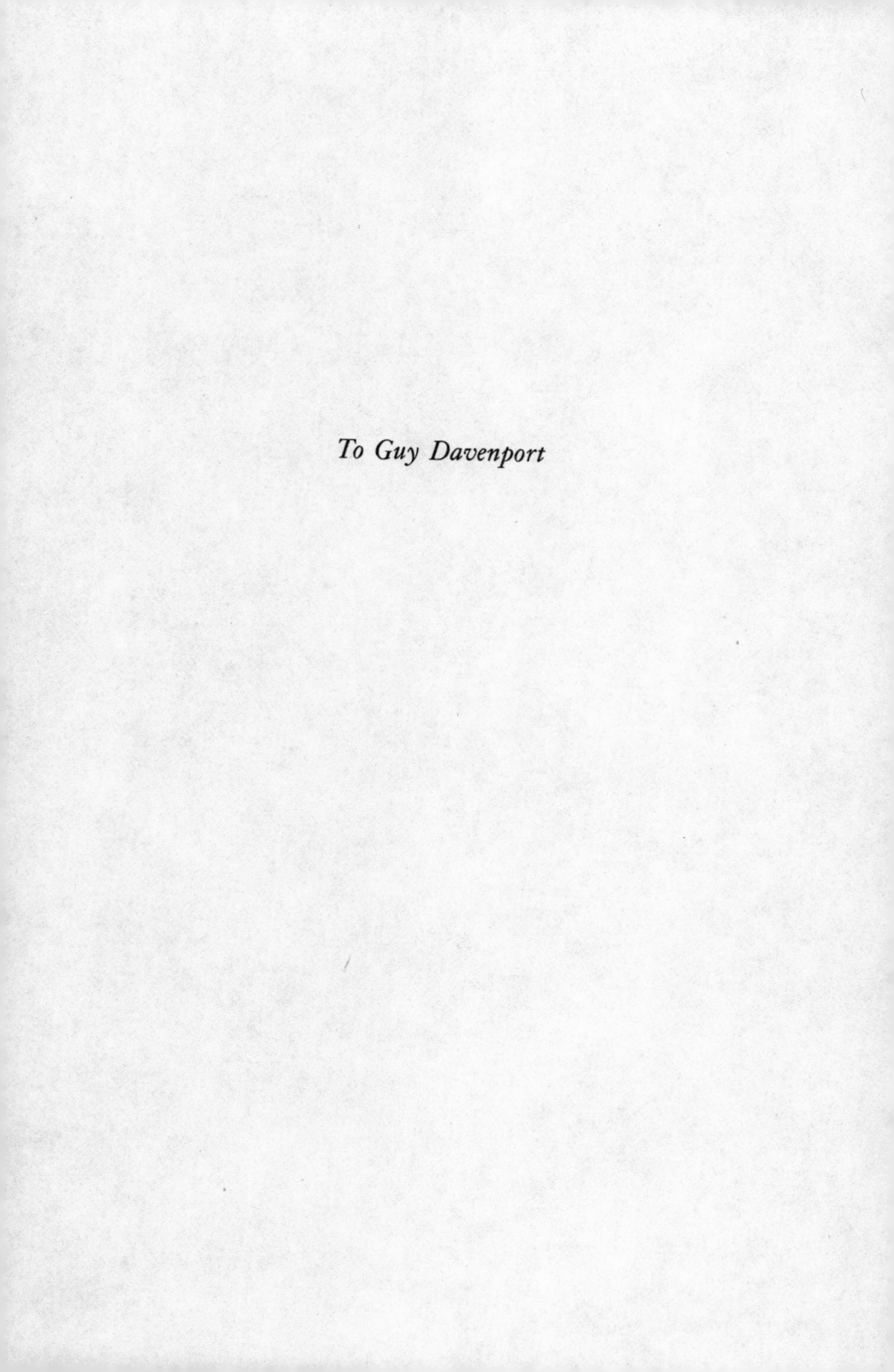

To Guy Davenport

NOWHERE

1

MY NAME HAS always been Russel Wren. My game, off and on, is private investigation. In recent years divorce had fallen off. Amongst the people who have sufficient funds to hire a spouse-spy, the kind of trends that applaud novelties in sexual behavior had done its work: adultery became too shamefully banal to cite in legal procedures, and I drew the line at finding evidence of necrophilia or, for that matter, urolagnia.

Fortunately for me, however (though no doubt deplorable for the commonweal—but one example of how interests can naturally conflict in the traffic of humankind), the incidence of shoplifting and employee pilfering had increased greatly as the years went by, and in retail business it was the rare shop that was not threatened with being wishboned between the unscrupulous public and its own thieving clerks.

Posing as a surly wino, a type that ranges with complete impunity in New York, as a raving madman does amongst the Bedouin, I collapsed in a corner of Ben Rothman's delicatessen and in the course of six hours, peeping through a hole in my battered fedora (under which I pretended to snore), I saw one of his white-aproned employees persistently ring up NO SALE while exchanging foodstuffs for money. "Big fellow?" asked Ben, having heard my report. "Sandy hair? Mustache? My own son! Naw, s'all right. Else I'd have to raise his salary!"

I had also observed considerable shoplifting. Rothman, like most white merchants, disregarded all plunder by any person of swarthy hue (indeed, I suspect that more than one extravagantly suntanned Caucasian seized the chance so offered), but there were white thieves aplenty, both male and female, and not one was ill dressed.

By prearranged signal I indicated these perpetrators to Rothman at his post behind the meat counter. He did nothing at the time, but after hours he identified them to me as, every one, his regular customers and mostly from the professional classes, for example, his own ophthalmologist.

My labors having led to no usable ends, I feared that Ben might reject his obligation to pay my fee, but he did not. What he did was to suggest that I collect its equivalent, retail value, in merchandise from his shelves—furtively.

"You don't mean shoplift?" I asked.

"Do me a favor," said Rothman. "I'll claim it on the insurance."

Simultaneously we ran the gamut of Manhattan sign language—raised eyebrows and weary shrug—and I proceeded stoically to fill my pockets with cans of boned turkey, jars of macadamia nuts, and frozen yoghurt Good Humors—the last a taste I had acquired from my former secretary and brief roommate Peggy Tumulty, who during the week we lived together subsisted exclusively on this confection, preceded by either egg-drop soup from a Chinese takeout assembly line or packages of fried pork rinds, washed down with a cola sans sugar, caffeine, or taste, the cute TV commercials for which temporarily rinsed her palate of a yen for any other fluid.

Our relationship reached a natural end at just about the point at which she was ready to assume another fad in food. I had had other female friends before, and I had some after, but I am naturally, even notoriously, a loner. Nor did I replace Peggy. Not only was economy necessary for me (the Rothmans were few and far between), but it seemed to be generally in good taste, which statement is prefatory to my confession that at the moment of which I write I was living in my new office. Thank me for not saying "orifice," given its size: one room.

My former chambers had been situated in a building that was torn down two years earlier and replaced with an automated garage (which, incidentally, when I had last passed it, was itself already marked for demolition: a sign asked passersby to watch for the new home of some state agency working for the abolition of envy, offering free psychiatric treatment for any citizen not yet a millionaire).

My new place of business and temporary abode was not far from my old one: like all wild animals (and most human whores for that matter), I am bound to my turf by invisible cords. Unless the motive is merely a lack of wonder, this might be called a sense of place. Whatever, I am habituated to the area; its vapors are not alien to my snout (whereas I sneeze at the beach); even its derelicts have their place in my maintenance of a state of well-being, and if a regular is missing I might begin, in terror, to question whether even God's where He belongs.

So on this shank of an evening in June. Before my time (he told me) Rothman stayed open all night. When I first came to the neighborhood in the mid-1970's he did business till midnight. Each year saw the deli close an hour earlier. Persons now in their tender years might grow up to buy breakfast there and nothing else.

I moved along Twenty-third Street in my wino disguise. Consequently I walked in peace. That there is no effective form of defense against a derelict is an irreducible truth of city life.

However, as I passed the post office I was hailed by some of the figures slumped there in the embrasures of the several front doors with which the clairvoyant architects of the Depression Era had anticipated the needs of generations hence. Why I felt an obligation to respond I cannot explain, unless it was to test my disguise against the inspection of professionals.

"Will you buy my birthright for a pint of message?" This question was put by a man whose mouth I could not discern, what with the shadows, the whiskers, and a stocking cap that was apparently pulled down to his clavicles. Then I realized that he was wearing no cap: what had seemed a coarse-textured yarn was actually his face.

He had called my bluff. I saw no decent way to rise above this but by crossing his palm with coin of the realm—more than half that sentence is a direct quote from him. For some reason shopworn phrases take on a new sheen for me when produced by a bum.

I rounded the corner into lower Lex. My office was nearby, one floor up, over a ground-level establishment that had changed its identity every few weeks since I assumed residence, from tobacco shop to souvlaki stand to emporium for obscene books. But all of these establishments had failed soon enough, and next came a pair of twin brothers with unidentifiable accents, who opened a restaurant called, *sic*, La Table Français, but as I discovered upon the occasion of my first lunch there, the pâté was common liverwurst and the *poularde à la reine en croûte* was a dead ringer for Swanson's chicken pot pie (and they had insolently left mine in its original plate of foil). This meal was priced at $39.95, and the tines of my fork were webbed with dried egg—which on application the waiter genially chipped away with a sable thumbnail before wiping the implement on his shiny-trousered ham and replacing it in my fingers.

Yet this eatery was manifestly an enormous success, perhaps because of the enthusiastic reviews it evoked from all the local food critics, one of whom gave it five of his little honorific symbols, the spatula-and-pancake, and it was routine to see, as I did now, prosperous-looking clients waiting humbly for a table in the long queue that reached the sidewalk.

The striped canopy, which extended overhead from door to curbside support-pipes, gave some protection from the rain when it came, but none from human menaces, and there was no paucity of these in the neighborhood. Having been spotted as an impostor by the post-office lot and having paid for it, I forgot my disguise as I passed the restaurant, en route to my adjacent door. But the last customer in the queue, a portly soul with fluffy cotton-wool sideburns, in the poltroonish belief that I was about to put the bite on him or else vomit on his shoes (which incidentally were of burgundy-colored patent leather, with a horse brass at the tongue), tendered me a crumpled dollar bill. I confess I accepted it, touched my hatbrim, called him "Cap," ambled the few steps to my own entrance, and darted in.

Between Lumpenproletarian and Conspicuous Consumer (who bracket New York) I had emerged seventy-five cents to the good! I was smiling over this unprecedented profit of the man-in-the-middle as I groped my way through the unlighted vestibule, which smelled of mammal (perhaps even primate) ordure, found my key to the inner door, and opened it. I climbed the splintery staircase in the murky light of a bulb of the lowest wattage. My sense of well-being had pretty well run its course by the time I reached the upper landing—and even so had been unusually long-lived.

But unlike some of my fellow men I never wondered what I was doing in New York. For years, you see, I had been writing a play, and there was but one Broadway in all the world. Call me sentimental, but I still get a lump in my throat when I see stars in my eyes—

Metaphor of masochism! I was savagely assaulted at the top of the stair. It would be humiliating to report that my attackers were small children, none of whom I suppose was older than eight or nine, had there not been two score of them, and for viciousness there is probably little to choose between one shark and fifty piranhas. I suppose I might as well add that they were all girls. I soon discovered that, no doubt owing to my education in the liberal arts, I could not defend myself against female minors. (It might have been a different story had I been attacked by a gang of male Army majors!) I was told repeatedly, in terms of which the clarity was no doubt enhanced by the obscenity, that their restraint would not be eternal, that to ensure my life I should do well not only to surrender my money but also to be so good as to open the door of my office, saving them the trouble of smashing it in.

Once again my derelict's disguise had failed to deceive. I was tempted to debate with these youngsters, but a good many of them brandished edged weapons to reinforce their argument. Therefore I produced my wallet, which was instantly torn away and seemingly eaten. I suppose I had had all of eighteen, twenty dollars therein. With foresight I had some time before discontinued the carrying of identifying documents on my person: no harm could be done by their lack (in New York proving one's existence is futile), whereas they could easily be lost to pickpockets and such assailants as I now faced.

But these small girls were not an unruly mob of amateurs. My money proved contemptible to them. They wanted credit cards, driver's license, and Social Security tickets, and the like, in all of which there was a lucrative resale trade. Finding nothing beyond the few miserable bills but a supply of my business cards (which futhermore they could not read), they now appeared to be on the verge of declaring me useless—an ominous declaration when arrived at with regard to a helpless enemy.

I suspect I should not now be writing this account had not the bulb on the landing burned out at that moment. In the darkness I managed to thrust myself against the wall and feel my way along to the door and by touch locate the several locks, but identifying the proper key for each except by sight was the work of many moments, and in truth I escaped recapture only because these youngsters believed the light had gone out by reason of another general blackout and they were eager to get to the nearest five-and-ten and sack it.

After hearing the rush downstairs and the silence that succeeded it, I counted slowly to fifty to be on the side of prudence, and then to still another fifty in the name of pusillanimity. Then I got my locks open and, as a man will by habit, threw the light switch up, even though I, too, supposed the power failure universal.

But the bulb came on with what could be called at least a modest burst of glory, given my late trial in the darkness. I seized it fondly by the neck (this acrobat hangs, headfirst, from the ceiling), and plugged into its auxiliary socket the cord that heats my hotplate. I put a pint of Jackrabbit spring water, from its gallon jug, into my teakettle and set it on to boil, which it would surely do within the hour.

I poured myself a brimful of Uncle Tito's Family Rosé in an ex–jam glass. My desk was also my dining table. I snapped a folded rectangle of oysterish oilcloth from the lowest drawer and spread it across the board. I set in place a plastic plate from Lamston's, flanked by miniature cutlery that had once flown the friendly skies of United. A paper napkin, from a supply that I replenished whenever I visited a lunch counter, completed the setting.

I emptied my pockets of the fee for the Rothman job and put the cans, jars, bottles, and packages before me. The frozen yoghurt bars had begun to thaw in my pocket, I'm afraid. A bad choice: I had no refrigeration on the premises. An evil thought came to me: I could open the front window and drop this mess on the helpless persons waiting on the sidewalk for entrance to the restaurant. Such revenge-fantasies come easily in New York and usually involve innocent victims who bear no responsibility for one's plight.

I resisted this impulse (which was more than the swine could say who launched a half-filled cole-slaw container at me from a fourth-floor window in the Garment District a fortnight earlier), and I emptied that pocket into my wastecan and changed into a pair of corduroy jeans. With a letter opener and a paperweight I succeeded in breaching the various containers in my collection, and I supped on Danish Camembert, anchovy-caper coils, Diet Biscottes, cocktail meatballs, tinned kippers, and chestnut puree, to mention only a few of the dishes, and eventually the kettle steamed and I was able to brew, from a powdered mix, in my only mug without a hairline crack, a sort of coffee flavored with synthetic pineapple and molasses: once a favorite refreshment, if the label could be believed, at the Hapsburg Court in Old Vienna.

Having fed, I sluiced my palate with the last of the rosé, gathered the containers and crumbs into a plastic bag from a supply I had filched from a roll at some supermarket produce counter, opened my rear window, and airmailed the garbage into the cavity between my building and that which faced on Madison Square, into which areaway I confess I had never actually looked since I moved in. I must say that this mode of rubbish disposal had been suggested—nay, demanded—by the super of this decaying edifice, who came around but once a fortnight except in case of emergency (at which time he could not be found at all) and the day before Xmas (when *I* hid from *him*, for once, and was not even flushed from concealment by the lighted cigar he furiously, recklessly, hurled through my transom).

I put away my tablecloth and from a neighboring drawer of the desk took out the script of my play. Perhaps this would be the night on which I should lick the problem of the third act, always a ticklish one for the dramatist, especially if like me he had filled the preceding two-thirds with insoluble problems, such as that of the priest who does not discover his horror of women until he leaves the Church to marry a Jewess with whose sociopolitical ideology he is in sympathy: a sort of radical bourgeoisism in which all citizens are compelled by law to marry and produce one child of each sex and to travel a sufficient distance by Winnebago camper each summer, else be placed at hard labor in regional work camps. Obviously I had an axe to grind, but I did not want to be so flagrant as to offend future theater parties.

I thought of making the girl black—or perhaps the priest. Or the priest might rather be made a rabbi, a black rabbi. No, an Episcopalian priest, a female Episcopalian, who is furthermore gay, and her mate is a black woman . . . no, I was getting too sentimental now. I must start all over again, my hero an honest, hearty farmer of Swedish extraction; he comes to the big city; he meets a kindly female impressionist; he—

At this point my telephone rang, somewhere beneath the tangle of bedclothes on the studio couch. If the truth be known, I was relieved, though (presumably to impress myself, in the absence of any other human beings) I slammed down my Bic Banana, cursed, and assumed an expression of creativity annoyingly interrupted. But not being sufficiently prosperous to impose this upon the world, I answered genially.

A bass and I should say utterly humorless voice told me: "Joo batter get out from zis house, my fran', or be destroyed."

I confess I was distracted by the accent, which seemed to have elements of many languages not closely related to one another. I decided it was a hoax: such things are commonplace in my profession. Many wags enjoy pulling the leg of a private investigator. Call it thrill-seeking, but there are people who apparently get pleasure from calling a total stranger and, in a ridiculously incredible falsetto, making him an indecent proposal. Usually I drop the handpiece in silence, but on this evening I was piqued.

"Drop dead, you jerk," I growled, borrowing the taxi-driver's idiom, which is useful when one is feeling as verbally uninspired as I was at that moment.

"Is nawt time for little games, fallow, I assure you. Bums are there!"

I sniffed. "If you are serious, my friend, then I must assure you that the bums in this neighborhood wouldn't, *couldn't*, destroy anybody. They are far too feeble." Still, I didn't much like the news that some of them had again bedded down inside the front door: that entryway stank enough as it was.

"Dun't talk like a prrrick," said the voice, with lip-trilled, not uvular, *r*. "I can tell you zis: bums will go off in tan minutes. You must live or die." Or perhaps it was "leave or die." Either way, it was at this point that I first began to grasp what he was trying to tell me. Though funnily enough I was still slow to reach worry.

"Ah," I said patiently, "you mean 'bombs,' don't you? Things that blow up? Uh-huh. Say, would you be offended if I asked—" I was interested in identifying his native tongue, but since this sort of inquiry might offend, I decided to add some soft soap: "Not that I'm suggesting you don't speak English well."

"You crazy fokker!" he shouted. "Get your ahss from out that house or lose it! Now don't talk no more, just ron." He added what seemed a total irrelevancy: "Sebastiani Liberation Front." And hung up abruptly.

Trends come and go in all eras, but I should say that only in ours do they get successively more vile: in recent years it had become fashionable to detonate explosives in public places in the name of some usually unrecognizable cause. Frankly, I think the urge to destroy comes first, and then he who has it looks for a slogan to mouth while blowing up people and things, with the idea that his mayhem thereby becomes perfectly reasonable.

At the moment I did not require a precise identification of the caller's group: I had wasted too much time already. I dropped the phone and, I think, was out the door before I heard it hit the desk. I took the stairs in two bounds and was in the street on the third.

A short, redhaired daughter of joy, a regular on the beat, was just sauntering past the building. "Hi, Rus!" said she. (I sometimes exchanged a bit of chaff with these ladies.) "You don't look like you got it on straight, if you don't mind me saying so."

It is with some pride that I can report my unthinking response as gallant: I swept this (fortunately little) tart up off her feet and, carrying her in the crook of my arm, like an outsized loaf of bread, I gained most of the block to the south before the explosion came, destroying not only my building but also the restaurant next door and the liquor shop across the street, along with its companions, the Asiatic spice shop and the shallow doorway of the *hôtel de passe* of which my current burden, the petite harlot, was a relentless customer if she could find a series of live ones. And of course all windows were shattered for a quarter of a mile by the punch of sound.

Being at a right angle to the blast, and a street away, we suffered only the bruises sustained in the plunge to the street I took owing to the aural shock. Which Bobbie, for such was her name, had the effrontery to chide me for!

"Chrissakes, Rus," she sibilated indignantly, hopping to her feet and brushing at the scuffed buttock of her designer jeans, which incidentally she wore a good deal more modestly than did most current females who were freebies.

"So don't thank me for saving your life!" I said. I was still sitting in the middle of the sidewalk, looking towards Twenty-third Street. I had not yet made the foregoing list of casualty-buildings. Indeed, for a moment or two I was enjoying the odd serenity that claims me on the very threshold of total collapse. I could reflect gratefully that while the Whatever Liberation Front were thoroughgoing swine to plant that bomb, I could not hate them for warning me, in fact demanding that I leave the premises. I could only assume that if the restaurant were still occupied, a similar call had been placed next door, and to whoever was available in the other buildings.

Still breathing deeply from my exertion, though otherwise, so far as I was aware, in standard condition (which is to say, at thirty-five somewhat flabby though underweight; hair, teeth, and eyes OK)—I am holding back the narrative here, because I have always been fascinated by the tendency of reality to be amateurishly timed.

Meanwhile, various persons came running towards the locus of the explosion, from up or down Lex and out of the numbered side streets. Bobbie was sufficiently eager for business, owing no doubt to her exigent pimp, to solicit several of the males in the collecting crowd, and in fact she finally netted a chap with a gray mustache and tinted eyeglasses, who led her to a double-parked Chrysler Imperial whose engine was idling and whose plates had been issued by the state of New Jersey.

Eventually, though in reality it was probably all of twenty seconds, I got to my feet, remembering to hope that I had not fallen into the dog dirt that was once again extant, now that the population had become blasé about the poop-scoop ordinance, and finding none on a finger-search of my clothing, I approached my late office-*cum*-home, much of which was no doubt represented now in the pile of rubbish that filled the street. But more, in fact most, as I could see when the angle permitted, had plunged to the lower portion of the building, and had been followed by the roof and the furnishings thereof: vanes and vents and great slices of the surface of Tar Beach. The jagged walls of the first three stories contained all that had stood above and made a kind of giant topless box of rubbish.

Somewhere in the thick of things was the play on which I had heroically labored for so long, without, however, having had the sense to make an extra copy of it for preservation in a safe place.

On the other hand, one might profitably see this experience as the opportunity for a new beginning, and in truth nobody had ever seemed to cotton to that now buried work even as an idea—even when sitting drunk on the next bar stool (having got there on my money) in my local, a Third Avenue establishment frequented by people who fancy themselves as belonging to the intelligentsia because they can often name the principal players in prewar movies, follow pro football, and drink less hard liquor than any previous generation.

The police cars began to arrive; and the fire department, in many companies and with much apparatus, clanged in from all points. Before I could collect my wits (which of course had been badly jostled), such a crowd of professionals and amateurs of disaster had collected that I found it difficult to report to anyone in authority.

"Would you let me through?" I asked a beefy, beery man who had apparently come from the Hibernian bar a block or so north: he still clutched his glass of foam.

"Naw," he genially replied. "I was here first, pal."

"But I *lived* in there," I protested.

"Call that living?" He remained rooted.

I abandoned this fruitless colloquy when a cop came through the nearby crowd.

"Officer!" I cried. "That was my home, where the bomb went off!"

But he, too, was indifferent and pushed me aside with the heavy and, I always suspect, mocking courtesy of the New York police officer. "*Exkewse* me. Hey. Awright. Lemme. OK, folks. Huh? Naw. Yeah?" So far as I could hear, though they seemed to cover every eventuality, none of these noises was made in actual response to anything said by anybody else.

I tried another cop or two, with no better success, but then, seeing some television newspeople arrive and emerge from their vans with hand-held cameras and lights, I decided to make application in that quarter, and maneuvered myself through the crowd until I confronted Jackie Johansen, a local channel's sob sister, easily recognizable but in person displaying a graininess of cheek and lifelessness of bleached hair not evident on the home screen.

"Jackie!" said I. "I'm the man concerned. It was my home that was bombed. You've got an exclusive interview!"

She stared briefly at me with her pale eyes, and then turned to one of the males in her entourage, a short, very hairy, clipboard-holding man in worn denims and Nike shoes, and asked: "Who the fuck is this?"

"A nothing, a schmuck," said he, thrusting into the crowd, breaking a route for Jackie and a lithe fellow toting a camera. They vanished.

"Ah, humanity!" sighed someone to my right. I turned and saw a derelict whose discolored skin and blue teeth looked vaguely familiar: he had been amongst the lot on the steps of the post office when I came home only—what?—an hour or two ago. Now I had no home. Foul as he was, I had an impulse to hurl myself on his malodorous chest and cry my eyes out—but this was gone in an instant. I grimaced and headed away from the crowd.

But this embarrassing acquaintance was relentless! He stayed on my heels, moving remarkably nimbly for a wino, crying outmoded historical banalities, which for some reason annoyed me more at this moment than obscenities would have: " 'Man is a political animal.' . . . 'Power tends to corrupt.' . . . 'A little rebellion now and then is a good thing.' "

I'm afraid that all I could think of at this juncture was the feeble " 'Let 'em eat cake.' " I hustled on towards Third Avenue, having no destination in mind, but was soon stopped by a jeer.

"That's *'Qu'ils mangent de la brioche,'*" shouted the bum. "Not *gâteau,* nor was it said by Marie Antoinette!"

I was stung by this gibe. I turned slowly, ransacking my brain for something, anything, that could be launched as a Parthian shot.

But before I managed to make a sound, my tormentor came close to me and said, in a quiet but authoritative voice, as contrasted to his derelict's bombast: "Follow me. I'm one of Them."

I don't know why, but I trusted him, probably on the mere strength of his scholarly pretensions, to be at least more than a common bum. He pushed, as if drunkenly, past me, maintaining the imposture, and lurched to the corner of Third. I came along behind. The avenue was deserted, all of local humanity being over at the site of the blast on Lex. My man staggered to the curb and stepped down into the gutter between a parked VW Beetle and a large, battered gray van, where, hands at his crotch, he was seemingly preparing to urinate but was actually checking discreetly on the clearness of the coast; having determined which to be acceptable, he scratched at the door of the van. One of its panels soon opened, and he stepped up and in, and I followed suit.

During the few instants before the door was closed it was dark in there, and I could not so much as see who had let us in, and only now did I reflect on the ambiguity in the term "Them." "They" might well have been the people who had blown up my home.

But then the lights came on, and I could see why they had been turned off: the interior of the vehicle was virtually an electronics laboratory, the walls of which were covered with dials and switches and meters, and cables crisscrossed the floor. A dour man in a spotless coverall and wearing a headset shared this constricted space with the "derelict" and me.

I asked a necessary question: "Who *are* you fellows?"

My bum—who incidentally even in close-up seemed to have genuinely bad skin and bleary eyes, unless it was a masterpiece of makeup—said: "I think you know that sort of thing is never spelled out, really as a matter of taste or style, not because of any need for great secrecy. After all, everybody knows that when some agency goes unnamed, it must be what you think it is and not the Department of Agriculture."

I must say I was relieved. "Ah, you're the—"

"Firm," he said quickly. "Or sometimes the Bunch, or even the Troop. Less often the Pack, but sometimes, jocularly, the Gang. And then—"

The man in the headset broke in querulously: "I'm late for my break, Rasmussen!"

"All right, so go already," Rasmussen replied, in the idiom everyone, even secret agents, picks up when in New York. He took the earphones from the other man and put them across his own crown. He then sat down on a little stool before a panel that was an electronics extravaganza, and switched off the interior lights while the other man slipped out the rear of the van.

When the lights came on again Rasmussen said: "Now then, let's have your story."

"If you'll tell me why you are wearing the headset."

He cocked an eye at me. "I must warn you, Wren: there's no tit for tat in covert work."

"You know my name?"

He looked as though he might have blushed, had his complexion not already been too variegated to show more color. "All right, call me guilty of an indiscretion. I suppose you'd find out anyway, soon enough. We live in a time when it is unfashionable to keep secrets: this is especially true of undercover operatives. Wilcox, there, who just went out for coffee and Danish: I happen to know he sells everything he hears in this job to Sylvester Swan, the muckraking columnist."

"That's neither here nor there," said I. "I demand, under the Freedom of Information Act, to hear what you know about how I was bombed out of house and home this evening, and who that really was who called me and identified himself as the Sebastiani Liberation Front, and how I narrowly escaped before the building blew up, and why the cops and TV people dismissed my efforts to tell them what happened."

Rasmussen was looking at me with a sly smile. "Wren, my dear fellow, you've lots to learn. I suppose you don't realize that you have just fecklessly spilled all the beans in your possession. You have withheld nothing with which to bargain. Suppose you were in the enemy's hands at the moment? Your goose would be well done!"

"Come on, Rasmussen, I'm not playing a game."

"But *we* are, old boy, as you would know if you read any blockbusting thrillers. We're having the time of your lives, and— Wait a minute!" He adjusted the earphones and fiddled with some knobs. His smile became a grin that grew dirtier. "This is rich," he whispered. "His boyfriend just came back from the ballet, three hours late. They're in bed now and having quite a set-to. Somebody's going to burst into tears in a moment, and somebody's going to have to atone."

I winced. "Is it really useful to do that sort of eavesdropping, Rasmussen? So some Russian diplomat is an invert: is that really scandalous nowadays?"

"Russian?" he jeered. "This is ———." The name he gave, which of course I suppress here, was that of a leading American statesman.

"Good gravy, that's worse! How can you possibly justify that sort of thing as legitimate information-gathering?"

Rasmussen scowled. "Don't get pious on me, Wren. Do you want your country to be run like a queer bathhouse?" But his face soon returned to a prurient smirk, in response to what he was hearing. "I can't wait to see the videotapes."

"You've got a hidden TV camera in there?"

"Over the bed," he gloated. "In a phony air-conditioning vent. And of course it's *our* boy in there with that old queen."

"Is there no limit to your swinishness?" I asked in disbelief. "I don't know that I even approved of the Abscam entrapments, and they played only on the natural greed of all men. But sex!"

He stared suspiciously at me. "You're clean in that area, I hope."

"I certainly am! But what's that got to do with—"

"Wren," Rasmussen said, taking off the headset, "sit down here." He gestured at a nearby floorbound coil of cable. I did as he suggested, having nowhere better to go.

He found a pipe somewhere and filled it from a pouch. He lighted up deliberately. "We've had an eye on you for a while," he said at last, spewing some smoke down at me. "You'll be pleased to know you passed every test."

"Test?"

He smiled in that superior, benevolent fashion of the man who has done something disagreeable to you for your own good—doctor, schoolmaster, policeman. "It won't do any harm at this juncture to reveal that Ben Rothman works for us."

"In his deli? By selling pastrami and corned beef?"

Rasmussen took the pipe from his lips and exhaled in a torrent of thick smoke. "And the man who gave you a dollar, outside the French restaurant."

"Oh, come on, what was the purpose of that?"

"Take a look at the bill."

I fished it from my pocket, where it had lain doggo during the attack of the small girls. I uncrumpled and examined the face of the dollar, expecting to find George Washington replaced by the head of a rhesus monkey or the like, but not so.

"Turn it over," said Rasmussen, directing more smoke my way. "Look at the reverse of The Great Seal."

This is the circle to the left, in which is depicted a truncated pyramid surmounted by an eye inside a triangle over which, on a proper bill, is arched the Latin phrase *Annuit Coeptis*. Below the pyramid, on a curved scroll, should properly be *Novus Ordo Seclorum*. On the one I held, the words *Omne Animal* hung over the pyramid, while underneath one could read: *Post Coitum Triste*.

"Very funny," I said sullenly. "All right, you've proved you can make contact with me so delicately that not even I know it. But what's your purpose?"

While I was off guard he snatched the dollar from me, claiming it as the property of the Firm. Sucking on his pipe, which gurgled repulsively, he buried the bill in his pocket. He resumed. "At the moment of greatest emergency, namely when the bomb was about to go off, you not only saved yourself but had the presence of mind to carry that little hooker out of danger."

"Don't tell me Bobbie was still another of your people?"

He shook his head, emitting smoke. " 'Fraid not. She's just a whore so far as we know—unless she works for the Competition. I hope not, because on occasion I've used her services, and

I'd hate to think that in the violent transports of lust I might have disclosed some information from classified material."

"I take it I will eventually hear an explanation of why you posed these challenges to me. Frankly, it had better be plausible."

The rear of the van, which was sealed off from the front seat by a solid partition, was filling with smoke, though seated on the floor as I was, I was still below the worst of it.

Rasmussen asked, "What do you know about Saint Sebastian?"

"Was not the person of that name, if indeed he existed at all, so pierced with the arrows of his enemies that he subsequently became the patron saint of pinmakers?"

Rasmussen scowled. "The Saint Sebastian to which I refer is the little country of that name—"

"Ah! The Sebastiani Liberation Front!"

He closed his eyes in chagrin. "I'm afraid this will get nowhere if you interrupt continually."

"But that's what the voice said on the phone. The only reason I was able to escape the building before it blew up was a call I got about a minute before the explosion: a man with a heavy accent, Slavic perhaps, but with also a bit of the German and God knows what else. On the other hand, I suppose it could have been faked." I peered sharply at Rasmussen: he or one of his colleagues would certainly have been capable of it.

"No news to us," he said disdainfully. "Naturally we had your place wired. That call was made by a member of an underground movement known as the Liberation Front of Saint Sebastian. These people are in the United States at this moment, on a fund- and sympathy-raising campaign for their cause."

"They have chosen a mightily ingratiating means of doing both," said I, showing my teeth. "How dare they come over here and blow up things and ask for *help!* Don't we have enough homegrown scum to do that sort of thing?"

Rasmussen leaned back and displayed a faint derisive smile. "Aren't we becoming a wee bit stuffy, Wren? Wasn't it our own Tom Jefferson who said the tree of liberty should be watered with the blood of tyrants?"

"But who chooses the tyrants? And how many tyrants are

found in Irish working-class homes, London department stores, Israeli kindergartens, and a highway junction near Nyack, New York? All of these have been the sites of unspeakable outrages by terrorist hyenas in the service of some cause for which perhaps some reasonable argument *might* be made, but to murder strangers in its name?"

Rasmussen shrugged. "It's all in a day's work to a pro, Wren. If I got into a tizzy over every little massacre, I'd never get anything accomplished." He grasped the bowl of the pipe and gestured at me with the stem. "Let me fill you in on Saint Sebastian. It's a little principality, tucked away in a kind of side pocket between Austria, Germany, and Czechoslovakia."

"I've *never* heard of a little country in the place you describe. There's Liechtenstein, of course, but isn't that near Switzerland? And San Marino's in Italy—"

"Shut *up*, Wren!" Rasmussen said coarsely. "In covert work we speak only when we have information to impart, never to be sociable."

He used the mispronunciation "coh-VERT," habitual with government types, but I decided to let that go for the moment.

He proceeded, "The place is ruled by one Prince Sebastian the Twenty-third, an anachronism, a dinosaur, an absolutist of the kind you don't nowadays find nowhere, nohow." He had turned folksy without warning: perhaps there are people who find that charming. "He has got away with it probably only because who cares about a tiny state of maybe seventy square miles, say thirty thousand souls, no raw materials of a strategic sort, and furthermore not on the main route to anyplace anybody would want to go, enclosed by high mountains. I mean, this is a little place time forgot, buddy-boy."

While wincing at his meaningless familiarity, I reflected that the same phrase had been uttered by me, on occasion, with reference to my hometown, a dreamy upstream Hudson hamlet where no doubt still today the village officials wear their pants an inch too short.

Rasmussen went on, after having sent my way a burst of smoke so noxious it might have come from the tailpipe of a city bus, "This prince is supposed to be some kind of nut, according to the few informants we have been able to find, a handful of tourists who have visited Saint Sebastian, and an old newsman, a stringer for some wire service, named Clyde McCoy. McCoy has apparently stayed there for years, due to the low cost of living and his high capacity for alcohol, cheap in Saint S. He's not exactly a trench-coated swashbuckler, I gather, not to mention that there's never been much that could be called noteworthy news from the place."

"*I* certainly have never heard of it," I iterated, though well aware that I would be annoying Rasmussen in so doing.

He glared at me briefly, pulling his lips back slightly from the pipe, to display two rows of rather spiky teeth: he was probably of that breed who eventually gnaw a hole in the hard-rubber stem. I seem to part with the rest of the human race in my instinctive distrust of a pipesmoker. "But then, how much do we hear of San Marino and Andorra?" he asked the ceiling of the van—in which incidentally I could spot no much-needed air vent. "Then these bombings began suddenly, as of last month, in certain American cities. I refer to those for which credit has been claimed by the Sebastiani Liberation Front, and not those others that have been the self-proclaimed work of the various other terrorist groups, though one or two explosions are in doubt, being boasted of by two organizations who have apparently no connection with each other, for example, when a series of small charges blew the genitalia off the nude male statuary in the National Gallery, credit was publicly taken by both the Amazon Army, whose cause should be obvious, and the Testosterone Society, an aggregation of militant macho men who performed the mutilation of marble, they said, to highlight society's daily severing of real gonads."

Rasmussen had the execrable taste to grin at this point: I suspected that the last example was apocryphal, his feeble essay at wit. I snorted, and he resumed.

"You can pooh-pooh terrorism in the interests of some schoolboy slogan about the perfectibility of man, but the fact is that violence is just about the only thing that will make you sit up and take notice. We're all in pretty much of a coma nowadays, wouldn't you say, what with mainlining, speedballing, herpes lesions, fear of getting AIDS from a handshake with a kid brother, dioxin-contaminated barbecue pits, over-the-counter

medicaments dosed with poison by embittered loners." He produced an anguished gasp: apparently he took modern life as
hard as any of us. "Hell, man, it *takes* an explosion to cut
through all that shit!"

I wondered again, as I had in the past, whether we were getting the finest types of men for our government bureaus or
whether they were going instead into the much more lucrative
field of pornographic videocassettes.

"Rasmussen," I asked, "would you mind opening a door or
turning on a fan?" I coughed and beat my hands. "Your pipe is
asphyxiating."

"Aha," said he, "you reveal a weakness."

"Yes. I'm afraid I breathe air."

He sighed and propped his pipe against a panel of switches
and dials. "My point is, if the Sebastiani Liberation group
thinks it worth their while to come all the way over here and
blow up a dump like the late building in which you made your
squalid home, perhaps we should return the favor and examine
what it is they are protesting against. Then we might throw our
weight to whichever side looks as though it's going to win, instead of getting entangled in ideologies, which is always a suck-
er's game. What I say is, let's take a look at this bozo close up,
this Prince Sebastian. What makes him tick? Maybe if Sebastian
comes up clean, it'll bring back the divine right of kings. World
could use a new angle on the whole political ball of wax: a rerun
of old-fashioned benevolent despotism might be the answer
we're all looking for. On the other hand, maybe it will make
more sense to fund this Liberation bunch, which might favorably impress various oil-rich fanatics in the Middle East." Rasmussen snatched up his pipe and puffed rapidly. "Well, Wren,"
he said around the stem, "you'll have a chance to pursue the
answer to these questions."

"Me?"

"We've decided to send you there," said he. "Isn't snooping
your profession? Obviously if you've survived in New York City
you know how to lie and cheat and dissemble: spying should be
just your meat."

I chewed on this remarkable proposal for a moment, then
said, "Don't think I'm not flattered by your offer, Rasmussen,

but really, I can't leave town at the moment. I've got to find a new home, and then I have to reconstruct my play. It's true that I have had some experience as an investigator, but that's pretty remote from being a spy, if you think about it. A principal difference is that if you do a bad job of private detection, it is not routine to be executed."

He failed to acknowledge these sentiments. "Your cover will be this: you're an American playwright who's gone to Saint Sebastian because it's a nice quiet place to hole up and lick your second-act problems."

I must say his information was uncannily accurate in assessing my dramaturgical difficulties. How he could have known about them was beyond me. Had I talked aloud in my sleep in the bugged room?

"Well, if you put it that way, I'll think it over." The fact was that with the winding up of the Rothman Deli job I had no employment. Indeed it would not have been easy to name a time when I had ever been overwhelmed with work. "I don't want to be vulgar," I said, "but am I naïve in assuming you folks pay some kind of fee to the free-lance?"

Rasmussen rose suddenly from his camp chair and hurled himself at the rear doors. I tried to follow him, but he opened the right-hand panel, leaped out, and slammed it in my face: furthermore, locked it from outside. After pounding awhile impotently, I went to assault the windowless metal wall that separated the rear compartment from the cab. The engine roared into life and started to move with a vicious lurch. I fell backwards, striking something adamantine with my head.

2

I was shaken awake as the vehicle hit a procession of the profound potholes with which Manhattan streets are pockmarked . . . except that I was not in the van or on a street anywhere, but rather in an airplane, aloft, and the bumps were caused by faults in the sky!

It was a commercial craft, and the approaching stewardess was a substantial fairhaired girl who wore a short dress of green jersey. She brought me a little tray which held a cup of café au lait and a plump croissant.

"Goot morning," said she. "Wilcom to Sebastiani Royal Airline, Meester Wren!" The bosom of her dress yawned open as she bent with the tray. I stared into her luxurious cleavage as something to do while I collected my wits. She asked, "Vould you like to skveese the breasts?" I should say her smile was more genial than sensual.

"Uh, no, thank you," said I, and then, courtesy being my foible even when far from home, I saw fit to add, "Perhaps another time. They look very nice."

"Oh yes," she said with vigor. "Mine body is beautifool." It would be hard to explain that this statement did not sound like boasting when it was pronounced. My natural taste in females is for a more slender sort of blond, but I must say that this statuesque person put me at ease, or at any rate at a good deal more of it than I could have claimed in her absence.

"Miss, please don't think me mad if I ask where we are, where I am. Did you say 'Sebastiani'? Is that what it would seem, a reference to the little principality of Saint Sebastian?"

She smiled grandly with the largest of white teeth and an

expanse of rosy lips: she was a spectacularly healthy specimen. "Ve vill be landing there soon."

I took a sip of the coffee, which proved hot and delicious and thus reassuring. "You may not believe this, but I haven't any idea of how I got here. When I was last awake, I was in a vehicle on a street in New York City."

She nodded sympathetically. "You had had some drinks before your friends brought you aboard, I think. You vent to sleep and only now have you awakened up. Vot puzzles me, sir, is how you have retained your you-reen all the night long."

"Pardon me . . . ?"

She frowned. "Don't you have to make peepee?"

I wasn't prepared for her frankness, which I began to suspect was habitual. I shook my head. I had had nothing to drink since the cheap plonk of my wretched supper: it seemed clear enough that that swine Rasmussen had drugged me. I would be mighty indignant when this flight touched down. Meanwhile there was nothing to do but eat breakfast. Both the coffee and croissant were excellent.

The stewardess said her name was Olga. She seemed to be working alone.

I asked whether there were any other passengers.

"Now, no. Your friends left in Vienna."

"Did one of them have a bad complexion?"

"To be sure," said Olga. She vivaciously sat down in the aisle seat. Her skirt was so short that her columnar thighs were now altogether bare. "I did not like him, forgive me!"

"Neither do I," I freely admitted.

She lifted the hinged seat-arm between us, leaned against me, and peered into my face. Her eyes were very blue. "Foreigners sometimes do not understand our vays. Ve do not have to screw under *every* circumstance. For example, rudeness is a reason not; opening the trousers first, or foul language, or violent seizings! All of these your friend did, forgive me."

"Let me apologize for him," said I. "He's not, thank heavens, typical of my countrymen." I felt some security in expressing this patriotic sentiment. "The average Yank, whom perhaps you haven't been fortunate enough to meet, is a hardworking family man whose simple idea of pleasure is to burn meat on a charcoal grill. He is definitely not a cryptofascist religious-fanatic war-monger, though he is, at work, no Nipponese zealot. He may even be something of a slacker, speaking industrially, but—"

"*You* can screw with me, to be sure," said Olga. She grasped the hem of her perfunctory skirt and raised it, lifting her bottom. She seemed to be wearing no underthings.

I have seldom been found lacking in carnal appetite, but no element in this state of affairs was propitious.

"I'll tell you," I told her, somehow sensing that it would not be considered a rejection, "I'd prefer, right now, to drink another cup of coffee and eat a second croissant."

I was right: she popped up, her skirt falling after a long and not at all unattractive moment, and smiling sweetly as ever, went to do my bidding. This time the croissant was accompanied by a fluffy pale mound, not a poisonously golden pat, of sweet butter and a little Limoges pot of an extraordinarily fragrant honey. Having delivered these, Olga sat down next to me again. She, too, exuded a lovely bouquet similar to that of the honey. I mentioned it to her, and she told me that both honey and scent traced their origins to a wild flower peculiar to the high meadows of her country. I must say that the associations the name Saint Sebastian had today were preferable to those of the evening before.

I could not forgive Rasmussen for the manner in which he had shanghaied me, but while finishing my breakfast I did remember the job for which I had been hired.

"Tell me, Olga," I said, gesturing with half a croissant, "about your prince."

"What is to be told?"

I nibbled and swallowed. "Is he loved by the people of Saint Sebastian?"

"Why nawt?" She laughed *hahaha.*

"Umm. But you know what I mean: is he *really* liked, admired, and so on, or does he simply hold power by brute force?"

"Ah," she sighed. "I could never know about that. My job is to be stewardess, and not to deal in social theoretics, you see."

It occurred to me to ask, "Do you even have the vote?"

"No, indeed, God be thanked!" Her negative enthusiasm seemed genuine enough.

I swallowed the remainder of the buttered and honeyed croissant and finished the coffee. They seemed to have a soporific effect. I barely had the energy to put another question.

"You are aware, are you not, of an anti-Prince Opposition? In fact, a terrorist group that blows up buildings in New York to get attention for its cause? The Sebastiani Liberation Front?"

Olga smiled prettily at me throughout my questions, in that fashion in which the questioned seems amused by some ad hominem reflections on the questioner and gives little heed to what is being asked. I wondered whether she was a nymphomaniac or merely weak-minded: I had known both sorts, sometimes even in combination, but never had they been so magnificently salubrious. I confess that Olga had an odd effect on me at this point: I would rather have trained her for some sporting event than taken her to bed.

I waved my hand before her eyes. "Did you hear me?"

She filled her great bosom with air and released it in a happy kind of gasp. "I am too beautiful for such matters. I vas selected for the job I have now soon after my breasts began to grow."

The gentle gong-sound that accompanies the seat-belt sign was heard, and Olga informed me that the airplane was about to land. She went to the little fold-down perch beside the door to the cockpit, giving me another vista of her breathtaking thighs. I reluctantly turned from this spectacle to the view from the window. I saw some neat checkerboarded farmland below, in various shades of earth colors, and then soon enough we were over clustered dwellingplaces, crooked streets, and free-form shapes of greenery, several of which surrounded bodies of water that reflected the cerulean sky, and on a higher elevation what seemed to be a crenellated stone fortress, and then the airplane made a great sweeping, banking turn and smoothly descended onto a very simple blacktopped landing strip, coming to rest nowhere near the terminal building, which in any event was too small to be equipped with an extensible gangway.

Olga opened the door, and I went to join her. To see outside, I had to lean around this magnificent specimen of young-womanhood, who was at least as tall as I. Beyond the airfield in that direction the farmland began, and in the distance I saw a blue range of mountains. I knew no more of the geography of this part of the world than I knew of its language, politics, history, or culture. Why Rasmussen felt it necessary to hustle me off so quickly, with no preparation or opportunity for research, made no sense, unless it could be explained by calling him a bureaucratic scoundrel and having done with it.

At this point a fairhaired functionary on the ground outside began to maneuver a portable stairway into place at the door of the aircraft.

"Good-bye, sir," said Olga. "I hope you did enjoy the flight anyway."

"Good-bye, Olga. You're a nice girl." On an impulse I added, "I regret not being in the mood to screw this morning. Perhaps another time."

"When you want!" she answered ebulliently, performing a little curtsy.

I went down the metal stairs and stepped onto the tarmac. The man who had wheeled the stairway into place was gone. Olga was still the only person I had seen since the night before, and no one was in sight on the airfield. The terminal building was a good half mile away from where I stood. Just as I decided that I would have to hike for it, I heard the distant racket of a noisy engine, and a vehicle came onto the field and rapidly approached me. When it got nearer I recognized it as an ancient station wagon of American make, a vintage model with a body of real wooden panels. It had been indifferently maintained: black smoke gushed from its tailpipe, and much of the wooden paneling was in a sorry condition, rotting or splintered. The windshield was cracked, the tires were bald, the front bumper was loose at one end. Instead of glass, plastic sheeting covered the driver's window. This was so dirty and discolored that I could not identify the person at the wheel until he stopped the car and cried out in a voice that seemed to come from the throat of a man with a mortal illness.

"You Wren?"

I could not see the speaker, but I confirmed the identification.

"Climb aboard!" The passenger's door was flung open. When I had rounded the old station wagon at the rear—the windows of which had been glazed with water-stained cardboard—I saw that the door had been opened so violently, and had been so feebly hinged, that in fact it lay on the runway.

I leaned down and looked in at the driver.

He fell across the seat in my direction, hand outthrust in greeting. "Clyde McCoy. Good to see somebody from Home."

Of course, he was the man Rasmussen had mentioned.

I thrust my hand in and shook his. "What should I do about the door?"

McCoy managed to sit up. He was a skinny, sinewy individual and dressed in a dark-gray suit that I suspected to be properly light gray. His urine-yellow shirt had surely begun life as white. The hue of his tie could be called grease-green. He left the car and staggered around the hood to reach the fallen door. He was one of those persons who owing to slightness of figure and lifelessness of hair could be any age. Using what seemed the strength of sudden madness, he lifted the door and got it back on its hinges. He closed it gingerly. Then he reached through the glassless aperture, found a twisted coat hanger that hung there, and fastened the wire to the upright post of the frame. This took a few moments of intense application in which he breathed in upon me, and when the job was done I felt half drunk.

When he returned to fit himself in back of the wheel I asked apprehensively, "You wouldn't want me to drive?"

He peered at me through lids that were almost closed. "It's understandable you think I'm under the influence. I suffer from a disease that resembles drunkenness so closely that my breath even seems to smell of alcohol. That's why I first came to this country. Saint Sebastian had the only doctor in the world at the time who knew how to treat this ailment. You know what he prescribed? Schnapps. Lots of it. You'd notice if I were to take a drink or two now I'd be sober in no time."

The vehicle was so old that its starter was mounted on the floor, and after making his statement McCoy began to look for it with the toe of his right foot, which was shod in a battered old shoe from which a section had been cut out, presumably to favor a bunion.

"I suppose you know that Rasmussen sent me," I said. "But what you might not know is that I've had no preparation for the assignment. I don't even have any money or a passport. And what language is spoken here? I want to get hold of a dictionary or phrase book."

"Don't worry about anything," McCoy answered. "I'll be back to normal in no time." He had begun to shake, but he finally got the starter's range and brought the engine into deafening life. The car jerked into motion and sped towards the terminal building.

It occurred to me to ask: "Don't I have to go through Immigration and/or Customs?"

The question fortunately came just in time to halt McCoy's head in its descent to the steering wheel. He lifted it and said, "Naw."

If we had continued on the current course we would have driven directly through the little terminal building. I urged McCoy to turn, which he did abruptly, lifting us on two wheels.

"But," I pointed out when the car had regained its equilibrium and left the airport on what was presumably the exit road, an unpaved, rutted lane, "am I not making an illegal entry? If mere rudeness is punished so severely, what about this?" I turned to see whether we would be pursued, but could not, owing to the cardboard in the back windows.

McCoy frowned. Looking at me, he forgot the road. I leaned over and seized the rim of the wheel with both hands and kept it steady.

I was worried. "Hadn't we better switch places?"

McCoy shook himself and reclaimed the wheel. "I'm fine. I just need a little pick-me-up and I'll even be better."

We were entering a town, shaking along a narrow cobblestoned street that wound past clustered stone buildings, going over an occasional bridge, also of stone. We passed through more than one quaint square around which were a bakery, a cafe, an *épicerie*, and sometimes a spired church. But human beings were not to be seen.

Finally McCoy pulled against a high curb, scraping, with an awful sound, not only the tires but the edges of the wheels as well.

"Got to stop this way," said he. "The brakes are pretty far gone, and except in the royal garages mechanics are in short supply. Except for foreigners, and of course the prince, cars aren't permitted in Saint Sebastian. Better slide out this way, so I don't have to undo that door again." He left the vehicle.

I slid over and out and stepped onto the stones of the next street I had touched after leaving the asphalt of Third Avenue, New York City. We were before a modest five- or six-story structure labeled, over its plain entrance, Hotel Bristol.

Once on his feet, McCoy magically gained a certain sobriety and positively loped into the hotel. I followed, entering a small lobby furnished with a high desk behind which were a set of birdhouse mailboxes and a panel from which hung outsized keys of dull brass. This complex was controlled by a stout person with a handlebar mustache. He wore an ancient-looking tailcoat, which I suspect would on closer examination have proved all but threadbare. His wing collar was none too clean, and the posy in his lapel was browning. He gave me a quick frown and then a slow, broad smile that eventually reached the gold tooth on the far left.

"Sir, without doubt you are Mr. Wren." He spun around, frighteningly fast for a fat man, and seized one of the hanging keys. He placed the key on the counter and rang the little domed bell there. From nowhere came a teenaged boy in a green monkey suit with brass buttons. He saluted me with two fingers and was about to pick up the key when, remembering I had no money in my pockets, I shook my head. Call me a tender soul, but I cannot stand to stiff a servitor.

"No, no," I said. "I'll find it myself. I have no luggage."

The concierge leaned onto his desk and, lowering his heavy head, winked ponderously. "He is available for more than carrying bags, sir."

For an instant I did not get his drift, being impatient to follow McCoy, who, oblivious to me, was already opening the grillwork door of the tiniest elevator I had ever seen.

"Then," my oily questioner persisted, "shall I send up a person of the remaining sex?"

"Neither," I blurted, and as he was beginning a response that I feared might well extend to zoological matters, I snatched up the key and stepped towards the lift. But I was too late. The feckless McCoy was already ascending in the little cage, his runover shoes just at the level of my nose, through the brass grille of the door.

It took an eternity for the elevator to return, throughout which I had an unpleasant wait, for the concierge renewed his importunities in a crooning, obsequious voice that was more repulsive than what he was suggesting.

The lift finally returned, and I took it to the fourth floor, being directed there by the number on the key. When I found my room, the door was open and there, before a rickety desk-table, stood McCoy, draining into his mouth the last few drops from an upended flat pint vessel. His lower lip was dippered out like that of a performing chimpanzee who has learned to drink Coke from the bottle.

He saw me when he lowered the now dead soldier. "All right," he said bitterly, "so I have a little snort now and again, so send me before the firing squad. Other people kill, torture, mutilate, yet never hear a word of criticism, but let me just take a little drink and I'm a criminal." He bent in the ever so careful movement of the drunk and deposited the empty bottle in a little wastecan under the desk. Then he went to an opened suitcase that lay on the bed and began to root through the clothing therein. "Rats," he gasped, growing more desperate and eventually hurling the valise's contents onto the coverlet. "Did you bring only one bottle?"

"I wasn't even permitted to bring a change of clothing," I told him indignantly, remembering my plight. "I assume I can get outfitted on one your local accounts."

"This is your luggage," he said in disgust. "It beat us here from the airport."

"Mine?" Except what I was wearing, tan corduroys and a knitted shirt in dark green, my own wardrobe, such as it had been, had perished in the explosion in New York. That Rasmussen had had time to collect the contents of this valise suggested that he had prepared for my mission far in advance of my being informed of it. The realization did nothing for my souring mood.

"Kindly get away from my possessions," I told McCoy. "I gather you have just drained the bottle the Firm included for my own medicinal uses."

McCoy sank to a seat on the edge of the bed. "If I don't get another drink I'm going to die."

And he had only just finished a pint of ardent spirits!

"What you need, my friend," I told him, "is rather a thorough drying out. I don't know whether Saint Sebastian has a chapter of the good AA folk, but you must take all possible measures towards eventual teetotalling. I'm no bluenose when it comes to drink, but—"

He had begun to shake violently. "You f-f-fucking idiot," he murmured. "I'm dying." With one great hug of his midsection he hurled himself onto the carpet, writhed fiercely, then went still and silent. I was relieved to see he had passed out: I should have been ill put to deal with delirium tremens.

I looked through the clothes provided for me. Alas, Rasmussen's taste, if he had selected them, was deplorable. The jacket was of that madras which is altogether innocent of India, in an awful blue-and-red plaid that has no reference to Scotland. The polyester trousers celebrated the principal bad-taste colors, kelly green, turquoise, and magenta. The loafers were of artificial leather and adorned with tassels. I had not traveled in some years, but I wondered whether the Firm's idea of typical American tourist attire was up to the minute in an age when quiche and *pasta primavera* had become popular even in the hinterlands.

I looked down at McCoy. Could he be genuinely ill? For the first time I actually thought about his having, good God, chug-a-lugged a pint of whiskey in the time it took me to rise on the elevator! I retrieved the empty bottle from the wastecan.

The label identified its late contents as having been no brand of potable spirits but rather an after-shave lotion cutely packaged to resemble a pint of Scotch. I sniffed at its neck: the odor was certainly lethal.

I knelt and searched for a pulse at various places on McCoy's body. I could not find one, nor could I find a house phone when I rose, and when I dashed down the hall to the elevator, there was no response to the finger I pressed repeatedly against the button.

I found a stairway behind an unmarked door at the end of the corridor and hurled myself down it, two steps per vault. Having

miraculously reached the bottom without breaking a bone, I
burst into the lobby.

The corpulent functionary behind the desk leered at me.
"Aha, I knew you would change your mind and want the boy
after all!"

"Quick," I cried, "a doctor! Mr. McCoy has been poisoned."

"That is not possible. He only just went to his room."

"Don't argue with me! He's dying of poison, I say. Call a
doctor!"

The concierge reached under his counter and brought up one
of those ornate brass vintage telephones, reproductions of which
are now sold in American discount stores. He barked into the
mouthpiece, "Constabulary!" When the connection had been
made, he said, "Hotel Bristol. One tourist has poisoned another.
. . . Yes." Having put away the telephone, he found an automatic pistol in the desk, brought it up, and trained it on me.

I raised my hands, but protested vigorously. "I'm no killer,
and for God's sake will you call an ambulance!"

The concierge rolled his eyes, and his upper lip came down.
"Our hotel is not a refuge for gangsters." From his left hand he
extended the index finger and waved it before my nose.

The police arrived promptly, two of them, on bicycles, which
they trundled into the lobby. These lawmen were uniformed as
if for an operetta: braided tunics, high glossy boots, caps like
pots, and very small holstered pistols. They carried truncheons.
The one in the lead had porcine nostrils and was about my
height but much wider. Without a word he produced a pair of
what proved to be handcuffs and attached ankle manacles,
linked by a chain so short that when the other constable had
knelt and fettered me with the lower shackles after the first had
braceleted my wrists, I was necessarily a hunchback.

I was bent (though not in the British sense), but not mute.
"You can't do this to an American national," I blustered, hoping
that they would not throw recent Iranian events in my face. "I
demand to see my consul."

The larger policeman struck me deftly on the crazybone of
my right arm, which was thereby paralyzed for many minutes.
"You have no passport," he said after a perfunctory search of my
person. "You have no other papers and no money. You are a

stateless vagrant, and you are a murderer. On the first charge you are sentenced to a flogging. On the second, to probable death: it would be unkind to predict another outcome to the Hunt."

I had to slow down the centrifuge inside my head, and choose which point to make first. "I'm not a murderer, for heaven's sake. *Flogging? Probable death?*" Already my neck was aching from trying to look up at him. "What's the Hunt?"

The smaller constable spoke for the first time. He had a soft, round, bespectacled face and looked like a village schoolteacher, but so had Heinrich Himmler.

"You will not find here the brutality of other countries," said he. "We do not sentence murderers to prison terms, and we do not perform so-called executions. We have the Hunt. We provide the condemned homicide with a revolver."

I was crippled by an utter lack of belief that this was happening. "Let's go back to the beginning, I beg of you," I said. "A fellow American, Mr. Clyde McCoy, by accident drank an entire pint of after-shave lotion. I rushed down here to summon a doctor, since there's no phone in the room—"

"The Hunt," said the pigfaced policeman, "consists of your being released with the pistol and our following your trail with the intention of killing you on sight."

"Just a moment, you policemen can only accuse me of a crime. You can't serve as judge and jury too."

Pigface put the end of his truncheon just under my nose and raised it, to give me a hog's snout as well. "Remember, this is Saint Sebastian, not the USA. We believe that only the policeman is capable of making these judgments, for isn't it only he who deals with the criminals and investigates the crime? Where is the judge all this while? In bed with his mistress! And the members of the jury are going about their little bourgeois affairs in safety and comfort. How can any of these people know of criminal matters as well as, not to say better than, the law-enforcement officer? And why should Sebastianers take seriously the so-called rights of those whose profession it is to damage those who observe the law?"

In this debate, if such it was, I was hampered by more or less agreeing with him, after years of residence in New York, where generally speaking the only citizen whose life is without hazard is the ruthless felon. But by the same token, *viz.*, being a New Yorker, I was culturally constrained to bring into use the word "fascist," which is literally meaningless except in a use peculiar to Mussolini, but which in Manhattan is regularly applied to any projected inconvenience.

The Sebastiani cops snorted in indifference, and the smaller said, "So why should we care what name be given the practice? The point is, there are crimes and criminals here as elsewhere, for roguery is natural to mankind, but there are no *habitual* criminals."

"We should surely see eye to eye on this subject," I said, "were *I* not unjustly accused, arrested, and restrained. There's the flaw in your practice!"

"And this is to demonstrate *your* flaw," the shorter policeman replied, and struck me across the kidneys with his truncheon. "You are helpless."

He had made his painful point, and I sensed that it would be politic for me to stay silent, but I could not accept the unfairness of it. "Won't you at least get medical help for my friend McCoy? There might still be hope for him."

"Aha," said the larger man. "You are the sort of pervert whose pleasure is bringing some poor devil to the threshold of death and then reviving him so that you can do it all over again?"

It seemed hopeless, and they were about to conduct me to the police station (by walking me in my bonds between them on their bikes, I assumed), where I would be given the aforementioned pistol and sent out as prey for the Hunt, when the little lift came down to the lobby and who should emerge but McCoy, not good as new, which would probably not have characterized him even as a child, I suspect, but certainly better than when last seen.

He lurched up to my captors and asked, "What are you scumheads doing to my friend? Get him out of those bracelets or I'll drive those billy clubs up your fat rumps."

Both officers blanched, and each contested with the other to be first to comply with the abusive demands.

While with twenty blundering thumbs they undid my various

restraints McCoy asked, "Why did you let them do this to you, Wren?"

"They're armed, for God's sake."

"Why," said he, "that doesn't mean anything. Look." He booted the larger officer in the behind. The victim looked only more miserable. He had hung the strap of his stick over his holster, and he failed to make a move towards either of his weapons.

"But they represent the law," I pointed out.

He gave me his bleary eyes. His breath stank of shaving lotion. "Only if you agree to let them."

"You mean what's legal or not is arguable in Saint Sebastian? That if I actually *had* murdered you I could righteously refuse to be arrested?"

"Murdered me?"

"I thought you were dying after drinking that stuff. I was looking for a doctor."

McCoy snorted. "It's that disease I told you I had. I didn't get the booze down quickly enough, so I passed out. But I came to when the alcohol had had time to take hold. By the way, somebody put the wrong label on that bottle. It's not Scotch but rye, and not a bad one. Decent booze is hard to get here unless you visit the prince. Schnapps is the local firewater."

Could there be such a malady? Perhaps I had misjudged him. But apart from that, he obviously had a stainless-steel gastrointestinal system.

My back ached. I was tempted to take a kick at the policemen myself, but I was still far from certain as to the rules or lack thereof in this situation. It would take me a while to lose my inhibitions against assaulting officers armed with guns and clubs, though that sort of thing was routine enough back home.

But complaining to the manager of the place one is currently living in is always permissible if not obligatory. I stepped up to the obese person back of the desk.

Before I could speak he crooned, "Ah, *now* you want a boy."

I lost such little patience as I had retained. "No, you pederast's ponce! How dare you accuse me of murder and put me through that humiliation?"

He stared at me for a while, I think to determine whether I

was serious, and then he called back the policemen, who were just rolling their bicycles out the door. My heartbeat became irregular. Despite McCoy, were they going to re-arrest me?

But when they reached the desk, the fat man came out from behind his protection and extended his hands.

"It's the pillory for me, I'm afraid. This gentleman charges me with exaggerated rudeness."

The constables assumed stern expressions and proceeded to put him into the arrangement of manacles and chains from which I had only lately been freed. I felt no triumph. Indeed, I tried to register my protest—all I wanted was a simple apology and, more important, to establish the truth that those who make accusations should have sound evidence in support—I was about to ask the policemen to free the concierge, but McCoy restrained me.

"Don't interfere," said he. "That's their way. I never make any trouble except when it's my own ox being gored. Besides, he *should* be punished. That's no way to run a hotel."

The policemen led the fat man away, riding their bikes on either side of him, at none too slow a pace even while still within the hotel, so that he was forced to perform a brisk trot, which was anything but dignified for a man of his bulk.

I said to McCoy, "Those policemen brought their bikes in here? In New York that would make sense, but I thought these people didn't steal."

"You haven't got the right idea yet," said he. "There's some theft here. What's different is that nobody can make a career of it, if he loses a hand for every conviction."

I took an extra breath. I had heard that that punishment, for which Xenophon had praised the younger Cyrus, was still being exacted in remote regions of Arabia, but in mid-Europe in the late twentieth century? This was turning out to be an appalling little principality.

"But are there still Sebastianers who would risk the loss of a hand for a bicycle, furthermore a bicycle that could easily be traced in so small an area and population?"

"It can't be news to you that human beings do things at which they can be hurt," McCoy said, with an appropriately cynical turn at one corner of his mouth. "Maybe *because* they'll get hurt." He frowned. "I wonder whether I need a drink to hold me until we get to the palace."

"Palace?"

"Uh-huh," he replied negligently. "The prince has invited us to lunch."

"The sovereign of Saint Sebastian? This is incredible."

"Don't make too much of it," McCoy said sourly. "Not that many tourists come here, the foreign diplomats left years ago, and he is afraid he might get assassinated if he sees his subjects, so he gets lonely." He started for the door. There was no one at the hotel desk now that the concierge had been arrested, but that was not my problem.

We got into the car and McCoy drove, inordinately as ever, down the cobblestoned street, all but grazing a skirted priest wearing a wide-brimmed hat and riding a shabby bicycle. In response the man of peace raised a warlike fist. He was thus far the only person I had seen at large.

Soon we entered upon a steep ascent that would have been an effort for a powerful new vehicle. At times the soles of my feet were seemingly higher than my chin, and the ancient car had a deeper cough and a more violent shudder for each yard of the road. But we finally reached the summit and rolled across a paved area large enough to be a parade ground and approached the palace, which without doubt was the castlelike structure I had seen from the air. It was massive and of a chunky stone texture, with narrow slits for windows and a roofline of crenellations, really more of a fortress than a palace, if one thinks ideally of the latter as being characterized first by stateliness. Sebastian's robust residence suggested it could hold off an army—not one armed with nuclear weapons, certainly, or perhaps even howitzers, but certainly swords, maces, and battleaxes, and maybe even flintlocks, would be no threat to anyone within its walls.

We arrived before a great entrance gate, but could not use it until its massive door was lowered over the moat, which, probably because I had been staring up, I had not noticed before. McCoy stopped the car by colliding with an abutment. He blew the horn, and hard upon the echo the enormous door, made of thick wood bound and studded with iron, began its creaking descent. I was disappointed, when it was altogether down, not to be able to see into a courtyard, for another large door intruded.

We crossed the drawbridge, found a winding staircase in the tower to the left, and climbed, emerging eventually into a windowless room. As yet we had heard or seen no living thing, but now two men, in even more gaudy operetta uniforms than the police had worn, entered through one of the several doors in the far wall. They were husky young officers with ruddy cheeks; except for their eyes (respectively ferret and hound) and noses (Roman and snub), they might have been twins.

"Good day, Mr. McCoy," said the one in the lead. "Perhaps you have explained the procedure to Mr. Wren."

"More or less," said my companion. He turned to me. "They search you, and then you put on the kimono."

The second officer assigned himself to me. He was the one with the beady bright eyes and large nose. "How do you do," said he, clicking his heels. "Mr. Wren. I am Lieutenant Blok. Please to come along to the changing room, if you will."

He led me to one of the doors. McCoy, lurching along behind the other officer, gave me a smirk. The changing room was a small chamber furnished with a chair and a plain table that held what looked like a stack of navy-blue towels.

I stood there and did nothing for a while, not knowing quite what the drill was, and not wanting to be notably quick in stripping myself before a man.

As if reading me, Blok after a moment asked politely, "Would you prefer a female guard?"

Funny, but this offer did not seem as flattering to my sense of my own virility as it might have. "Certainly not," I replied, and in no time at all was down to my briefs—the rather gaudily striped pair I had purchased, for a song, from a sidewalk vendor's cardboard box on Fourteenth Street: how could I have known, upon donning them two mornings ago, that they would not be doffed until I was in a castle in a foreign land, about to meet an absolute monarch?

As each of my few articles of clothing came off it was handed to Lieutenant Blok, who examined it carefully. He now received my socks, which after two days might well have been a bit high.

"You must understand," I said to this spotless officer in his shining boots, "I was whisked over here—" and then I remembered that as a secret agent I should probably not volunteer such details, though Rasmussen, with the same negligence that had characterized this assignment from the first, had failed to give me any such instructions. "I'm an impulsive traveler," I said. "I jumped on the plane before I had a chance to shower."

Blok made no reply, just continued solemnly to inspect the socks—as if one could conceal a lethal weapon there, despite the sizable hole in each toe.

And I'm sorry to say that I finally had to surrender even the striped drawers for the same search, and then was obliged to bend and spread my nether cheeks, should I be concealing a vial of explosive.

3

When Blok finished his inspection he bowed and left the room, and immediately in came a little officer resplendent in braid and wearing a sword. He clicked his heels.

"Mr. Wren, I am General Anton Popescu, commander of the Life Guards." He took from the table what turned out to be, when unfolded, a rather handsome ankle-length robe of thick soft stuff, a kind of velour without excessive sheen, in a blue I now would call not quite as dark as navy. I put on this garment with considerable relief, and was next provided with a pair of sandals of soft black calfskin, soled with crepe rubber.

When I was dressed, the little general, who wore the thinnest of mustaches and whose hair was brilliantined and parted in the middle, opened the door through which he had come, bowed, and swept me onward with an expansive gesture. I found myself in a marble-floored corridor, the walls of which were lined with magnificent tapestries.

McCoy was waiting there, wearing a robe like mine. He said sardonically, "I see you weren't carrying a grenade up your keister."

I addressed the general. "These tapestries are splendid."

"Indeed they are," he told me. "When Leo the Tenth heard about them he demanded that Raphael make similar designs for the Vatican."

"Do you mean—"

"To be sure," said Popescu. "And for those the master was paid ten thousand ducats. These he did for the rewards of piety and the gratitude of Sebastian the Fifteenth."

"The history of this country goes back that far?"

"Good gracious," said Popescu, running a finger along one side of his mustache. "This country was venerable by the time of the Renaissance. There were Sebastianers who went on the First Crusade with Walter the Penniless, though to be sure few survived the journey through Bulgaria. They were wont to plunder the lands they passed through, you see, and sometimes the people who lived there took countermeasures. Sebastian the Third himself went to the Fourth Crusade: his Byzantine souvenirs can be found amidst the palace collections."

As I dimly remembered, the Fourth was the farcical crusade: en route to smite the infidels, the Western Europeans stopped off to assault their fellow Christians at Byzantium and sack that great city. But it would scarcely be politic to make this point at that moment. Instead I indicated the nearest tapestry, on which was depicted a kneeling haloed individual about to have his brains bashed out by the boulder held high over the head of the person behind him.

"Who's that poor devil?"

"Saint Stephen, being stoned," said the general. "You know those old martyrs!"

McCoy was either blasé from having seen the tapestries too often or, more likely, had no taste for the fine arts. He was biting his lip and staring longingly down the corridor towards what one would assume was the expected source of his next drink: he had not had one for a good twenty minutes.

We went through a doorway into a large chamber, the walls of which were lined with dark-red silk against which were hung ornately framed oils, all of which were immediately recognizable.

I asked Popescu, "Isn't that a copy of 'Aristotle Contemplating the Bust of Homer'?" The original of which was of course one of the Metropolitan's most publicized possessions.

"In fact," said the little general, wiggling his mustache-lined upper lip, "*this* is the original, done by Rembrandt for his patron Prince Sebastian the Nineteenth. If you have seen another elsewhere in the world, it is surely derivative of this."

"Rembrandt was here?"

"Ah, my friend," sighed Popescu, "he was but one of the many painters to the court of Saint Sebastian."

I stared at the other walls, recognizing Botticelli's "Birth of Venus" and then one of the finest of the many portraits of Philip IV done by the great master whom he kept at the Spanish court.

"Velásquez was one of them?"

"Certainly," said the general, indicating the polished brass plate on the picture frame.

I peered in close-up and read, "Portrait of Sebastian XV, by Diego Rodríguez de Silva y Velásquez, 1599–1660."

"This is remarkable," I disingenuously noted. "Are you aware that this very face, in its many depictions, is elsewhere in the world invariably believed to be that of the Spanish monarch Philip the Fourth?"

The general gestured. "It does not surprise me at all. There have been many such misrepresentations throughout the centuries. No doubt it should be flattering to know that the world so envies us."

I nodded at the "Botticelli" across the room. "Now, that superb canvas is elsewhere called 'Birth of Venus' and sometimes, jocularly, 'Venus on the Half Shell.' " Popescu remained sober. "I believe it is the Uffizi which has an excellent example of it, which, naïfs or prevaricators, they call the original that came from the brush of the sublime Sandro."

The general shrugged with all of his tense little body. "There you are, eh? And don't ever think those wily Florentines naïve, my dear chap! Though it is true enough that Sebastian the Fourteenth more than once made an ass of Lorenzo, who between you and me was not all that Magnificent. . . . As everyone knows, the model for that picture was Queen Sebastiana the Third, done by Botticelli when he was her court painter and perhaps something more." He gave me a significantly cocked eyebrow.

"Remarkable! A nude depiction of a reigning princess?"

General Popescu smiled in pride. "Our rulers have often been notable for their lack of shame."

"They've all been called Sebastian or the female version?"

"No," said Popescu. "There have been Maximilians, Ferdinands, and at least one Igor."

"And surely amongst the princesses' names were Isabella and Carlotta?"

"Indeed," said the general. "I see you've done your homework."

We went through two more rooms hung with the pictorial treasures of the Renaissance. McCoy had long since disappeared.

Finally Popescu said, "Forgive me, but I must take you to the prince. He does not care to wait for his meals!"

He led me to a doorway and stepped aside. I went through it and was met by a horse-faced lackey wearing a green tailcoat, buff knee-breeches, white stockings, and buckled shoes. He held a tall staff, which, as I stepped across the threshold, he lifted and thumped buttfirst upon the floor.

He cried, "Mr. Russel Wren!"

Good gravy, I was in the throne room! There, at the far end of a crimson runner, on a three-stepped stage, sat Prince Sebastian XXIII, or anyway it was to be presumed that the distant figure was he: I would have to walk an eighth of a mile to be certain, between two ranks of trumpeters who, hard on the final echo of the stentorian announcement of my name, raised their golden instruments to their lips and began to sound a deafening fanfare. When these musicians were at last done, my head remained, for almost the entire trip down the carpet, as a cymbal newly struck, and the prince was a growing but tremulous image, so agitated was my vision.

He wore a golden crown and red, ermine-trimmed robe.

As I reached the last ten feet of the red runner, it occurred to me that I must make the traditional gesture of obeisance that was probably expected of everyone, even an American democrat, who finds himself before a throne, but still shaky from the fanfare and utterly unprepared for this moment—wretched Rasmussen, to ship me over without adequate training!—I made a fool of myself: I forgot about bowing, which in fact I had not done since appearing, with powdered hair, in a grammar-school re-enactment of Cornwallis's surrender at Yorktown, and instead plucked an imaginary skirt at either side of mid-thigh while dipping at one knee. In a word, I curtsied.

This performance was greeted with explosive laughter from the throne. "How do you do, Mr. Wren," said the prince, still shaking with mirth. "Welcome to my country."

"Thank you, sir."

His plump face was the kind that one assumed had been almost beautiful as a boy, and he still had rosy cheeks and long-lashed dark eyes. With a hand to steady his crown, he now stood up. He looked to be of medium height. The long red robe concealed the particulars of his body, but there could be no doubt that he was very corpulent.

"Shall we go to lunch," he said, without the implication of a question mark. Lifting the robe slightly, so that the hem would not trip him up, he descended the stairs. When he stood beside me I saw that he was not nearly so tall as I had supposed when viewing him from a lower level: the eminence and the long robe had created an illusion. In reality he was much shorter than I. Which is not, however, to say he lacked that mysterious presence called royal.

A liveried lackey preceded us to the dining room, which was not so far distant from the throne room as I should have supposed, given the size of the palace. The dining room itself was enormous, with a table long enough to have fed dozens. A little army of formally dressed servitors was lined up in silent ranks.

An aged man, festooned with gold chains and keys, shuffled up to meet his sovereign. But what he had to say was reproving. "You shouldn't be wearing that crown. It's not at all the thing to wear at table, it really isn't."

"You old fool," Sebastian said, "it's my crown and I'll wear it when I please. Don't interfere or I'll have you flayed." So much for the words: his delivery, uncertain and even a bit fearful, was at odds with them.

The old man came forward then and, putting out his tremulous hands, took the crown from the prince's head. "Now, you just eat your lunch like a good boy, and we'll say no more about it." He gestured to one of the servingpeople, a young man with large ears, and gave him the crown, which was golden and encrusted with bright gems. It was the first I had ever seen in use, and frankly it did not altogether escape vulgarity: the jewels looked synthetic.

Sebastian made no resistance, but he stamped his foot once his head was bare. "I did so want to wear it for once while eating. You are a withered old person, a feebleminded dotard." His short dark hair showed the impress of the crown.

Immune to the abuse, the old man limped to the head of the table, pulled out the stately chair there, and said, "You just sit down and have your ice cream, young man, and no more nonsense."

I was amazed to see the prince promptly do as told, though he was still muttering peevishly.

He said to me, "I suppose you wonder why I tolerate the insolence of this wretched old thing, but he's been my personal retainer since childhood. There's no one else I can trust, you see."

I had not been told where to sit, and not wanting to call attention to myself—it's strange how the presence of royalty makes bad taste of what would otherwise be routine—I shyly slid out the chair on Sebastian's right and sat down.

The prince picked up a large soup spoon and began to bang it on the tabletop. This sort of infantile demonstration was familiar to me from visits to my married sister, whose daughter, my niece, was an unusually disagreeable baby as well as one of the ugliest children I had ever seen, a dead ringer for my jawless, flap-eared brother-in-law.

"Ice cream!" Sebastian was shouting. "I want my ice cream." These complaints went on for some time, no doubt because Rupert moved so slowly. But at last the old retainer wheeled up to the table a trolley on which, embedded in a tank full of crushed ice, was what would appear to be a canister of vanilla ice cream of the capacity of several gallons. Amidst the chains with which he was hung, Rupert found a golden spoon. He plunged this implement into the container and carefully gathered some ice cream within its bowl. He brought the spoon up but did not taste its contents before inhaling the aroma with quivering nostrils. At last he took the spoon's burden between his desiccated lips, chewed awhile, rheumy eyes rolling, and then brought up from behind him, in his left hand, a shallow silver vessel and, turning away from the prince, but towards me, deliberately spat out the melted residue of what he had been tasting. This was not a palate-piquing spectacle.

The prince cackled maliciously. "I look forward to the day when someone *has* poisoned it, you ancient swine, and you fall to the floor and die, foaming at the mouth and writhing in agony."

Rupert's dried-apple countenance stayed noncommittal as, using two spoons, he built, within a capacious golden bowl, a Himalayan peak of ice cream. Sebastian watched the project with every appearance of mesmerization. When the mountain had at last been sculptured to Rupert's taste, the old man lifted a gold sauceboat high as his shoulder and poured from it a stream of butterscotch syrup onto the summit of the vanilla Everest. From other golden vessels he took, in turn, whipped cream, crushed nuts, chocolate sprinkles, those edible little silver beads, and finally a garishly red maraschino cherry.

When Sebastian saw that the dish had been completed, his importunate cries became more shrill, and when the old retainer at last delivered it to him he fell upon it with a ferocity for which the word "attacked" would be a euphemism. So swift was his work that for an instant I believed he was using no tool but rather shoveling it in with both bare fists. But after my eye adjusted to the motion I could identify, along with the spoon in his right hand, a fork in his left, and though he ate so rapidly, he employed these instruments with the deftness of a surgeon.

No sooner had the last spoonful gone from bowl to prince than a lackey whisked away the former and old Rupert supplied his sovereign with a napkin the size of a beach towel. Sebastian made vigorous use of this linen sheet, but in point of fact I saw not the least besmirchment of his mouth after the furious bout with the elaborately garnished ice cream.

For a few moments after the withdrawal of the empty bowl Sebastian sat with closed eyes, his expression one of momentarily weary sweet sadness, suggesting the well-known post-coital effect, but then his eyes sprang open and he looked at me for the first time since I had sat down.

"It is probably not easy to accept the display you've just seen as not gluttony but a heroic effort to allay it."

"Indeed."

"By eating a sweet course as opener, one kills a good deal of the appetite for the rest of the meal," said the prince, earnestly compressing his several chins against his upper chest. "It's an American technique."

"Sounds like it," I could not forbear saying: I really had lost some of my awe of him after witnessing the foregoing scene.

"And the infantilism serves an emotional purpose," he went on. "Being royal is to be deprived of the warmer human feelings. You may not be aware of it, Mr. Wren. It was not my mother the queen who gave me suck, but rather a peasant wet-nurse whom I never knew, and I was reared by nannies and servants. In a word, that mound of ice cream topped with the preserved cherry might well represent the royal dug I was denied."

In America a grasp of basic Freudianism was now enjoyed by millhand and shopgirl: it was instructive for me to hear such platitudes from an absolute monarch.

I offered, "Or perhaps that of the wetnurse?"

Sebastian stared above my head. "No, the whipped cream and other embellishments would suggest a higher class." He fluttered his long lashes: he really had very nice eyes. "In any event it's a theory that derives from the studies of a certain professor who was not appreciated at the University of Vienna, but my great-grandfather saw the fellow's possibilities and brought him here. Froelich?"

"Or perhaps Freud, Your Royal Highness?"

Sebastian shrugged. "Perhaps."

"He became quite well known."

"For this theory of the substitute tit?" The prince smiled. "Is it not extraordinary what frivolous enterprises will succeed in the world beyond Saint Sebastian? My great-grandfather's interest in the professor was due to their common keenness for collecting classical antiquities and Jewish jokes."

At that moment Rupert rolled the trolley to the tableside, and I was pleasantly surprised to become aware that a footman was discreetly laying a place for me, with a plate bearing a gold relief of the crown, heavy gold cutlery, and a napkin of linen a good deal finer than any stuff I had worn against my skin: the serviette was embroidered with the crown, and the cutlery showed it in cameo.

On Rupert's trolley were several footed vessels the bowls of which were spanned by golden-brown domes of pastry. With a spoon from his dependent gear the old retainer broke through one of these and tasted whatever lay beneath, then put the bowl before Sebastian.

The prince scowled at it. "You old sod, you have spoiled the looks of this dish, as well as the surprise."

"A pity," said the imperturbable Rupert. "But I could hardly taste it without breaking the crust."

The prince seized a spoon and smashed the remainder of the pastry, churning the fragments into the contents of the bowl, which seemed to be a clear soup. He then dug into this mix with much the same urgency with which he had ingested the ice cream. He had emptied the first bowl by the time the lackey had placed mine before me, and before I penetrated the crust, Sebastian's empty vessel had been removed and Rupert had served a second order.

When I broke through the gossamer puff-pastry dome, I inhaled a celestial aroma which I could not have begun to identify until I saw, in the first spoonful of amber broth, black morsels of what could only be the priceless truffle, of which there were approximately as many pieces as there are noodles in a packet of my usual soup, Lipton Cup-a: I trust it is not bad taste to wonder what each of these bowls would have cost in New York.

Sebastian drained four or five of them into his gullet, and we did not converse during this performance, which had no sooner ended than Rupert returned with a trolley load of the largest poached salmon I had ever seen and a sauce in which at least a pound of beluga caviar figured.

It was during the fish course that I remembered that McCoy was not there. But it seemed impolitic to ask the prince about him, or indeed anything else, for with his last bite of the salmon, he turned eagerly to the new dish brought by Rupert, an enormous salver on which reposed dozens of tiny ortolans, which is to say birds the size of, uh, wrens: morally no different from cooked chickens, perhaps, or, speaking pantheistically, no more pitiable than a stringbean that has been boiled to death. Yet, this spectacle for me was fraught with pathos, and in fact I lost such little hunger as I had had.

Sebastian however seemed only just to be hitting his gustatorial stride with the small birds, seizing each by its hairpin legs and plunging it beakfirst into his mouth, biting it off at, so to speak, the little knees and discarding the legs of one en route to the next: quite a pile of these limbs began to accumulate alongside his plate. Apparently he could deal internally with the bones and beaks.

When a footman offered me a similar dish, I waved him off, but I did begin to sip the champagne I had been served by another.

Perhaps it was the diminutive size of what he was eating that reminded Sebastian of his own childhood. In any event, after the second dozen of the ortolans, he suddenly stared at me with misted eyes and said, "Like the old heirs apparent to the French throne, I was most savagely treated as a child. I was whipped bloody by my tutors, viciously slapped and pinched by my nurses, and the detestable old jackal who stands behind me at this moment was cruelest of the lot. My boyhood, Wren, was a living hell. It was intended to be, of course. That's the only sort of thing that develops the ruthless, vengeful qualities of character so necessary to a ruler."

"But now, Your Royal Highness, you need answer to nobody," said I.

"How wrong you are! Commoners never understand these matters," said the prince with a profound sigh. "I am in reality a helpless prisoner of tradition!" In a lugubrious manner he sucked two more little avian delicacies off their dead legs, but then quickly cheered up when more dishes arrived.

No doubt it would be as exhausting to read more of this meal as it was to sit there throughout it sans appetite. I couldn't have kept up with Sebastian at the most esurient moment of my hollow-bellied adolescence. I had no taste for the succession of dishes that arrived on the trolley, which never stayed long at rest: the game course (hare); the roast; the vegetables, which came in separate servings and included things like cardoons, salsify, baby artichokes no larger than plums; a profusion of salads; savories of cheese, mushrooms, bacon; and puddings and pastries and fresh fruits, each second or third course divided from the next by a palate-refreshing sherbet; and finally a great platterful of so-called *friandises*: bonbons, petit fours, candied chestnuts, and the like.

The prince said no more, seeming indeed to forget me as well as all else, in the transports of what could only be called his orgy, though again, as with the initial ice cream, he dropped or dripped nothing from his implements and, so far as I could discern, had not even a sheen of grease on his lips, which were thin for such a plump face. He did, when in the so to speak thick of things, breathe rapidly and stertorously, and his eyes when not rolling were closed.

How long this spectacle went on I cannot say, for though eating no more I continued to swallow champagne, my supply of which was ever replenished by my personal footman, but with little consequent peace of mind or, inexplicably, any reaction to the alcohol.

But I was taken by surprise when Sebastian ate a final chocolate cream, lowered his chin and produced a shattering belch, then, raising himself slightly, whitening knuckles on the ends of the chair-arms, flatulated even more loudly.

I tried to stick my nose into the champagne glass, but unfortunately it was of the narrow gauge called a flute. However, it might be of some interest here to note that the prince's farts were, in my limited experience of them, not noisome: explain that if you can without embracing the assumption that his bowels were as regal as his blood.

As the echoes of this report were still reverberating amongst the high vaultings overhead, Sebastian looked at me and said, "For some time now I have been bored with the affairs of state, from which a monarch cannot relieve himself short of abdicating. But I have no one to whom to turn over the crown. I am myself an only child. I have not yet married. By modern tradition the sovereign weds only a Sebastiani commoner. Until the late Renaissance we took wives or husbands from the other ruling families of Europe, but usually this meant that the consort was from a much larger and more powerful country than our little state, and too often it happened that the wedding was but a prelude to an attempt by the larger country to annex our land. We repelled all such, but at an awful price in Sebastiani lives. Sebastian the Eleventh was our Henry the Eighth, beheading as he did four queens in succession and all for the same crime: conspiring to betray their adopted country to the advantage of whichever German or Bohemian or Rumanian kingdom they came from."

The prince signaled to Rupert, and the old retainer brought him another glass of mineral water. He drank it down in one prolonged swallow, and then changed his position in the chair and farted again, this time producing a peculiar vibration that made the crystal glassware tremble.

"I know I should marry some healthy peasant," he resumed, "and impregnate her several times in succession, for my parents were irresponsible in producing only me—which is why I must take such precautions to ensure my safety: I am the last of the line. If I make no heir, this splendid little land will fall to the rabble."

Now, I am democratic to the marrow, and if I rail against the vile herd, or in any event that version of it all too oppressively evident in New York City, my objections have nought to do with matters of social class, my own being none too exalted. Yet, I confess that sitting at the prince's table, and more important, drinking his champagne, I was inclined to take his problem as having much the same value as he himself put upon it.

"Good heavens. Then you must by all means and with all haste find a bride, sir, for I have had my own personal experience with your enemies." I began to tell him about the Liberation Front bombing, but royalty has (or anyway this example of it had) small patience with the narratives of commoners, and Sebastian spoke as if I had been sitting in silence.

"Luckily," I was saying, "I took seriously the voice on the phone, and ran from my building, for—"

"The difficulty," said Sebastian, "is that I cannot endure the prolonged company of women. Unfortunately, tradition demands that the prince go through an elaborate series of wedding ceremonies, and then make at least some pretense of sharing his life with the princess, insofar as official functions are concerned."

"Aha," said I, in lieu of a better response. Obviously the prince was immune to charges of so-called sexism, which in New York were so easily brought by the kind of viragoes I dated, when my crime was so minor as to express a preference for a plain bagel as opposed to one of which honey, dates & nuts were constituents.

"I'm afraid that artificial insemination is not possible, owing to the many restrictions precedent places on the royal semen," said the prince. "The sovereign's spunk is considered virtually sacred. The sheets are burned if I have a nocturnal emission in bed, for example."

I drank a half-fluteful of champagne.

Sebastian was frowning into the middle distance. "I expect there's nothing for it but to get cracking, repugnant as my life will be thereafter, until there are sufficient children to make extinction of the dynasty unlikely, and then the princess might be dispensed with."

I choked on a draught of champagne. "She will be put to death?"

After a jolly laugh, Sebastian said, "No, that sort of thing has not been done in ever so long a time. It would now even be out of date to send her to a convent. No, she'll have a pretty villa in the country and an adequate staff: perhaps not sumptuous accommodations, but neither will they be mean. My own mother enjoyed such lodgings for many years."

I was so relieved to hear that he would not, when done with her, execute the poor woman who married him that I could respond almost blithely to the plight of his maternal parent.

"How nice."

"Rare indeed," said the prince, "is the great man who has not found a boy's flesh much sweeter than that of any female. Socrates, Caesar, Frederick the Great: there are few exceptions, and those who pretended otherwise were surely hypocrites."

To make some expression of what in the Aesopian jargon of those groups who seek to promote the acceptance of their own special tastes was called "freedom of choice" would be truistic to the point of lèse majesté under the current conditions: the prince hardly required my permission to pollute the choirboys of the country he ruled absolutely, not to mention that he was not misguided in finding many celebrated sodomites on the rosters of prominent men. But it was ludicrous to suppose that the likes of Napoleon, Mark Twain, and General MacArthur, to take a disparate lot, had been fraudulently hetereosexual. But remember that my purpose was not an inquiry into eroticism.

I drew on my store of trivia: "And England's Edward the Second and Ludwig the Mad of Bavaria." The prince frowned quizzically. I explained, "Two more for your list: I was responding to your theory with respect to great men."

Sebastian shrugged. "I am *always* right. Perhaps it's a pity. Sometimes I walk upon the palace wall and look down and see my subjects in the town below. I think how happy they are to be wrong in most of their opinions and judgments. How comfortable a lot, whereas I must carry the burden of perfect wisdom to my deathbed." He rubbed his hands together: I had not previously noticed how chubby they were; so fat were his fingers as to look as though inflated. He wore no rings.

He smiled at me and said, "But you do not yourself have a taste for boys."

"Yes, that is true, Your Royal Highness. I cannot explain it, but I seem to prefer women. It takes all kinds, I expect." I made a happy-go-lucky flinch. "Would you mind telling me how you knew?"

"*You are not a great man,*" cried the prince, preparing to chuckle. "And while the pederast has a keen sense of humor—he must have, given the joke he is perpetrating on nature!—he is usually the entertained and not the entertainer." He gave vent to his risibilities, with the sound of boiling water.

"Aha." Until one has been put in his place by a royal personage, one has not experienced the ultimate in that exercise: the difference in rank is so commanding that to be reminded of it is not offensive. The bootblack envies his busier colleague at the next stand, not the captain of industry in whose lobby he works. But the analogy is inadequate, for it is not impossible that a shoeshine boy can become a chairman of the board, whereas blood can never become blue by gift or effort. Thus far I had seen in Prince Sebastian not the ghost of an admirable or even decent trait, yet he was the reigning prince: not so long ago in the history of humanity, such a figure was believed to have been the personal selection of God and to be able, with a touch of his hand, to cure scrofula.

On the other hand, I was getting lots of free champagne and I felt an obligation to be companionable. "Uh, given this unhappy chore—that of marrying a person of the opposite sex—what would be your criteria for a prospective wife?" I smiled politely. "Should I come across a suitable candidate somewhere, perhaps back home." I had several ex–girlfriends I would have liked to sic on him.

"Americans? Oh good heavens, no!" he cried. "I cannot endure them. They speak in conundrums when they're young; when they're old, in homilies."

In my unsuccessful effort to understand that statement I concluded that I probably did, after all, feel the champagne more than I had realized. "Yes, well, perhaps you might tell me what kind of woman you would find least repulsive: blond, brunette, tall or short, full-bodied or slender, and so on?"

He had widened his eyes early in my list. "Obviously you are not aware that blonds are held in contempt in my country." He leaned back and snapped his fingers. The signal brought Rupert to the table. It occurred to me that this meal had gone on for hours, a long time for an old man to be on his feet. Sebastian merely breathed heavily in his direction, and Rupert drew a silken handkerchief from his sleeve, held it to the prince's nose, and Sebastian blew a blast that would have been as shattering as his flatulations had it not been so muted. When this episode was brought to a close, the ancient retainer wadded the cloth carefully and carried it out of the dining room.

The prince leaned confidentially towards me. "I wanted to get rid of him for a moment. He must go to burn the handkerchief that carries the royal snot. . . . The fact is, Rupert is not as young as he once was. He really makes a cockup of the job. I need a younger and more vigorous man. I could never trust any of my contemporary subjects." He slapped the top of the table. "Wren, would you like to be my principal body-servant?"

I pretended to ponder gravely on the matter, while my pulse raced in horror.

"Naturally," Sebastian went on, "I wouldn't expect you to perform all the duties done these many years by Rupert. You would not be required to attend me at stool, wiping my bum and so on, except in emergencies, midnight alarms, that sort of thing."

"Sir, you are too good."

He shrugged genially. "I am aware that times have changed, and that these warm, personal attentions that so characterized one's association with underlings in the past are now considered too quaint for words! One thinks something precious has been lost, but perhaps I'm hopelessly romantic. In any event, a lackey can always be found for the tasks for which you feel yourself too good."

"Sir, I—"

"No need to make up your mind on the instant," said the prince. "I can imagine how staggered you must be at the magnificence of the proposal. Here you are, an obscure tourist, a historical nobody, and without warning you are offered the opportunity to be as near a royal personage as anyone could be, short of a sexual partner, a role you can never play, owing to your advanced age."

I endeavored to rise above my disappointment at the limitations of the offer. "Indeed, sir, sire, I am overwhelmed. But might I ask about your earlier reference to blonds? They are despised in Saint Sebastian?" Experience has taught me that the most effective way to distract an unwelcome importunity of any kind is to ask a question.

The device worked with Sebastian. "Indeed they are," said he. "They are the butt of the typical Sebastiani joke. They must stay in their own areas at places of public entertainment, and are barred altogether from cafes and restaurants except those exclusive to themselves. They may pursue any profession, but usually they voluntarily confine themselves to the callings considered inferior by others, for example, the practice of law."

"Attorneys are blonds?"

Sebastian nodded. "You must understand that litigation is discouraged here, and that criminals are not allowed to have counsel. Thus a Sebastiani lawyer has virtually no work. His principal function is to provide a figure to be derided by those who have useful occupations."

"The first Sebastiani national I met was a blond young woman, as it happened. She is an airline stewardess."

"There you are," said the prince, waving his fat hand. "Politics is against the law here, of course, as is its brother profession, journalism, else they might make excellent pursuits for the Blonds, who by the way some years ago successfully petitioned me to command that their designation be spelled with a capital *B*. This was during the time of their Blond Pride campaigns."

Rupert had returned by now. The prince sneered at him and said, "You vile old creature. I've just offered your job to Wren. Now, what do you think of that?"

The venerable retainer remained dispassionate. "I think it's time for your nap. Tell this person to leave."

Sebastian laughed wrily. "Well, there you are, Wren. I'm afraid that ritual makes slaves even of princes."

I was not eager to remain. I lowered my champagne glass and stood up. "Thank you, Your Royal Highness, for everything. You can be sure I shall treasure this memory." This time I remembered to bow. I also thought I remembered that one was never to turn one's back on a monarch, that he who was departing must keep his front towards the person of kingly rank, bowing while walking backwards, all the way to the exit. I had doubts as to my ability to do this successfully on a route as long as the one that lay between my place at the table and the distant door through which we had entered this vast dining room.

I finally, boldly, presented the problem to the prince.

He pondered on it for a moment. "Why don't you go back for ten or fifteen paces, until you leave our immediate vicinity, after which you may discreetly turn and proceed on your way without giving the appearance of rejecting the sovereign." He looked at Rupert. "Wouldn't you say that might suffice?"

"Certainly not!" snapped the ancient retainer, standing behind the prince's chair. He had yet to address me directly.

Sebastian chuckled. "I could have predicted his reaction. Those who serve adore ceremony, which gives them something to do, you see. And they are overjoyed when the person in power is himself obliged to obey the commands of custom and tradition. Since he's done nothing all his life but abase himself before royalty, Rupert must believe that rituals are of the utmost importance, else he has wasted his life. Is that not so, Rupert?"

The old man remained expressionless.

I compromised and backed almost half the long way to the

door, going slowly so that I would not trip. In the anteroom I encountered General Popescu, who had presumably been waiting all this while, sitting in an uncomfortable-looking straight-backed chair.

On our way out to the gate I asked him whether he knew what had become of McCoy.

"I'm sure he's done what he usually does when he comes here," said the little general. "He goes to the royal wine cellars, finds a bottle or two, and empties them."

"The prince tolerates such behavior?"

Popescu's mustache moved. "He must. Any guest is protected by the immutable laws of hospitality."

4

MᴄCᴏʏ ᴡᴀꜱ ᴀᴛ the changing rooms, looking in better shape than had been his on our arrival. We got back into our proper clothes, reclaimed the car, and roared down the hill to town. The engine was too noisy for conversation, and McCoy was the sort of driver who drives as fast as the wheels can turn without losing their adhesion to the road.

Not far from the hotel we went through a square in the middle of which stood a pillory. My quondam enemy the concierge was fixed to it by wrists and ankles. Around his neck hung a wooden sign into which was burned the following legend:

I WAS RUDE

Before him a group of urchins, the first children I had yet observed in this country, were making what I saw only in a dumb show but were undoubtedly jeers and catcalls.

McCoy paid no attention to this spectacle. Arriving at the hotel, he scraped to a stop in the usual manner and left the car. But instead of entering the building he staggered several doors down the street and entered a shop identified on its front windows as the office of a cable service. From an inside pocket of the ancient jacket he took a sheaf of papers and presented it to the clerk, a balding person who wore rimless eyeglasses.

This man's acceptance of the manuscript was given reluctantly, with an audible sigh. "Mr. McCoy," said he, "I'm afraid—"

"You really should bill New York," McCoy said hastily. "I'm a mere wage slave of the imperialists." He threw up his arms, displaying infamous sweat-stains, and left briskly in the peculiar stride that looked as though it were but prefatory to a tumble but apparently never was.

Before I could follow, the clerk leaned on the counter in an attitude that I think was intended as beseeching and said, "I appeal to you, sir, as a countryfellow of Mr. Clyde McCoy! I am sorry to say he owes me a good deal of money. Several times a month he files lengthy cables to America, yet never does he pay me for transmitting them. He insists that I should bill the publications in reference. But when I do, my bills are ignored."

I crawl with shame when Americans bilk foreigners (while, with my cultured principles, shrugging it off when the swindle goes the other way, as it does mostly). "I'm no authority on the subject," I told him, "but he might well be right. I should think the *Times* or Associated Press or whomever he works for are honorable firms and would pay their debts. Perhaps you don't know the proper form for billing them."

The clerk frowned. "Those names are unknown to me." He peered at McCoy's latest manuscript. "This goes to *Crotch: The International Sex Weekly.* Is that printed by an honorable company?"

"I can't say I'm familiar with it," I confessed. But added quickly, "Which by no means implies that it does not enjoy respect in its field." I was drifting towards the door: I didn't want to get enmired in McCoy's problems.

"Perhaps," said the clerk, "you would kindly use your own influence to aid me in this matter. Be assured that in gratitude I will see that your own cable traffic is never interrupted."

Had I been better situated I might have upbraided him as an insolent puppy, for making a threat, but I had not forgotten that Rasmussen had furnished me with no money whatever.

I therefore lifted my finger to my brow, as if in affirmation, and was about to step out the door when, behind me, he added, "I will also introduce you to some pretty boys."

I stopped and turned. "No thank you, but perhaps you could tell me why since I arrived in your country it has more than once been assumed I am of the pederast persuasion?"

The clerk nodded briskly. "You see, female Blonds are everywhere available in Saint Sebastian. They are expected to give you their bodies. There's no romance in that state of affairs! But to have a boy is to violate nature, to partake of the forbidden. Now, that's exciting!"

"It's against the law?"

"Of course," said he indignantly. "What country would be so degraded as not to condemn the vile crime of sodomy?"

"What of the brunette women?"

"They're usually married."

"And no doubt adultery is considered a heinous crime—?"

"Except with Blonds, of course."

I went to the hotel, where a new concierge was behind the desk. In every way he seemed a twin to his predecessor, whom I had only just seen in the pillory, his gray-spatted shoes protruding through the lower apertures.

When I reached my room I found McCoy sitting on the edge of the bed. I soon learned, by asking him to leave, that it was his own room as well.

I asked incredulously, "You mean we're supposed to share it?"

His response was bitter. "*You're* complaining? It's my *home.*"

I looked around the walls and saw the wardrobe, the screen hiding the bidet and washstand, but nothing that could be considered personal possessions of his. The suitcase assigned to me had been placed on the floor.

"That's not even a double bed."

McCoy proved more thin-skinned than I expected. "You're none too fragrant yourself," said he. "May I suggest you take a long bath?"

"I'd like nothing better," I spat. "But where *is* the bathroom?"

"End of the hall, far right end. The WC's the other way."

"You don't have a private bath?"

"For God's sake, Wren, you think you're working for a profitable industry? Economy's the watchword these days. I can hardly keep body and soul together on what I'm paid—*when* I'm paid, that is, which at the moment hasn't been for months."

"And," said I, "they're always trying to cut appropriations further."

"They're not making much right now. At least that's their excuse."

"What does that mean? Graft or extortion money?"

McCoy frowned. "It means circulation is down and therefore

so is the income from ads. That's what they say, anyhow. I wouldn't know, being over here."

It occurred to me that we were speaking at cross purposes. "Aha," I murmured. "You mean that smut paper which provides your cover. I'm speaking of the Firm."

McCoy jerked his head indignantly. "OK, so they're easing me out in favor of a Johnny-come-lately like yourself, but do you have to be so damn superior? I was in Paris before you were born, junior. There was a time when I knew 'em all: Ole Ez, Gertie, Hem. I shared many a bottle of Jimmie Joyce's favorite *urine d'archiduchesse* with him: 'swhat he called a certain Swiss white."

I raised an eyebrow. "I thought you were World War Two. You're naming the Paris gang of the Twenties." His eyes rolled, but not in embarrassment. "I'm not displacing you in any sense," I went on. "I'm regularly a private investigator in New York. I'm just on temporary assignment here—without my consent, I might add. Rasmussen really shanghaied me."

"Don't know him," said McCoy. "Is he the new publisher?"

We were getting nowhere. "Forget about the porn!" I pleaded. "I'm one of you. I'm a fellow agent."

"I don't have the slightest idea of what you mean. I got a cable this morning from Mortie Rivers, managing ed. of *Crotch*, asking me to meet you at the airport and put you up for a few days. He didn't send any funds, needless to say, not even what they owe me, so this is the best I can do. I don't think it's nice of you to sneer."

I was touched by his appeal. "Forgive me," I begged. "I didn't mean to belittle your hospitality, which in fact has been more than generous. I wonder whether this 'Rivers' could be one of Rasmussen's masks?" McCoy continued to show puzzlement, so I finally had to say, "I know this is in execrable taste and as unprofessional as if a mobster were, with reference to his own associations, to use some term invented by the hacks of the communications media, 'Mafia,' or 'Cosa Nostra,' but I see no alternative to saying *CIA*."

"Who?"

"We work for it, don't we, you and I?"

"I didn't know there was such a thing in reality," said McCoy, whether disingenuously or not I couldn't say. "I always assumed the name was something invented by ex-Nazis when they transformed themselves into left-wingers. The genuine outfit was called the OSS. I never worked for it, but I understand they did a good job against the Krauts."

"That was during the Second World War," I said. I began to suspect that years of boozing had given him irreversible brain damage. But whether or not he would acknowledge it, he was my only local contact. "I thought I should compare notes with you on the prince."

"Why?" asked the veteran journalist.

"Well, for God's sake, he's the boss here, isn't he?"

McCoy shook his head. "Nobody pays any attention to him. He's stayed up there in the palace for years."

"He delegates his authority?"

"Naw. He doesn't have any real authority."

"Then who has?"

"Nobody," McCoy said. "Or maybe I should say, anybody who claims to have it—until of course it is challenged, as I did with the cops. Authority's usually just an idea, anywhere, except in those countries which maintain large standing armies for the purpose of policing their own citizens."

I was dubious. "Can't any individual then take the law into his own hands?"

"Maybe. But who would want to?"

I pondered on this for a moment. "Ambitious people."

"You won't find any of them here," said McCoy. "Money isn't used in Saint Sebastian. Everything's done on credit."

"Wait a moment. Just now the cable clerk complained to me about your overdue bill."

"That's because a cable goes out of the country, and foreigners want to be paid for their services." He thought for a moment, then said, "Hey, maybe that's why Mortie hasn't sent me any money for a long time. That little bastard ain't sending him my dispatches! Lend me a little something, willya, Wren?"

"Very funny," said I. "But tell me: are you serious? One doesn't pay for anything here but rather puts it on the tab?"

"That's why I came here during the war," McCoy said. "Went over the hill. That and the free cooze, of course, if you like blonds. Used to be a lot of ex-GIs here. The others all fucked themselves to death. Now you take me, I haven't got one up for several decades, and I consider myself the better for it." He stood up and uncertainly supported himself with a hand to the edge of the little table. "I just filed my month's work, Wren. I intend to relax for a while, wet my whistle somewhere in peace. I trust you'll take that bath before going to bed tonight. We'll be at awful close quarters."

I rose above the insult to ask a few more questions. Among them was why he wanted to be paid for his work for *Crotch* when he couldn't use the money except of course to pay for the cables?

"I import something decent to drink when I can afford it. The local schnapps is horsepiss."

"One more thing. Everybody here speaks English as a matter of course, but the self-characterized Liberation Front spokesman who phoned me a bomb warning in New York had a heavy accent that sounded Slavic. The stewardess on the plane this morning spoke English like a German. Is there a Sebastiani language?"

"How do I know?" McCoy growled impatiently.

"You've been here since World War Two and you can't answer that question?"

"I'd only *ask* it if I didn't know what they were saying," he told me, and staggered out the door.

What an intellectual loss he was. Unless of course that was part of his cover, which he maintained even when closeted with me. I decided to go out in search of more information about the country, but first I must spruce up my person.

In the valise that had been provided for me I searched without success for a bathrobe, then looked in the tall, dark armoire against the wall opposite the bed, which held what was presumably McCoy's wardrobe but could easily have been mistaken for a week's collection made by Goodwill Industries. I could find no robe here, either, but my colleague did possess (no doubt a souvenir of earlier, more ambitious days as a journalist) an ancient, stained trench coat. I stripped to the buff and donned this garment. My next search was for slippers or clogs or scuffs, something with which to protect my feet on the hike to the bathroom, but could find nothing suitable. McCoy owned several pairs of runover shoes, all wing-tipped and in a color that might be called pus-yellow, but they were too small for me. Finally I put on a pair of galoshes, which, large enough to go over shoes, could more than accommodate my feet.

Behind the catercornered screen that concealed the bidet and washstand I came upon the only towel on hand and a sliver of hard gray soap. So attired and accoutered, I went along the hall in the other direction from that which would take me to the elevator. My galoshes were buckled, and taking a leaf from the book of the old movie heroes, I had tied together the ends of the trench-coat belt.

The bathroom was at the farthest termination of the corridor, and so to speak camouflaged behind a closet full of mops and pails. From behind its locked door issued an extraordinary voice lifted in song. My initial annoyance at having to wait, in dirty trench coat and loose galoshes, while someone else soaked his hide for God knows how long, was soon assuaged by successive renditions of every familiar aria in the literature of the Italian grand-opera tenor: "Celeste Aïda," "La donna è mobile," "Vesti la giubba," and so on, in a Mediterranean extravaganza that went on, I should say, for the better part of an hour as I leaned against the slanted mops and brooms and listened to the golden sound. But at such times one does not tick off the minutes.

The bathroom door at last opened and, swathed in a crimson dressing gown made from sufficient cloth for Ringling's big top, an enormous man emerged. There was not enough room for the both of us in the mop-thronged anteroom, and I was forced to step backwards into the corridor. But I had been so enchanted by his magnificent voice that I did not resent this enforced courtesy.

I bowed as I backstepped. "Sir," I said, "that was the most extraordinary sound these ears have heard. Surely you cannot be a mere bathtub performer."

He shrugged in the classic Italianate manner. A thick white towel was around his neck, and he carried a striped sponge bag. His hair was covered with a bathing cap of pink rubber. The lower half of his face was all black mustache and beard.

His silence suggested he had no English. I therefore found

employment for the most useful of terms in my limited Italian vocabulary (one can go far on just these two): *"Maestro, complimenti!"*

Now he smiled radiantly and tossed his fat hand at a jaunty angle. He swept out and rolled down the hallway as if on parade-float wheels.

I entered a bathroom redolent of the subtle aroma of steam and the bolder scents of soap and cologne. The tub, mounted on high, gilded legs, was of heroic proportions—as it had had to be to hold its most recent occupant. Having taken off the trench coat, I sought a hook on which to hang it, but rare indeed is the sanitary facility, in America or Europe, which meets every simple need: so saith Wren's Law. Eventually I folded the garment into a parcel and placed it on the marble-topped dressing table, and there noticed, as I had not previously, that the other object thereupon was a tape recorder. The cassette inside it was labeled: "All-Time Greatest Hits of Enrico Caruso."

When I got back to the room after my bath, I found a rusty razor, a mangy brush, and a mug containing a cake of brothel-scented shaving soap, and I brought this ancient equipment into play, with ice water, to clean away a day's whiskers at the washstand behind the screen. I combed my damp-blackened hair (normally it is light brown) and donned a keen combo of synthetics: lime-green shirt; lavender trousers supported by a white plastic belt joined by an outsized brass buckle bearing the logo of Coors beer; the madras jacket, the fabric of which had the texture of crepe paper; and loafers made of cordovan-colored imitation leather.

I went down the hall and rang for the elevator. When the car finally arrived, however, it was filled to capacity by the enormous man who listened to Caruso while bathing. We now exchanged helpless but amiable shrugs, and I used the stairway.

I didn't know which of the twin concierges was at the desk, and decided I didn't care.

But he told me. "Mr. Wren, sir! I am now rehabilitated."

"It wasn't my idea that you be put in the pillory."

"It did me a world of good," said he. "And the institution also serves to meet the needs of youngsters, who, without the occasional malefactor to taunt and deride as he sits helplessly restrained, might torture animals or mutilate one another. As it is, we have little juvenile delinquency in Saint Sebastian."

"Indeed yours is a remarkable country," said I. "I wanted to ask you where I might go to find out more about it, whom I might interview—?"

He closed the lid of one eye, leaned across the desk, and spoke in a hoarse whisper. "The public library."

At this point the elevator finally reached the ground floor: unreasonably, it traveled more slowly with a heavier load than with a light one. The large man deboarded. I failed to mention earlier that he wore tennis clothes: V-necked white sweater, white linen shorts, white knee socks, and sparkling white sneakers. Again we exchanged gestures: this time a slight bow on my part and an inclination of the head, with a horizontaled forearm, on his.

I turned back to the concierge. "The public library?"

He put a fat finger to his lips, and virtually shouted in the direction of the large man, who was moving out the street door, a can of tennis balls in a rear pocket and dwarfed by the massive ham underneath, "A male brothel? But of course, my dear sir!"

"What are you doing?" I cried.

The door closed behind the vast figure of Caruso's fan. The concierge returned to his stertorous whisper. "We must be discreet."

"About the public *library?*"

He gave me a long stare, then threw up his fat hands. "Well, sir, if you are not concerned for your own reputation, then who I am to be worried?"

"Let me get this straight: there is something wrong with going to the library?"

He rolled the vein-webbed whites of his eyes. "Far be it from me to reflect on your tastes, sir, but you are an unrepresentative tourist. You have no apparent interest in sex, you are never drunk, loud, or abusive, and you've had only that one slight brush with the law, which I hasten to say was entirely the result of a misapprehension of mine."

"You mean that most visitors to your country act badly?"

He made his oiliest smile. "And why not? It's what we're here for."

I frowned. "Be that as it may, tell me how to get to the public library."

"Number Four, the Street of Words. The boy outside knows the way."

Though I didn't understand whom he meant, I went to the street. At the curb was a kind of rickshaw with a husky fair-haired young chap between the traces. He wore running shorts and a singlet in gold-trimmed blue.

"Please to tal me how to go, sair," said he.

I gave him the address and asked whether he had a sister.

"Many and brothers as well." His ingenuous broad face shone with good feeling. "You require dem for sex?"

"No thank you. Is one of the sisters named Olga?"

"Sure."

"Would she work for the Sebastiani airline?"

"Sure."

Wondering whether he might simply agree with anything asked of him, I climbed into the rickshaw's seat. He picked up the twin shafts and, swinging the vehicle around, headed uphill at a smart pace. Soon this became a trot: he was stronger than the engine of the ancient Minx I had driven when I was an impoverished young English instructor at State. Having reached the summit, we began to roll downhill at a greater rate of speed than the superannuated Beetle, for which I traded the Minx, could have attained under similar conditions. Such was our progress up and down several steep elevations.

Finally the young man, who was not even breathing heavily from his labor, turned into a little street narrow as an alley, lined with quaint little houses, some leaning at an angle, all decorated in Central European gingerbread, with miniature, one-man balconies attached here and there to the upper stories, and tiny shuttered windows like those in cuckoo clocks. He pulled me in front of the fourth house and lowered the traces, putting my seat at a downward angle from which it was simple to slide out. Despite the downhill speeds, I had felt secure in his hands, and the vehicle did offer a comfortable ride. At such a moment Saint Sebastian had much to recommend to a veteran of the choice of transportation evils available in New York City.

I walked to the somewhat undersized front door of the house

and knocked thereupon. In a moment it was opened by a slight, short man with very dark, intense, yet benign eyes.

"I'm sorry to trouble you," I said, "but can this possibly be the public library?"

"Indeed." He bowed and beckoned me to come in.

It was a strange library, however, judging from the entrance hall and then the front parlor of the house, which was furnished in a slightly shabby, old-fashioned bourgeois style, fringes on the lamps, tables with curved legs, and antimacassars on the ponderous overstuffed chairs. The only books in view occupied the four shelves of a relatively narrow cabinet with glass doors.

The volumes in this cabinet were of a uniform binding in dark green. I bent and read the dim gold lettering on the spine of the first: *Encyclopaedia Sebastiana*, Volume I, A—Austria."

I asked the librarian, "May I?"

"Certainly."

I opened the uppermost of the glass doors and removed Volume I, opened it at random, saw the heading "Airplane," and began to read.

> AIRPLANE. The swiftest means of covering great distances in the shortest time. Its advantages over the bus, the train, and the various private vehicles are, in addition to speed, cleanliness, availability of toilets, and, strange as it might seem, according to statistics, safety; but it should be remembered that the normal passenger on an airplane never feels really secure. Most of us have our hearts in our mouths from the moment we take off until the landing is made, for though accidents might be rare statistically speaking, when one does happen, it's terrible, often resulting in hundreds of deaths . . .

I turned to the librarian. "Would you know who wrote the entries in this work?"

"Yes indeed. The original edition was a product of a committee of Sebastiani scholars at the turn of the century, but the *Encyclopaedia* is ever in the process of being revised."

"By contemporary scholars?"

The man's smile became smug. "The finest. Perhaps you would like to observe them at work? They are just upstairs."

With a certain eagerness I said I would, and he led me up a

narrow staircase to the next floor. I had expected here at least to see a collection of shelved volumes that might reasonably be called a library, but I encountered none in the room to which my guide conducted me.

This chamber, which fronted on the street, was furnished with a large table around which sat a dozen or so men, each of whom was reading in a green-bound volume of the sort that was in the bookcase downstairs. "Our visitor would like to learn how the *Encyclopaedia* is edited."

The nearest scholar smiled at me. "Quite simply, really. Every morning each of us picks out one of the books and reads in it until he comes to a passage with which he does not agree, and then, using a red pen, he rewrites that portion between the lines or in the margins, then tears the pages out and sends them upstairs to the typists, who prepare clean manuscripts for the printer."

"May I assume," I asked, "that in such cases you have come upon some information that is outmoded? Which must happen all the time with scientific subjects. For example, the entries on the exploration of space."

Another of the scholars chuckled. His fringe of hair was sandy in hue, and his spectacles were pince-nez from which dangled a grosgrain ribbon. "As it happens, we have no entry whatever on that subject, not having been able as yet to find anyone amongst us who knows anything about it."

A whitehaired man spoke up from farther along the table. "Perhaps *you* would like to do it."

"Me?"

"Or you might choose any other subject, if you don't want to do one from scratch, which can be quite taxing. I tried my hand at that as a young fellow, but soon gave it up. There was virtually nothing that interested me sufficiently to warrant the effort of writing an original article upon it. But revising what's there can often be very entertaining."

"Yes," I murmured. "You have interesting and, so far as I know, unique criteria for this enterprise. In the outside world, if I may use that term, scholarship is expected to be, anyway to have a go at being, objective. Yours would seem greatly conditioned by the personality, the character, of him who does it. Am I putting that fairly?"

"Yes, you are," said the whitehaired man. "But why are you concerned with being fair?"

I chuckled. "That's true. Why, indeed? I don't know any of you, and you all look utterly incapable of doing me either good or ill."

They all joined in good-natured laughter, and one of them said, "Be assured that we are absolutely inconsequential and that what we do has no value whatever. Only two copies of each volume are printed: one goes in the bookcase downstairs and the other is used up here. Furthermore, no one ever consults the downstairs set."

"No?"

"Well, if you think about it, why would they? The *Encyclopaedia* contains simply the arbitrary opinions of a number of individuals: anyone else's would be as good on any subject."

"Then of course," I said, "the question is obvious: why have such an encyclopedia?"

"The answer," the whitehaired man said genially, "is that we are the scholars of Saint Sebastian. What else could we do?"

I shook my head. "That's not as good an answer as you apparently believe it, sir. You might seriously pursue the facts, the truth, in the various areas of human enterprise, and record them, it, as carefully, as objectively, as possible."

"That sounds like more work than we have stomach for," said the sandy-haired man.

A watery-eyed scholar at the far end of the table cried, "It's great fun to be totally irresponsible, whereas being careful about truth is a dreary way to live." He bent over the book in front of him. "This is lively writing, much better than if lots of facts were given." He began to read aloud, " 'The tallest building in the world is a Woolworth five-and-ten in New York City. It's really tall, a whole lot bigger than any structure in Saint Sebastian. Big buildings are all right if you like to be way up high, but you might not care to live next door to one and have it block the sun from your roof all winter. But summer, now, that's another matter entirely. The shade provided by the skyscraper might be darned welcome.' "

I shook my head. "For at least half a century the Woolworth Building hasn't been the tallest, and it never was a five-and-dime. The person who wrote this entry apparently wasn't even aware of the Empire State Building, let alone the World Trade Center, not to mention a structure in Chicago that is taller yet. The other remarks, while perhaps true enough, are pretty obvious and banal, are they not? Are they really worth giving space to in the national encyclopedia?"

The whitehaired man looked at me in gentle reproach. "You do have strong opinions, sir. And forgive me if I say that you yourself are not without bias, are you? if you cannot name the tallest building because it's in Chicago and not New York. But I take it that your point remains that our encyclopedia might be inadequate?"

"With all respect, sir."

"And do you have a suggestion as to how we might remove that inadequacy?"

I sighed. They would have a massive job. "You might take a look at the *Britannica* or the *Larousse*, the *Brockhaus*, and so on. I don't think the *Great Soviet Encyclopedia* would be, all in all, much of an improvement on your own, but most of the major cultures have pretty good ones."

"These are already in existence?"

"Of course."

"Then why should we seek to duplicate what's there?" he asked.

I thought about this for a moment and had to admit to myself that I could find no reason, after all. "I'm sorry," I said. "I suppose what you do does serve the only need you have—and anything that does that, anywhere in the universe, can be said to be successful. . . . In fact, if I might accept your flattering invitation to contribute to your invaluable work of reference . . ."

"By all means, sir!" said the older scholar, and the others cried, "Hear, hear!"

"What I'm thinking of doing is an original entry." There were more sounds of encouragement.

I was taken by the librarian into a smaller, adjoining room, seated at a desk, and given a sheaf of quality foolscap and an old-fashioned fountain pen of the kind I had not seen since childhood. Its point glided across the heavy, creamy-textured paper as a keen blade skims over black ice. What I wrote was as follows.

> WREN, RUSSEL, born not so many years ago that he cannot still be called young, should be universally acknowledged as America's foremost playwright in the last quarter of the twentieth century, but in reality he has been infamously neglected by the *soi-disant* major critics, who however have some slight justification in that as yet his work has never been produced.

When I returned to the roomful of scholars and presented the little paragraph to the man with white hair, he read it eagerly and then, with every sign of approval, gave it to the man next to him. When this second reading had been completed, the two nodded at each other.

"Superb!" said the older man. "We are delighted. But I must point out that it is, after all, a revision of an existing entry."

"How can that be?"

He bent over the volume before him, flipped through the pages until he had arrived at the one he could use as evidence, and handed the book to me. "See for yourself."

It was midway along the right-hand page, in the *W*'s, between Sir Christopher and a bird called the Wren-Tit:

> WREN, RUSSEL, a shabby private detective in New York City who poses as a playwright to gain sexual favors from women and bluff his fellow man.

"So you see," said the elderly scholar, "you have provided an obviously much needed revision."

"I don't suppose you could tell me who composed this entry," I asked, tapping the book with an offended forefinger.

He looked around the table. "Anyone here?" But they all of them shook their heads in negation.

At length a skinny man with a prominent wen on his nose pursed his lips speculatively and said, "That wouldn't have been Mr. McCoy?"

"Perhaps," said the whitehaired man. "He's done most of the American entries, for obvious reasons."

"Good heavens," I cried. "You people unwittingly took quite a chance. I assume you didn't know that McCoy had AIDS."

But my spite went for naught. They had never heard of the ailment despite the local prevalence of buggery.

The slight, dark librarian then conducted me to the third floor, where a battery of male typists made manuscripts of the revised entries for the encyclopedia.

My guide told me that these were regularly taken by himself to the royal printing house. He went now to a metal strongbox, painted bright red, on a table near the door, opened its hasp, and peered within.

"Filled. We might go there now, if you'd care to come along."

Outside, I suggested we take the rickshaw, which was waiting at the curb, for the seat was wide enough to accept the slender man along with me, and the blond in the traces was certainly strong enough to pull the two of us. But my guide told me the printer was just along the street a few steps away.

The printer's shop proved to be in an outbuilding, originally no doubt a stable, behind the house at the end of the street. A large hand-operated press, glistening disc cocked at the traditional angle, dominated the room, and sawdust covered the floor. A stocky man in an inky apron and a handmade paper hat was setting individual pieces of type in a composing stick: he did this with remarkable speed, plucking what he needed from a shallow horizontal box of pigeonholes.

"That's nice to see," I told my guide. "When I was a boy there was still a fellow in my town who did job printing on a hand-powered press when he was not occupied with Linotyping the weekly paper. By the way, do you have a newspaper in Saint Sebastian?"

"Broadsides," said he, "when the occasions present themselves, but not on a regular schedule of any sort. Is it true that elsewhere in the world, newspapers are published every day and at the exact same time of day, whether or not there is anything of note to report?"

"And television and radio newscasts, as well," said I, "relentlessly. And weekly magazines and papers, in addition, though of course by the time a week has passed, it would be unusual were nothing to have happened."

He shrugged. "No doubt the problem is frequently addressed by invention."

"That does happen at times, but if they're caught at it there's hell to pay." I saw him frown, and added, "But perhaps the practice is routine in Saint Sebastian?"

"It surely would be, but we do not bother with news in the first place, you see."

His smugness irked me. "But you do bother with an encyclopedia."

"It cannot bother many if only one copy is available for reading, and of course we do what we can to keep quiet about the existence of a public library."

The printer was now locking up a chase in which many sticks of type had been brought together to constitute a page. After the fashion of craftworkers everywhere, he found it easy to ignore laymen.

"Yes," said I, "and I confess I cannot understand why, unless the idea is simply to keep the populace in a state of ignorance. In which case there would be no sense even to have something called a public library."

"The idea, I should say, is rather to make it necessary to expend some personal effort in relieving one's ignorance," he told me. "Not to force-feed information to the reluctant."

There might have been some sense in this had a genuine library been at the end of the obstacle hunt, or even one encyclopedia of substance and not such a farcical product as was being fabricated by the scholars of Saint Sebastian, but as a guest in the country I did not make these points aloud.

The printer finally turned. He winced at the sight of the red box. "That's not filled *again?*"

The librarian cringed and said apologetically, "Well, that's our job, isn't it?"

"Speak for yourself," the printer growled. Then he stared at me and asked rudely, "Who's this one?"

"I'm from New York," I said, choosing from amongst my various identifications (nationality, profession, religious preference, etc.) the one I supposed would make the quickest impression on a national of a tiny foreign country.

But I immediately lost the advantage.

He demanded, "Where's that?"

"*New York?* Why, in America. You've heard of America."

"Don't be insolent," said the printer. "What's new about it? Where's Old York?"

"England. But the Old isn't nearly as well known as the New."

"I don't like new things of any kind," said he. "They're never really reliable, no matter what you say. Would you consider this new place as more reliable than the old one?"

"Certainly not. But is that a reasonable criterion?"

The printer cleared his throat angrily. "Name a better one! If you go about irresponsibly naming things 'New,' then you should expect to defend the practice sooner or later. You say New York is well known. For what?"

For no good reason I was altogether on the defensive, and when my back is to the wall, like most people I resort to dollars and cents. "Money! I understand you don't use any in Saint Sebastian, but please believe me when I say that elsewhere it makes the world go round, with the exception of totalitarian-collectivist lands, where brute force, realized or implied, would seem to be the catalyst."

The printer resituated the paper hat on his head. "Do you have a lot of money?"

"As it happens I have very little."

"Why, when you live in its capital?"

"Aha," said I. "That is a somewhat rude but not irrelevant question. I always expect to be given some in the future. A play written by me might have a great success, making me a rich man overnight."

He thought about this for a moment. "And life as a rich man would be to your liking?"

"I assure you it would, not because I yearn for possessions. Indeed, I might even own fewer things than I do now—or did before my home was destroyed. Incidentally, that was done by extremists from Saint Sebastian, so not everyone here thinks this country is a paradise." Going on the offensive made me feel better.

He simply ignored my later point and focused on the earlier. "What would being rich do for you?"

I welcomed the opportunity to sort out my feelings on that subject. "Services! One could hire people to take clothes to the cleaner's and to wait until the machines were free at the Laundromat. . . . Just a moment: if you were rich enough, you could wear clothes until they were soiled and then simply throw them away and send your flunky to the shops for more. Having one's own chauffeur-driven limousine would be basic, but what of getting from your apartment to the car? Such a routine journey can be fraught with discomfort and even danger in New York. With money one could hire a team of bravos to carry one to the curb! These same men, preferably conspicuously fearsome-looking plug-uglies, would accompany one everywhere and forestall, by their appearance alone, most of the abuse which is a quotidian feature of life in the city: the vicious responses of cabdrivers to imaginary encroachments; the thrusting shoulders of sidewalk thugs; the threats of those who find you, if unarmed and harmless, the principal author of their social disenfranchisement; and even the fishwifery of well-upholstered matrons who cannot forgive you for falling victim to their umbrella-tips. In restaurants such bullyboys could command the attention of the same blind-and-deaf waiter who is hired specially by one eatery after another, whichever you choose to dine at that day, to serve cool steak and warm ice cream, to bring Bulgarian claret and charge you for Mouton, and to replace a greasy fork with one which displays dried marinara sauce."

The printer was staring at me with a raised eyebrow.

"Mind you," I went on, "there are free radio psychiatrists, and museum food has got more elaborate in recent years, and at certain gathering places notables are sometimes to be glimpsed, trading gossip and/or punches, and one who's fascinated by fresh-made pasta and picketing against gentrification need never be lonely."

The printer shook his head. "It's obvious you suffer from an exaggerated case of envy. You lust for what you cannot have, and envy has vitiated such force as you might originally have had. My advice to you is to settle in Saint Sebastian and learn and practice a craft: printing, if you like. I can always use an extra apprentice. Or carpentry, shoemaking, masonry, cooking or baking, distilling schnapps, brewing beer. There's plenty to do, none of it characterized by the hateful competitive strife typical of, by your account, your home principality."

I passed up the opportunity to quote the legendary bon mot of the circus employee who gave elephant-enemas, "And leave show business?" I simply told him I'd think about it, thanked him, and left.

On his own exit the librarian, who I now decided greatly resembled the author of *In der Strafkolonie,* had plucked, from a pile near the door, a copy of a one-sheet newspaper.

I asked him, "Is that a broadside?"

"Yes, indeed," said he, presenting it to me.

It bore a headline of modest size: "The Case Against Training Birds to Speak." I read it aloud, and asked, "Is that a current problem here?"

"At least one person thinks so," said my companion, "else he would not have written this."

"The subject is characteristic of the broadsides?"

"I'd say so. Natural history is a favorite topic. There was one last week that considered what might happen if mice were as large as pigs."

I lowered the paper. "Have you ever heard of a long story entitled *Die Verwandlung?*"

"No."

"Have you ever read *I Promessi Sposi,* the *Thesmophoriazusae, Gammer Gurton's Needle, Wilhelm Meisters Wanderjahre,* Ghalib's ghazals, or, for a change of pace, the frothy entertainments of the late Thorne Smith: *The Night Life of the Gods,* perhaps, or *Topper Takes a Trip?*"

"Never."

"I suspected as much. It is no doubt desirable in Saint Sebastian for a librarian to be—forgive my candor, which is intended to be scientific, not abusive—to be, in a word, ill read."

"I'm quite illiterate," said he, with a smile I should have called proud. He nodded at the paper in my hand. "I can't read a word of that."

"Uh-huh. And it doesn't strike you as strange to have such employment as you do?"

"Not at all. You see, I am therefore utterly unbiased. One book is as good as another to me."

"You don't really have many books at the library, do you?"

"Not now."

"At one time there were more than the *Encyclopaedia Sebastiana?*"

"A good many," said the librarian. "I gave them all away."

The rickshaw man was waiting at the curb. His head was down and he seemed to be dozing as a horse might in the same situation.

"To whom did you present them?"

"I gave one to each person, but sometimes, when I was told that several constituted a set, I gave those that belonged together to the same person, relying on his honesty, for of course I was unable to identify the titles except by ear."

"Extraordinary," I said. "And may I ask why you disposed of the collection of the public library of Saint Sebastian?"

"It seemed to make little sense to keep all the books with me, who could not read, when they might each find a good home with someone who would make use of them."

"Yes, but people generally do not reread the same volume constantly unless it's a religious scripture and they are fanatically devout," I told him. "Most readers go from one book to the next."

He was shaking his head. "Not in this country."

"Come now, you don't mean to say a Sebastiani reader remains with the *same* book?"

"With all respect," said the librarian, "if your practice is otherwise. But my literate countrymen believe that, going from one book to another, the reader can never get more than the most superficial sense of what the author has taken the pains to write."

I was not insensitive to the point being made, having myself in my pedagogical days taught a survey-of-world-lit. course at State, in which in the space of barely eight months the students were obliged to pretend they had read the major works of some twenty centuries (I confess their instructor had to fake a few himself). "There is much to be said for that argument if the books concerned are masterpieces," I noted. "But *every* volume in the library? Would you not have had some titles of negligible value: the mendacious memoirs of film stars, the apologias of ex-statesmen, once famous muckrakings made pointless by time, first-aid manuals for personality disorders now out of fashion, and the kind of narratives our forebears found risqué but which nowadays would anesthetize with ennui a novice nun?"

"Sebastiani readers do not make such distinctions," said the librarian. "If a book is printed and bound, it's good enough for them."

It occurred to me to ask, "Would the books concerned have been the work of Sebastiani authors?"

"Indeed they would," said he.

"Might it be possible for me to meet one or more of your writers? There are some extant?"

"Certainly. The pink house just there is their quarters." He indicated the building next to the library.

"When you say 'quarters,' do you mean they live there in a kind of colony?"

"Of course. That is the law."

"When you say 'law,' do you mean that they are obliged to live there?"

"Not unless they want to practice that profession," said the librarian. "No man can be forced to become a writer, but if he does become one, he must live here and not amongst the populace."

"What is the purpose of that law? For whose benefit was it enacted? The public's or the writer's?"

"Both, I should think," the little librarian said. "Thus neither is polluted by the other."

"I'm not sure what that means. By 'polluted,' do you mean—"

"I'm sure it's a fancy way of saying 'bored,' don't you know," said he. "But here we are." We had reached the doorstep of the two-story building in pink stucco. "The authors will be having their . . . let me see, which meal will it be? Breakfast, Post-breakfast, Lunch, ah yes, this would be Postlunch without a doubt. I'm sure you will be most welcome in the dining room."

5

WE ENTERED the pink house and went upstairs to a dining room that occupied most of the second floor. Its central feature was a large round table, at which about dozen men, one or two young, one or two old, but most of them in middle age, sat silently drinking what would seem from its color, and the shape of the glasses, to be sherry.

"Gentlemen," said my sponsor, "you have a visitor from New York. I know you'll want to make him welcome."

One of the writers, a flabby-cheeked individual with the melancholy eyes of a hound, gestured with his forefinger. "There's a place there, next to Spang."

I assumed it was Spang, a sallow, longlipped man, who moved so that I might slide into the chair beside him. But when I said, "How do you do, Mr. Spang. I'm Russel Wren," he replied, in a high-tenor voice, "Oh, I'm not Spang. I'm Hinkle."

"Since when are you not Spang?" asked the sad-eyed man who had first spoken to me.

"I've never been Spang. He's deceased."

"If that's so, then why have you never mentioned it before?"

"There's never been an occasion to do so," said Hinkle. "You've never called me Spang before."

"But *I've always thought you were Spang.* Can't you get that through your thick head? Simply because I've never had to use your name before doesn't mean that I was not certain what it was."

"Well, what do you want me to do, for God's sake?" Hinkle asked. "Change it to Spang so that your usage is legitimized?"

The flabby-cheeked man smirked. "Well, aren't we getting toplofty?"

I looked towards my neighbor on the left, but he did not return the favor. He was a beetle-browed sort, with a hard-looking jaw. He stared malevolently into his sherry.

No one did anything about getting me a glass. The librarian had taken a silent leave.

I began, "You see, my own work has been for the theat—" but was interrupted by a curly-headed author across the table, one of the younger men.

"Leave it to you assholes to make an issue of something so inane. Who cares who's Spang and who isn't?"

Hinkle said, "You wouldn't be happy if someone got your name wrong, Boggs."

"I couldn't care less!"

"All right, then, I'll call your bluff. From now on, I'll refer to you as Sprat."

The curly-haired man frowned. "Now, wait a minute. That's insulting. I don't have to take that sort of thing."

"You phony," Hinkle growled in disgust. "It's simply a name I made up out of the blue. What's insulting about it?"

"It's the name of a tinned fish, as you very well know!"

Some of the others were sniggering now. A well-constructed young Blond waitress appeared behind a serving cart full of soup bowls. She began to distribute the soup, starting with me, then moving on in a counterclockwise direction towards Hinkle.

"You're being oversensitive, Boggsy," said a man whose dark hair was plastered flat to his scalp and parted in the middle. "My name is Merkin, but I've never been embarrassed by it. It was good enough for my old dad and it's good enough for me."

"Of course that's an archaic word," said the only man yet to have addressed me, viz., he who had directed me to a seat. "You'd feel different if you were called Cunthair. I think Boggs has a point."

"Well," said Merkin, " 'bog' meant 'shit' in the olden time, did it not?"

Someone else asked, "Verb or noun?"

I saw with astonishment that the large-nosed author next to

Hinkle had slipped his left hand up under the skirt of the waitress as she bent to place his soup before him, and was obviously massaging her buttock. No one but me, including the young woman, paid any attention to this.

When I looked again at Boggs, he was plucking up a roll. He proceeded to hurl it at Merkin. Merkin with amazing speed lifted a fending palm, and the roll bounced off it and soared to fall into the soup which the waitress had placed before the large-nosed man while he was fondling her behind.

The victim seized the nearest basket of rolls and began to hurl them one by one at Boggs, who ducked some but was hit by several. When the fusillade had ended, Boggs asked the man next to him to pass the boat-shaped glass dish that held olives, black and green, and sticks of celery.

The author with the flabby cheeks protested. "Now, hold on, Boggs. I'm fond of olives and don't want to eat them off the floor."

Boggs carried the dish to this man and emptied it on his head. "Eat your fill, then, Buzzle."

The waitress had now reached the man on my left, but the cart was empty. There had been just enough bowls for each of the regulars. My presence had thrown off the count. With an extended finger she enumerated the bowls she had served, shook her head, and burst into tears.

Buzzle had been furiously gathering up as many of the olives and celery sticks as he could, after they had rolled and bounced off his head, no doubt with an angry intent to launch them at Boggs, who had returned to his seat, but the weeping girl distracted everyone for the moment.

Hinkle was first to speak. "You idiot," he cried to her, and then he shook his head at various of his colleagues and even at me. "It's an outrage that almost every day our meal is marred by some stupidity on the part of that Blond." He addressed her again. "You fool!"

She sobbed into her hands and then peeped out with two blue eyes. "Is brinkink twelf as alvays."

Merkin shouted, "Count them, you silly bitch!"

When she did as instructed, most of the writers joined her in pointing at the bowls and announcing the numbers aloud, in chorus. They arrived at twelve.

"I don't understand it," said Hinkle. "There *are* enough bowls." They repeated the process, this time without being joined by the waitress, who stood silent and humble alongside her cart.

I finally said, "May I explain? You see, I am the ex—" At this point Buzzle hurled two handfuls of olives at me, and Merkin began to pelt me with rolls. I was also the target of odd names as terms of abuse: "Barber!" "Dentist!" "Accountant!" And so on.

For a moment I was taken aback to be so treated when I was supposed to be their guest, and I crossed my arms across my face and sank beneath the table, out of the line of fire. But then, since I hadn't really been hurt, indignation soon became my dominant emotion. I came up fighting. I lifted my bowl and hurled the soup across the table into Boggs's face. I picked up from the floor some of the rolls thrown at me and fired them at Hinkle, Merkin, and Buzzle. I snatched up olives and celery and dashed them into the face of the grumpy-looking man on my left, though in truth he had not been one of the aggressors against me.

"You shits!" I cried. "You call yourselves writers?" Perhaps this had nothing to do with the issue at hand, but surely one need not justify what one says when exercised.

Eventually it struck me that from the moment I went on the offensive, the authors became peaceable, and by the time I had committed several acts of violence against them they had begun to assume expressions I could not but identify as admiring, perhaps even downright obsequious. For example, the man on my left wiped his face with a napkin, rose, and came meekly to me.

"Sir," said he, "please accept my apology for having offended you as apparently, though without intention, without indeed having, to my memory, been aware of your presence until this moment—unless, to be sure, it was that very ignorance for which you gave me what was surely a merited punishment and if not was yet no doubt deserved according to that principle enunciated by the Bard, *videlicet*, which amongst us could escape the noose were justice to be honored more in the observance than the breach?" He offered his hand. "Your servant, sir. I am Barnswallow."

"Wren," said I. I transferred to my left hand the roll I had been holding and shook with him: he had a weightless but clinging sort of grip, which one half expected to have to scrape away.

"Welcome to our little convocation," he said. His paunch hung over his belt. It now occurred to me that all these authors wore matching navy-blue three-piece suits, most of which were rumpled, stained at the vest, and sprinkled with dandruff at the shoulders and even the lapels. Barnswallow was one of those whose vests were unbuttoned so as to offer a modicum of liberty to their extra flesh.

Hinkle was next to offer his welcome. The others around the table were beaming and intoning, "Hear, hear."

I finally lowered my roll to the tabletop. I was not yet prepared to be extravagantly genial, but I did say, grudgingly, "Well, all right, I suppose I can accept the apology. But I'll strike back if I am the recipient of any more aggression. I realize I am an uninvited guest, but you might simply have asked me to leave."

"Excuse me, Mr. Wren," said Hinkle. "It would have been rude by our lights to ask you to go, you see. As it was, we proved you were welcome by treating you as badly as we treat one another!"

Again the "Hear, hear"'s were sounded around the table.

"All right," said I. "I'm willing to put the misunderstanding, if such it was, behind me. Now please resume your usual activities. I assume these lunches are normally the occasions for discussion of your works in progress?" I sat down now, as, following my lead, did those writers who had sprung up earlier.

"Actually," said Boggs, across the table, after the chair legs had stopped squeaking, "we talk almost exclusively about inconsequential matters, as it happens. Never do we mention to any of our colleagues what we're working on at the moment, lest he steal the idea and complete the work before the man can whose original idea it was."

"Then you don't trust one another?"

Buzzle snorted. "Certainly not! We writers are the most unscrupulous people in the country. We're well known for that.

Not only will we steal one another's ideas. We mingle with the crowds in the marketplace, shoplifting and picking pockets. If someone is still naïve enough to invite any of us to dinner, we'll swipe what we can: silverware, family heirlooms small enough to slip into a pocket, dirty underwear from the bathroom hamper—"

"Male or female underclothing?"

"Either," said Boggs. "As long as it's been worn recently."

Whether or not I was supposed to take him seriously, I decided that these were the most unattractive people I had met thus far in Saint Sebastian. Indeed, the Blonds, though cretins, were, all in all, the nicest. When I went on the attack, the waitress had slipped out of the room. Now I espied her peeping from the swinging door that obviously led to the kitchen. I had not previously seen her face straight on: it bore a notable resemblance to those of Olga and Helmut.

When she determined that the soup course was so to speak over, though most of it had been splattered across the table, she re-entered the dining room, transporting, with high-held wrists, a large trayful of loaded plates. So as to keep the peace—for despite their avowals of friendship I did not trust this lot—I waved off the dish she was about to place before me.

"You don't care for roast stoat?" asked Hinkle. "They can probably rustle you up something else, then: perhaps some of yesterday's badger."

"Actually, I've already eaten and within the hour," said I. "I shouldn't have taken the soup. But please go ahead, all of you. I'm here as an observer. Don't mind me."

I cannot justly complain, for I had told them to proceed, but I must say they fell to their plates with an ardor, even a ferocity, that astonished me. For a few moments the table was a mise-en-scène of flashing cutlery and gnawing teeth. Juice dripped from chins, fragments of food fell from flying forks. Boggs's knifework was so savage as to wound his index finger, and his blood dribbled to join the other fluids staining the tablecloth. With closed eyes one would have heard a troop of hyenas demolishing a carcass. Before I had completed an ocular circuit of the company, those first served were displaying empty plates.

I addressed Hinkle, who had long since devoured the last morsel of his own portion. "You fellows are quite the trenchermen. Do you work up such appetites at writing?"

He patted his protuberant belly. "I've never made up my mind about the chicken or the egg: maybe gluttons are naturally attracted to the profession, for some reason. If so, bless me if I can see the connection."

The waitress was now going around with red wine. After every four persons, she began a new bottle, for the glasses were large and she filled them to the rims.

I asked, "Do you people drink a lot?"

"Not during the week, except after eleven A.M." said Hinkle, lifting his goblet and emptying it in one long draught. When he lowered the glass he looked around for the waitress. She was detained. Barnswallow's hand was between her legs.

"And sex?"

"Yes," said he, "with anything." He gestured with his glass at the waitress.

"By the way, don't you have any female authors in Saint Sebastian?"

"If you can call them that. They write nothing but pornography."

"Are you serious?"

"Is that so surprising, given the filthy imagination of the typical woman?" Hinkle was now growing annoyed with the failure of the waitress to fill his glass, but Barnswallow was working ever more furiously under her skirt, to which activity she seemed indifferent, whereas he was gasping stertorously. It was an ugly spectacle to me, but his colleagues were seemingly oblivious to it.

I wasn't eager to start more trouble, so I made gentle application to Hinkle.

"It isn't her fault. Why don't you ask Barnswallow to unhand her?"

Hinkle shrugged. "We're never critical of one another in such a situation."

"You were only just throwing things and insulting each other!"

"That was only personal," said he. "This is principle. Can't you see that? A Blond's a Blond!"

I turned in my chair, so that I could not see Barnswallow from the corner of my eye. "I suppose it's none of my business. . . . Tell me, what do you write?"

"I do children's books. Each of us has his own specialty. Boggs for example does books and articles explaining how things happen in the natural sciences: how the porcupine throws its quills, how the basilisk paralyzes its intended prey with a fixed stare, and so on. Buzzle's latest work is a series of profiles of three great men who were afflicted with chronic diarrhea: Mohammed, Molière, Marx."

I frowned. "Just a moment. Can that be true? How does he—"

Hinkle made a superior smile. "Pure assumption. Else we *couldn't* say, according to Buzzy. Molière, for example, was awfully cunning at it, leaving not a shred of evidence."

"Neither, I should imagine, did the other two. Also, I happen to remember from my scouting days that a porcupine certainly does not throw its quills, and that a basilisk can paralyze with a glance is a quaint old delusion of the Middle Ages, if I recall the footnotes in my college edition of Shakespeare."

At this point Barnswallow finally released the waitress. She came to Hinkle with the wine bottle.

I asked her for her name.

"Inga."

"You're not by chance related to Olga and Helmut?"

Her answer did not take me by surprise. "Sure."

Hinkle was not offended by my negative comments. Still smiling proudly, he went on. "Hozenblatt, over there, is our modern historian. He is best known for his comprehensive study of the concentration camps in which the Jews exterminated the German and Austrian Gentiles, 1938 to '45. Currently he is at work on a book in the same vein, this one concerned with the Siberian forced-labor camps in which anti-Communist zealots confine benevolent secret policemen."

I retrieved one of the overturned sherry glasses and asked Inga to fill it with table wine. "Thank you," I told her, and added, sotto voce, "I'm your friend."

She made her blue eyes into veritable saucers and asked in a loud voice, "You vant to screw?"

But no one, including Hinkle at my other elbow, showed any

sign of having heard this. I still had not got used to the utter lack of sexual shame in Saint Sebastian.

"No, thank you," I told Inga, and turned back to the writer of children's books. "Tell me, Hinkle, what kind of thing do you write about for kids?"

He was pleased by the question. "All manner of informative subjects, actually, from economic theory to contraception. Then, on the entertainment side, surveys of nightlife around the world, the *caves* of Paris, the after-hours joints of New York, the transvestite bars of Istanbul, and so on."

"And do the children understand this material?"

"Well, of course, *nobody* understands economics," said Hinkle. "I expect they get some profit from the rest of it. But if they don't, what does it matter? They're just kids."

"Some of you have British-sounding names: Merkin, Boggs, *et al.*, and everybody in the country speaks fluent English, though so far as I know, you're a considerable distance from Great Britain."

Hinkle narrowed his eyes. "You're not speaking derisively, are you?"

"Certainly not!"

"Because an awful lot of people do, if they know you're an author. Which is why we all of course use pseudonyms, some of which are British. As to the use of the English language throughout the country, you'd have to look in the *Encyclopaedia Sebastiana* for the whys and wherefores. But my understanding is that at some time in the early nineteenth century the then reigning prince decided to simplify the matter of language, the choice of which in conversation had become trendily arbitrary. It was chic, especially among the better class of ladies, to address a person in an exotic tongue. The other would of course endeavor to one-up the first by replying in an even more obscure language. The universal use of English seemed the answer, for what is it but a compound of many other tongues, beginning as German, taking on Latin from the Romans, then French from the Normans, and so on, and eventually even collecting such exotica as *pajama* from Persian by way of Hindustani and *goober* from Bantu?"

During the course of the foregoing remarks I had emptied my

glass. I rose now and pursued Inga, who was at the turn of the table with her bottle. While she poured, I was addressed by the nearby Hozenblatt.

"I say, Wren, perhaps you could settle this argument I'm having with Smerd. I maintain that Montenegro is a peak near Kilimanjaro in Africa, whereas he insists it's a very dark wine of the Jura. What do you say?"

"Neither. He was a Latin American singer of the bossa-nova era, now almost forgotten."

Smerd was a husky, powerful-looking man, whose constant expression seemed to be a scowl. I asked Hinkle what sort of thing Smerd wrote.

"He's our muckraker. He exposes people, often literally, as when he's researching the prevalence of dirty feet. He's not above knocking you to the ground, tearing off your shoes and socks, and prying your toes apart, looking for toe jams."

I glanced again at the author in question, but my eyes were attracted to a man on his left, a big fat jolly writer with a high-colored face and watery eyes. He had taken the bottle away from Inga, a new bottle, and putting its mouth to his, lifted its base into the air.

I asked Hinkle who that was.

"Riesling," said he. "Our literary critic."

When I looked again at Riesling I saw him emptying the bottle unto the very last drops, to catch which, on his protruded red tongue, he held the neck perhaps a foot overhead. Then without warning he hurled the bottle at Merkin, who however caught it easily. Riesling roared-wept with laughter.

"No doubt, despite his jovial appearance, he wields a savage pen?"

"Not at all," said Hinkle. "He writes only praise."

"Surprises keep coming," I said. "What kind of thing does he write about?"

"Poetry is his great specialty."

"There are many Sebastiani poets?"

"Not one," Hinkle said.

"How's that?"

"Riesling writes essays, even long books, about great poetry that has never been written."

"Nobody ever tries to write poetry?"

"They'd keep it a secret if they did," Hinkle said with feeling. "Riesling had sworn to murder anyone who tries. Even Smerd, strong and brutal as he is, is scared of Riesling in that regard."

My second glassful was now gone. I twitched a finger at Inga, and when she came to me with a newly opened bottle, I took it from her and tried to ape Riesling's stunt. But for the life of me I couldn't swallow in consecutive gulps more than about a third of the contents. The critic really was a remarkable talent.

As I drank, Hinkle identified the rest of the authors and their genres. As it happened, only Blond women wrote fiction, and according to him it was all obscene.

"Explicit hardcore sex, eh?"

He snorted indignantly. "There's no normal, decent crotchwork, if that's what you mean. This is real *filth*. The heroine is saved from some peril by the big, handsome, and wealthy nobleman, who then asks for her hand in marriage. The one I read made me puke my guts out. I wouldn't want one to get into the hands of any daughter of mine, I tell you."

When he had finished, I asked, "Are there many Sebastianers who read books? If so, where do they get them? Not at the library."

"Various places," Hinkle said. "Whichever would be appropriate to the theme of the particular book. My own, for example, are distributed where children congregate: playgrounds, birthday parties, and so on. Hozenblatt's tomes, being so heavy, are stacked in gyms used by weight lifters. The female porn is made available at hairdressing salons."

"And Riesling's criticism?" The large, jovial man fascinated me. It looked as though he seized life and made it groan.

Hinkle shrugged. "The fact is, it's never been printed." He leaned closer to me. "Some say, never been written. None of the rest of us has ever seen it, I know that."

"Remarkable! But he seems happy enough, doesn't he? Is he telling us something?" I took another swallow of wine. "And does anybody do playwriting, which I raffishly call my own racket?"

"No one," said Hinkle.

"Then the art would be another good subject for Riesling!" I cried. I was feeling the wine now. I looked across at the critic. He had got Inga to bring him another enormous plate of food, great forkfuls of which he was shoveling into his open mouth. His eyes were closed in bliss.

"Hey, Riesling!" I shouted. He opened his watery eyes but continued to eat. "Catch!" I hurled the bottle at him. With horror I watched him do nothing whatever to seize or deflect it. It struck him squarely in the forehead and bounced off as if it, or his skull, were made of rubber. He closed his eyes again and went on eating.

I shouted his name once more, and then:

> "Shall I compare thee to a summer's day?
> Thou art more lovely, and more temperate . . ."

The critic immediately dropped his loaded fork, went to his armpit, and brought out a large automatic pistol. His first shot broke the glass in front and slightly to the right of me; the slug continued past my forearm with a hideous whistle.

I didn't wait for another. I plunged to the floor and left the room on running hands and feet. I hurled myself down the stairs and dashed out the door of the pink house and leaped into the waiting rickshaw, ordering Helmut to depart on the double.

But, looking back, I saw I was not pursued. The life of the Sebastiani authors, however intramurally passionate it was, never crossed the threshold to make contact with the great world. And no doubt that was best for the country.

Once we were beyond the Street of Words, I directed Helmut to pull over to the curb. Riesling's attack had returned me to sobriety. I realized that I should sit quietly somewhere and try to make some sense of what I'd seen and heard since arriving in Saint Sebastian. I might use Helmut as a sounding board. He was so stupid that I would not appear foolish no matter what nonsense I bounced off him; also, he had no personal axe to grind.

We were on a street of low wooden sheds, each separated from the next by some distance; no people were in view or in hearing.

"Here's how it looks to me," I said towards Helmut but really to myself. "The prince is a pervert, an eccentric, and so on, but as rulers go, he's far from being the worst imaginable, because he has no effect on the country."

"Sir vill vish—"

"Please, Helmut, I'm trying to follow a train of thought. You wouldn't understand, but I have been sent over here from my country to find out what happens in yours. If we like what we see, we will give you money."

"Is interesting place," Helmut said, pointing to the sheds. He picked up the shafts. "You should look."

"What is it?" I asked. "It resembles the fireworks factory that was at the edge of my hometown when I was a child."

"Yass," said Helmut, pulling me into a graveled lane that went amongst the little frame buildings.

"You mean it *is* a fireworks factory?"

The establishment of my childhood had been surrounded by a high fence topped with barbed wire and everywhere posted with warnings as to the explosive nature of what was made therein and the danger of fire. Here there was nothing to restrain the layman or -child from wandering about the premises, not even an informational sign.

Helmut stopped before a certain hut, which was distinguished in no way from its fellows, lowered the shafts, and went to the door of weathered wood, saying "Come, please," and I did as asked.

Inside, along three of the four walls, were workbenches at each of which sat a middle-aged woman. The one nearest me, her gray-blond hair in a bun, was pouring what would seem to be gunpowder through a funnel into a stout red cardboard tube. She did this none too carefully, for a dusting of the black powder covered the tabletop.

"Very interesting," I told Helmut, and turned nervously away. "I really must get back to the hotel."

Ignoring me, he went to the center of the room and pushed aside the rough-woven rug that lay there, uncovering a trapdoor. He bent and grasped the recessed ring that was its handle and pulled up the door, revealing a wooden ladder that descended to some space below. He beckoned me to follow and went first. Curiosity overcame my apprehensions. There was an earthen smell at the bottom of the ladder and no light whatever for a moment; then Helmut produced an electric torch from somewhere. He led me through a low, narrow tunnel whose ceiling and sides were braced with timbers. Just as it occurred to me that I should probably worry about being asphyxiated, we turned a corner, went through a crude door that resembled the end of a packing crate, and entered a chamber lighted by several kerosene lamps atop a coarse wooden table and, I was relieved to see, ventilated by a vertical pipe going up through the ground above. Nevertheless it was not the kind of retreat that would have appealed to the claustrophobe.

Camp chairs were arranged around the table, and Helmut, with a new authority and in a new accent, asked me to choose one and take a seat.

He stood before me. "Olga will be coming along in a few moments," he said. "Along with the rest of the Revolutionary Council. We haven't been able to get together with you until now, because each of us has a demanding, and of course degrading, job he or she must perform for at least ten hours a day or night. It is not generally known, I think, that one of the major problems in making a revolution is merely scheduling the conspiratorial meetings—if the persons involved are flunkies in their society."

Temporarily dumbstruck by the transformation, I sank onto one of the chairs and stared at the hard-packed earth between my feet.

At last I looked up. "You're telling me that *you* and your sister are leaders of the Sebastiani liberation movement?"

Helmut sneered. "The belief that we all look alike is but another manifestation of the bias against us. We are siblings only in the ideological and not the biological sense."

This was a familiar plaint of oppressed minorities, and, so far as I was concerned, usually justifiable enough. On the other hand, *these* people had blown up my home. I reminded Helmut of that outrage.

He moved his square chin. "A man posing as an agent for the owner of the building assured us it was not only unoccupied but scheduled to be demolished."

"The individual in reference was undoubtedly that swine who does janitorial work around the place," said I.

Helmut's nostrils flared. "In Saint Sebastian he would be a Blond."

"No doubt," I said. "But I hasten to assure you that such a chap in New York City is a social pariah only by reason of his own personality, not because of before-the-fact prejudice. I've seldom seen a black super in a white building. Finally, an Afro-American friend of mine, with a Harlem super of his own kind, had the same complaints as I. Along with one that remained unique: *his* super used a passkey to slip into the apartment and eat all the fresh fruit."

Helmut shrugged. "If you remember, you did get a telephone warning as soon as it was discovered that you were on the premises. We had no motive to wish you harm."

But I did not hear him offer to compensate me for the loss of property. He displayed the solipsist self-righteousness that has always kept me from wholeheartedly admiring the ideologue even when I give general assent to his proximate aim.

At that moment a woman came in from the tunnel. She was tall and full-figured, wore rumpled dark slacks and a shapeless gray coat; her hair was gathered within a beret, and she wore spectacles.

I assumed she was a hitherto-unencountered member of the Revolutionary Council—until she seized my hand, yanked it up and pushed it down, and said, "Good day, Brother Wren. We meet in other conditions than yesterday's."

I leaned forward and squinted. "Olga? Can it be?"

She laughed coldly. "Is that not a vile role I must play?" Then in came several other men and women, all of whom were fair-complexioned. They sat down on the camp chairs, but Olga remained standing.

"We'll make this brief," said she. "Rudy and Margit and some of you others are supposed to be on duty right now. Fortunately, the conviction that we all look alike helps us at such a time. *They* never quite know who's who." She directed the last comment to me.

I was still trying to habituate myself to the new Olga, who was even more remarkable than the new Helmut.

She continued. "Brother Wren, as some of us know already,

has been sent over by the US government to determine how best to aid our movement."

At this point I recovered sufficiently to interrupt. "Excuse me," I said, "but that's not quite the case." The Blonds all turned and gave me uncompromising stares. In the modest refulgence of the kerosene lamps their eyes were darker than the normal sky blue. They were all rather large people. I quickly edited my statement. "That is, it might be premature to put it as you have. Anyway, I am a humble information-gatherer, not a policy-maker."

Olga resumed as if I had not spoken. "We want arms that are light and portable: automatic rifles, machine pistols. We don't need planes. Sebastian doesn't have an air force, and he doesn't have any armor, so we don't need tanks. I suppose if we had artillery we could shell the palace, but then we'd have to go to the expense of rebuilding it, for we will want to maintain a commanding structure up there for the executive offices of the democratic government to come. It's the highest point in the city and figures too importantly in the ruling symbolism of our country to dispense with."

She was an impressive figure, standing there before us, though her clothes were drab. I do not ritualistically gasp in admiration at the sterner sort of woman (who has always, beginning with my grade-school gym teacher, an iron-jawed bruiser named Bertha Dirkwalter, tended to be impatient with me), but I had to admit that Olga was morally more prepossessing now than when posing as an airborne airhead.

She went on. "Annaliese, Hans, and I, as the Subcommittee on Arms, have drawn up a list of the weaponry we require from America." She nodded at one of the other women, attired and spectacled as soberly as herself but underneath it all, one could discern, another Valkyrie only slightly less handsome than her leader. "Please give Brother Wren that list."

Annaliese opened her blouse, reached within, and brought out a sheaf of papers, which she handed across to me. They were warm from contact with her flesh, which, judging from the set of her shoulders, was ample.

"I'll look these over," I said, placing the papers on the table. "But again I must remind you that somebody with more authority than I will make the judgment as to any aid, military or otherwise."

"Of course, we will require a good deal more than arms," Olga said, as usual making no acknowledgment of my reservations. "We'll need one hundred million dollars to begin with. I won't waste our time with a list of specific allocations: we're quite capable of making the dispersals ourselves. If you must justify it to your people, tell them the largest single outlay will consist of bribes to those around Sebastian. His advisors and ministers are so corrupt that we might well bring him down bloodlessly: that should appeal to you Americans."

"In which case you wouldn't need the arms," I pointed out.

Olga's fair face darkened. "I'm afraid that, on the contrary, weapons must always, if deplorably, have the highest priority. For it is likely that as soon as Sebastian is removed, our neighbors will see what they will interpret as our time of weakness in which they might strike with success."

The other Blonds murmured their fervent agreement with this analysis, and Annaliese smote the tabletop with her fist.

Intermittently I was still having seizures of astonishment at the change in Olga.

I said, "As I think you have reason to know, I was transported to Saint Sebastian in a comatose state and had not been well briefed beforehand. I'm not sure I can remember your abutting neighbors. Austria? Czechoslovakia, one or both Germanies?"

Olga proceeded to pronounce names which, never having heard them before or seen them written, I can reproduce only approximately. "Gezieferland on the north, and to the southeast, Swatina."

"My ignorance of these countries is absolute. I take it they are as small as Saint Sebastian? What sort of regimes do they have?"

"Tyrannical," said she. "One is ruled by a king and the other, a grand duke, two scoundrels who are in fact cousins to Sebastian."

"Why would they be eager to attack this country?"

"They have no Blonds of their own," said Olga.

"They would like to enslave you for their own purposes?"

"Need you ask?" She made a gesture of impatience. "It's time for our people to get back to their jobs before they're missed.

And I'm sure you are eager to get to the cable office to contact your principals with our demands."

I winced. "Just a moment. You're speaking of demands now? Or was that a slip of the tongue?"

Olga said coldly, "Not at all, Brother Wren. I'm afraid we must hold you hostage until we receive an affirmative response from your government."

6

THERE WAS LITTLE QUESTION that I could be easily restrained by the large Blond men, and therefore I attempted no physical resistance.

But I could say, "I find your tactics leave something to be desired. Remember, I am first the man whose home you destroyed, along with the script of a play that might have been produced on Broadway, making me rich and famous. Then I am literally kidnaped by an agency of the US government, drugged, and sent over here. As if that isn't enough, you now inform me that I am to be used as a pawn in your game. You certainly know how to attract sympathizers."

Oblivious to my remarks, the Blonds rose from the table. Helmut remained at the door; the others left.

"There's nothing personal in it," said Olga. "You should not take offense. The individual cannot be respected in such an effort as ours, else nothing would be accomplished. Our country is already badly behind the times. Who else in the world is governed by such a degenerate as Sebastian?"

"Ironically enough, some of the newest nations in the so-called Third World might provide a rival or two," said I. "But even if I agreed that you Blonds are in a peculiarly subservient situation in Europe, even if you might require brute force to depose the prince, why must you work your will by violent means on foreigners, strangers who have no proper involvement in your affairs?"

A sneer hardened the shape of Olga's full mouth. "Do you think anyone would even hear of us, let alone care, if we were nonviolent? You have just admitted you are here only as result of

our bombing your home. Then we were successful! Why should
we be concerned with your inconvenience, even your pain? Did
you care about ours?" She sighed in impatience. "Wren, the hu-
manistic platitudes belong in the schoolbooks. They have no
meaning in the real world."

This argument, like all the effective ones in my experience of
life, was not original, but except in the hands of geniuses, inno-
vation tends to be little more than thrillseeking. In any event, I
had virtually exhausted, for the moment, my capacity for debate
on the subject at hand: Aristotle to the contrary notwithstand-
ing, I am not to any degree a political animal: I just wish people
would be quietly nice and fair to one another and there would
never be any riots, revolutions, wars. I am aware that hope is
weak-minded, but I am confident that it is normal amongst the
rank and file of all nations, creeds, and breeds.

Helmut was still there. No doubt he was to be my private
guard, and so far as I was concerned, husky as he was, he would
be sufficient even though unarmed. Were he as stupid as I had
originally believed, I would have assumed I could easily outwit
him. As it was, I seemed to be a prisoner.

Imagine then my pleased surprise when Olga spoke to her
comrade in a strange tongue, and he nodded (rather sullenly, I
thought) and exited into the tunnel. I reproduce her speech as
well as I can; I never saw written Sebastiani.

"Helmut, alley yets. Idge lee manazhay."

I intended to wait until he had had time to reach the surface,
and then to overpower Olga by the most expeditious means,
using as much force as was needed: despite the current trends, I
dislike using violence against women, but this was not the moment for the gentlemanly restraint shown by the heroes of
World War II films, who are unable to punch even a female
Nazi.

To kill time, I asked her about the local language: who spoke
it, when, and why?

"What you just said to Helmut was at the threshold of intelli-
gibility for me. It seemed some combination of several modern
European tongues."

Olga was staring at me, a new emotion behind the lenses of

her severe spectacles. She said, "You are not altogether unattractive."

"Uh, thank you, Olga. Neither are you. In fact, you're beautiful, even as you're dressed right now, which I gather is supposed to be antiseptic."

"You don't have one of those New York diseases, do you?"

"Pardon?"

"Herpes or that peculiarly virulent new strain of gonorrhea?"

"Good heavens, no!"

"Then I want to screw." She began to remove her clothing. "This may not be impeccable revolutionary practice, because you really must get off that cable without delay, but I have normal sexual appetites, and who knows when such a moment will come again?" Her long skirt was already off and hanging over one of the chairs. I noted for what it was worth that irrespective of her outer attire, the overabundance of the revolutionary's garb or the brevity of the stewardess's uniform, underwear was unknown to Olga.

I was about to protest in the name of my natural modesty when it occurred to me that such a moment as this would beautifully suit my intention to escape. In another instant Olga would be starkers, whereas I had not yet even pretended to begin to undress, a lack of preparedness which she had not yet, in her egocentricity, noticed.

But the fact was that when Olga had stripped to the altogether, she was not as easy to leave as I had anticipated. Indeed, in a sexual career of some dimension, I had not seen the like of her body, for which "magnificent" would have been an inadequate term. I began, all but involuntarily, to remove my own clothes. . . . Having no intention of catering to those who hold a book in one hand, I omit the details of the succeeding moments, except to say that Olga proved to be even more of a handful than she looked: I might even go so far as to say that her performance led me to question whether I had ever previously had any encounter which could be called carnal.

I was not aware of how much this experience had taken out of me until I heard a snapping of fingers and an impatient voice saying, "Come along, Wren. The Revolution can't wait while you snooze," and opened my eyes and saw that Olga was all dressed while I still lay on the tabletop, feeling as though I were a half-melted stick of butter. It was chagrining to me to remember that not so long before I had been planning to jump her while I was dressed and she was naked!

I creakily climbed down and retrieved the clothes I had dropped on the floor. Bending my back was an exercise in anguish.

"Let's go," she nagged.

"You're stronger than you think," I wincingly murmured as I secured my belt, which now could be cinched one hole further on the skinny side.

However, once I was attired, I reflected that we were on terra firma now, and not in the horizontal situation in which she had a natural advantage (please, no feminist outcries: whoever *contains* another is perforce boss!). She was big and strong, but I was wiry and had studied the martial arts for at least four sessions with an Oriental whose dojo shared the second floor of a ramshackle Garment District building with a bathhouse staffed by his female countrymen, adepts in that art of pressure-point massage called *shiatsu*, which is not obscene (I should say, not *necessarily* obscene) and had the polka-dotted belt to prove it.

I assumed the fighting stance taught me (not sans pain) by my slant-eyed *sensei*, and said, "I'm not going to be kept your prisoner, Olga, but I will promise, after only a little more investigation—for frankly I'm eager to get home—to return to the USA and make a thorough report to my superiors on Saint Sebastian. Be assured that your argument will be well represented, if you'll answer only a few questions. First, if you Blonds are as clever as you obviously are when you drop your masks of subservience, why have you taken so long to make your move? So far as I can see, the prince does little to enforce his will on the populace. Such power as he possesses seems to be used exclusively for self-protection. The security measures at the palace would bring bliss to a paranoiac. I have not encountered any soldiers or any policemen but a couple of low-comedy municipal constables. So who enforces the tyranny of which you complain?"

Olga's face had taken on a very bland, very blond mien. "And what else would you like to know?"

"Well, what's puzzling me is, I haven't yet met many examples nor have I seen much evidence of a Sebastiani middle class. In America, even in New York, most of the people you see at any given time, unless you constantly frequent the venues of the lumpenproletariat or the watering places of the plutocrats, are those in the middle: they work at something during the day and come home at night; they are usually married and probably have offspring; it is they who give the plurality to whichever presidential candidate, after he and his rivals have so strenuously curried their favor. The news is published and/or broadcast for them. Most kinds of entertainment are offered with them in mind, and cars, refrigerators, and home computers are designed to meet their existing needs or create new ones. This kind of people has been conspicuous by its absence thus far in my Sebastiani experience. I've seen a few jeering urchins; a clutch of scholars, a gaggle of authors; some hotel personnel, *et al.*, and most recently, a band of revolutionaries. But where are the ordinary folks, the regulars, the normal population, the crowd, the mob, the herd, elevated over the centuries of growing enlightenment in the Western countries, from Spenser's 'rascal many' to 'the people' of the social reformers, and finally, at least in the US, to the sort of human beings who fill the stands at the Super Bowl—which as you undoubtedly know, flying to the States as you do so often, is the major public event of any year in my country."

Exhausted by speaking so long while standing in the karate position, thighs at right angles to my calves, fists at the ready, I straightened up to receive Olga's answer. But as soon as I was off guard she kneed me in the stomach and, as I buckled, struck me with a right cross that would have felled any of the current contenders. I blacked out as I fell, but came to not long after meeting the floor.

Olga stooped, lifted me to her back, and with the fireman's carry transported me along the tunnel to the overhead trapdoor. Riding comfortably along on her back, I expected her to carry me up the ladder with the same ease in which she had negotiated the tunnel, but my awakening was rude. She put me on my feet, back against the ladder, and continued to slap my face long after it should have been obvious I had regained consciousness.

"Will you stop?" I cried, fending off her hands. "And don't

attack me again! I subscribe to an ancient moral code by which a man cannot strike a woman. I tell you it was a better world when that was in force." I woozily, sorely climbed the ladder to the room where the women were making giant firecrackers. No doubt it was from this source that the makings had come for the bomb that destroyed my home.

Olga emerged and then closed the trapdoor behind her.

"Wasn't it careless to have left that open all this while?" I asked.

"No. They would never come in here. They're scared of the gunpowder." She hooked her arm through mine. "We're going to the cable office now. Don't try to escape unless you want to be permanently crippled."

She had been an animal when undressed. I still felt half lame. I was disinclined to test my strength against hers once more. Beyond this consideration, it was not unpleasant to be so closely clutched by such a woman as she: her right breast rubbed my left biceps at each step, and occasionally I was brushed by the arch of her Lachaise hip. Hers was the most generous body with which I had ever been intimate. I believed it unfortunate that she was so obsessively political.

We walked through the town. I cannot explain why our route was more or less flat when the rickshaw ride had been as if on a roller coaster, unless it was that Helmut had taken a circuitous and undulating journey for the purpose of flexing his muscles.

I tried again to talk to Olga. "I wish you would give me some explanation as to why you Blonds are in the existing situation. You are all splendid physical specimens of humanity, and I suspect that the members of the Revolutionary Council are not the only intelligent members of your breed. How is it, then, that you are servants to those whose masters you should be? Are you aware that only a half-century ago a dictator named Hitler, in a country not too far from here, made your type his ideal?"

At last I had said something that provoked a response from her. "And was not Hitler himself dark-haired, sallow-skinned, narrow-shouldered, and pudgy-bellied? And were any of his close associates blond or, for that matter, even physically fit?"

"But is it your implication that attractive, healthy, fair-complexioned persons are at natural disadvantage in Europe or, for that matter, the human race? I don't think that blonds are losers in Scandinavia, or in American show business."

But Olga had returned to silence. Perhaps she was the woman-of-action type, to whom matters of rationale were boring. I'll admit that despite my job (which I always think of as temporary), I tend to look for a theoretical place in which to file each phenomenon. We made an odd but complementary couple.

Had the pace she set not been so demanding, I might have enjoyed the walk more as we passed a series of colorful open-air markets. At the largest of these, all manner of food was for sale, great wheels of golden-fleshed, red-rinded cheese, plump artichokes, sleek aubergines, striped melons, blushing pears, wicker-encased demijohns of ruby-red wine, jugs of foaming cider, and eviscerated pheasants, woodcock, and hares, suspended from boothfront hooks. The food stalls were attended by outsized women, with great thick red arms and strong, raucous voices, in which they exchanged abuse and cried the virtues of their wares, which included generous displays of the fruits of the sea (though so far as I knew, Saint Sebastian was nowhere near saltwater): bins of corrugated green oysters, blue-black mussels, the little marine hedgehogs called sea urchins, living langoustes and crayfish, huge crosscuts of tuna, tiny prawns, tentacular squid . . .

In a contiguous square was a riotously multicolored flower market. Here the vendors were winsome girls in the years of pubescence, their faces fresh as the blossoms they sold. Then on into an entire street lined on either curbing with birdcages, tended by short black-haired men of cheery mien, who exchanged whistles, chirps, squeaks, with the fowl that were their wares: minuscule finches, high-crested cockatoos, peevish-eyed parrots, a laughing magpie, and warbling canaries.

But one conspicuous lack distinguished each of the markets from those elsewhere in the world: no customers were in evidence!

"There you are," I said to Olga. "Who buys the goods offered for sale by these merchants? Again I ask, where is the *public?*"

By now we were turning into the familiar street in which the Hotel Bristol was situated. We had passed no fellow pedestrians during a twenty-minute walk, and no vehicle had used any of the nearby roads.

Olga's response was to nod towards the hotel and jerk my arm. "There'll be time enough to send the cable. I'm feeling lustful again. You're not as sexually ineffectual as I supposed, though probably part of your allure for me is simply that you have dark hair and are puny."

I overlooked the slur in my amazement at her appetites. Perhaps she had revealed her exploitable weakness. After the workout she had given me in the underground room, such legendary satyrs as Victor Hugo and John Paul Jones would have needed time for recuperation, and therefore it was not likely that I would be capable of soon again being distracted from an intention to escape.

So I showed a burst of false enthusiasm, brought her arm more tightly against my side (where a rib was still sore from the pressure of her steel thighs), and insofar as it was ever possible with Olga, pretended to take the initiative in a vigorous stride into the hotel.

When the concierge saw Olga his face contorted in revulsion, and he said to me, "Blonds are not permitted to enter the hotel except in the role of a servant."

I was caught by surprise, but Olga said immediately, "I am nurse." She reached into one of the capacious pockets of her coat and produced a small purse, which in turn yielded a document encased in glassine. "Is license." She showed this to the concierge, who waved it away in disgusted assent. Yet Olga found it needful to go further. "Will give enema," said she. "He has tourist constipation." No doubt it could have been predicted that in Saint Sebastian the complaint suffered by visitors to other countries would be reversed.

No sooner had the elevator doors closed on us than Olga seized and opened my belt buckle and pulled my trousers to my ankles. I defended my drawers, but with two quick hands at the elastic in back, she was rapidly baring my fundament. The last-named was pressed against the rear wall of the car, and it could anyway not answer her needs, so soon she abandoned that phase of the assault and went again to my groin, this time with a combination of feint and brute power, and succeeded in exposing it just as we reached our destination, the fourth floor, and the door opened on Clive McCoy.

"I see it hasn't taken you any time at all to go bad in a permissive society," said he with a dirty smirk.

Olga pulled me off the elevator and in the hallway continued to try to undress me as though we were alone and behind a closed door. She was utterly devoid of shame. I suppose it was the presence of my alcoholic countryman that gave me the strength to hold my own against her for a few moments, and then, when the tide was turning back in her favor, to knock her out with a punch to the jaw that almost broke my knuckles.

McCoy had stayed in the hall to watch the ruckus, and when Olga was down he gave me a hand of applause. I pulled up and secured my clothing, and was immediately contrite: I knelt and examined my opponent for serious damage. I found none. She breathed regularly.

McCoy jeered. "Don't worry, a Blond has an iron jaw and a granite head. I should have known you were an SM man."

"Put a sock in it, McCoy, and give me some help. How can I keep this woman from molesting me without having her actually arrested or really hurting her?"

Wryly he shook his head. "How to get somebody to do something they hate and still have them love you. That's a Yank for you! But over here that kinda shit don't go. Want somebody off your back, you drop 'em."

"Come on, be serious. I've got a problem." Despite Olga's ruthless using of me for her own purposes, sexual and political, my basic sympathies were still weighted towards her cause.

"I'm telling you," said McCoy. "You don't have to put up with anything from a Blond. You can throw her out the window."

"I'm afraid I don't subscribe to the Sebastiani code, and I must say I am appalled to know that you do. Even though you've lived here for years, you still call yourself an American."

"Pigshit," McCoy growled. "Did you not ask my help?"

"I regret that," I said frostily. Olga made a sound. She was becoming conscious. I had to slug her again or flee. I really do hate to hit a girl, especially one with whom I have recently had intimate congress—though now that I think about it, would an utter stranger be more appropriate?

I fled. I ran down the hall and around the corner and into a veritable wall consisting of the large body of the man who listened to the recorded voice of Enrico Caruso while bathing. He was about to let himself into what I assumed to be his room.

"Per favore, signore," I pleaded, exhausting my store of ready Italian, "can you give me refuge? I'll explain this as soon as I can."

He performed a (given his figure) necessarily generous shrug and gestured, with a rolled-out palm, for me to proceed him into the room. Then he swept in behind me and closed the door before Olga had reached that section of the hall, though I could hear her running footfalls. With another similar gesture he indicated I should take a seat on the sofa, a decent-looking piece of furniture upholstered in flowered brocade. We were in a comfortable sitting room. My Mediterranean friend appeared to have a suite for himself. One of the several doors undoubtedly led to a bedroom, and another set, louvered, he now opened to reveal a neat little kitchenette of the type I once enjoyed in Manhattan (if you can say that about a combined roach resort and mouse spa in which the fridge was on permanent defrost whatever the adjustment and only half a burner worked on the quarter-sized stove).

The large man had been carrying, somewhere beneath my line of sight, which was focused first on his huge hairy face and now on his massive middle body, a string bag full of groceries. This he now placed in the little sink and began to empty. There were several elongated boxes of the size in which spaghetti was packed, a handful of greenery, a great wedge of cheese, and some other surely edible items.

Next he brought me a tumbler full of red wine, carrying in his other large hand a raffia-wrapped vessel of gallon capacity. With an amiable display of very white teeth, he pantomimed Bottom's Up, then went back to the kitchenette I could hardly see when he stood before it.

I thought I should wait a while before speaking, lest Olga be listening at doors, and therefore I drank my wine in silence. The big fellow refilled the glass occasionally without my asking, but his principal effort was applied to cooking spaghetti in a giant-sized pot and grinding, with mortar and pestle, enough garlic to scent the room, and then what from the bouquet I could identify as basil (having had, a few years previously, an affair with a married woman who would rather cook for me than go to bed: her husband was OK at sex but a slob when it came to cuisine, said she, "with this food revolution exploding all around us").

By the time my friend served up the *pesto genovese*, on a side table which became dining-sized by the elevation of two hinged panels, I was a bit pissed from having gulped the wine into a stomach lately agitated by my passionate encounter with Olga. He had given each of us a mound of greenflecked spaghetti that rose from tabletop to eye-level, and now, before I could so much as approach my portion with a weary hand, he had reduced his own by half, in the consuming of which he lowered his head, tucked the fork into the side of the heap, and shoveled violently while his lips produced a suction that a Hoover might have envied.

I finally wound a few strands onto my fork and ingested them: very tasty. I took another slug of red.

"I haven't been over here for long," I said, "but I've already been exposed to a number of Sebastiani phenomena, and thus far what I've learned seems to cancel itself out in every respect. The prince is in theory a tyrant from a much earlier epoch, but in practice he is apparently harmless. He does nothing but eat rich food. His sexual tastes are pederastic. None of his subjects can be in want, for they enjoy unlimited credit.

"Now the Blonds may be second-class citizens and condemned to the menial work, waiting on tables, pulling rickshaws, and so on, but according to the prince they also practice law and certain other professions that are more or less honorific elsewhere. Their women are obliged to have sexual relations with anyone who asks them, but the only Blond female with whom I am acquainted virtually raped *me*, so one might question how onerous they consider the obligation, for I was all but a stranger to her. And it should be noted that the Blonds are splendid physical specimens, tall and strong and comely, unlike any other oppressed people on record."

During my remarks the large man nodded frequently but con-

tinued to gorge on pesto, refilling his own plate and raising his
heavy eyebrows when he looked at mine, still loaded from the
first serving. To be polite I gobbled up a few lengths and washed
them down with another flood of wine, which I saw was, according to the label, a local estate-bottled vintage of something
called Valpolifella (*sic*) and could be characterized as being red
and wet.

I resumed. "The scholars of Saint Sebastian are lazy buffoons,
and the male writers are a pack of swine. Incidentally, the pornography is allegedly written only by Blond females, but I
haven't checked this out for myself, and I must say I wouldn't
place much credence in the unsupported word of any of the
scribblers I have met. On the other hand, again I can't see that
much actual harm is done by any of these gentry, for only a few
people read, and according to the official librarian, himself an
illiterate, what each reads is the same book, over and over again.

"The law-enforcement procedure is ridiculous. People are
punished harshly for rudeness, but on the other hand, anybody
can accuse anyone else of any crime and be believed by the
police."

My host raised a full tumbler of wine and poured it down his
throat with the sound of a flushing toilet. He smacked his lips
and rose to carry his empty plate to the spaghetti pot, which had
remained on the stove, looked within, and finding nothing left,
sighed massively and went to the wardrobe, where he removed
the jacket and vest of the black serge suit he wore, but retained
his white shirt and dark necktie. He put on a maroon silk dressing gown and tied its tasseled belt around his tremendous midsection. After politely bowing to me, he loosened his collar,
strapped across his eyes the black sleep-mask he took from a
pocket in the robe, and lay down upon the bed, which sagged
until its mattress-springs almost touched the floor.

Obviously it was time to terminate my exterior monologue. I
had got some profit from drawing up the oral bill of particulars
with respect to the country I found myself in. I had confirmed
my suspicion that Saint Sebastian was an unusually difficult
place about which to generalize. No doubt this was true of every
society: e.g., how to characterize a city shared at once by the
South Bronx junkie, the gilded tenant of Trump Tower, the cop

from Queens, and the Broadway headliner? But I had yet to see a significant relation between any two of the Sebastiani milieus, including the court and the Blonds, each of which would seem to have only a theoretical reality for the other. And I thought I could remember from my college reading of history that it is never the oppressed people which make a revolution, but rather the class between the rulers and those at the bottom: *viz.*, the very class which was not in evidence in any large numbers in Saint Sebastian . . . but then, human beings of any kind were in short supply, owing to the current contrast to the clamorous Manhattan throng amidst which I normally pursued my destiny. On my first day in the capital city I had seen, all told, not as many mortals as one would encounter in a midday walk from my old loft to Rothman's delicatessen.

Rothman's Deli! Never when it was accessible did I dream that one day in a far-off land a mental reference to it would move me to nostalgia. Given the difference in time, back home it would be morning now, and the customers would be coming in for their fresh bagels and bialys, milk-blue coffee in bone-white containers, and sweating prune Danish. The street criminals would have wiped the gore from their switchblades, put their Saturday Night Specials on safety, and slunk, or more likely swaggered, to their lairs for a well-earned rest. The tarts were in bed at last to sleep, and the derelicts had not yet risen from their doorways. Here and there a leashed dog would be enjoying his matutinal bowel movement; a few would even be doing it legally, below the curb. The vehicular traffic would not yet have begun to accelerate towards the homicidal mania of noon. Perhaps the odd cabdriver would suggest, with spasmodic gestures and abrupt sounds, the hysteria that would claim him absolutely later in the day, but seen so early the display might be taken for harmless, even charming verve. And at this hour the sidewalk pedestrian undoubtedly ran the least risk all day of being called "motherfucker" by another human being who was an utter stranger to him.

In short, I was astonished to discover that I missed New York, perhaps not to the degree that I was ready to sing that fatuous song rendered, at the behest of the Tourist Bureau, by show-biz celebs who love Gotham so ardently as to reside in California, but I did identify in myself a homesickness, if it could be so termed, for the quotidian life of Manhattan as opposed to what I had thus far encountered over here, where everything was so *foreign*. Could I have been turning into what, as a man of culture, I had, my adult life long, despised: *viz.*, the provincial xenophobe?

I pushed away the now cold pesto, went to the door, opened it a crack, and took the lie of the land. It would have been less kind to awaken the enormous man from his nap, I thought, than to leave quietly without tendering my thanks. I had decided to repair to the cable office, if I could elude Olga, and send a message to Rasmussen demanding that he withdraw me from this country where I could not be protected from its capricious nationals. . . . No, such a negative appeal would never succeed with a sadistic superior. I had it: I would rather employ some such strategy as more than one grim wit had suggested "we" should have done in Vietnam: i.e., simply declare victory and leave. I would assure Rasmussen I had seen enough to write an authoritative report on Saint Sebastian, and suggest what American policy should be towards the little principality: neglect, and rather more indifferent than benign.

7

"AH," SAID THE CONCIERGE as I passed through the lobby, "I do hope you are now eliminating your stools painlessly, my dear sir, and will not again require the services of your Blond colonic irrigationist."

"By the way," I replied, "did you see her leave?"

"I have not," said he. "But I'm sure she has done so if she's not with you. She would certainly know the consequences if found in the hotel without authorization."

"Would you mind telling me what those consequences would be?"

He frowned and then said, "I really haven't the slightest idea. It's the sort of thing one says."

"Much of Sebastiani existence consists in such statements, does it not? You people speak on the extravagant side, but so far as I can see, the reality is much tamer."

He looked crestfallen. I hastened to say, "I'm not criticizing, mind you! It's certainly preferable to a state of affairs in which violence is commonplace, as it is where I come from, where furthermore it's fashionable in certain milieus to pretend that at any given time the situation is all that it should be." Already I was less homesick. "I once lived in an apartment building every tenant of which was robbed at gunpoint, in the lobby, by a band of neighborhood thugs who were contestants in an all-city mugging competition. When our hooligans lost to the Kip's Bay team, the victims were indignant and gave the criminals a consolation party."

"Well, then," he said bitterly, "isn't everything always more colorful in New York?"

I had perhaps gone too far and hurt his feelings. "I wonder whether you get my meaning?" I asked. "I'm flattering you, by contrast."

His greasy smile instantly reappeared. "I understand perfectly. Now would you like a boy?"

"No, thank you, and kindly never ask me that question again. What you might do however is tell me why I see so few people wherever I go in Saint Sebastian? And most of those people I do encounter are working at some kind of job that serves the public. But no public is in evidence." I specified the open-air markets.

He thought for a moment, the tip of a finger at his pursed lips. "I have it! Those who sell fruit buy pets from the bird people, who in turn purchase cheese, and so on." He wore a self-congratulatory expression, which I did not wish to darken by expressing dubiety.

I left the hotel. Unless Olga was still looking for me in the hallways upstairs, she had made an exit unobserved by the concierge and might attempt to waylay me in the street. I hugged the walls of the building on the short route to the cable office and saw neither her nor anyone else.

The bespectacled clerk was at the counter when I entered the office.

I obtained a cable form from him, as well as the stub of a pencil, unpleasantly marked as if by gnawing. The feckless Rasmussen had not provided me with a code in which to communicate with him. True, what I had to say was hardly the information that men would kill to get, but to be plainspoken in this context would seem unprofessional and might, if discovered, be used by the Firm's congressional critics as a pretext for appropriation-cutting.

The message I came up with was crafted from bygone slang of the 1930's and '40's, which would be instantly intelligible to any Yank however young, owing to nostalgia-film programs, but would surely be nonsensical language to one who had learned his English abroad.

SCREWBALLS VS. GOOFS. WOULD
NIX MOOLAH FOR ALL. UNCLE

DUDLEY FEELS LIKE SAP, WANTS
TO TAKE POWDER.

I handed the form to the clerk. "Please send this literally, letter by letter. Don't worry if it doesn't seem to say anything understandable to you, even if you think you're fluent in English."

He took it and held it high, in two hands, for a perusal. When he was done he winced and shook his head. "I'd think the Firm might have come up with a better code than this."

"What do you know about it?" I asked hotly. "That's impenetrable, if I do say so myself."

"I'm afraid no one else would," said he. "It's pathetically pellucid. You dismiss them all as eccentrics and wouldn't give money to any of them. You feel like a fool and want to go home."

I scowled at him. "Are you another ex-GI who was stranded here when the war ended?"

"I'm too young for that. But I have seen many of your motion pictures, including the excellent Boston Blackie films starring Chester Morris. Also those of Mary Beth Hughes, Jane Frazee, Vera Hruba Ralston—"

"Just a moment," I said, narrowing my eyes. "What do you take me for? You're making up those names. I'm a native American filmgoer, yet I've never heard of these people."

"So much the worse for you," said the clerk. "May I suggest you visit one of our cinemas during your stay in Saint Sebastian and acquire an education in your own movies. We have the very latest. Showing at the moment is the latest in the series about Rosie the Riveter. There's a new Western starring Johnny Mack Brown, and others with Charles Starrett, Bob Steele . . ."

These names being meaningless to me (I who, along with everyone else of a certain culture in New York, regard myself as a scholar of the films of Bogie, Bette, Coop, Hitch, *et al.*), I asked, "Are you speaking in some kind of code?"

He sighed. "What can I say if the leading artists of your own country are unknown to you, except that frankly I am shocked. Those names are household words in Saint Sebastian, I assure you. Every child can recite them and more."

"But *are* there any children in this country?" I asked resentfully. "I've seen hardly any."

"Of course you haven't," said the clerk. "They're at the cinema all day."

I concluded that he was pulling my leg for certain. "And these moviehouses are everywhere, though I have yet to see a marquee?"

"Indeed they are," said he. "And they have no marquees. Public advertising of any kind, beyond the simple descriptive legend on a shop window, is illegal in Saint Sebastian. Everybody knows where the motion-picture houses are. There's one close by wherever you live, generally in the same street, and weekly schedules are sent to every household and of course posted in the outer lobbies of the cinemas." He smiled. "Oh yes, the movie theaters are in buildings which were formerly schools and churches."

"Aha." I was still far from sure he was not jesting. "That's why one sees so few people on the streets? They're all at the movies?"

"Except for those of us who are not so fortunate," said he, making a lantern jaw of self-pity. "I can't go until after business hours."

I leaned on the counter. "You're telling me that most of the population of this country, adults and children, spend most of their days at the movies?"

"Sure Mike!" he said with energy. "That's where all the bozos are, and the tomatoes and the small fry too. I don't mean maybe."

However reluctantly, I began to believe him. It was at any rate established that he was conversant in jargon that could have fooled me. I was embarrassed, and briefly considered, with a purpose to regain some ground, performing my Cagney imitation, but soon decided that that was all too routine even amongst native Americans who did not have the exotic cinematic lore at his command. I must be more ingenious to hold my own with this fellow. I decided I had no choice but to invent, to cut from the whole cloth, an actor who never existed, and to imitate him for the cable clerk.

"Tell me who this is." I screwed my mouth up, made one

eyelid sufficiently heavy to lower itself halfway, and spoke in a droning tone: "If you mugs think you can make a monkey outa me you got rocks inna head."

The clerk narrowed his eyes. "Just a minute. . . . That's not Barton MacLane? No, let me . . . Jack LaRue? No . . . Charles Bickford?"

"You'll be guessing all night," I told him triumphantly. "You see, I—"

"No, no, give me another chance! Did I hear a little bit of accent? Eduardo Ciannelli?"

"Believe me, you should give up," I said quickly. "It's an actor who made only a couple of low-budget pictures by comparison with which a Republic horse-opera was *Aïda*. Uh, his name was, uh, Ben Spinoza."

"Latin type?"

"You could say so."

The clerk snapped his fingers. "Yes, of course! He's playing in a film that just opened at the Linden Street cinema: *Gats 'n' Gals.*" He pouted. "I haven't been able to get there yet because of this damned job of mine."

I started to say, "That's imposs—" but decided it was really beneath me to keep this up. Instead I said coolly, "Please send this cable as soon as possible."

"To the Firm?"

I had yet to mention to whom it would be sent. Again I wondered whether this know-it-all was more than he seemed, but I decided against asking him, for whether or not he was, he would be certain to pretend to be—if that syntax will hold. Perhaps he had got that modus operandi from those old American movies, in which the heroes are invariably yea-sayers whose strides are jaunty, whose fedoras are cocked over one eye, and whose initially saucy girlfriends eventually go soft ("Aw, you big lug," etc.). But then I was thinking of the mainstream pictures: God knows what went on in the obscure B flicks so popular in Saint Sebastian.

"Yes, the Firm, Washington, DC."

"Isn't it rather Langley, VA?"

Again I was briefly suspicious, but on reflection I decided that McCoy had probably used the same channel of communication

with the home office, a shockingly primitive one for an intelligence agency of a major world power, but no doubt that was
just the point: the enemy would never look for such simplicity,
which made impotent their computerized decoders. Anyway, it
was a theory.

I sighed and told him to proceed. "Say, while I'm here: what's
your position on the Blonds?"

"Aha. Well, personally I am incapable of bigotry. I think a
fairhaired individual is quite as good as anybody else. I wouldn't
want one for a friend, maybe, but—"

"Just a moment. You wouldn't?"

"A man has a right, has he not, to make the pals he chooses? I
don't have the slightest interest in the culture of the Blonds.
Why should I be forced to have an intimate who plays chess, a
game I have never been able to understand; eats vegetables,
which I loathe; and never has a cold, whereas the one I feel
coming on at the moment will continue for months."

"Those are typical Blond tastes and traits?"

He grimaced. "They really are a pack of baboons. I say that
without prejudice, of course. They are welcome to any advantages they can wrest from decent people."

"Do they have much of a resistance movement?"

He laughed and used another locution that must have derived
from an old Hollywood production on a rube theme. "Gee whil-
likers, I wouldn't see any reason why. They're the happiest
bunch you'll ever see, and why not. They don't do any work."

"They lie around and play the banjo?"

He frowned. "No. They play things like the cello and bassoon. Really dreary stuff. They're very boring people and much
too lazy to want to change a social arrangement that suits them
more than it does the rest of us." He looked at the cable form.
"If you're going to leave us soon, you should make the most of
your remaining time here."

"What would you suggest?"

He seized the pencil stub I had put back on the counter and
put its end in his mouth, which explained the toothmarks on it.
"Well, the Lido, if you like to swim. Longchamp, if you bet on
the ponies. The Prater can be fun if you enjoy carousels. A
cruise through the canals is a pleasant way to spend the after-

noon. Picnicking in the Bois can be delightful, as is motoring to the nearby countryside to see the Summer Palace, the Greek amphitheater, or the great mosque erected during the Turkish Occupation, which is now the Museum of Quilts. Or may I suggest a visit to the Bourse. In the third cellar below the trading floor one can find Roman baths, their reservoirs and conduits still in working condition, their mosaics exquisite."

I said, with obvious irony, "Saint Sebastian is then a microcosm of Europe? Surely you have as well your own Versailles, Brandenburg Gate, and Erechtheum with a Caryatid Porch?"

He shrugged in satisfaction. "We are peculiarly blessed, I must admit. For that reason we Sebastianers are not great travelers."

"Also, on leaving the country one's overdraft and credit balance must be paid, no?"

"In fact that would be against the law."

"To leave the country?"

He shook his head. "No, no: to discharge one's debts *in toto.*"

"Can you be serious?"

The clerk spoke gravely. "It would be a profession of lack of faith in one's countrymen. No crime could be more heinous. Every Sebastianer has a God-given right to be owed money by others. Only in this way does he establish the moral pretext for running up his own large debts. Else our economy would collapse."

The dismal science has never been my strong suit. Whenever I've tried to understand how, in the same world, filled with the same people, buying and selling the same things, there can be regular periods of great prosperity, followed immediately by recessions, my brain spins on its axis (this would make sense only if the good times resulted from the purchase of Earth goods by visitors from Mars, who however on the next occasion took their business to Jupiter).

"If you say so," was my response. "But tell me: who makes these policies and/or laws? Not the prince?"

"Golly all get out," said the clerk, in an as usual without-warning resort to vintage-film idiom, "I think they must come down from the old days, most of them, but there is a legislative body that probably does something, though don't ask me what.

Oh, and there are some ministers. If you're interested in that sort of thing, you should stop at Government Square, just around the corner."

"All right, I shall." Ordinarily I'd walk a mile to elude the so-called social studies or those who practice them, but until officially relieved I was on a fact-finding mission—and I had no strong interest in seeing the derivative sights aforementioned (which suggested too strongly for me those scale models of the Taj Mahal, the Sphinx, the Eiffel Tower, and so on, constructed to lure tourists to otherwise colorless American backwaters). "Just tell me two more things. If the churches have been transformed into movie houses, what's become of the clergy? Yesterday I saw a man in priest's garb, riding a bicycle."

"They're now projectionists," he said enthusiastically.

"I suppose those at the top of the hierarchy, the bishops and so on, are film critics." I was joking only by half.

"Certainly not. That's illegal in Saint Sebastian! Anyone saying more than that he either liked or disliked a movie would be arrested and flogged."

I raised my brow. Now and again the ways of this country were not altogether foolish. "My last question concerns the language I heard some people speaking. In fact they were Blonds. What might that be?"

"It's some slang used only by Blonds. We call it Sebastard."

"It has ancient origins?"

"Naw," sneered the clerk. "They invented it so we wouldn't understand them when they spoke to one another in front of us. But who would want to know what a Blond was saying anyway?"

He gave me directions as to how to reach Government Square, and I left the cable office. The square proved to be that in which the concierge of my hotel had been pilloried, which I had seen when McCoy drove me back from the palace. The punitive device had another occupant today: shockingly, a boy who looked to be no more than nine or ten.

I stopped and spoke in commiseration. "You poor lad. What could you have done to deserve that?"

"Played hooky," said he in his voice of high pitch. "But I'm sick of Ken Maynard movies, and anyway I didn't want to sit in school all day in this nice weather. I wanted to go down to the river and mess around, fish or something." He had a saddle of freckles across his nose.

"I used to catch tadpoles when I was your age. I have degenerated since. You want me to let you out of this thing?" The gates of the pillory were secured with loose bolts that looked as if easy to dislodge.

He shook his head, on which the hair was cut high above the ears. "I could get out any time I want, these holes are so big." Wiggling his hands and feet, he demonstrated that fact for me. "But they'd just catch me again, and next time the punishment would be worse. Know what it is? You have to eat *pesto!*" He made a horrible face.

I continued across the square to what in New York would have been a multiple dwellingplace of modest size. With its half-dozen stories, it was the largest building hereabout. I could see some sort of placard on its front doors. If government was to be found on the square, this seemed most likely to be where.

When I reached the sign, which was crudely made of cardboard and inscribed in felt-penned capitals, I read:

> W.C.—3RD FLOOR FRONT
> CHAMBER OF LEGISLATORS—3RD FL. FRONT
> MINISTRIES—ATTIC
> COURT OF JUSTICE—CELLAR

Nearby, on the wall of the building, was a proper brass sign which discreetly proclaimed the presence, in the same edifice, of Dr. C. Moritz, Podiatrist; Mellenkamp & Co., Novelties; The Brockden School of Ventriloquism; and the House of Costumes.

Of the governmental tenants, the Court was most quickly reached from the ground floor. The one-car elevator at the rear of the little lobby seemed indifferent to my button-pushing, and therefore I went beyond it to a staircase and descended to a dank basement corridor, which was dimly lighted by a naked bulb of small wattage that hung from the ceiling on a badly frayed wire. I groped my way along the hallway, trudging here and there through pools of standing water and more than once hearing scurryings that could have come only from rodents of a fairly substantial size.

I had begun to assume I was in the wrong cellar for the Court, or else the handwritten sign outside had been the work of a practical joker with unfathomable motives, and was about to turn back when a door opened in the crepuscularity just beyond me, and an ancient man, with a parchment skull around which were a few unruly wisps of white hair, shuffled forth. His judicial robes were tattered.

I was amazed that he could see me, given his rheumy eyes and the feeble available light. "*Now* you come," he said peevishly. "Now, when I've got to go piss. Well, you'll just have to wait while I go to the toilet, which means climbing the stairs, for the lift is once again out of order, and then at my age you have to stand there till the prostate gland decides what to do, holding that shriveled wick that's no earthly good for any other function."

"I was simply going to observe the court at work," I said. "Please don't feel any need to hurry on my account. I'll just go in and sit down. Is anyone else there?"

"Certainly not," said he. "We dispense swift justice here and don't make people wait around."

"Then I'll come upstairs with you and look in on the other branches of government while you're in the toilet."

He made a gesture of indifference. Going up the stairs at his side required more patience than I had anticipated, so slow and tottering was his climb, but when I offered him a hand or arm, his rejection, with a horny elbow, smote my ribs that were still sore from the calipers of Olga's steel thighs.

To make some use of this time I asked him about the court: was it civil or criminal?

He grunted disagreeably. "What a dumb question. Criminals have no place in a court! They are dealt with by the police."

"But is it not possible that the police might sometime punish the wrong man?"

"It's also possible that a person might be struck by lightning or have some other kind of ill fortune, contract a mortal illness, and so on, but that sort of thing is not an occasion for a resort to a court of justice."

"Then what does your court deal with? Civil lawsuits?"

By now we had climbed perhaps four steps, each of which the

old jurist gained in a most precarious way, teetering interminably on the metal binding at the edge of the tread and arresting a backwards fall with a desperate grasp of the rail, applied only at the last moment it could have been effective. After witnessing this procedure repeatedly I at last took my heart from my mouth: he was actually in no danger of falling.

"I don't know what that term means," said he. "What I adjudicate are private differences between individuals. For example, a man acquires a new possession, say a pocketknife, and proudly shows it to a friend. The friend disparages it, so the owner of the knife hauls him into court on a charge of envy. The defendant, on the other hand, tries to prove that his criticism of the knife had to do only with objective standards of quality: the workmanship is shoddy by comparison with other knives sold for the same amount of money."

"Suppose you decided in favor of the plaintiff in this example?"

"If the decision went against the defendant, he would be obliged, for a certain length of time, to wear a placard on his back announcing to the world that he was an envious person."

"The same kind of thing, then, that the person arrested for rudeness must undergo."

"Not at all. Rudeness is a crime against the state," said the old judge. "Envy is a personal matter. An envious man is not put into the pillory."

I couldn't see the distinction. Therefore I asked him another question. "Do you have insurance companies in Saint Sebastian?"

"No," said he. "It is against the law to wager on someone else's misfortune."

"Then what happens to the man on whose sidewalk a pedestrian slips and breaks his collarbone and subsequently sues the property owner: a routine occurrence in the States—?" Something like that happened to a retired postman who lived next door to my uncle's sister-in-law's second cousin's friend: the uninsured ex-mailman was the defendant; the victim claimed he had dislocated his spine; I never learned of the outcome.

"Yes," said the old man, toiling up the third-to-last step to the ground floor. "The victim would surely be sued by the property owner."

"Can I have heard you correctly? The *victim* would be sued? Wouldn't he be doing the suing?"

His glare suggested such annoyance that I was concerned lest he become distracted and lose his tenuous grasp of the railing and plunge backwards down the stairs. "Are you trying to bait me?"

"Forgive me, sir. I'm honestly trying to understand the workings of your law, so different from ours. In America, and I think many other places, the injured party is the plaintiff."

"And so with us," the old man told me, his anger subsiding, or rather turning into what would seem contempt. "In the episode you have projected, the property owner would have been humiliated by someone's having been injured on his sidewalk. It would only be right that he sued the fellow who was responsible, *viz.*, he whose back was injured."

"But what of the victim? First he hurt his spine and is perhaps permanently disabled, and then he is sued. Is that justice?"

The judge's brow descended. "Yes," said he. "The person you speak of sounds as if he might definitely be the kind of unfortunate whose specialty is making the people around him totally miserable. One more such outrage might well prove him to be the kind of troublemaker we would want to eliminate from our society."

I repeated, "Eliminate?" The problem with ingenious systems of justice is that they inevitably have their ugly aspect.

"It's often the only answer," said he. We had at last reached the lobby, where he stood sourly contemplating the door of the out-of-service elevator. "And Gezieferland, believe it or not, dotes on such people: they're always after us to send them more losers. Sometimes they even threaten to go to war. The idea there is that we'd beat them savagely and thus their entire population would again suffer the kind of loss they live for."

As I remembered from Olga's remarks, Gezieferland was another little country, north of Saint Sebastian. "Are you saying that you exile these so-called losers to your northern neighbor?"

He nodded, and proceeded to refer to the southern neighbor mentioned by Olga. "Swatina takes off our hands anyone who makes a public menace of himself: say, walks along the street speaking violently to an invisible companion or exposes a part of himself that might disgust others, such as a back covered with pimples or an enormous belly. There are scoundrels, male and female, who will commit this crime at the beach and play portable phonographs and eat gluttonously while dripping with sweat. Lying to the south of us, Swatina has a warmer climate than we and consequently a longer beach season. Indeed, the visitor to that wretched country sees nothing but striped umbrellas and hideous naked bodies."

My physical impatience was making me uncomfortable. I could not endure creeping up two more floors in his company. Therefore, with thanks to him for helping me to a new understanding of Saint Sebastian, I hastened to a narrow flight of upward-leading stairs and climbed to what Americans would have called the second floor, but which, in the European style, was the first: of this I was reminded by the painted *1* on the wall of the landing. This meant that the old judge would have an even longer climb to the toilet than I had first supposed.

It seemed nonsensical that the governmental agencies would be put on the upper floors when a costume business, a school of ventriloquism, and the novelties of Mellenkamp occupied the more accessible offices. I thought that on the route upstairs I might just stop off at one or more of these establishments and talk with the people who worked there, but on each landing there was a locked door between the stairway and the business floor, as well as a sign forbidding entry and warning the would-be trespasser that attack dogs patrolled the premises at all hours.

At the third (actually the fourth) floor, the door to the landing stood open. To shut it would have been preposterous: it consisted of an empty frame from which the panels had been removed. I went along the corridor, passing the toilets (which had no doors whatever and therefore no designation as to the sex of their users). I arrived at a door marked CHAMBER OF LEGISLATORS. I opened it and stepped inside.

What I saw was a largish room filled with canvas cots of the folding, Army type, each of which contained the recumbent form of a markedly shabby man. The odor of the place was very unpleasant. As I stood there, surveying the place, I felt a hand plucking at my trousers in the area of the knee. It was the man on the nearest bunk.

"Hey, buddy," said he, continuing to yank at me, "gimme some dope." He seemed not much older than I, but he was in miserable physical condition, and he obviously had not washed his face in time out of mind: the dirt was ingrained.

"I don't have any," I said, and pulled away from his grasp.

"How about a drink?" When I shook my head, he asked, "Then have you got a cigarette at least?"

"Sorry, I don't smoke."

"Then what *have* you got for your legislator?" he asked. "It better be good, if you want me to scratch *your* back."

"I'm a visitor, a foreigner. Are you really a legislator?"

"If you're not one of my constituents, go fuck yourself," said he, letting his head fall back on the unspeakably filthy pillow.

As it happened I was not offended, but I *was* curious. "You have no interest in maintaining friendly relations with other countries?"

He replied without bothering to raise his head. "I might or might not have, according to my needs at the moment, but being nice to you would have nothing to do with the matter in any event."

"You mean because I come from a country that has a long record of rewarding those who insult it?"

"I don't know or care which country you belong to," said the recumbent legislator. "I'm speaking universally. And that has exhausted me." He closed his eyes and almost immediately began to snore, denying me the opportunity to ask him a final question.

Therefore I put it to the man in the next bunk, a person quite as filthy as the first and as disagreeable, who sneered at me and said, "Keep going. I heard what you said to Filtschmidt."

"I merely wanted to ask why you have no fear of being arrested for rudeness."

"Because we're legislators, you cretin. Why should we create a law to which we ourselves are subject?"

By now these people had succeeded in irking me. "According to my information," I said with a sneer of my own, "you have no power whatever."

He covered his eyes and wept, the tears running abundantly from beneath his hands to drip on the dirty, caseless pillow, as if he were squeezing water from a concealed sponge. When at last he spoke, he did so through sobs.

"I have never been addressed so cruelly." He wept some more. "Oh, how could you?"

I had enough. "Stop that sniveling, you ninny. You reserve the right to be nasty to others, but you can't take your own medicine."

"But that's the only way of doing it!" he howled. "You're punishing me for being human, and it isn't fair!"

"If you were brighter," said I, "you would understand that my punishing you is only human, as well, and it's really not fair of you to call me unfair."

At least he stopped crying. Now he simply looked baffled. I decided that further traffic with the legislators would not be fruitful, and I left the smelly dormitory, found the stairway again, and climbed until I reached the attic. Judging from the many steps I encountered, the attic was three or four stories above the legislators' chamber, but I found no indication en route that I was passing other floors and saw no means of access to them if indeed they were in place.

At the top of the stairway was a door of which the top panel was frosted glass. Scotch-taped to my side was a typewritten notice, which read:

BEYOND THIS DOOR ARE THE ROYAL MINISTRIES. ALL PERSONS ARE HEREBY WARNED THAT ANY VISITOR MAY BE ASSAULTED AT ANY TIME AT THE WHIM OF THE MINISTERS, WHO ARE NOTHING IF NOT WILLFUL.

This news was not reassuring, but I had expended too much energy to turn back now. I opened the door and walked down a brightly lighted corridor of which the walls were painted a cheery apple-green. The hallway was carpeted in a slightly darker version of the same color. These premises were the most attractive I had yet found in the building, and but for the sign outside I would have assumed I had succeeded in penetrating not a governmental office but rather one of the business floors I had elsewhere been denied admittance to.

The first door on my right, made of solid wood and painted in a jolly French blue, was labeled: MINISTRY OF IRONY. I decided to go along the hall to its termination and see what the other ministries were called, before choosing which to enter first. The next, on the left, with a door of bright orange, was the Ministry of Disaffection. Then came, on the right, the Ministry of Clams. On the left again, the Ministry of Allergies. The doors to the foregoing were painted, respectively, blue-green and brick red. Finally, at the end of the hall, neither right nor left, but facing the visitor, was a zebra-striped black-and-white door labeled: MINISTRY OF HOAXES.

I confess I could not resist applying first at the last-named. I was rewarded by the sight of a very comely redhaired young woman, who sat at a receptionist's desk in an anteroom furnished with deep chairs and an outsized sofa. These pieces were upholstered in salt-'n'-pepper nubby tweeds. Here and there on the walls were hung *trompe-l'oeil* still lifes which at any distance at all you could have sworn were real: the dead pheasant, next to the game bag and fowling piece, seemed really to be decaying. "How do you do," I said to the receptionist. "I'm a visitor to your country. I wonder whether you'd be willing to tell me something about this ministry? Am I correct in assuming that its work is rather like that of what in America we call the police bunco squad? Do you deal with the kind of misrepresentation by which honest citizens are bilked?"

She smiled at me. "We don't *police* hoaxes, we practice them. For example, we spend the money allocated to us for one purpose on something else entirely. We pretend to be a vast bureau with hundreds of employees, but in reality there's just me and Albert."

"Albert's the minister?"

"No, he's the bouncer." And then, no doubt owing to my puzzled expression, she explained. "Some people—though by no means all—are resentful when they discover they've been tricked. If they bring their complaints here, Albert is the man who deals with them."

"I see." More brutality. "Well, thank you for—" I realized that I was beginning to smell a nauseating odor. . . . Of course, that pheasant in the fool-the-eye painting *was* real and decaying!

What an unpleasant place the Ministry of Hoaxes had proved to be. However, male pride with respect to the redheaded receptionist would not let me leave on a sinking note. I took a conspicuously deep breath and winked at the picture.

"By George, that's so clever you'd swear it was phony."

"It is," said the young woman. "Step closer."

I obeyed her and found, after all, only a painted bird. "It's so believable," I confessed, "that I was sure I could smell it."

"You could," she said in what I was finding an insufferable smugness. "The odor is piped in through a vent."

"What's the purpose of such a thing?"

She extended a glistening underlip. "Look, duping people is our job. If you have a complaint, talk to Albert." Before I could discourage her, she pressed a bell push mounted at the edge of her desk, and immediately a door opened behind her and a man came out of the inner office.

But to my relief I saw he was a small, frail-looking person, a good ten to fifteen years older than I. He wore a genial smile. I recognized that the hoax here was that one would be threatened with "the bouncer," and then harmless Albert would appear and discuss your problem in a reasonable, even sympathetic way, utterly unlike any governmental employee I had ever met back home, beginning with the mailman, who, since my failure to reward him lavishly enough one Xmas, had habitually left my packages in the entryway corner where winos urinated.

"How do you do, sir?" Albert greeted me. "Do you have a complaint?"

"Perhaps I do, at that," I replied. "Doesn't government, any government, practice enough hoaxing in the ordinary course of its activity as to make pointless a special ministry for the purpose?"

His smile became even warmer. "But don't you see how useful it is to have one government agency which candidly states, boasts, that its function is solely to gull the citizen. We practice pure hoaxing for hoaxing's sake, with no ulterior motive. We don't pretend to deal with national highways, for example, or the exchequer, agriculture, or whatnot, and then instead play cards, drink beer, and read thrillers the day long, as they do in Gezieferland. No, we do our job straightforwardly and we're

proud of it. You have any contact with us, and you'll be bamboo-
zled or know the reason why. Speak to any Sebastianer and you
will find that we are that ministry most trusted by the public."

As with so many of the phenomena I had encountered in this
country, what had seemed utterly preposterous at the outset had
a milligram or two of reason in it when more closely examined,
but rarely if ever enough to bring it even into the neighborhood
of the desirable.

"Very well," I said, "you have explained it."

His smile grew cooler. "But you're not yet convinced, are
you?"

"Oh, I wouldn't say that—" At this point Albert gave me a
powerful one-two punch to the midsection. As I bent to favor
the pain my legs gave way, and I crumpled to the carpet. I did
not genuinely pass out, but, appropriately enough for this office,
I simulated unconsciousness so that he would not give me a taste
of his heavy shoes, which in close-up looked as though they
might be capped with metal.

After he returned to the inner room, I laboriously regained
my footing and limped to the exit door.

"Thank you for calling at the Ministry," the redhead said
behind me. "We're always glad to help."

I decided to pass up both the ministry that dealt with irony
and that whose business was disaffection, for I believed, projecting from my experience at Hoaxes, that I could imagine more or
less what they were up to. But I must say I was curious about
the ministries of, respectively, Clams and Allergies, if for no
other reason than their incongruity with each other and, indeed,
everything else.

The office was like that which I had only just left, but this
time the receptionist was a young man with a handlebar mustache.

"Good afternoon," said he. "May I help you?"

After identifying myself, I asked him what was the precise
function of his ministry. "Clam fishing is obviously one of the
important pursuits in your country. I wasn't even aware that
you had access to any ocean and was amazed at the variety of
offerings at the open-air seafood market."

"We have no coastline," said he. "Our only water is the river, which of course provides no clams. Trout, eels, gudgeon, and some other freshwater fish are caught in the river by individuals for their own private use and are not sold to the public. That display in the market is artificial: the seafood is made of plastic."

After a moment I nodded. "Uh-huh, that would explain the absence of any odor. . . . OK, then: you have no clams in Saint Sebastian."

"That's correct," said he. "Which is why we have the ministry."

"I confess I haven't the beginning of an understanding."

"Aha," he said, flicking the left tip of his mustache, as if dislodging a fly. "Nothing could be simpler or more effective as an instrument of government than a ministry of clams. It has but one function: it is the bureau of last resort, to which all insoluble problems are sent, to which all unanswerable complaints are forwarded. If nothing can be done about something, for example a plague of locusts at a time when there is an inexplicable absence of the kinds of birds that eat large insects and atmospheric conditions forbid the use of insecticides. If the crops are destroyed the farmers can curse fate, but for their emotional well-being they really need some human agency to blame. The Ministry of Clams serves such a purpose. Accepting denunciations is our job. Look here."

He rose from the desk and opened the door to the inner office. I came to the threshold and looked in. The sizable room I saw was filled from wall to wall with metal filing cabinets, with just enough space between their ranks for the drawers to be opened.

"Those cabinets," said the mustachioed receptionist, "contain the complaints received for the past thirty days. On the first of next month they will be emptied for the reception of a new consignment."

"Your efficiency is breathtaking," I said. "How do you manage to deal with such a volume of work in only a month?"

"By doing nothing whatever about it but filing the papers!" he cried. "Is that not beautiful?"

"And the complainants are satisfied?"

He frowned. "No, one cannot make such a statement, for human beings, whatever their situation, are *never* satisfied. Trying to make them so is a waste of effort, perhaps even a mockery of the human condition. Have you ever known any social problem that was truly solved?"

"Let me think. Of course, the child labor that was the disgrace of the early Industrial Revolution. Humane laws did away with it."

"And the result was a child population consisting of illiterate dope addicts supported by government handouts."

"Oh, come on. You exaggerate."

He nodded soberly. "You're right. Those who became criminals were very prosperous."

"Living in New York has made me a monster of cynicism," I said, "but surely you go too far."

"I'm speaking not of your country," said the young man, "but rather of mine, as it was back in the Dark Ages, before the Enlightenment, which brought among other things the Ministry of Clams."

"Am I right in suspecting that your so-called Enlightenment was not all that far in the past?"

"Indeed you are," said he. "For some reason, it is the fashion to call that period the Sixties, though in fact virtually all the important reforms happened rather in the Seventies."

"And what role does the prince play in all of this?"

"None whatever," said the young man. "I doubt that he even knows of the existence of our ministry."

"Remarkable!" I exclaimed. "Do you receive many complaints with reference to him?"

"Never. It's impossible to complain of the prince. He's beyond it all, like the flag."

I told him I had never yet seen the flag of Saint Sebastian.

"No, and you probably never will. I have never seen it though I'm native born and work for the government. I believe it's kept in some top-secret place along with the Constitution. I've never heard who has access to them. Maybe they don't even exist!"

"Like the poetry of which your leading critic writes," I suggested.

"Isn't that fun?" he asked, smiling with a set of horsey front teeth.

"Just two more questions, if you will. Why do you use the word 'clams'?"

"To suggest the ministry's true function in its name would strike a negative note. We could have called it something else, I suppose: the 'Ministry of Aubergines,' for example, but that sounds too frivolous. The 'Ministry of Rust,' on the other hand, has an ugly sound. No, we think 'Clams' strikes the right note. There's the pleasant connotation 'happy as a clam.' And any suggestion that encourages the populace to be discreet and not circulate gossip is welcome: I refer of course to 'clamming up.' Fortunately, most Sebastianers are innocent of your World War Two GI term for the female organ, unless like me they have been instructed by Mr. McCoy: the 'bearded clam.' "

Embarrassed, I said hastily, "Yes, he's a scholar in the vocabulary of vintage obscenity. In fact, at the moment he's putting together a comprehensive lexicon of indecent terms for the press of one of our leading universities. . . . My other question pertains to your artificial fish market. Why do you have such a thing?"

"Because it is colorful," said he. "Because fish markets are traditional, and why should we be denied one simply because we are far from any coast and wish to be self-sufficient and eat only those foods we find or grow in our own land? But mostly so that we might have fishwives."

"Fishwives?"

"Who can scream more loudly or demonstrate a more authoritative use of invective? Having such a spectacle available at all times is a healthy thing for a society."

I thanked the young man for his eloquent presentation. "Could you give me some idea of the function of the Ministry of Allergies? I'm not sure I have enough time for a visit there."

He grimaced. "I'd stay away if I were you. It's an unpleasant place. I wouldn't work there on a bet, though I realize it's necessary, for even in salubrious Saint Sebastian some people fall ill, some even die, though of course everything concerning death is kept under the hat."

"Could you explain?"

"If a certain person doesn't show up for several days, without having left some message as to his whereabouts, the assumption is he's dead."

"His near and dear, however, surely know?"

"Certainly not," said the young man with the mustache, "unless they, or someone else for that matter, has been present at his death, which after all could happen from a bolt of lightning or by falling off a mountain. But you can be sure that, if so, they would keep mum about it, for nothing is more severely punished than to speak of such a matter."

"But most deaths result from illness, I'm sure, and not accidents."

"*Allergies,*" said he, "which are, all of them, at bottom but one: an allergy to living."

"All matters pertaining to illness are the business of the Ministry of Allergies?"

"Yes."

"And death as well?"

He shook his head. "No. Death has its own department: the Ministry of Irony."

As usual I was taken by surprise. In this case I had too easily assumed that at Irony the bureaucrats sat around exchanging cynical wisecracks.

My final question was as to the function of the Ministry of Disaffection.

The young man piously rolled his eyes at the ceiling. "You must not pass it up."

"Really? Well, then, I'll stop by." I thanked him and left.

I went along the hallway to the orange door. Just as I was about to touch the knob, it receded, and a thin, sour-looking woman of about fifty years of age appeared in the narrow opening between the door and frame and said, with a kind of melancholy peevishness, "We don't want any."

"I'm not a salesman, madame. I'm a visitor from abroad."

"But we don't *want* a visitor," said she. "What good would you do us?"

This was a challenge. "I neglected to mention that I'm an American. My country is thinking of giving money to yours."

"Money wouldn't do us any good," she said, shaking her head of iron-gray hair tightly pinned. "We'd just spend it."

"I believe that's the idea with money."

"If we spent it, we wouldn't have it long, so what would be the point of receiving it in the first place? If it was just one gift, however large, it would soon be gone, and the lack of money, after having had a taste of it, would be degenerating. On the other hand, if you continued to provide money, we'd become your helpless parasites in no time at all."

"OK, then," I said with all the good nature I could summon up. "Forget money. I just want to be your friend."

She frowned for a while, as if in thought, and then said, while shutting the door, "I don't see any profit in that."

8

ON MY WAY DOWNSTAIRS I encountered the ancient judge, who stood catching his breath on the landing at the entrance to the third floor. Apparently he had not yet reached the toilet, for he was facing in, not out. He stared disapprovingly at me, giving no indication that we had met before, and therefore I did not seek to converse with him now.

As I went along the street I came to a building which was identified, on a polished brass plate alongside its front door, as The Linden Street School. The cable clerk had mentioned this institution. Curiosity took me inside its entrance hall, which proved to be a lobby decorated with colorful posters of coming cinematic attractions.

"Come along, come along!" said an impatient voice. "The feature is just starting." This command was directed to me by a woman dressed as a nun, who stood at a curtain-draped doorway. When I approached she held the curtain aside and switched on the small flashlight she carried and preceded me down the aisle. I had never before received this sort of service at a movie house, but could recall seeing the like in vintage films, in which a hero, seeking to hide out till some ill wind blew past, took similar refuge in a cinema, as in real life did our latest successful presidential assassin.

I wanted to continue on to my habitual place, rather nearer the screen than would be the taste of most, owing to a mild myopia, but the stern sister forced me to take an aisle seat no more than halfway along, reminding me that I had "a job to do." I had no sense of what she meant until I sat down. Immediately I was asked for permission to go to the toilet. My eyes not having as yet adjusted to the darkness, I could not identify either the sex or the age of this personage in the seat next mine, but the voice was that of a child.

"Why do you ask me?"

"Because you're the monitor!" said the person whose small body was climbing over my legs before I could begin to stand up.

I became aware that all this while there had been images on and sound emanating from the screen. I now took conscious note of these and saw that the black-and-white Coming Attractions were just ending in a riot of giant display type, followed by exclamation marks and printed on the diagonal. Whatever was on its way to this theater next would be SHOCKING!!!

But then the titles began for the feature, and I was incredulous when I saw, after the name and logo of the studio had come and gone (for the record, "Puma Productions" and a cougar who bared his fangs at the camera), "Ben Spinoza . . . in . . . GATS 'N' GALS," the actor and title I had created from thin air so as to defend myself when speaking with the cable clerk!

By now my vision was clearing, and therefore I could discern, when the nun returned her, fingers pincered on her ear, that my toilet-bound neighbor was about eight years old, had a short butcher-boy haircut, and was dressed in the kind of smock worn by French schoolchildren.

While the girl climbed back to her seat, the nun upbraided me for letting the child out of the aisle.

"For a person of your age to be taken in by such an old ruse is ridiculous," said the sister. "Nobody leaves their seat *till the end of the picture!*"

After she left, the little girl said, "Sorry. I didn't mean to get you in trouble. But I really hate gangster pictures."

I was touched by this manifestation of decency in a human being of such a tender age—before I reflected, New Yorkly, that if you don't find it in a child, you won't see it anywhere.

"What kind of movies do you like?"

"Where the ladies are rich and have servants waiting on them and wear pretty clothes, and where the men have their hair combed and wear those coats with the long backs and fancy shirts and they help the ladies into carriages and they go to places with shining candles and dance in two lines, one for the ladies and one for the men."

How I used to hate it when at her age I would be trapped at a costume picture with such tedious sissy-scenes, which one must endure so as to reach the swordfights.

"It takes all kinds," I told her.

Gats 'n' Gals proved to be somewhat better than I anticipated. Its morality was oversimplistic, but it was a relief, after all these years, to see criminals presented as deplorable creatures while the men of law enforcement were courageous, honorable, and even courteous (while routinely wearing their wide-brimmed fedoras indoors, they doffed them when a woman entered the room). The dialogue would provide more grist for the cable clerk's linguistic mill: cigarettes were "coffin nails"; women, "twists"; cars, "chariots"; and clothes, faces, and dollars were, respectively, "duds," "mugs," and "simoleons." Spinoza was a middle-sized chap, on the slender side, but with a thrusting jaw. At one point he fist-fought two thugs who (in addition to being giants) pressed into service as weapons a series of found objects, chairs, lengths of pipe, and an axe, but with the use of only his two hands Ben eventually "closed out their accounts," to quote a line of his partner, another G-man, who is subsequently shot in the back by a dastardly, toadlike ruffian, but who has recovered sufficiently by the end of the film to receive a hospital bedside visit from his winsome sister, who has fallen hard for Spinoza, but in the convention of the time had behaved snippily towards him until he appears now, with a box of candy for the invalid and a boyish grin for her. "I'll bet I know who'd make a swell best man!" says she, simpering at her brother, whose eyebrows rise in a benevolent amazement that is surely also ingenuous.

No sooner had "The End" appeared on the screen than I was treated as an inanimate obstacle not only by the little girl from the seat next me, but by all the children in the row: they climbed, vaulted, swarmed, over me and pushed into the general congestion of the aisle, which was clogged with other children and, farther along, the adults who had occupied the seats more distant from the screen.

I detained, against his will, the last child to leave my row, and was informed by him, in answer to my question, that this was a toilet break and not the end of what he thought of as the school-day.

"There are more movies?"

He portrayed disgust with his mouth and nose. "Where've *you* been all your life? We don't get out till five. We've still got to watch a chapter of a Tim McCoy serial, an Edgar Kennedy comedy, and some dumb girls' picture with singing and dancing!"

He wriggled away and plunged into the aisle-traffic before I could ask him more. I waited until the throng had passed and then left my seat. Before I could reach the street, however, I was stopped by the stern-faced nun who had chided me earlier.

"Because of the allergies that are going round, we'll be short-handed for monitors again at the evening session, and you'll have to stay."

"Excuse me?"

"I think I'm speaking clearly enough," said she, lengthening the lines that ran from the base of her nose to the mouth. She was one of those persons who have forever the power to make one feel feckless. "You have a job to do."

"As it happens, Sister, I am an American visitor who just wandered into the school by chance."

This information made her no more genial. "Then tell me if you can," said she, "why your films are of such poor quality. Some are scratched badly, and many break during a screening, and Father has to stop the machine and splice the film. At such times the children can become quite unruly. Even our adult-education groups get restless."

"You must understand, I am not connected with the American film industry and have little technical knowledge, but I wonder whether your troubles might not be due to the age of the pictures. From what I understand, the movies you show are almost half a century old. *Gats 'n' Gals*, for example, obviously dates from before World War Two."

She squinted suspiciously at me. "Can that be true?"

"Oh yes. I can assure you that if indeed he is still alive, Ben Spinoza is quite an old man. Those boxlike cars are seen only at the exhibitions given by collectors, and the clothes worn by both criminals and law-enforcers would nowadays not be seen publicly on anyone except perhaps the kind of alternative-sex people who go to parties given by celebrity designers."

The nun looked even more grim. "I wonder whether Father knows this." She beckoned to me. "Come along."

I supposed I was not really obliged to obey her, but, as I say, her air of authority was that authentic kind that requires more of an effort to dismiss than to honor. I followed her black habit and white cowl through a little door and up a flight of stairs and into a projection room in which were twin movie machines, other pieces of equipment, and a balding man wearing a round collar. The last-named sat at a table in front of a film-editing device: two reels separated by a glass screen. I vaguely remembered seeing a smaller version of such a gadget in the "den" of an uncle who was familially notorious as a home-movie bore, who with his intrusive camera would delay holiday meals until the food grew cold and never fail to catch for eternity any minor embarrassment within the 360-degree purview of his lens, while missing altogether the local events of great moment (tornadoes, presidential motorcades, circus processions with prancing bears).

The nun spoke. "I'm sorry to bother you, Father, but this American has quite a story to tell."

The priest continued to stare silently into the glass window of the machine before him, while slowly turning the right-hand reel by means of the little crank attached to it.

I didn't like the implication that what I had to say might be questionable, and bridled when the sister made it even stronger. "You won't believe this, but I really do think you might want to hear it." She gave me a bleak look. "Go ahead."

"I don't have earth-shattering news to relate, I'm afraid, but the American films you show are of an earlier era and do not reflect the current life of my country."

Without looking up from his gadget the priest said, "I'm well aware of that."

I looked at the nun. She said, "*I* wasn't." She made a quiet exit.

"An usherette doesn't have to be," murmured the man of the cloth, shaking his head at something he saw in the little screen. "I don't know how many more splices this will take." At last he looked up at me. "That's the only trouble, the physical condition of many of these pictures. We could use some new copies. You don't suppose that when you go back home you might look for somebody who could make copies of these fine films? We don't have adequate equipment for that job over here. No doubt they might elsewhere in Europe, but we Sebastianers don't like to admit our weaknesses to anyone nearby."

"I suppose I could do that," I said. "But could you tell me where you get these films nowadays?"

"Aha." He had keen eyes under metal-rimmed spectacles and was losing his hair at those two places on the crown just above the temples. "Your USO and Army people left them behind when they went home after World War Two. It seems that Mr. McCoy had access to them. Were it not for these pictures I don't know what our Enlightenment could have come to."

"I confess I find it curious that the clergy of all people would condone the exchanging of schools and churches for cinemas."

The priest laughed merrily. " 'Condoned' is too mild a word, my dear fellow! We were positively ecstatic to do so. For the first time in a century we have full houses!"

"And the movies are also a substitute for school?"

He frowned. "The choice of words is not appropriate. The movies are not substitutes! If anything, church and school were the substitutes. They were poor imitations of life. Now we can see the real thing."

"Old American films are the real thing?"

"Yes, of course," the priest said forcefully. "The virtuous are shown to succeed, the evildoers invariably come to grief, and the general philosophy that informs every picture is that there is a common good, which is recognized by everyone—including the wicked, who of course are opposed to it, but they *know what it is.* Believe it or not, before the Enlightenment, Sebastiani society had no such standards or beliefs. The church had utterly different aims from the schools, and the code one learned in each was utterly confounded by one's experience of life. And the government received no respect from anyone, which of course is still true, but now the government is *intentionally* performed as a farce, and is quite effective."

"Namely, it does nothing."

His smile became ever more radiant. "Exactly! And are you aware of what an achievement that is? Unprecedented throughout history! Not even the Austro-Hungarians were able quite to pull that off."

"And everything is run on credit."

"One of the most brilliant schemes man has ever devised!" said he. "And not all that different from the old way of exchanging pieces of paper, if you think of it. A bank note has no intrinsic value, nor has a check. And it has been a long time, has it not, since the coins circulated in any country have had much value as metal? All the foregoing means of payment are essentially no more than credit, eh?"

Until now, being in my peculiar situation, I had not thought of an obvious question, *viz.*, "Who decides who gets most credit?"

The priest had gone back to his movie-viewer. He now looked up with a quizzical expression. "Credit is unlimited for everybody."

"Then everybody is rich?"

"Far from it," said he. "We have fewer rich people than we formerly had, and of course many fewer of the poor. But some of those who *are* rich are richer than they were previously, and there are still *some* poor people."

"And could you explain that, Father?" It might seem ridiculous that I so addressed a projectionist, but the fact was that, like the nun, the priest seemed to retain all the authority he would ever have had.

"Personal taste," he said. "There really is an enormous variation amongst human beings. One exercises his vanity in quite another way than that of his neighbor: one by accumulation, the next by deprivation. But of course most Sebastianers, so as to allay envy, are somewhere in the middle."

"Then vanity and envy were not eradicated by the Enlightenment?"

The priest grimaced at me. "Are you really so naïve, or should I take that question as derisive?"

I admitted, "I really can't decide."

His brow cleared. He accepted that answer in good humor, perhaps because he understood that it was no more or less than the truth (unless I am being too sentimental in my assessment of him, as those reared as liberal Protestants tend to be with respect to a celibate clergy).

"I'll withdraw the question and put another," I told him. "What do you think of the Blonds?"

"They are all God's children."

"I meant their situation in society."

He shrugged. "I don't know what to say beyond 'There it is.'"

"Are they not condemned by the mere fact of their birth? Is a person responsible for the color of the hair with which he was born?"

The priest stared at me. "No, of course not, but he certainly is for that which he retains as an adult."

"What does that mean?"

"Most of us are *born* with fair hair," he said resentfully. "Our parents dye it throughout childhood and then when we become adults we either continue the practice ourselves, if we have any self-respect, or go rotten and allow it to return to what it was, which gives a moral weakling a further excuse to make nothing of himself. Nobody expects anything of the fairhaired, you see. It's a self-fulfilling kind of thing."

If this was true, then the argument of Olga and the other liberationists was necessarily compromised, but now the negative side of my basic sense of priests came into play: were they not professional defenders of whichever status was quo, provided it included them?

"The Blonds, then, deserve what they get?"

"I'd put it another way," said he. "They get what they give every evidence of wanting."

"Thank you, Father. I've profited by our little talk. By the way, in your current job do you still take confessions?"

"Of course. People nowadays call them in on the telephone, thereby being able better to conceal their identities and at the same time allowing us to transmit their remarks on the radio."

"You don't mean the confessions are broadcast?"

"Yes, indeed, and the program is perennially the most popular. The excitement is in what each show will bring. No one knows. They're not rigged or edited in any way, but go on as

they come over the phone. You might get twenty or more innoc-
uous ones or nothing more than impure thoughts before a really
filthy story comes along. You never can tell."

"By 'filthy' you mean . . . ?"

"Do you think I would repeat such smut aloud?" he asked
indignantly.

"I haven't heard television mentioned since I got here," I said.

"The radio engineers are working on it," said the priest. "But
it'll be a while before it gets to be more than a novelty."

I thanked him again and left. On the main floor I encountered
the nun again. She was directing the traffic of children and
adults on their return to the auditorium, but left off for a moment to ask me, though I was foreigner, to serve again as monitor for the next picture, which starred someone named John
Boles, but I expressed my regrets and departed from the building.

No sooner had I stepped into the street than two men moved
against me, one from either side, and in a pincer-play conducted
me to the curb, against which a long black automobile that
might have been a vintage Mercedes suddenly swooped in from
nowhere. The rear door was flung open and I was pushed inside, one man climbing in after, and the other going around to
enter from the opposite door. My captors were of a similar
height and weight and wore identical black suits.

This sequence had occurred too swiftly for me as yet to have
reacted, pondering as I had been, at the moment of capture, on
the educational system of Saint Sebastian, but I was ready by
the time the car started to roll.

"How dare you?" I demanded first of one man, and then
turned and repeated it to the other. Their being dressed identi-
cally was taxing: I found I had to guard against the tendency to
repeat to either whatever I had said to the other, though they
were separated only by the width of my person. Only by the
rigid application of self-discipline was I able to establish a style
in which the first part of any utterance was addressed to the
man on my left and the second to him on the right. As for
example, what I said next.

"Who are you?" Turn. "And where are you taking me?"

The questions were answered with twin silences. The car was

being driven by a man with thickset shoulders and a neck that was as wide as that part of his head I could see before it vanished into his hat. The car was moving too swiftly for me to attempt an escape from it while it was in motion; therefore I persisted in my attempts at conversation, this time taking a more leisurely tack.

"Do you know"—turn—"this is the only car I've seen on the streets"—turn—"other than that of Mr. McCoy, the expatriate American journalist"—turn—"whom you may"—turn—"know, given"—turn—"the small size of this country."

Neither of them acknowledged any of this, and soon the car entered a courtyard and pulled up before a gloomy-looking stone building of fortresslike construction: those few windows it had were narrow and barred. The two men hustled me into its grim dark interior, along several tunneled corridors ever grimmer and darker, and finally into a room that was grimmest, and darkest, of all, illuminated at the moment only by whatever light could penetrate the slit-window high on the wall, though a lamp with a mesh-covered reflector hung from the ceiling directly over the single piece of furniture in the room, a stark straightbacked chair.

I was pushed violently towards the chair and told to sit upon it. The overhead light was switched on. The bulb was more powerful than I expected; I sat in a cone of intense light, and the heat of it was comforting, for the men soon left the room. How long I sat there I could not say, but finally the door opened and in came a person I could hardly see: he remained in the shadows beyond the circle of light.

Suddenly he said in a harsh tone, "You've been frequenting a Blond."

"I'm a tourist."

"You're an American agent."

"May I ask who *you* are?"

"The State Security Service of Saint Sebastian."

I suspected my best move would be to tell the literal truth, up to a point. "By chance I encountered the stewardess of the airplane that brought me here. 'Frequenting' is scarcely the word for my distant and brief acquaintance with her."

"You did not fuck her? Blond females are nymphomaniacs."

He came closer, but I still could not see him except in outline. "Oh, you fucked her," said he, "or vice versa."

I took the courage to say, "I'm not going to speak to anyone I can't see." After a delay he slowly moved into the edge of the light, and I saw that he was—or had been, for his hair was now dark, and his accent had been lost—the rickshaw-puller known as Helmut.

"Was it not you who took me to the fireworks factory?"

"I was giving you enough rope," said he. "You see, it has been my conviction from the first that you came to our country with a favorable bias towards the Blonds. I was putting you to the test, and of course you failed—or rather, I should say you succeeded beautifully in confirming my theory."

"Why would I be favorably disposed to them when it was they who blew up my home in New York?"

He smiled sardonically. "Because cultured Americans adore those who abuse them in what is represented as a good cause."

"I assure you I am still happily enmired in the Me Generation," I cried with false enthusiasm. "I'm a monster of self-interest and have been denounced as such by a series of do-gooder women, for I am often attracted to social activists, if they have long legs and nice breasts." I was trying for a joke here, but without undue conviction that I would succeed. My lack of faith was appropriately rewarded: Helmut threatened to connect electrodes to my testicles and send a powerful current through them."

"You don't seem to understand," said he. "You're in the hands of the dreaded security police. You are dead to the outside world when you're in here, and vice versa. We can wash your brain like a handkerchief, flushing away your memories, hopes, ideals, and . . ." He searched for a word, did not find it, and murmuringly repeated "ideals." Aha! I thought, there's his usable weakness, a poor command of terms, but he soon confounded me by saying quickly, "And principles, values, convictions, and if I've left anything out with regard to the superego, you can be sure it will wash away as quickly as the rest."

"And you think my government will sit idly by while this is going on?"

"Certainly not," said he. "They'll launch nuclear missiles at us." His grin was unfunny. "Why, you poor schmuck!" he said, pretending to more compassion than he felt.

I decided to counterattack, though naturally in an extremely subtle way. "I think you're better-looking with blond hair."

He scowled. "Why should I care what you think?"

"I only just discovered that all Sebastianers are born blond."

His expression changed to one that might have been called uneasy. "That's common knowledge. We're all in the same boat to start with. Those who are content to stay there deserve to drown. Not much is asked, after all: just a little dye, but you see they're too lazy even for that."

"Not everyone is cut out to be blond all his life," I said, cunningly perverting his point, "but I think you could do it to advantage."

"Dammit," said Helmut.

"It's the shape of your jaw." I suggested a square with my fingers and thumbs.

I had got to him! He hung his head for a moment. "You might be right, but it's the political thing, you see. Were it simply aesthetics . . ." He showed a regretful pout.

"To be sure," I went on, "fair hair doesn't stay all that light on the adult head. So-called blond men usually have a head of dirty brown, if not snot-green."

He raised his chin further than required. "As you saw me with the rickshaw, that's entirely natural." He pointed at his scalp. "*This* is the dye-job."

"Then indeed you have beautiful hair."

He peered narrowly at me. "Are you a bugger after all?"

It was the "after all" that caught my interest. "Certainly not. I assume the concierge assured you of that truth. Does he not work for you?"

"Naturally," Helmut said. "Concierges are always police spies by tradition, as you very well know. Their mystique demands it. . . . Look, it's kind of you to admire my hair, but that doesn't alter the fact that we must force a confession out of you. I'm afraid that the means by which that will be done are extremely cruel. I say 'I'm afraid' merely to be courteous. Actually, I enjoy that phase of my job more than any other. I am that relatively rare person who is authorized to carry out his most outlandish fantasies in his everyday work."

"You do this in support of the status quo?"

"No," said Helmut. "I do it because I enjoy having the power to remove someone's freedom and to bring him pain."

"But you don't want to see the prince deposed?"

He shrugged. "I couldn't care less. My job is to ferret out dissenters and to frustrate their efforts. The means I employ represent my own interpretation of the work. I have infiltrated the liberation movement and can identify every one of its ring-leaders. I could at any moment round all of them up and bring them here. But the fact is that, as you could see, they are a pack of harmless, ineffectual clowns here at home. Their bombs are used only in America. I would dearly like to torture them, en-joying the bringing of pain as I do, but alas! how can I do that when I already *know* all their secrets?"

"You can't do it to me, either," I said, rising from the chair. "Because before you can torture me, I confess!"

"Oh, no you don't!" he cried. "You cannot."

"But I have already done so, you see. Any torture you submit me to now would be contrary to the international standards of interrogation. You would reveal yourself as being a selfish sadist rather than a zealous investigator. Your authenticity would be shattered!"

Helmut threw his hands up. "All right, all right, you've made your point. But can't we just talk, at least?"

I had him on the run now. "Perhaps, if you'll just apologize for submitting me to this ordeal."

He spoke impatiently. "Consider it done. But your responsi-bility hasn't ended. What are you confessing *to?*"

"To being an American agent."

"OK. Now confess what sort of mischief you had planned to wreak in this role."

"None whatever. I'm on a fact-finding mission. But just a mo-ment: Olga knew that. Why didn't you, if you have infiltrated the movement?"

He looked sheepish. "Well, all right, so I miss a few things. I don't get the rest I should, and I work darn hard, pulling that rickshaw, so I admit I catch a few winks whenever the opportunity offers itself. You don't know how boring it is to listen to revolutionary rhetoric. Another thing that limits the effectiveness of this agency is the lack of a name that can be used easily and gracefully, like Gestapo or KGB. It's awkward to pronounce the letter *S* five times in succession, and the term Five Esses, which we've tried to get people to use in recent years, simply doesn't sound serious."

I was still standing in the circle of light. "That's your problem," I said. "Having kept my end of the bargain, I'm leaving."

He clasped my arm and pleaded, "Look here, old fellow, can't you stay awhile? I could really use the company. You're someone I can talk to. This is a very lonely job. We might drink a beer or two and play some cards. I'll take you home for some of the best goulash you ever ate. Afterwards we'll listen to my brother-in-law play the concertina. And, say, my wife has another sister who's unmarried. You'll like her. She's—" He suggested, with cupped hands, a pair of enormous breasts, to carry which the woman would need a frame of the same kind.

He was about to resume when the door opened and one of the black-suited men came in.

"Sir," he said, "the revolution has begun."

"Of course it has," Helmut said derisively. "Led by that ridiculous Olga, no doubt."

"In fact, yes," said the man.

"I don't know why you've chosen this moment for your little joke, Stanislaus," said Helmut. "It's been a long day. Mr. Wren and I are going home now to a good dinner."

"It's not a joke, sir. The Blonds have taken the palace and captured the prince. Others are going around to all the government facilities. They'll be here at any moment. What shall we do, sir? Surrender or fight?"

"Hold them off until I wash this dye out of my hair!" cried Helmut, dashing for the door.

9

I ENCOUNTERED no one at all on my uncertain exit through the grim dark passageways of the building of the SSSSS (a name easier to write than to speak). When I finally emerged I had no idea of where I might be. However, when I rounded the first corner, I saw The Linden Street School at the end of the street. I had been only a block from where the security people had picked me up, and it was a short walk from there to the hotel.

As I passed the school I glanced through the glass-paneled front doors and saw that the audience was once again entering the auditorium from the hall or lobby. It would seem as if news of the revolution had not yet reached them—or they were simply indifferent to it.

But changes had already been made at the hotel. For one, its name, according to the replaced brass plate on either side of the entrance, was now The Hotel Blond. I was confronted by the concierge, whose hair was now a mass of tight yellow curls and who had exchanged his tailcoat for a resplendent uniform tunic, draped with braid and bearing an embroidered legend on the left breast: again "The Hotel Blond." I suspected that he had not only been the classic concierge in serving as police spy, but had typified the traditional police spy by being a double agent.

"Halt!" he cried from behind the desk. "Your identification!"

"Come off it."

He flushed and brought, from under the counter, the Luger he had drawn on me once before, then with his free hand he banged the little domed bell before him. In a moment the bellboy appeared, the same whose flesh he had tried to sell me on numerous occasions. The concierge ordered him to search my person, which the lad proceeded to do, and though presumably a catamite he was discreet enough with his hands. He wore the old uniform with a newly embroidered Hotel Blond breast patch.

Next the concierge lifted the telephone and tried to reach the police but had no success. Lowering the instrument, he spoke to me as if I might be sympathetic.

"I suppose we must be patient. The changeover is not quite complete."

I asked sourly, "What are you charging me with this time?"

"Refusal to identify yourself to an officer."

"You're an officer?"

"Do you not see my uniform?"

"It's the costume of a hotel flunky!" I cried. "Whom are you trying to fool?"

"I'm afraid your troubles are growing," he said with false regret. "*Everybody* in any kind of uniform is perforce an officer of the Revolution. It is a grave offense to insult one of us."

"Just a moment. A mailman is an officer?"

"Certainly. As is a nurse." He moved his heavy head from side to side. I suspected that though obviously he had been prepared with clothing and signplates, the Revolution had caught him with insufficient time in which to bleach his dark-dyed hair and that that which crowned his skull was a wig.

"This bellboy wears a uniform!" I pointed out.

"And he's an officer," shouted the concierge.

"Do you admit that the last time I saw you, a scant few hours ago, you showed quite another attitude towards the Blonds?"

He addressed the lad, who had withdrawn from me. "Lieutenant, what was consistently my position on the Blonds when they were a despised and oppressed minority?"

The boy clicked his heels. "Sir, you always admired them and in so doing took an enormous risk."

"There you are," the concierge said smugly.

I grimaced. "Your effrontery is breathtaking. As to the 'lieutenant' here, how recently was it that you were trying to peddle him for sexual purposes?"

"Oho." The large man moaned in pleasurable anticipation. "I wouldn't want to be in your shoes when I get hold of the police!

Sexual inversion is of course counterrevolutionary, as is inde-
cency with respect to a minor. The lieutenant is but seventeen
years old. To have made importunities to him is the foulest of
crimes. . . . Indeed, you are such a heinous criminal, all in all,
that I am justified, as a colonel in the Revolutionary Blond
Army, to sentence you to death on my own authority." He
raised the Luger to point at my head. It might have been a bluff,
as so many things proved to be in Saint Sebastian, but I was not
inclined to put him to the test.

Fortunately, I did not have to, for Clyde McCoy reeled into
the lobby at that moment, leaned across the counter and dis-
armed the concierge, and spoke to me.

"*There* you are. I've been lookin' for you, sport. Thought you
might have located a source for something to drink by now."

"You haven't heard of the revolution?"

"Huh? Oh, that. That's *their* business."

"What will become of the prince, do you think?"

McCoy shrugged. "They'll probably knock him off." He took
the clip from the Luger and returned the weapon to the concierge, who smiled obsequiously and thanked him. The bellhop
had disappeared.

"You are curiously unimpressed," I told the veteran correspondent. "You don't expect your own status to be altered?"

McCoy gave me his bleary eye. "I took the poet's advice many
years ago and abandoned excessive expectation about anything.
That philosophy has left me untouched by human hands, if you
know what I mean."

"But with all respect, McCoy, is that any way to live?"

He groaned. "You call this living? I haven't had a drink for an
hour!"

"The Blonds have closed the wine shops and taverns?"

He squinted at me. "Is *that* the reason? I thought they just ran
out of goods, which happens a lot. The distillery breaks down."
He turned and lurched towards the door. "Come on."

In truth, I had nothing better to do, not to mention that in
such a time I felt secure in McCoy's presence, the drunk tending
to enjoy the status of a holy idiot in most cultures or anyway
someone who is given a wide berth (except on the iconoclastic
pavements of the Big Apple, where he might well be set on fire).

I followed McCoy out to his car and was about to take my chances with the passenger's door when he directed me to enter by way of the window. I did so, sliding headfirst through the aperture, then falling inside. Meanwhile he inserted himself behind the steering wheel, and soon we were roaring and rattling up the hills towards the palace.

When I saw what our destination would be, I asked, "You think it's the opportune time to go there?"

"Damn right," said McCoy, setting his jaw. "I'm not going to let them get away with this Prohibition shit."

"You can stop them?"

He scowled at the windshield. "I'm an American, for Christ sake."

It was so strange nowadays to hear the term used in that way —though it was no doubt routine in the movies shown by the priest.

We gained the summit and shortly thereafter scraped to a stop against the wall overlooking the moat. We left the car and climbed the spiral staircase in the tower. The old journalist displayed an impressive spryness. No doubt he was energized by the expectation of getting a drink from the stores of the deposed monarch.

When we reached those corridors through which I had been conducted by General Popescu on my previous visit to the palace, I saw that the walls had been denuded of the so-called Old Masters.

We still had not seen a Blond, or, for that matter, anyone from the ancien régime, but when we finally reached the first of what had formerly been the sumptuously furnished antechambers to the throne room but now was empty except for a desk of gray metal, atop and around which were a number of matching accessories, intercom, wastecan, telephone, there sat a young fair-haired woman. She wore a suit of some gray material with a slight sheen, a white blouse, and a black bow tie. Her hair was pulled into a tight bun at her nape. She was wearing no jewelry and no makeup.

I had assumed that McCoy would continue and perhaps even intensify the truculence with which he had greeted my suggestion that the new leaders were teetotallers, but in fact he now turned on an old-fashioned charm, or in any event, what he obviously intended to be taken as such.

"Sweetie," he crooned, so to speak quasimodoing his body, lowering his head to leer on the level of her own, "Could I ask you kindly to let me see Who's in Charge?"

She nodded crisply and bent over a chart that lay flat on the desk pad. She stabbed at a certain place with the eraser of an unsharpened pencil. "I can give you five oh five P.M., Wednesday the twenty-fourth."

"Honey," said McCoy, "that's next week."

"It's next month."

"Now, darling," said the veteran newsman, "I'm Clyde McCoy, pool correspondent for a number of important American wire services and TV and radio networks. I'm *sure* you folks would want me to give you a good send-off in the dispatches I send back to the States."

"One moment, sir," said the receptionist, and she threw a switch on the intercom and spoke into it so rapidly that I could not grasp a word. She was answered with a grunt.

She nodded. "You may proceed."

"Thank you, snookums," said McCoy, and we opened the door behind her and entered the next room. This was another of the chambers that had been hung with the royal collection of bogus paintings. Like the one we had just left, it was now furnished only with a metal desk. Behind this one sat a young man dressed in a suit of the same material as that of the girl next door, a white shirt, and a black bow tie. He was ex-Lieutenant Blok, of the old palace guard, the officer who had strip-searched me just that morning. His hair was now blond.

He asked brightly, with a touch of arrogance, "May I help you?"

McCoy used another style this time. He swaggered up and rested one buttock on the edge of the desk. "Maybe you can, sonny-boy, maybe you just can. I wanna see the Big Fellow."

"And who would that—"

But McCoy interrupted with a pointing finger. "Just call me through, junior, and I won't report you for having pecker tracks on your fly." He winked, got up, and did not bother to wait for

Blok to execute the orders; the latter at the moment was con-
ducting an anxious inspection of his trousers.

In the third room, the last of the antechambers, was an excep-
tionally large and husky man, whose blond hair was clipped
close to his outsized skull. He looked uncomfortable in the gray
suit and black bow tie and out of place at a desk.

He asked, in the hostility-tinged though technically neutral
voice of a professional in the craft of bringing people to, or
keeping them in, order, "What do you fellows want?"

The versatile McCoy made another change of tone or tune.
He barked, "You call this security?"

The big man's eyes lost half their diameter. "What do *you* call
it?"

"Swiss cheese," said the journalist. He pulled a pen from an
inside pocket of his wretched jacket and pointed it at the large
Blond. "If this was a gun, you'd be a memory."

"Yeah, but you wouldn't get any further unless I pressed this
button," the large man said, reaching under the desktop.

McCoy found a piece of paper in his breast pocket and unfolded it. "All right. That'll go in my report."

"Report?"

"He and I are doing a security check," said McCoy, nodding
at me. "You just squeak through—unless I decide otherwise."
He put the paper onto the desk and scribbled on it. "Now hit
the button."

The big man did as asked. One of the double doors swung
open, and we passed into what had formerly been the throne
room of Sebastian XXIII.

Now the long chamber was in the process of being subdivided, like one of those contemporary office floors, by the intro-
duction of standing panels of opaque corrugated plastic. An
army of carpenters was so occupied. Meanwhile desks were in
place, in a regular pattern throughout the vast room, and gray-
suited Blond functionaries were already seated at them. Every
one at whom I looked was speaking on the telephone, perhaps to
a colleague in the same room, for when one hung up, the rest of
them did the same. The throne was gone, as was even the dais
on which it had stood. The entire corps of gray suits was now,
simultaneously, stapling sheaves of paper.

I stopped at one desk and asked, "Where's Olga?"

"Olga who?" The young woman continued to use the stapler.

"Then who's in charge?"

"Of which department?"

"The whole country."

"I'm sorry, sir," said she. "That's not my job."

I started to leave, but on second thought tarried to ask, "What *is* your job?"

She put a finger to her cheek. "I haven't been told yet. I was just hired."

"At the end of the day?" I asked. "Without warning? I see a movie, and when I come out, a revolution has occurred?"

She gave me a sympathetic sad smile. "I don't know about that. But as my old teacher, Sister Thérèse, used to say, 'In the movies you lose all track of time, don't you?'"

I left her. It was then that I observed that McCoy was no longer in the vicinity. I scanned the area but saw only gray suits and workmen carrying panels of corrugated plastic.

I left the throne room and went through more barren halls, looked into more chambers, and saw more gray desks and people who, except for their hair, matched them, and now computer terminals were beginning to appear on the desktops, but I did not encounter anyone from the ruling group of Blonds whom I had met in the subterranean room at the fireworks factory. To the naked eye this revolution looked as though it had succeeded only in transforming the palace into a branch of IBM.

Finally, in one of the marble corridors I met someone I recognized: Popescu, now apparently an ex-general, for he was wearing coveralls and pushing a longhandled broom.

I had no wish to embarrass him, but I was desperate for news as to what had taken place. "General," I said, "I—"

Tears sprang from his eyes. He dropped his broom and embraced me. "You *remembered!* Oh, how kind!"

"It was only this morning," I said. I stepped back: he stank of sweat. "Was there much fighting? Did you resist? Is the prince dead?"

Popescu shrugged. "It was astonishingly quick. It happened after lunch, when we were all taking our siestas."

"But the palace guard?"

"Undoubtedly there would have been bloodshed had they been attacked with routine weapons, but you could well imagine how terrifying it was to confront an invasion of movingmen carrying metal office furniture and computer equipment, followed by one shock wave after another of clerks wearing vulgar lounge suits cut from synthetic stuff, and black bow ties."

"The prince was captured?"

"One assumes so," said the ex-general. "One is reluctant to ask too many questions. I trust I won't be harmed if I do a good job at this." He brandished his broom and even managed a smile.

"Would you know a big Blond named Olga?"

He shook his head.

"She was the leader of the liberation movement."

"I'm afraid I've never heard of it."

With some impatience I said, "They're the people who made the revolution. You know, the Blonds."

"Not this revolution, with all respect."

"But all the people working here have fair hair."

"Indeed. As everyone knows, Blonds make the best bureaucrats. They have the sort of docile temperament that is ideal in such a situation, and are especially good at such routine tasks as using the telephone, the Wheeldex, and the computer terminal."

"Then who *did* lead the takeover? Who's the boss now?"

"Gregor."

"Who in the world *is* he?"

"He's the man in charge," Popescu said curtly, and began to apply his broom to the floor between us. "He'd not be likely to notice anyone in my lowly position: at least, I pray he won't." He gave me a fearful wince and moved on.

"But I'm an American," I cried. "Where can I find him?"

He told me which turns to make, then returned to sweeping the floor he had lately strode in polished boots. I followed his directions, arriving at last at a suite of interconnecting rooms, the last of which was made, walls, floor, and the stupendously large bathtub embedded in the latter, of white marble with prominent blue veins.

An obese body was lowering itself into the tub as I entered. Obviously these were the royal quarters, and the prince was quite OK, though apparently not attended by any of his former people or anyone else.

"Your Royal Highness!" I began to apologize.

But I had had a rear view. When the huge rump had disappeared below the surface of the water, followed by half the massive block of flesh that formed his back—the oversized tub must have been a yard deep—the head turned and the profile I saw was not that of Prince Sebastian but rather that of my acquaintance from the Hotel Bristol, the enormous and silent but affable lover of Caruso and pesto!

He now spoke for the first time. "Meester Ran. Please to take seat." He gestured at a scroll-armed bench, a kind of Roman thing, against the nearest marble wall. His accent was not Italian.

I did as asked and said, "You are Gregor?"

His body made a movement that caused the water to be agitated briefly. "And you," he asked, "are from the Firm?"

I neither confirmed nor denied this as he found a sponge and a cake of soap in niches in the tub above the waterline, and began to abrade one against the other.

Instead I asked, "I am told that you are running this thing."

He made a moue. "I halp Sebastiani pipples."

"The Blonds?"

"Bluns, everybody." He had worked up a supply of lather sufficiently generous to hide his hands.

"But you are not yourself a Sebastianer."

"Nor you," said he.

"That's true, but I haven't made a revolution."

He began to soap his shoulders and hairy upper chest with the lather-laden sponge. "Not ravolution, but improved efficiency."

"What have you done with the prince?"

"He laft."

"Where was he taken?"

Gregor began to work soap into the thick black hair atop his head. "Wherever he wants."

"Who are you?" I asked.

"Gregor," said he. He left his soapy scalp to pick up the floating sponge and push it in my direction. "Wash my beck."

I rose abruptly, but rather to show my resentment than to

obey his command. "While the liberation movement was playing its naïve little game, you simply walked in and took over the country, didn't you? But what I want to know is, *why?* Surely you must have seen that it is a place of no consequence in the greater scheme of things."

He smiled broadly, displaying the gold teeth at either end of his dental range. "*You* was going to." He shook the sponge at me again. "Scrob my beck!"

"The joke's on you," I said. "I was just about to make my final report that the place is worthless. You've got a white elephant on your hands. Don't you know that nobody works? Most of the populace spends its days at the movies, and the economy runs on credit. The country's too small to be of strategic value and has no useful raw materials. What can you use it for?"

"Example of democracy in action," said he. He gave me a stare of some duration, then whistled and in a moment and from nowhere appeared three stocky men with the faces of plug-uglies. They stood glowering at me. They were not Blonds. They were much more formidable-looking than the old black-suited secret police of Helmut's.

I went to the tub, crouched on the marble floor, and accepted the sponge, which under the circumstances felt slimy but probably was not literally so, and did as ordered. He had quite a growth of hair on his shoulder blades.

"Is that sufficient?" I asked after I had scrubbed for a while.

"Sure," said Gregor.

I returned the sponge to him and got to my feet.

"See," he said, grinning up at me. "I ain't so bed a guy! At least you din't never have to wash my balls!" He laughed so heartily that he almost lowered his face into the lathered water. When he recovered his breath he said, "So you can go in peace, Ran. Sebastiani Airline got a night flight leaves one hour. So long and have a nice day."

"I'm being expelled?"

"I don't believe you was ever here, you know?" Gregor said, not unkindly. As one might say, he was only doing his job.

"Well, obviously you've won," I said, "though I'm not sure how or what. Do you intend to put a lot of people to death as counterrevolutionaries?"

He smirked. "You got crazy ideas. We ain't going kill any-body. Put them to work on public projects! Make life better for pipples."

"What kind of work?"

"Farmss."

"Huh." I tweaked my chin. "I never thought about it—there's a New Yorker for you—but obviously they must have some do-mestic sources for food, since I was told they didn't import much."

"Nice farmss beyond airport," said Gregor. "All the way to the base of mountains, and farmers work hard, don't sit in mov-ies all day. We make more farmers."

This was beginning to make sense. "And if you grow a sur-plus of food, you'll export it, no doubt?"

Gregor rose dripping from the tub. He had a remarkable body, fat but not soft; perhaps when younger he had been one of the super-heavyweight power-lifters for which his culture was famous. I half expected him to order me to give him a toweling, but I was wrong. He had a nice sense of proportion; he had already made his humiliating point.

He answered my question. "They don't need all the food they got. They going to plant flowers."

"I'll be damned. You're not going aesthetic, are you, Gregor?"

"Poppies," said he, with a slow smug smile.

I was even more damned now, but I did not say so. Instead I chuckled humorlessly. "I didn't know you guys use the stuff."

"Not us," said Gregor. "But *you* sure as shit will!" Now his laughter was so violent as to shake his vast body, watching which was as if to await an eruption of Mount Saint Helens. The marble room continued to ring for some time after he had stopped. His bravos were slow to join him in mirth, no doubt because they were deficient in English, but one of them brought him a towel.

Unfortunately I had no rejoinder, expecting as I did that the Western world would end not with a whimper but a fix. I changed the subject. "Mind telling me what became of Sebas-tian's collection of art?"

"Confiscated," Gregor answered. "Is nawt right for one man to have all expensive stuff. Give to pipples." He spread wide his treetrunk legs and went between them and under the great projection of his belly to dry his crotch, vigorously tumbling his genitals in a towel.

"But which people?"

"Hell's bells," said he. "We are all pipples, ain't we?"

He did not seem to be aware that the artworks were counterfeit. It was my one pitiful score off him and secret at that, but it was a point on which to leave.

"Good-bye, Gregor. I can't say it's been a pleasure, though to be courteous I suppose I should thank you for the pesto. Where'd you learn to make that?"

"Travel lots of places," said he, gesturing. "Gosh, I like to pick up some culture. Food! Opera!" He abraded his breech with the towel. "See you next place, Ran."

"Only in the funny papers, Gregor," said I. "I'm not a pro at this. I know it'll give you only more contempt for me to hear it, but I'm essentially a playwright."

He was drying his armpits. "Hey," he cried, "you could stay here and write some plays."

My chance had come at last! Who knows what might have become of me had he not added, "Nice plays to show pipples how to behave themselves."

"Pity," I said, "but my work is the degenerate stuff that would have just the opposite effect: Manhattan slice-of-life, characters who pay two-thirds of their income for an uncomfortable apartment and the remainder to a psychiatrist, who forsake parents, spouses, close friends, to search for someone who can *really* love them."

He put a twist of towel into one ear socket. "Be good for bad examples."

"I doubt it. See, I make them sympathetic. I'm afraid I would be a subversive element."

He scowled at me. "In all the world, only an American would boast of that."

"Then maybe there's still some slight hope for us." I left before he could change his mind.

10

IN MY EAGERNESS to leave the palace I forgot about McCoy and remembered him again only when I saw his car just across the drawbridge. He was sitting behind the wheel, drinking from the neck of a magnum.

He grimaced at me as I slithered into the car via the window. "This was all that's left. They already poured out most of the old brandy and other spirits. They got gangs at work on that, at the drains of the royal laundry. Fucking barbarians!"

"I'm supposed to leave the country on the next plane," I told him. "You'd better come along."

He let some more wine run down his throat and made a pickleface. He handed the bottle to me. "Did this go bad? Taste it."

I did as asked, then looked at the label: it was the legendary Romanée-Conti, the biggest of the reds, too costly for anyone but reigning monarchs, sitcom stars, and defense counsel for the downtrodden. "It's just too good for you, McCoy. What about leaving Saint Sebastian?"

He reclaimed the bottle. "God, I don't know. And leave everything I've built up over the years?"

"Which is what? A crummy hotel room?"

"Shit, I'm not ready to go Stateside just yet."

"It's been forty years since that war ended!"

He gulped some more wine. "I wonder if *Time* or the AP could use a Continental smut correspondent on a regular basis?"

"You could always ask," I said. "But let's get going. I'm supposed to catch the plane within an hour." I told him about Gregor.

"One of the things I'd miss is this old bucket of bolts. I hear they got all-metal station wagons now—?"

"Yes, I think since before I was born. No doubt you'll find everything has been changed since you left, but the same is probably true of every other place. I hear Paris and London have been stacked with glass skyscrapers since I was there on summer vacation, via Icelandic Airlines, less than twenty years ago." McCoy's presence brought out the nostalgia in me.

"Jesus," he said. "If I went home I might be spotted by the old lady or one of the kids."

"You've got a family? Your children would be older than I!"

He took the bottle from his mouth and swallowed loudly. "You know how it is. They been taken care of. Military allotment."

"Wouldn't that have ended years ago?"

"But they got the GI insurance, I'm sure. Just before I went over the hill from Germany to here, see, I found a dead Nazi of the right size, hung my dog tags around his neck, and dressed him in my uniform. The ball-'n'-chain would've got ten grand. That was real mazooma in those days."

"You could avoid her part of the country. But I think it's imperative that you get away from here. Gregor and Company aren't your kind of people, McCoy. You see what they've done with the prince's cellarful of drinkables, and I hardly think they'll look kindly on the sort of writing you do. Let's head right for the airport."

"I have to stop by the hotel and pick up my stuff," said he, hurling the now empty bottle from the window and starting up the catarrhal engine.

We hurtled downhill. When we reached the bottom we proceeded to pass most of the places with which I had had some association during my short time in Saint Sebastian. Already these had been altered or were in the process of changing. Of the open-air markets, only a stall selling potatoes was open for business. The birds had disappeared, along with the fake fish and the fishwives. The pillory was gone from the square, and a number of workmen were erecting a scaffold that looked ominously as if it might well become a gallows. A cul-de-sac that greatly resembled the old Street of Words was now signposted as Truth Lane. At the moment the pavement in front of the writers' pink building was being scrubbed, with soap and brush, on hands and knees, by what looked from my distance like some of the authors I had met, Spang, Boggs, and poor sybaritic Riesling, provoking whom I now regretted.

When we reached the hotel a Blond functionary, in gray suit and black tie, was behind the desk.

"Mr. Wren," said he, and handed me an envelope he had taken from one of the pigeonholes behind him.

It was a cablegram from Langley, VA.

> NOBODY NAMED RASMUSSEN AT
> THIS ADDRESS, AND NOTHING
> CALLED THE FIRM. BE ADVISED
> IT IS ILLEGAL TO IMPERSONATE
> AN EMPLOYEE OF A FEDERAL AGENCY.
> THE COMPANY

This was Rasmussen's idea of a joke.

I peered at the man behind the desk. "Aren't you Helmut?"

"Formerly. I've made a successful transition. Of course, I would have liked to be a secret policeman for the new regime, but I failed to pass the entrance exam."

"A difficult test?"

"Yes. I was supposed to throttle one of my old colleagues with my bare hands."

I shudderingly changed the subject. "You did a good job in washing the dye from your hair, unless that's a wig. Which reminds me: what became of the old concierge?"

"Transferred."

So despite his desperate efforts to climb onto the revolutionary bandwagon the fat opportunist had not been able to save himself.

"Do you now manage the hotel?"

"No, sir. I simply work here. One of Mr. Gregor's associates is in charge. Do you wish to see him?"

Helmut made a swift movement below the counter and brought up a sheet of paper. "Your bill, sir."

This was one obligation I could scan with a light heart. "Haha! I see you charged me two hundred dollars a day. I'd certainly object, if I actually had to pay that, for I have merely shared the room in which Mr. McCoy lives permanently, which is not even equipped with a bathroom, nor with twin beds. Not to mention that I haven't stayed overnight in it. And then, haha, I would scarcely be paying you in US currency."

Helmut's expression remained impassive. "But you're leaving the country, sir. I'm afraid your credit is effective only while you remain here, and we have no currency of our own."

"Well, I don't have two hundred dollars."

Helmut smiled sadly. "If you will notice, the meals make it a bit more."

I had quickly glanced at only the first line of the bill. I now raised it for a more careful study and saw the following itemization:

Café complet, Sebastiani Airlines		$ 15.00
Lunch at Palace	(prix fixe)	65.00
	champagne	110.00
Late lunch, House of Authors	(visitor's rate)	45.00
Pesto & jug wine		35.00
Movie *(Gats 'n' Gals)*		7.50
	subtotal	277.50
	service	41.63
	value added tax	27.75
	NYC sales tax	23.59
	Total room & board	570.47
	Revolutionary surtax	57.05
	Grand Total	$627.52

"I don't know where I should begin," I said, with the overwhelming sense of defeat I get when outrage exceeds a certain limit (this of course was a daily phenomenon on the city streets). "Perhaps by simply pointing out that charge which is among the least in money but the most heinous in its moral status, namely, New York City sales tax. I'm here, not there."

Helmut said patiently, "But you're *from* there."

"Look, Gregor has asked me to leave the country. That, conjoined with the fact that I have no money whatever, should be enough to close the discussion."

"Oh, I *am* sorry," said Helmut, "but it was Gregor himself

who just phoned me to ask that I be sure to collect payment from you before you left. I'll have to call the manager."

He depressed a new bell push that had been installed at the edge of the desk, and in a trice a thickset man, with heavy eyebrows and a forehead that began an inch above them, came through a rear door and glowered at me.

Fortunately McCoy returned at the same moment, stepping off the elevator with a faded green duffle bag in one hand and my suitcase in the other. "I brought your shit, too," said he.

"Oh, I didn't wan—" I caught myself and, taking the valise from him, turned to the new manager of the Bristol Hotel. "I don't have the money for the bill," I said, "but as a man of your sophistication must surely know, it is traditional in such cases for the hostelry to confiscate the luggage." I put the suitcase on the countertop and opened it. Quickly extracting the knitted shirt and old cords, which McCoy had thoughtfully included, I said, "Here's an entire wardrobe for travel, in the most fashionable American colors, every item guaranteed to be of a synthetic material that will look new eternally." I began to disrobe and add the items I had been wearing to the collection, and I donned the clothes in which I had been shanghaied.

I had finally made a sound judgment. An expression of delight came over the simian features of the manager as he inspected the gaudy garments, the madras jacket, the plastic shoes, the Day-Glo socks, etc.

He grunted his assent, and McCoy and I left the hotel. The veteran journalist was subdued and drove to the airport with none of his usual verve.

As opposed to the informality in which I had landed, we were now obliged to run the gantlet of a number of Blond functionaries in gray suits, with an occasional glimpse of one of the thugs imported by Gregor. An exit visa was waiting for me, but it had to be examined and stamped by one official after another in the terminal building, and when that process was finally completed, I was taken into a lavatory and forced to undergo a humiliating spread-cheek strip search, more thorough than that conducted by Blok: this one was managed by a Gregorian wearing a rubber glove.

McCoy, for whom no exit permit was ready, had been separated from me and taken elsewhere in the terminal. Under the old regime he would not have suffered this ordeal of red tape, but he was displaying a new docility. When he had not reappeared by the time I was finally ready to be led out to the airplane, I protested. The gray suits appealed, in what had apparently been established as the line of command, to the nearest of Gregor's men, and the latter's continuous brow came down over his small eyes as he drew a wicked-looking sap from his back pocket and raised it to strike me.

But McCoy saved me one more time, reappearing from a door near at hand and, in the imperious style of old, shouting at the secret policeman. The man was startled, but no doubt hearing what he took as the note of authentic authority, he complied.

To me the vintage newsman said, "Look, Wren, I've just had a phone talk with Gregor. He can use my professional skills, as it happens. He offered me the job of Minister of Information. I'll be writing about the achievements of the revolution."

My expression must have reflected my thoughts.

"I don't care what you want to call it," McCoy said defensively. "I'm too old to go back to the States at this late date. This is a good job. Turns out that though Prohibition will be in effect for most of the population—except on certain holidays honoring phases of the revolution—you can drink all you want if you're an insider."

"Do you realize what you're going to have to write?"

He let his mouth droop on one side, presumably to indicate wryness. "Piece of cake."

Suddenly I saw the light. "It was *your* idea, wasn't it? How'd you talk Gregor into it?"

"Hell, man, I'm an old pro! I assured him that in the dispatches I sent out to the world I would naturally fail to mention any atrocities committed by his crowd while exaggerating or inventing altogether the vicious outrages of the opposition, if there was any opposition: if there wasn't, I'd invent one. Were he to find it necessary to massacre people en masse, I would present such events as counterattacks against forces that far outnumbered his own small band of gallant freedom fighters. I assured him I could also be counted on to honor the principle of revolutionary modesty and denounce the cult of personality, exalting only those members of the prevailing power elite and expunging the names of persons who, despite their contributions, had been outmaneuvered by their comrades."

I realized I had underestimated the old fellow, but did wonder why he had wasted so many years at sex-reportage and not the kind that had a greater sway amongst persons of culture.

"All right, McCoy. Though much younger than you, I'm already too old for expressions of moral indignation."

"Fuck you too, Wren," said he, but rather blithely, without spite.

Two of the gray suits led me out onto the field where the airplane, a propeller-driven craft reminiscent of the old Icelandic machinery, was waiting. I climbed the steps, entered the cabin, and saw several recognizable persons.

I greeted the stewardess, who was back in the old familiar abbreviated uniform. "Back at your post, I see, Olga."

She gave me the synthetic smile of the profession and the ritualistic welcome-on-board, then went forward, to the cockpit, with a trayful of coffee and cups.

I moved along the aisle to my favorite midship area and said good day to my nearby fellow passengers, the ex-concierge of the Hotel Bristol and the catamite bellhop for whom he had served as ponce. They were both now in subdued mufti.

I did not expect the man to be embarrassed, and he was not. "Well, Mr. Wren," said he, "soon we'll all be making our fortunes in New York."

"Frankly," I said, not without a tinge of bitterness, "I expect you will be quite at home there in no time."

"Yes," said he, hovering on the verge of a smug simper, "I've been offered a position as maître d'hôtel at Les Cinq Lettres." This was one of Manhattan's most expensive and therefore most publicized eateries, visited at least once a year by the human-interest reporter on each TV channel's news team, who ordered a conspicuously *nouvelle* dish—say, sea urchins on artichoke pasta, blueberry-vinaigrette sauce—and was wry about the astronomical price.

"And him?" I indicated the former bellboy.

"My son," said the concierge, "has been hired by Mr. Rasmussen for his male burlesque theater."

"Your son . . . Rasmussen . . ." The astonishments continued to be greater as the sequence proceeded, for at that moment
the man himself, Rasmussen in the flesh, emerged from one of
the forward toilets. He had coarsely saved the zipping of his fly
as an exhibit for his fellow passengers.

"Rasmussen!" I cried, going up the aisle. "You—"

He looked up from his crotch. "Wren! The very man I wanted
to see. I just flew in, and I'm flying right back out with this load
of Sebastiani boat people." His complexion was as bad as I remembered.

"Are you or are you not CIA?"

"I never said we were. I always said Firm, not Company."

"Then what's the Firm?"

"Private enterprise, babe."

"Don't call me babe. You've used me, you've taken advantage
of my patriotic feelings."

"The term you're looking for is 'jerked off,' I believe," he said
grinning. "Actually, if you were really patriotic, you ought to
commend me."

"For what?"

"What do you think, you dork? For bringing Saint Sebastian
into the democratic camp."

"Gregor is a totalitarian!"

"I don't mean that shit," Rasmussen said, rubbing some dandruff from his sandy hair. "I'm selling them a lot of seconds in
stereo equipment, surplus canned goods, recalled models of certain cars, and, hey, can you beat this: a big stock of Nehru jackets, in storage in Jersey for fifteen years. And you helped. You
oughta feel some pride."

"Oh, yeah? Well, I'll expose you, Rasmussen! There are inves-
tigative reporters who would kill for such a story as I can give
them."

He laughed negligently. "You're welcome to try, but I think
most of the media are in my pocket. See, we got the big star.
Prince Sebastian signed an exclusive contract with us."

"Sebastian the Twenty-third?"

"Of course. I already got him booked with dinner theaters,
women's-rights organizations, and self-realization groups across
the country."

"Then he's been allowed to leave here?"

"It's part of my package deal with Gregor and Company."

"So you're a talent agency?"

"Among other things. We're a conglomerate, babe."

No doubt they published *Crotch*, the paper for which McCoy had been foreign correspondent, as well. I didn't ask. I was still seething. But there was nothing I could do about my hunger for revenge until we reached home, and frankly I had my doubts as to what I could do even then, for Rasmussen was obviously much closer to the ruthless center of the New York mainstream than I was likely ever to be. He could even afford to eat in such restaurants as the one in which the concierge would be maître d'. And he also could hold his own with the likes of Gregor. The people who know how to handle themselves seem to be similar, irrespective of ideology.

"I assume it was you who got him"—I indicated the former concierge—"his new job. Well, then, I—"

Rasmussen interrupted. "Isn't he the *perfect* mater? Subservient to a clique of the initiates, yet mercilessly abusive to the humble stranger who wanders onto the premises under the erroneous impression that it is a foddering place."

"What I was going to say was, if you would render such aid to a foreigner, perhaps you'd do a favor for a fellow American whose life you've disrupted in the interests of a commercial scheme of questionable morality. I don't suppose any of your enterprises are involved with the theater?"

"Why, they certainly are!" said he. "We bring a lot of shows to Broadway."

"Broadway? You don't mean it!" One's opportunities come in the most bizarre ways. What a grueling experience I had had to undergo to meet a producer at last!

"I don't know whether I've mentioned this, but I am essentially a playwright."

Rasmussen leaned very close to me and poked me in the chest with a rigid forefinger. "Let me tell you something, Wren: so is everybody."

I had briefly become obsequious, but I bridled now. "You bastard you! You owe me something."

He took a step back, and his eyes widened to show even more

discolor. "Where'd you get the spunk all of a sudden? I like that, Wren. It'll take you farther than that habitual bitterness of yours. Read your Nietzsche and you'll find that all the world's ills can be traced to *ressentiment.*" He reached into an interior pocket and brought out a rectangle of pasteboard. "Bring your stuff up to the office when we get back. I can't promise you more than a reading, but I'll tell you this: it'll be read by somebody who's fluent in English."

He gave me the card, which proved to be something called American Cousin Productions, with an address in Shubert Alley.

Not wishing to be near the concierge, I took a seat up front, but had not sat there long when Olga emerged from the cockpit with her tray. When she reached my row she stopped and said coldly, "I'm sorry, sir, but this is the First Class section."

"I'm being ejected from the country," I said. "*Your* country, which has just had a revolution in which you, the leader of the liberation movement, obviously played no part. And which has left you in the same position as before."

"At least I don't have to pretend to be a cretin any more," said she, with what I must admit was a certain dignity. "Now, unless you can produce a First Class ticket, you must return to the Tourist section."

"I don't have a ticket of any kind."

"But if you *did* have one," she said stubbornly, "it would be Economy."

I sullenly got up and she moved on. Farther along the aisle I encountered another familiar face: that of the cable clerk.

"Yes," he said, before I could speak, "I'm exiling myself while it's still possible. I'm heading for Hollywood. I want to take a tour of the stars' homes, see where some of my favorites live: Ginny Simms, Gloria Jean, Bob Burns: I love to hear him play the bazooka."

"A forward-looking project," said I. "But did you know that your former sovereign is soon to become a popular lecturer in America?"

"That big palooka will take the cake!" the clerk told me enthusiastically. "He's triple threat. Call him anything but late for breakfast. Who you think's flying this egg-crate?"

It took me more than a moment to get any sense out of this mishmash of outmoded jargon. Then: "You're saying the prince is our *pilot?*"

"You ain't just bumping your gums together. It's ceiling zero, visibility zero, and we're comin' in on a wing and a prayer."

As he spoke it came to my attention that the aircraft had begun to move: I had been subliminally aware that the engines had been idling for some time. Olga came along and insisted I take a seat and fasten the belt, and then upbraided me for putting a suitcase in the overhead rack.

"It's not mine!"

"A likely story," said she, and demanded that I put it under the seat in front of me; if it didn't fit, the takeoff would be delayed while the case was ejected.

"It's yours, isn't it?" I angrily asked the cable clerk, across the aisle.

"Not on your tintype," said he. He moved his head to indicate the ex-concierge. "Belongs to that hepcat."

Therefore I did as ordered. The case must have contained stolen metallic things from the hotel, clinking and heavy as it was, and I had the greatest difficulty in moving it with no aid from anybody. But when it was lowered, it did fit under the seat.

"Now," said Olga, scowling down at me, "extinguish your cigar, cigarette, or pipe."

"As you can see," I said derisively, "I'm not smoking."

She brought a pack of cigarettes from the pocket of her tunic. "Take one of these and light it." She gave me a cigarette and a folder of matches, and actually forced me to take a puff or two, again threatening to stop the aircraft unless I complied.

I obeyed her, but I did demand an explanation.

"It is one of the new regulations of the People's Airline," said she. "Gregor has warned us that the punishment will be stern for any failure to enforce any rule. Since nobody on this flight was smoking, it was impossible to observe the regulation. You were the obvious choice to bring about the proper state of affairs. Now put the cigarette out, so that we might take off promptly."

The takeoff, when it came, seemed professional enough.

When the plane was level again, the intercom came on in a rush of static, and someone, presumably Prince Sebastian, said something through the auditory fog, but as on every flight I have taken throughout my life, only the odd word was comprehensible. I gather our altitude was specified in thousands, and the phrase "on your left" would suggest that the passengers were urged to look out those windows for a view of something on the ground.

That the ex-sovereign of the country was now piloting a commercial airliner was not as remarkable a fact as it would have been only a day earlier, for one result (perhaps the only) of my visit to Saint Sebastian was a diminishment of my capacity for wonder, already weakened by several decades of adult life in the known world before I ever heard of this little land it was easy to call preposterous. Perhaps too easy. Did things make any more sense elsewhere? Or, to be fair, any less? It was true that where I came from you could get more or less fresh fish (allowing for the fact that most of them came by truck, in bumper-to-bumper traffic, from Boston), and not plastic. On the other hand, not New York nor any other American jurisdiction, to my knowledge, had a department of hoaxes, though obviously almost any of the existing bureaus could be, with justice, so labeled. The same might be said with respect to a department of irony, and if you got right down to it, was there not a crying need for a government agency that rose above pedestrian meanness to the grander, more generous view: *viz.*, the vision of human problems as allergies? If the Saint Sebastian of old had been ridiculous, it was not *altogether* ignoble. But the stress must go on the penultimate word, for the country's shortcomings were obvious, and it might be asked whether this had really been a feasible way for human beings to live—though not by one who had ever had occasion to travel by Interborough Rapid Transit.

Derailing such a train of thought, perhaps in the nick of time, Olga appeared with a trayful of glasses filled with a liquid off-puttingly colored in a vermilion that looked as if it might glow in the dark.

"I trust you have an alcoholic alternative," I growled.

"Drink this," she ordered. "It was developed for the Sebastiani space program." She lowered the tray from the back of the seat ahead and deposited the glass on it.

"You can't be serious."

"The project may not have gone farther," said she, "but the orange drink was a beginning, anyway."

"You *are* serious. Do I detect a note of nostalgia? Are you already looking back on the old regime with a certain fondness?"

She frowned and went along the aisle.

I put the glass onto the tray, slid out of the seat, and went forward again, passing Rasmussen, who had taken his place in first class and was, of all things, reading a paperback edition of *The Aspern Papers*. Perhaps naïvely, I could not resist returning to comment on this phenomenon.

"This is disgusting," said he, putting a finger to the cover. "Publishers can't even spell anymore." I confess I have never been able to decide whether or not he was jesting.

I continued unopposed into the cockpit, through an unlocked door; hijackers were not feared on this flight. The first person I saw was old Rupert, the prince's butler. He sat in the co-pilot's seat and wore a 1920's Lindy type of leather helmet, the flaps of which were buttoned under his withered chin, the goggles pushed up on the forehead. He turned and sneered at me.

Crammed into the pilot's place was the stout figure of Prince Sebastian XXIII. He wore a green uniform trimmed with gold. Clamped over his billed cap, World War II–style, was a set of earphones.

Though the noise of the engines was considerable up here, Rupert was audible, though he seemingly spoke at no more than his normal volume.

"Go away," said he. "His Royal Highness is engaged."

At this the prince turned. "Wren, old chap! Welcome aboard. I'm afraid we'll have to pig it as to food until we reach New York, but I did manage to bring along a few bottles of Bollinger, a pound or two of sterlet, a cold grouse, and some other things my cooks were able to put in the hamper before they were packed off to become refrigeration mechanics."

I had an odd feeling of disequilibrium.

"Sire," said Rupert.

"Can't you see I'm speaking to Wren?" Sebastian asked in annoyance.

"Sire, we are losing altitude."

"Then pull us up, you old dog."

"But where, sire, is the joystick?"

Sebastian shook his head at me. "The ancient sod hasn't been in an aircraft since the Fourteen–Eighteen War."

"Which side?" I soon had cause to regret my question, for the airplane continued to descend, at an ever steeper angle, yet the prince answered me at length.

"The Central Powers, I'm afraid. But you see, we were surrounded by them, and the Hungarians, who could not whip anyone else, would have been only too eager to punish us if we had not declared ourselves their allies. My grandfather made the necessary decision but of course had to pay the price at Versailles: our so-called empire was dissolved. On the other hand, this was no more than a formality, for our only overseas possession, claimed for the Crown by the Sebastiani explorer Giovanni Dori in 1611, an unpopulated island very near the magnetic North Pole, had long since proved to be only a flat iceberg and, unbeknown to the geographers, had melted during one unusually warm winter. Fortunately we were ignored by all the major powers during the Second World War, though it was touch-and-go at one point, when Marshal Goering sent a team of emissaries to inspect the pictures in the royal collections. Luckily for us, Germans have no taste in art: they soon went away and we were not molested."

"Sire," Rupert said again, but in the same tone of gentle impatience, though I was about to scream by now.

"Haven't you watched me at all, you fool?" Sebastian asked. "One simply pulls back on the wheel!"

I sighed as the old retainer clutched the device before him. In a moment the leveling-off could be felt.

"Of course, he was never much of a pilot, I gather, and was said to have crashed our only airplane on his solo flight. It was not repaired while the war was in progress."

"Highness, how is it that you can fly this airplane?"

"I did such things when I was younger," said he. "I raced cars and boats and could fly any aircraft. All this is in the royal Sebastiani tradition, like sodomy."

"Pardon?"

"I've been deposed now," said the prince, chuckling. "I'm not obliged to be a bugger anymore." I confessed I did not understand. He explained: "I no longer have to take measures against creating bastards, you see?

"Nor need I now get married!" he added. "I'm a free man, for the first time in my life."

"Is it true you will make a series of public appearances in America?"

He nodded. "Having to make a living is new to me. I was going to send Rupert out to work, but then how could I get along? Tell me, is Rasmussen a good talent agent?"

"He's wily enough," I said. "But tell me, Highness, why did Gregor permit you to leave the country?"

"While Saint Sebastian has for a long time existed on credit domestically, we have of course sometimes been required to use money abroad—for my food and drink, for example. I could not abide the swill eaten and drunk by my subjects. And for the odd piece of machinery—for example this airplane—I have always paid cash, and I get it from my accounts in Switzerland. Gregor would like to have access to that money. I agreed to give it him if I were allowed to leave unmolested."

The airplane hit a bump in the road of wind, and had I not clutched the back of Rupert's seat, I might have tumbled.

Recovering my balance, I said, "But, sir, why would he take your word? Once you're in America, you can ignore him with impunity."

Sebastian looked at me with an expression of disbelief. "My dear Wren, I am a prince of the royal Sebastiani line. It would be impossible for me to break my word. And what of my poor subjects? A scoundrel like that would take revenge on them. If the exalted are not trustworthy, then the world would indeed be a hopeless place."

I was amazed to learn that being a parasite did not disqualify a man from having principles. Whether they would survive in his new life of show business was to be seen.

I was about to say something, probably the sort of banality

with which fate provides us on the unwitting brink of a catastrophe, when an explosion occurred somewhere aft. Perhaps Gregor had had second thoughts about letting us go, having found another means of getting to the Swiss accounts, or maybe there was still another group of the disgruntled who made their case with explosives.

Up in the cockpit I was hurled to the deck as the nose lifted violently, then thrown against the ceiling as the balance shifted the other way. Something or someone was suddenly on top of me. Ungodly noises were being produced, the loudest by myself. All was swirling, then dark, then blazing bright, then fragmented, then in horizontal striations. . . . Enough of this: we crashed.

I found it remarkable that I was conscious all the way down, instead of fainting away as I had always supposed was one's obligation, and that in fact after such a fall I was totally conscious. And had apparently—though only tomorrow would tell, for I bruise easily but slowly—sustained no damage whatever.

True, I had fallen only a few feet. What had obviously happened was that, as is my wont, I had lowered my head to rest on my arms, which were crossed on the top of the desk, to ponder on possible solutions to my persistent problem with the second act of my play. At some point, weary from a day's undercover work at Rothman's Deli, aching from the subsequent drubbing I had taken from the gang of little-girl thugs, I had dozed off, my chair had slid slowly backwards, and I fell . . .

Saint Sebastian, and all that went with it, had been but a dream, if not a nightmare. My home, such as it was, had not been destroyed: I was sitting amidst it at the moment. I stood up. Yes, the dog-eared sheaf I called my play was still on the desk. For the first time I could admit that it was a vapid thing, whereas, judging from the dream, I had untapped riches in my unconscious. Now that the Rothman job had come to an end I was at liberty, with more than ample time to begin another play —about a Utopia that was probably not admirable except, like life itself, by chance, but which, like most phenomena, seemed better when it had receded into the past.

But meanwhile I sensed, from the bleak light that penetrated my front windows, that dawn had come to Manhattan: always the best part of the day if you are awake to see it, for the simple reason that so few others are.

I lurched to the window, in a stride reminiscent of the imaginary McCoy (funny how certain items are retained from dreams), threw up the sash, and a pane fell from the rotted wood and went to shards on the pavement below, which fortunately was deserted, else I should have provided another entry for the local list of deaths-by-falling-object: in winter concrete cornices drop, and when summer comes the air conditioners fall like rain. The sidewalk was otherwise reasonably clean this morn, as was even the gutter: indeed I saw Mr. Rat's whiplike tail as he scuttled away with the last morsel of edible filth. A flock of lugubrious-looking starlings was on the edge of the building across the street. I saluted them and cried, "Hey, you slugabeds! Why aren't you up with the Wren?" As it happened, I was in a uniquely fine mood, for no reason at all, as if responding to a posthypnotic suggestion.

Gee, what a nice place the New York sidewalks would be if most people were kept always at the movies!

But when I went to make that matutinal cup of coffee that forms the bedrock on which is mounted the day to come, my mood changed abruptly. The hot plate was still plugged into the socket that hung from the ceiling, but its coils were quite cold, which meant that they had been burned out or the fuse had blown. The fusebox for all the circuits in this wretched building was in a cellar the door to which was locked to keep, as the super said, surely comprising me in his term, "the assholes out." I could easily gain entrance using the all-purpose skeleton key I had provided myself with from Krachlich's Third Avenue hardware store (which offered a full range of burglar's aids), but the fusebox itself was locked more elaborately. Not to mention that Mr. Rat, his stout wife, and their multitudinous offspring made their home down there and at any moment would be, as McCoy might have said in his vivid vintage lingo, tying on the breakfast feedbag. . . . Funny how one can become attached to a supposititious personage, but then, I am in life a lonely man. I wish I could again afford a regular girlfriend: the incessant bickering keeps one on the qui vive. Almost every day I read somewhere that a bachelor's life expectancy is alarmingly short.

I can't function in the morning without my caffeine fix, I
don't care what the doom-crying nutritionists say. Unless I
wanted to mix my instant coffee with the tepid water from the
lavatory tap, I had to go out to breakfast. I searched my pockets
for the money I remembered was not there: I found only a
crumpled business card, which I hurled to the desk in frustration. I went through the spare clothing I maintained in a heap
on the studio couch, then to the garments that hung on the nails
driven here and there into the woodwork. But could locate not
so much as a single verdigrised relief of Honest Abe. *Merde!*

I went back to the desk and picked up the card so that I might
ball it and fling it cursing, an event from which, like most of us,
I get a wan satisfaction, and I glanced at it and—good gravy!—
saw the legend thereupon: *Our American Cousin Productions, 1 Shubert Alley, NYC,* a 944 number, and *Norman Rasmussen, President.*

But before I could even begin to reconcile reality with dream,
my telephone rang. I answered it warily, and this time heard a
tenor voice with a local accent.

"There's supposed to be a bomb in your building. Better get
out."

I snorted derisively. "Sure there is."

"Whadduh yuh, *arguing?* Bomb squad's onna way. Get out
right now."

"Who are you?"

"Getcherass outa there and you can have my shield numbuh."

"You're a cop?" But the distinctive Celtic-tinged speech of the
NYPD, even when the speaker himself is Italian or Jewish, was
unmistakable. "All right, I'm leaving. But tell me this, officer:
why do people do this sort of thing?"

"C'mon, *willyah?*"

I abandoned my attempt to elicit some judgment on these
terrorists, if only a pungent epithet, but I suppose cops say
"scumbag" only on TV these days. Alas, I had lingered too long
in what proved a vain pursuit: I was still in the doorway downstairs when the bomb went off, projecting me onto the sidewalk,
where however my fall was cushioned by the small but firm
body of Bobbie, my friendly neighbor streetwalker.

"Jesus, Rus!" she protested, rising quickly and dusting her
clothing, a slack suit in a subdued color, with her hands.

I got up slowly and looked at my building. It was still standing, nor could I see any flame or smoke. "It's different from the dream," I said.

"Are you on something?" Bobbie asked, anxiously peering at my eyes.

"A bomb just went off in there! Didn't you hear it?"

"You're kidding. That was a backfire over on Madison." Bobbie went into her purse. "Take a look at my new ad, Rus. How you like the writing?"

I accepted the newspaper clipping and read: "Virgin college girl newly arrived in town. Need quick money to pursue Ph.D., and therefore must sell maidenhead to highest bidder." This was followed by the address of a mail-collection service in Chelsea.

"It's clever, Bobbie, but do you think it will fool anybody?"

"You'll see," she said. "I'll get all kinds of answers. The kinda people who read *Crotch* like stuff like that. The kinda people who go to prostitutes are *romantics,* Rus! If you don't know that, you don't know much."

"Do you ever see any articles in there by a man named Mc-Coy?"

She sneered. "I never look at the front part of that piece of shit. I read good stuff, Rus: Harlequins, Barbara Cartland, you know."

"I guess it was a quixotic question, Bobbie. Looks like you're just getting in from a hard night. How about buying me a cup of coffee?"

"Sorry, I don't buy nothing except for Smoke."

"He's the chap who drives the ornate Caddie, wears the big white sombrero?"

"That's my lover-boy. I hope you don't have no criticism."

"Not me," said I. "He has about him the aura of a Renaissance wit. That's all too rare these days."

"You want to panhandle, you go along Gramercy North. That's where the Jewish doctors are."

"Hey, that's an idea."

She frowned. "I don't know, Rus, sometimes I think it oughta be better than this. But then I think, *Where?*" She shook her head as if to clear it, then sighed, took the ad from me, put it in her purse, and came out with a quarter. "Here you go."

I was genuinely touched. "Gee, Bobbie, that's nice of you."

"What the hell. Support the arts!" She gave me a wink and a smile and assumed a sprightly stride as she crossed the street to her hotel.

The bomb destroyed only the WC on my floor, as it happened, and the super, speaking for the absentee slumlord (frankly, I had always assumed they were the same individual), refused to install another, so long as there was a "perfectly good crapper in the cellar."

An anonymous caller informed TV newsperson Jackie Johansen that the bombing was the work of a group which deplored the detonation of explosives on the premises of persons who had no responsibility for the supposed injustices suffered by the bombers. As there was really no other means by which to attract the notice of the press to this organization, the world should expect more of the same.

I haven't yet got in touch with Norman Rasmussen: I started the new play but soon ran into a problem with the second act.